LEWIS SHINER

This special signed edition is limited to 750 numbered copies.

This is copy __625__

# HEROES
# AND
# VILLAINS

BOOKS BY LEWIS SHINER

NOVELS

*Dark Tangos* (2011)

*Black & White* (2008)

*Say Goodbye* (1999)

*Glimpses* (1993)

*Slam* (1990)

*Deserted Cities of the Heart* (1988)

*Frontera* (1984)


COLLECTIONS

*Heroes and Villains* (2017)

*Collected Stories* (2009)

*Love in Vain* (2001)

*The Edges of Things* (1991)

*Nine Hard Questions about the
Nature of the Universe* (1990)

# HEROES
# AND
# VILLAINS

THREE SHORT NOVELS
AND A FABLE BY

# LEWIS SHINER

SUBTERRANEAN PRESS

The following stories originally appeared in *Subterranean Magazine*:
"Doctor Helios," Fall 2013, © 2013 by Lewis Shiner
"The Black Sun," Summer 2014, © 2014 by Lewis Shiner


Interior design by Lewis Shiner
Set in Bembo


ISBN 978-1-59606-840-7


Subterranean Press
PO Box 190106
Burton, MI 48519


www.subterraneanpress.com
www.lewisshiner.com

*For Bill Schafer, patron of the arts*

*And, as always, for Orlita*

# TABLE OF CONTENTS

# INTRODUCTION

G ETTING HOOKED by an action movie is a very particular
experience. In the course of two hours, you make an emotional
connection to a set of characters, then watch them take on bad guys
who have all the advantages. It's a philosophical struggle made visible,
and the final catharsis always comes at a cost. I'm a tough audience for
this kind of picture, but I love it when it does work for me—*Jaws,* say,
or *Star Wars,* big movies that also have brains and heart.

In early 2004 I had my own blockbuster idea. Two words: Vampire Lawyers. I never considered writing it as a novel because I was
not interested in scaling literary heights with this one. It wasn't in
the idea's DNA. This was about car chases, ticking clocks, and things
blowing up in slow motion.

Filming a big action movie, however, is a much more expensive
and collaborative enterprise than writing a novel, and not something I could do in my study. Thus I sent my finished screenplay to
my hotshot (but nice) Hollywood agent and also to a major pro-
ducer who was a fan of my work.

And that's where our two very different ideas of heroism collided.

"No actor in Hollywood is going to want to play this guy," they
told me. The reason? When things started to go sideways, his first
reaction was not to get a bunch of guns and start killing people. The
hero as mass shooter de jour, brought to you by the NRA.

That was the end of my blockbuster. I put the screenplay on my
website in case anybody was interested and went back to my day job
and my literary ambitions.

IT ONLY TOOK ME ten years to figure out that there was a third
alternative. That if I turned a page of screenplay into a page of prose,

I

I would have about 25,000 words. There's a name for this art form: the novella. I'd never written one before, but I suddenly realized that it was the perfect vehicle for a movie in prose. I could have all the CGI and exotic locations I wanted. My heroes could be regular human beings instead of Lethal Weapons. Maybe best of all, I didn't feel the obligation to high seriousness that I did when writing a full-blown novel.

Stephen King's *Different Seasons* reinforced the connection. Here was a book I admired that spawned three feature films from its four novellas.

That in turn led me to consider the novella as a possible solution for a few other story ideas that had backed up in my mental queue. Which, incidentally, gave me something to do on my breaks from the highly serious and immensely long novel that I was in the process of writing.

Given a few ups and downs and false starts, that's pretty much what happened. Bill Schafer of Subterranean Press encouraged me from the start and published the first two of the resulting stories in his online magazine. And within two days of my finishing the final draft of the last piece, I had his contract in hand for this book.

ALL ALONG I've thought of these four stories as a group. They all played out like movies in my head as I wrote them, and I tried extra hard to pile on the visuals and the action. Together they make a kind of Saturday matinee, starting with a black-and-white newsreel, continuing with a creature feature and a cartoon, and winding up with a spy thriller to top the bill.

If they also share some concerns about the abuse of power, I hope that doesn't distract too much from the business at hand: good guys and unabashed bad guys, gun fights, car chases, races against time, things blowing up—and maybe even a happy ending or two.

# THE

# BLACK

# SUN

T HEY ALL KNEW the man who had invited them to this anonymous Paris conference room. They had all seen him perform as the Amazing Adonini, and some had been fortunate enough to study under him or to otherwise know him in his off-stage life as Ernst Adler. The thinning white hair, the white goatee, the deep lines that put his mouth in parentheses, all were to be expected of a man in his seventies. What no one had anticipated was the hint of fever in his faded blue eyes, the slump of his shoulders, the faint tremor in his long, thin fingers.

"Gentlemen—and lady—thank you all for being here," he said, in English that still held the brittleness of his native German. "I know that it was a sacrifice for many of you to come on such short notice. I have one additional favor to ask before we proceed. You have all taken the Magician's Oath, and I must insist that everything I tell you today be held under that covenant. If you do not feel you can comply, I must ask you to excuse yourselves now."

The twelve magicians at the table all nodded or spoke their assent, and Adler relaxed visibly. "Paco," he said, "would you get the lights?"

Paco, under the name of Francisco de Sevilla, was Spain's greatest magician. His black hair was still lustrous in his fifties, though his waistline had suffered from his success. As Paco stood up, Adler switched on the magic lantern that sat in front of him. Paco flicked off the bank of switches by the door, and the room went dark save for the glowing cone of light from the projector.

Adler inserted a glass slide and a man's face appeared on the wall at the front of the room. The face was middle-aged and the eyes smoldered with anger. A dark forelock fell across the man's forehead and a toothbrush mustache sprouted from his upper lip.

"I assume," Adler said, "that most of you know this man. President

4

Hindenburg appointed him Chancellor of my country a year ago this past January, and since then he has ruthlessly extended his power by any and all means available to him."

In a quieter voice, he said, "Because illusions are our craft, we magicians are less susceptible than most to the claims of spiritualists and occultists. Yet I must tell you what I have seen with my own eyes. This man Hitler is evil, evil in a sense that approaches the absolute, even the supernatural.

"To be more specific, he combines a homicidal rage and bitterness with a personal charisma that is terrifying to behold. He believes he has been wronged, both personally and politically. Because of what the German people have suffered, from the savagery of the Versailles Treaty, which sought to punish us for all the sins of the Great War, to the runaway inflation that recently bankrupted our entire nation, many have come to accept his vision of themselves as victims.

"He has made no secret of his intentions. Under the pretense of Lebensraum—'breathing room'—he plans to rearm Germany and forcibly advance its borders to the east, which will likely precipitate another global war. And I believe that he must be taken literally when he says that he means to murder the entire Jewish population of Europe."

"Preposterous." The booming voice came from Hermes, an upper-class and well fed Englishman in his late thirties. "Herr Hitler has performed an economic miracle in Germany. This nonsense about mass extermination is mere rabble rousing. We're speaking of millions of people, here. It's not even possible, let alone financially tenable."

The ensuing silence was both long and uncomfortable. Hermes broke it himself by demanding, "What do you mean to do, assassinate him? In violation of every principle of our brotherhood?"

"No, sir," Adler said. "I do not intend violence of any kind. For one thing, it would only make a martyr of him. For another, I myself am morally opposed to it." He cleared his throat. "However. I *do* propose political intercession in the affairs of a sovereign state, which you, among others, may feel is an inappropriate use of our skills. If that is the case, I would excuse you from further discussions, with sincere assurances of no ill will on my part."

Again the room was silent, except for the faint humming of the magic lantern. Finally Hermes got to his feet. "A long way for a damned waste of time," he said, cramming on his hat as he made for the door.

"I should also mention," Adler said, "that what I am about to propose is assuredly dangerous. The odds of success are poor and there is a significant chance of physical harm or even death. I am old enough not to care, especially when I consider the millions of lives at stake, however, many of you have barely begun your adult lives, let alone your careers. I am not asking for commitment at this point, but anyone who is not willing to consider that sacrifice, or anyone who has other reservations, is welcome to depart now, with my thanks for listening this far."

Two more men quietly rose and left the room.

When the door closed, a woman's voice spoke up. "If you're not going to assassinate him, what then do you propose to do?" She spoke English, as they all did, although hers had an American accent. She was dark-haired and shapely, and as the Great Belinda she was one of the few women to headline in a field where her sex was generally consigned to the role of assistant.

"Ah, Cora, that is indeed the question, is it not?" Adler changed the slide in the lantern. The new photograph showed a long line of soldiers in similar light colored shirts, some in matching trousers, others in darker jodhpurs. They wore fatigue caps and marched in tight formation. The camera had caught them with right arms held high in salute and left legs thrust forward in mid-goose-step.

"Germany today is a police state with three different kinds of police," Adler said, "which is at least two too many. The first were the Sturmabteilung or SA, the stormtroopers, also known as the Brownshirts. Hitler recruited them to attack dissenters at early Nazi rallies." The next slide showed a man with a round, heavily scarred face, graying hair and mustache, and a warm smile. "Ernst Röhm, commander of the SA, wants to sidestep the restrictions on the size of the German Army by expanding the SA. The regular army, the Reichswehr, understandably feel threatened by this. Also they are concerned about the fanaticism of the Brownshirts, who are known to viciously attack bystanders who fail to give the Hitler salute. They burn down Jewish businesses and turn Communist rallies into street brawls. They are common thugs and bullies.

"Röhm is also well known to be homosexual. This was not a problem in the past, although it is becoming one now as the country turns increasingly prudish, reflecting the pathologically repressed sexuality of Hitler himself.

"So that is one tension, between the Reichswehr and the SA."

His next slide showed a man in a solid black uniform, his face obscured by a high peaked cap. "Next we have the Schutzstaffel, the dreaded SS, originally an elite paramilitary group within the SA that was charged with guarding Hitler. They are now completely independent, and pledge their loyalty to Hitler alone." The shadow of Adler's finger extended into the light to point out the twin lightning bolts on the lapel of the uniform. "Note the runes. I will have more to say about that in a minute."

He changed the slide again. "Under this man, the SS grew until it now fills the role of both internal security and public police for the entire country." The face on the wall might have belonged to a stereotypical accountant: weak chin, round glasses, receding hairline, an even smaller version of Hitler's miniature mustache. "He is a former chicken farmer named Heinrich Himmler, and we will return to him shortly as well. For the moment, note one more tension, which is that the SA feel that the SS have undermined their power.

"Finally we have the Geheime Staatspolizei, the Gestapo for short, the Secret State Police, the creation of Hermann Göring." The next slide showed Göring to be dashing, in a small-eyed, barrel-chested sort of way, with the breast of his expensive, tailored uniform plastered with medals. "The Gestapo have taken the tactics of terror and intimidation that the SA and SS developed and turned them into high art. Göring created the Gestapo out of the Prussian police on his own whim. Just last month, after numerous clashes of jurisdiction, Hitler took them away and put them under Himmler's command. Göring was not pleased, nor were many of his officers."

The next image showed a heavy man with stiff, brush-cut white hair, a skeptical expression, and a mustache with huge curves at the ends. "Technically Hitler is only Chancellor, which makes him subordinate to this man, Paul von Hindenburg, President of Germany. Hindenburg appointed Hitler to his current position, though Hitler had not performed that well at the polls, and there is evidence that Hindenburg now regrets his decision. Unfortunately he is old, getting weaker by the day, and is not expected to live out the year."

Adler took a sip of water and shifted in his chair. "In short, we stand at a crossroads, a unique moment in history. Hitler's three most powerful subordinates all despise each other and are maneuvering for position. The man who put Hitler in power is looking for a reason to remove him. Hitler is at this moment more vulnerable than he has ever been, or likely will be again. Left alone, he will doubtless move to consolidate his power, and do so in a ruthless and violent way. We must act quickly to take advantage."

He placed the slide of the chicken farmer in the machine once more. "Luckily for us, Himmler is the Achilles Heel of the Third Reich. Although he is ruthless, well organized, and absolutely loyal to Hitler, he is also...a believer. He believes in visitors from outer space, a hollow Earth, the magical power of runes, mental telepathy, resurrection of the dead, and the superiority of the Aryan race, among other delusions."

The next slide showed an engraving of a castle as seen from the air. The walls formed a narrow triangle, the long sides intersecting in a large, circular tower. "This is Wewelsburg Castle, in the Westphalia district of Prussia. It is Himmler's headquarters, which he intends to restore as a sort of Black Camelot, complete with a

Round Table. He sees himself as a pagan, Teutonic King Arthur on a mystical quest.

"And that, my friends," Adler said, "will be his undoing. And Hitler's as well."

OUTSIDE THE HOTEL, Cora watched as Paco, Robertini, and Gideon got into separate taxis and sped away. The sun was setting and the rainy spring afternoon turned from gray to black.

"Do you have time for a coffee?" Adler asked.

"Certainly," Cora said.

They found an outdoor table under an awning where no one could overhear them. "Five of us," Adler said. "More than I had feared. Fewer than I had hoped."

"Against the five of us," Cora said, "what chance does Nazi Germany have?"

Adler smiled with little conviction. "I thought Gideon's ideas for the endgame very clever."

"Clever, yes, but also very strange. Like these French Surrealists. If I may say so, Gideon himself seems strange, perhaps even a little... unstable."

"Perhaps. I have heard stories. However, he is a brilliant mimic and we need him. And who among us is without his idiosyncrasies?"

"I suppose," Cora said. She would also keep a watchful eye, for very different reasons, on the escape artist Robertini. He was just the sort of very physical, very intense, very serious man that she was attracted to, and there was no room for such feelings in their undertaking.

"Speaking of idiosyncrasies," she said, "this will cost you a fortune. Can you really afford it?"

"I am older than I ever imagined I would be. I have no family. What else am I to do with my money? Tell me, have you heard of this man Gandhi, in India?"

"I've heard the name. I know little about him."

"He is trying to better the lives of the peasant class, and I think he means ultimately to end British rule there. He said something to the

effect that violence may appear to do good in the short term, yet in
the long term it can only do evil. I have spent many sleepless hours
thinking about Germany in that light. To fight the Nazis on their
own terms would plunge the world into a frenzy of violence that
would surpass even the Great War. I asked myself what the alternative could be, and this is the result. Like the fable about putting the
bell on the cat, once I had come up with the idea, there was no one
else to put it into action.

"But what of you, Cora? Paco has good reason to fear Fascism—it
is a constant threat in his own country. Gideon and Robertini are
both Jewish. But you, my dear...I am more grateful than I can say
for your commitment, although I do not understand why you are
willing to take the risk."

Cora considered for a moment, then said, "Compared to your
idealism, this may seem rather petty. Back in Brooklyn, when I was
in high school, my best friend was Jewish. Her name was
Rebeccah, and I always thought she was beautiful. She herself,
however, hated her nose, which had a bend in it, like a tiny eagle's
beak. She thought it made her look Jewish. For her sixteenth birthday the only thing she wanted was plastic surgery, and her parents
reluctantly gave in. Except the surgery had complications, two small
perforations in the septum that they were unable to repair. After the
surgery, whenever she breathed through her nose, there was a whistling noise. From shame, she always breathed through her mouth,
and even then you could sometimes hear it. She began to avoid her
friends, me included, no matter how hard I tried. The last time I
talked to her parents, they said she wanted no contact with anyone
from her past.

"All I can tell you is that the memory of Rebeccah has haunted
me ever since. What is the power of this hatred that can infect its
own victims? That can turn a person against her own beauty and
cause her to mutilate herself? It might surprise you to know that I
have also experienced prejudice, for being a woman in a man's profession, for daring to think for myself and manage my own affairs.

And now that I have lines around my eyes and a body that is feeling the effects of thirty-eight years of gravity, I am considered old and of no further use."

"I assure you, you are more beautiful than ever..." Adler said. Cora waved away his objections.

"You're kind, and I digress. The point is that men like Hitler, whose currency is hatred, do nothing but poison minds and destroy lives. Even as indirectly as they did Rebeccah's."

Adler nodded. "When you deliberately appeal to the worst in human nature, human nature sinks to meet you. Which reminds me, when was the last time you were in Germany?"

"Two years ago. Has it changed so much?"

"Berlin especially. You had best prepare yourself for a shock."

"Well, then," Cora smiled. "We shall have to change it back again."

SINCE HE HAD BEEN old enough to read, Robert Sándor had idolized the Great Houdini. For his twelfth birthday, his father had taken him to Budapesst to see Houdini perform the effect he called "the upside down," his famous Chinese Water Torture Cell escape. From that night on, Robert began to introduce himself as Robertini the Magnificent, to the endless amusement of his friends.

Like Houdini, Robert was Hungarian, Jewish, small for his age, and fiercely competitive. With his father's help, he found an after-school job with the local locksmith in Kesztolc, and on weekends he hitch-hiked to Budapest to loiter in Hungary's only magic shop. He spent the rest of his time practicing, initially on all the locks in the house, then on all the locks in the village. He never succumbed to the temptation to take anything, and became a local legend when, after accidentally setting off the alarm in the town bank, he took the time to secure the doors before he fled. Everyone knew who was responsible, though he left no evidence, and his father gently suggested that he might want to be more careful in future. Before he finished secondary school he had obtained a booking with a vaudeville company and, with his father's reluctant permission, he left home for good.

Robert was on tour in England on the night in late 1933 when
the Greenshirts of the Hungarian National Socialist Agricultural
Laborers' and Workers' Party outlined a Star of David in petrol in
the field next to his parents' house and set fire to it. The fire spread
to the house and his parents and youngest sister were killed. By the
time the news reached Robert and he was able to return to
Kesztolc, their bodies were already in the ground and Robert's heart
had become a small, cold thing.

Now it was Sunday, 27 May, 1934, and Robert and Paco stood
outside the Swiss Wing of the Hofburg Palace, in the exact geo-
graphical center of Vienna. They occupied a lop-sided courtyard
thirty meters on a side, surrounded by four-story-high white walls
that offered only a single narrow passage as an exit. A perfect place,
Robert thought, to be trapped like rats.

In Adler's grand plan, this was Phase 1, and he had not asked
much of Robert: merely to rob the Weltliche Schatzkammer, the
Secular Treasury of the Austrian Empire, containing the crown jew-
els of the Hapsburgs, among other priceless treasures. Not to mention the fact that he had to do it in broad daylight without being
detected or even suspected.

Robert's own plan had taken shape over three days. He'd spent
those days wandering through the interlocking white plastered
rooms wearing a series of disguises, pretending to stare into the
two-meter-high, glass-fronted mahogany cases filled with gold and
precious stones and carvings and ceramics, while in reality figuring
out the elaborate alarm system, the walking patterns of the guards,
the size and make of the various locks.

He had not shown undue interest in the item labeled Heilige
Lanze, the Holy Lance, located near the Imperial Crown.

The lance point—it had no shaft—was leaf-shaped, 35 centimeters
long, and five centimeters across at its widest point. It was formed
largely of iron that had oxidized centuries before into a dark brown,
with the exception of a sleeve of gold that wrapped the middle third
of its length. Inscribed on the sleeve were the words "Lancea et clavus

domini," lance and nail of God, referring to the belief that the sleeve enclosed a nail from the Crucifixion. It was a complex construction, the outer blades bound to a central shaft with wire, the shaft eventually expanding at the bottom to a socket that would fit a wooden pole.

Adler had insisted that a mere replica of the lance would not be convincing enough, and that the best counterfeit his fabricators could manage would only deceive from a distance. His first requirement, therefore, was the putative original.

Robert checked his watch. It read 3:25. He smiled at Paco who, like him, was anonymous in white coveralls, and said, "It's time."

Paco's return smile was forced. "Can I change my mind?" he asked. His German was accented but passable. "This is clearly insane, what we're doing."

"I see you haven't forgotten that confidence is everything," Robert said. "Come on, let's get started."

Robert, whose German was fluent, carried the clipboard. He led Paco through a wooden archway the color of dried blood, topped with the coat of arms of the Holy Roman Empire, an eagle with elevated wings.

Robert walked straight to Room 11, where the Imperial Regalia were kept, and approached the nearer of the two guards. The boy was scarcely over his teenage spots, clearly uncomfortable in his red blazer and white turtleneck sweater as he towered 30 centimeters over Robert.

"Who's in charge here?" Robert asked in a bored, mildly irritable tone. "We're supposed to perform an inspection of the alarms."

"What, now?" the boy asked.

"Yes, now," Robert said. "Half an hour ago, in fact."

The boy caught the eye of the guard at the other end of the long room and tilted his head. The other guard nodded. On his first visit, Robert had quickly determined that only one of the two guards in each hall could leave his post at any given time.

The boy took them to a small office where a paunchy, white-haired man wrote laboriously in an oversized ledger. He had a cigarette in one hand, for which there appeared to be no room in his overflowing ashtray.

"Dieter," the boy said, "these men are here to look at the alarms."

Dieter did not look up. "Not now."

"Sorry for the inconvenience," Robert said. "I'm afraid our instructions require us to—"

"Perhaps you didn't hear me."

"With all due respect," Robert said, "I believe your supervisor is Herr Grauerholz, who in turn reports to the Antiquities Committee. If you would call the number on this work order, I think you might prevent Herr Grauerholz from himself getting a call that he might find most upsetting."

The color went out of Dieter's red cheeks and he glanced up briefly before snatching the clipboard and making the call. Robert was able to hear Adler's voice on the other end, screaming. When there was a momentary pause, Dieter said, "Jawohl, mein herr," then the screaming resumed. Finally Dieter was able to say, "Right away, mein herr," and hang up. The hand that put the earpiece back on the hook trembled slightly.

Dieter looked at the boy. "Give them what they want and get them out of here."

Robert repressed a smile. "If you could just sign here on the order?"

The boy, now all jangled nerves, took them to the alarm box. "I don't have the key. Perhaps Dieter…"

Robert briefly flashed his hotel key. "I have the master." He palmed it as he turned toward the box, replaced it with a pick, and had the gray metal box open in two seconds.

"Er, will there be anything else?" the boy asked.

"Your name?" Robert demanded.

"Peter, sir."

Robert sniffed. "Peter. We will call you if we need you."

Five minutes later Robert felt as much as heard a hush go through the museum, followed by the murmur of excited voices, all repeating the same phrase: "Mein Gott, der Führer!"

•

GIDEON HAD MADE his reputation with a unique combination of comedy and sleight of hand. His innate gift for imitation had earned him several playground beatings as a child in Minneapolis until he'd learned to defuse the anger of his victims by discovering a coin in an ear or a chosen card in a deck. By the time he'd graduated to impersonating Charlie Chaplin and W. C. Fields, he was also juggling, producing doves, and performing two dozen different cigarette tricks.

He understood that there was something not quite right with him. The urge to mock would take him at inopportune moments, driving away everyone who attempted to get close. At first he'd believed that someone would eventually care enough to see past his defenses. Now there were times when he scarcely remembered the name he'd been given at his Brit Milah. He was only Gideon now, and Gideon was so many faces and voices that no one would ever pin him down again.

He did not consider himself a hero—the opposite, in fact. He had volunteered only because it was the Amazing Adonini who asked, a man who was spoken of in the same breath as Hermann and Keller and Blackstone and Thurston, a man whose recognition and respect Gideon craved.

Gideon made up for his barely adequate German with a repertoire of flawless regional accents. It came down to how you held your mouth and tongue. Impressions amounted to the same thing on a larger scale. Once you spotted the trick of posture, the gesture, the rest was easy.

The key to Hitler was his ungainliness, his discomfort inside his own body, his inability to find something to occupy his hands. Then the madman inside would ignite and he would forget his body entirely. Gideon had been doing Hitler for over a year now, since the man had been made Chancellor, so he had the wig, nose, mustache, and trench coat already. He even had a pair of thin glass scleral lenses to turn his brown eyes to the clear blue of Hitler's, although for the current purpose they would have been overkill.

He and Cora had arrived half an hour early and sat in the parking area outside the museum in awkward conversation. Though she was ten years older than Gideon, she had an unrepentant sensuality and self-confidence that he found most alluring. He sensed that Cora did not particularly like him, and he knew she resented his request that she wear a low-cut dress so as to provide the maximum possible distraction. Her reluctance notwithstanding, she had in fact done a remarkable job in that area, such that Gideon's own distraction was doubtless making her discomfort worse. Even the blonde wig and heavy makeup she'd affected as a disguise added to her—unfortunately false—air of availability.

Finally Cora glanced at her watch and let out a sigh of relief. Gideon verified that it was 3:35 and they got out of the car.

"Anyone who knows the first thing about Hitler," Cora said, through a falsely radiant smile, "knows that he would never be seen in public with a woman whose tits were hanging out."

As they strolled arm in arm past the vast, curving neoclassical façade of the Neue Berg section of the palace, people gaped at them in astonishment.

"Well, whoever they think we are," Gideon said, "we seem to be having the desired effect."

They wound their way through the maze of passageways and courtyards to the Swiss Wing, where they simply stood in the sunlight and pretended to converse while Gideon stared at Cora with a wolfish Hitlerian grin. A crowd quickly gathered in the portico outside the Secular Treasury, making only a halfhearted attempt not to stare. Although Austria had not yet joined the Reich, Hitler had been born here, had invented himself right here in Vienna, and curiosity about him was boundless.

Gideon let his gaze drift over the faces in the doorway. Still no sign of Paco. Suddenly the enormity of the risk overwhelmed him. If things went wrong inside, armed guards would descend in swarms, Gideon's disguise would be penetrated in seconds, and all four of them would be arrested and asked questions they could not answer. A drop of sweat trailed into Gideon's right eye and he realized that he was speaking nonsense that only sounded like German. Cora raised one eyebrow, as if concerned that he might fall apart at any moment.

He wondered if her fears were justified.

ROBERT FLIPPED THE SWITCH that disabled all the alarms. A red light flashed on the panel and his heartbeat sped up to match.

He nodded to Paco, whose job it was now to help spread the Führer rumor and then get himself into a position to make eye contact with Gideon.

Robert returned to Room 11. The older guard had joined the throng at the entrance while Peter remained on watch, standing directly in front of the cabinet that held the Lance. He shifted from one foot to the other as if he needed the toilet, gazing longingly toward the front entrance.

"Go ahead," Robert told him. "I'll watch things here."

"If Dieter found out, I'd lose my job."

"Take a quick look. No one will ever know. When will you get another chance like this?"

The boy hesitated, torn between irresistible forces. Robert jerked his head toward the entrance and smiled. The boy melted. "Just for a second, then," he said, and bolted.

A second was all Robert needed. He picked the lock on the case, opened the glass front, took out the Lance, replaced it with a replica from his pocket, and had it locked again in virtually a single motion. By the time Peter re-entered the hall, Robert was at the far end, tapping one of the cabinets with a middle finger in the way the doctor at the clinic had tapped on Robert's chest when he'd had the influenza as a boy.

Peter was radiant. "Is it all right? Did Dieter..."

"No," Robert said. "All is well."

He made his own way to the front. Paco stood in the crowd at the doorway, looking into the museum. Robert nodded to him, and

Paco in turn nodded to Gideon. Robert caught a glimpse of Cora in her costume and had to force himself to look away, a slow smile spreading across his face. He switched the alarms back on and then, for spite, made one more trip to Dieter's office.

"Everything is working," Robert said. "Sign here."

Dieter grunted and signed.

"And here."

Dieter signed again. Robert resisted a diabolical urge to keep going and tucked the clipboard under his arm.

"What's all the commotion out there?" Dieter asked.

"I don't know," Robert said. "Perhaps a clown doing tricks for the children?"

THAT NIGHT at Vienna's Westbahnhof railway station, Robert paused at a news kiosk. He set his worn leather satchel on the concrete floor and reached for a copy of the *Neue Freie Presse*.

An older man in a broad-brimmed fedora appeared beside him and placed an identical satchel next to his. "Gruss Gott, mein herr," the man said. Robert glanced at Adler, nodded, and looked away. Adler purchased a packet of Atikah cigarettes, picked up Robert's satchel, and disappeared into the crowd.

THE DAY AFTER the Weltliche Schatzkammer robbery, Adler settled on his final target. And so, he thought, begins Phase 2.

He had been a month in the central German hamlet of Neuenbeken, a long way from any major cities, but only 30 kilometers from Wewelsburg Castle. It was a small enough village for everyone to know everyone else and for strangers to attract suspicion.

His cover identity was Ernst Ackermann, newly retired dock worker from Hamburg, living on a hectare of gently rolling forest land outside town, arriving by bicycle in the warm summer mornings at the library or the greengrocer's or at the café for leisurely conversation. With his hair cut close to his skull, his goatee shaved, a pair of foam rubber pads in his gums, and an artificial scar across the top of his nose, the likelihood was small that anyone would recognize him as the Amazing Adonini. Instead the locals thought him a good sort, if perhaps a bit dim. If anyone cared to look further, they would find a complete set of impeccably forged documents for Ackermann in the appropriate government agencies.

His target, Rudi, was the 11-year-old son of Mayor Glöckner. Rudi was solitary and melancholic, given to long walks in the woods carrying a copy of *The Sorrows of Young Werther*.

The spring had been the driest in memory, part of a world-wide drought that was turning the American West into a wilderness of dust. The heat even permeated the forest, and the fallen leaves and pine needles crackled with Rudi's every step, making him easy to follow. He was sitting under a beech tree, reading, when Adler appeared before him.

The boy started and dropped the book.

Adler smiled, held up a single cautionary finger, and wordlessly took a gold sovereign from his shirt pocket. He tossed the coin into his mouth, swallowed it with comic difficulty, then pulled it out of his right ear. Looking puzzled, he then removed a duplicate from his left ear.

Rudi laughed.

Maintaining his distance and his smile, Adler wiggled one of the coins so that the sun, directly overhead, flashed repeatedly into the boy's eyes. "Listen to my voice," Adler said, "and my voice only."

CORA HAD ALWAYS loved Berlin. In daylight, as she strolled past the fashionable shops on the Kurfürstendamm, it seemed unchanged. The sidewalks thronged with tourists and well-off locals, all overdressed and in high spirits. The streetcars clanged and the architecture dazzled the eye, from the majesty of the Brandenburg Gate to the onion domes of the New Synagogue to the elegant Bauhaus apartments of Maeckeritzstrasse.

It was at night that the difference became inescapable. A few of the most famous clubs and cabarets remained open: Werner Fink still satirized the government at Die Katakombe; the Residenz-Casino, the "Resi," still offered telephones and pneumatic tubes at the tables so that strangers could send gifts and invitations to each other; the Haus Vaterland still contained five stories of themed restaurants, musicians, and cinema, with a giant dance floor under its lighted dome.

What was missing was the sex.

The Eldorado, famous for its transvestites, where Cora had seen Marlene Dietrich perform; the Hummingbird, the Silhouette, and the Adonis-Lounge; the Café Dorian Grey, the Mikado Bar, the Auluka Lounge, the Monocle-Bar, the Zauberflote, and on and on and on, all of them closed under Göring's orders, part of his mission to crush Berlin's wild, decadent, anarchistic, anti-Nazi spirit.

It was true that the great sexual license of Berlin had amounted, in the end, to the freedom of rich tourists to rent the bodies of the nouveau pauvre and use them as playgrounds for their erotic fantasies. There had always been a desperate quality to the revelry, embodied most tragically by Anita Berber, the stunning, androgynous, voracious nude dancer whose appetite for sex, cocaine, morphine, chloroform, ether, and alcohol left her dead of old age at 29.

And yet, and yet...so many had found liberation there, including her friend Kurt, who had come to Berlin from the Bavarian countryside at age 16 and discovered the beautiful woman inside him, and found the lovers of both sexes who adored that beauty. Or Fritzi and Franzi, the two girls who never slept with anyone but each other, who had transformed themselves into mirror images, with their tuxedos and pasted-on mustaches and boy's haircuts parted on opposite sides, Fritzi with a monocle in her right eye, Franzi with a monocle in her left. And there were the things that Cora herself had done that shocked her now to remember, even as they gave her a wistful smile. She had spent so much of her life in the single-minded pursuit of her career that Berlin's frank and easy-going sensuality had seduced her before she knew it.

She started at the Resi, making no effort to disguise herself. A glass of overpriced champagne, a slow stroll through the tables, and then she moved on. At each of her old haunts she let herself be seen, and seen to be scanning the faces around her. Finally she returned to her hotel, exhausted and dispirited, as the sun rose.

On the third night, she made a final stop at the Kleist Casino, where the dim lights, tiny crowded tables, and dark red walls were as tawdry as she remembered. Almost immediately she saw a man in his fifties, handsome and dark haired, dressed as always in his black suit, like a mortician. Poor, sad Michael, who had been Kurt's lover for 27 days and never stopped pining for him. He was so happy to see Cora that he burst into tears.

"I'm sorry," he said. "It's just that seeing you brings back those days, which I miss so much." She squeezed herself into a chair at his table and he clutched her hand feverishly.

"I saw," she said. "So many of the old places are gone."

Michael shook his head sadly. "If it were only the cabarets and the newspapers I would not care so much. Starting one year ago, they began to round up the Jews, the gypsies, the communists, the Jehovah's Witnesses, the schwulen like me, and send us to the Konzentrationslager, the KZ. For Berlin it is in Oranienburg, but there are others. Esterwegen, Dachau. Nobody knows how many people they have."

"Oh, no. Not Kurt...?"

"No, not Kurt. Not yet. But we live in fear now, every day."

"Can you get word to him? I need to see him. It's very important."

"If you were anyone else I would tell you I don't know where he is. For you...I will try."

A FARMER HAD FOUND Rudi wandering, terrified, in the road at the edge of town. Rudi said that he had fallen while climbing a hill and had struck his head a glancing blow on a rock. When he woke up, he said, he was completely blind.

The doctor was summoned but no physiological cause was found. There was no bruise, though Rudi reacted in pain when the doctor touched his temple. Mayor Glöckner personally took him to the hospital in Dusseldorf, where a baffled intern suggested that perhaps the blindness might be "hysterical" in nature.

The owner of the village café, whose name was Kuefer, had taken to having the occasional cup of tea with Adler. Rudi had been blind for four days when Kuefer finally mentioned the incident.

It was Friday, 8 June, and they were sitting at an outdoor table, though the sun had not yet driven away the last of the morning chill. Kuefer, who affected a beret and a walrus mustache, grew damp around the eyes as he talked. Adler listened sympathetically and let him go on for some time about the anguish of the boy's mother, the desperation of the father, the sense of terrible injustice that had gripped the entire village. All the while he put on a show of increasing discomfort.

"Well," Kuefer said, "we can discuss something else. I can see that this is making you uneasy."

"No, it's not that, it's..."

"What?"

Adler shook his head. "No, never mind, it's too ridiculous."

"What is?"

"I hate to even mention it, because I don't believe in such things myself. I used to be a bit of a gambler, a card player. One night a couple of years ago this fellow from India was losing badly, and was badly drunk besides. He had no money left and offered to put this sort of large metal talisman on the table to cover his bet. 'It's magic,' he said, very serious. The thing was very strange looking, old rusty iron and a collar of gold. At that point the hand was down to just him and me, and I had already won a good deal of his money, so I agreed. He lost, of course, and I probably would have thrown it away and not given it further thought except for two things."

Adler paused, waiting to set the hook.

"Yes?" Kuefer said. "What things?"

"Well, first of all, when I touched it, I felt...I don't know how to describe it. A sense of power. Almost an electrical charge."

"And the other thing?"

"The look on his face when he lost it. There was sadness, yet there was also...relief. As if a great burden had been lifted from him. We both left the game at that point, and he taught me how to work it."

Kuefer leaned forward in his chair. "And did you? Work it?"

"No," Adler said. "As I say, I don't really believe in such things. Besides..."

"Yes? Gott im Himmel, man, tell the story."

"Well, the Indian shipped out the next day. And I heard, later, that there was a terrible storm soon after the ship left Hamburg, and that he was washed overboard and drowned. So I decided that even if it was real, maybe it was best to leave it alone."

"But you think it could cure Rudi's blindness?"

"The doctors say Rudi's condition might be in his mind. So as long as Rudi believes the thing has power, maybe that would be enough. But it's probably a foolish idea."

Kuefer leaned back in his chair, chewing on a fingernail. "I think it's a very good idea. Do you honestly believe there's a danger to you from using it?"

Adler shrugged. "This seems harmless enough. And the cause certainly justifies the risk. I know I'm only a stranger here, but I would like to be of service if I can."

"Oh, I know you're all right," Kuefer said. "I pride myself as a judge of character. I'll talk to the Glöckners. Come back here tomorrow morning with this 'talisman' and we shall see."

FOR TWO DAYS Cora kept up her search. On the third day the telephone woke her at 11 AM and Michael's gloomy voice said, "Tonight go to the same place at the same time we met. Yes?"

"Yes," Cora said, and Michael hung up immediately.

She spent a long time choosing her clothes and applying her makeup, remembering Kurt's acid tongue. He had always been elegant, whether dressed as a man or a woman, and he expected the same of everyone else.

Yet when she saw him that night in the Kleist Casino, she hardly recognized him. He wore a white shirt, khaki pants, and sleeveless sweater, the bourgeois uniform. His hair was short on the sides, longish on top, parted on the right—a haircut not unlike Hitler's. He stood up as soon as he saw her and hugged her fiercely. "How beautiful you look," he whispered.

She held his face in her hands. The fire of his wit still burned in his eyes, but like an abused animal, he couldn't hold her gaze. "And you," she said, "look so very different."

"Yes," he said bitterly. "I am very männlich now."

He was alone—poor Michael had apparently failed to get himself included. When Cora reached for a chair, Kurt said, "Let's walk."

Even at two in the morning, the Kleistrasse hummed with traffic, the westbound cars partially obscured by the trees in the median. They passed hotel after hotel, then turned north toward the Tiergarten, Berlin's version of Central Park, a kilometer or so away. Cora's attempts to reminisce the way she had with Michael only made Kurt withdraw. "It makes you unhappy, thinking of the past?" she asked.

"No, on the contrary. I cannot believe I was so lucky to have been the age I was and to have been in this place. Never before in history has there been such a time for men such as I, and there may never be such a time again. It was like Camelot in the legends, one glorious moment surrounded by darkness. I would not have missed it for the entire world."

"But it ended so soon."

"Moments pass," he said quietly, "even the most glorious. All you ever have of anything is memories, whether of your first love or the words you just spoke. There is no 'now,' only, always, the past."

Cora felt a sudden shock of grief, as if the years of her happiness had only that moment fled from her, never to return. Kurt's despair was contagious. She felt bereft and alone. "And the future?" she asked.

Kurt showed her a tight-lipped smile. "Here comes the future now."

Cora looked up to see five drunken SAS in brown shirts and jack boots stagger down the sidewalk toward them. Kurt seized her upper arm and dragged her up against the nearest shop front to make room. As the men passed in a haze of beer fumes, Kurt raised his right arm in the Hitler salute. One of the Nazis slowed, staring at Kurt as if he sensed something out of kilter. Kurt kept his gaze focused in the middle distance and his arm extended until the man shook his head and moved on.

"One night," Kurt said, "a friend of mine gave a gang of them das Zeigen des Vogels, you know, the middle finger. They beat him so badly that he was in the hospital for a month, and they gave me a solid thrashing too, for being with him."

"They're animals," Cora said. "I don't know how people put up with them."

"Who's going to stop them?"

They walked on in silence. In the distance Cora saw the greater darkness of the Tiergarten. Finally she said, "What if you could change things?"

"What, get rid of the Nazis? You are going to loan me maybe your magic wand? 'Hey, presto!'"

"I'm serious. What if there were a way?"

"If I truly believed it possible? I would do anything."

"Do you still have your political connections? There must be some kind of organized opposition to..." She trailed off, suddenly afraid to pronounce Hitler's name. "To the ruling party." It's affecting even me, she thought.

Kurt lit a cigarette and shook his head. "You're too late, by more than a year. As soon as Hitler came to power, he outlawed all of the left-wing parties, from the Communists to the Social Democrats. Ernst Thälmann, our Presidential candidate, was arrested a year ago March. He's still waiting for a trial he will never get. Clara Zetkin, our great theorist, died in exile last June. Ernst Toller, the great playwright and organizer, is in exile too. Hitler is ruthless and utterly efficient. It was like 1919 again, when they murdered Kurt

Eisner, Rosa Luxemburg, and Gustav Landauer within two months of each other."

"You knew Toller, didn't you? You were friends?"

"Friends only, if that's what you're asking."

"If you can get a message to him, tell him he must return to Berlin. He must be here on the night of the summer solstice. That would be a week from next Wednesday, the twentieth of June."

"What happens then?"

"I can't tell you. But you must be there too, and everyone you know. And here's what you must do..."

ON SATURDAY, Adler arrived at the café early, to find Kuefer already waiting for him. "No improvement, then?" Adler asked.

"None. It's a measure of their desperation, I suppose, that they were eager for you to see the boy. I've brought my car. We can have tea later. If you are successful, perhaps we will have schnapps."

"I make no promises..."

"Understood, understood. Let us be off."

The Glöckner house was two stories, half-timbered, perhaps hundreds of years old, lovingly and expensively maintained. Inside, the wood floors shone with polish where they weren't covered by Oriental carpets. The furniture was new and comfortable, the ceilings high. Mayor Glöckner, who had let them in, said, "Herr Ackermann is here, Rudi."

The boy had already risen from the couch, sightless eyes staring straight in front of him, hands half-raised defensively, a look of fear and longing on his face. His mother stood beside him, wearing a nearly identical expression.

"Hello, Rudi," Adler said.

Rudi gave no indication that he recognized Adler's voice. "Good day, sir."

Rudi's mother half-heartedly asked, "Can I get you something to drink? Tea or coffee?"

"No, thank you," Adler said. "I am only here to try to help."

Mayor Glöckner tugged nervously at the fingers of his right hand. "So...how does this work?"

Adler shrugged apologetically. "I hope Herr Kuefer made it clear that I am in the dark about all this. I have never used this...thing... before, so we must figure it out together."

From the look that the Glöckners exchanged, it was clear that Kuefer had erred on the side of optimism.

Adler crossed to a low wooden table in front of the couch, piled with magazines and neatly folded newspapers. He took a canvas bag out of his jacket pocket and set it on the table. "Sit down, Rudi," he said gently, "and try to relax."

Rudi sat. His muscles stood out like tent poles stretching canvas.

"Would you draw the curtains, please?" Adler said. "And turn off the lights?"

The summer sun was strong enough that the room was still illuminated. Adler drew out the spear point in such a way that the muted sunlight glinted off the gold collar. The Glöckners gasped.

"As I understand it," Adler said, "this is an instrument for focusing and amplifying the will." Adler was using his own will to modulate his voice and gestures, to keep them simple and ordinary and not arouse suspicions of theatricality. "So I think we should all do that now. We must focus our wills on the thought of Rudi being able to see again."

Adler let them all stand in silence, concentrating, for half a minute, then he asked, "Rudi, do you feel anything?"

"No. Maybe. I don't think so."

"We must try again. There were words one was supposed to say. Let me see if I can remember...ah, yes. Yes, I have it. Jantar Mantar Jadu Mantar."

A moment later, the Mayor said, "Anything, Rudi?"

"Nein, Papa."

"Jantar, Mantar, Jadu Mantar!" Adler said.

Kuefer, fidgeting, said, "Are you sure those are the words?"

"I think so," Adler said. "One last time. Everyone concentrate, really hard.

"Jantar!

"Mantar!

"Jadu!

"Mantar!"

Rudi, whose post-hypnotic instructions had been waiting on the third repetition, blinked rapidly. "Papa...mama!" He leapt to his feet. "Papa! Mama! I can see! I can see!" He ran to his mother and threw his arms around her.

"Gott sei Dank," Frau Glöckner whispered, as tears rolled down her face. It was not a sentiment that was encouraged under the anti-Christian, pro-pagan Nazi regime, and she glanced apologetically at her husband.

The mayor dismissed the lapse with a shake of his head and a huge smile, then shook Adler's hand fervently. "It's a miracle. How can we ever thank you?"

"Please," Adler said, "it's nothing. We must not speak of it again."

TWO WEEKS after the heist in Vienna, Gideon received a parcel wrapped in brown paper at his Dusseldorf rooming house. Inside was the uniform of an SS-Hauptsturmführer, more or less equivalent to the rank of Captain, complete with the red armband with the white circle and black Hakenkreuz, Hitler's reversed swastika.

The sight of it so thrilled and terrified him that he immediately put it on and gave himself the Hitler salute in the mirror. He goose-stepped across the room and back, heels slamming into the floor, prompting his downstairs neighbor to rap on her ceiling with a broom handle.

Also in the package was a complete set of forged papers for a fictitious officer named Otto Mueller, including orders for him to report to Reichsführer-SS Himmler in person at Wewelsburg Castle.

He sat on the edge of the bed and watched the papers rattle in his trembling hands.

•

PADERBORN WAS THE NEAREST big city to Wewelsburg, and six days a week the workmen queued up outside the cathedral in the city center at six AM. Most mornings there were forty or so of them, and they were all dressed in dark blue coveralls with Hakenkreuz armbands and an identity card from the Reichsarbeitsdienst, the "voluntary" labor service, pinned to the breast. These were the supplemental workers, taken on an as-needed basis, as opposed to the permanent work staff that lived at the castle full time.

The week before, Paco had photographed one of the identity cards with a tiny camera hidden in the palm of his hand, and then sent the picture to Adler's fabricators. Now he had an identity card of his own, and his own blue coveralls and armband. They had arrived in a package on Friday afternoon, along with a note containing a code phrase that meant that Adler hoped to reverse Rudi's hypnotic blindness the next day.

The clock was running.

Paco got on line at 5:45 Saturday morning. Dawn had pried open the sky in the east, letting in another hot, dusty day. Paco blended in easily enough with the other workers, a full third of whom were Untermenschen like himself: Poles, Turks, Serbs, Hungarians, Czechs. All of us good enough for manual labor, Paco thought, as long as we didn't try to interbreed with the Herrenvolk, the master race.

A blond, hawk-faced German in his forties stood next to him in line. He looked Paco up and down and said, "Where did *you* come from?"

"Madrid," Paco said affably. "But that was a few years ago."

A Turk behind him sniggered.

The hawk face got red and Paco held up one hand. "Relax," he said. "The Ministry sent me." He flicked his identity card.

"The fucking Nazis don't like surprises, that's all," said the hawk-faced man.

Paco picked up the hint. "Well, I don't like the fucking Nazis, so I guess that makes us even." The Turk laughed again.

"Nobody likes the fucking Nazis," the hawk-faced man said. "But only an idiot says so to their faces." He turned away, still irritable, although apparently satisfied.

Paco's father had been a magician before him, and Paco had gotten his start by helping to fabricate his father's illusions. The clean smell of newly planed lumber, the cool perfection of polished chrome, the flow of solder over hot copper, all these things had a certainty that Paco loved, an enduring simplicity that was the opposite of the stage performance. For Paco, being on stage was one opportunity for failure after another. Not so much the sleights—constant practice made those reliable enough. It was the force that made him nervous, the vast array of gestures and vocal cues that let you dictate a sufficiently distracted victim's choice of card, of a number between one and ten, of a color, of any set of options you could name.

Most of the time, anyway.

If he'd had the choice, he would have been a carpenter or an electrician. However, his brothers had no aptitude for magic, and his father wanted so badly to have someone carry on the name. And so Paco, who had spent his life pleasing everyone but himself, found himself this early morning in Paderborn looking forward to a few days of honest labor with his hands.

At precisely 6:00, two long, canvas-topped trucks pulled up to the curb. Paco, having watched the ritual from the shadows of the cathedral, knew what to expect. A soldier at each of the tailgates, wearing the black uniform and the helmet with the lightning runes, checked badges, paying little or no attention to the names on the clipboard that he carried. Paco followed the hawk-faced man and stood in line for the second truck. Seven men got in ahead of him, flicking away their cigarettes before they climbed up, taking their places on the metal benches along the sides.

The soldier, little more than a boy, with full lips and sad eyes, stopped Paco with a hand on his chest. He read the name from Paco's badge. "Bilbao?" He looked at his clipboard. "There is no Bilbao on this list."

Confidence is everything, Robert had said. "They told me to report here this morning. They said my name would be on the list."

"It is not on the list," the boy soldier said. "Step out of line and stand over there."

Paco hesitated, wondering if he should try to make a break for it.

"Oh, shut up, for fuck's sake, Willy." It was the hawk-faced man, from the rear of the truck. "Quit trying to act like a big bully. I can vouch for Señor Bilbao from Madrid."

Willy blushed and gestured angrily at the truck. "Get in."

The hawk-faced man held out his hand and pulled Paco up. As they walked, bent over, toward the front, Paco said, "Danke."

The man snorted. "Fuck the Nazis."

Wewelsburg was a 20-kilometer drive away, most of the distance over a fine new asphalt roadway. A large window let Paco see into the cab of the truck, and past the driver and out the windscreen. They were in rolling countryside, dotted with trees and carpeted with grass that had yellowed in the relentless drought. The land rose in waves until finally Paco saw the castle in the distance, white stone and a blue slate roof atop a high hill, as if it had sprung from one of the Grimm brothers' fairy tales that Hitler loved so much.

The road bent and twisted in narrow switchbacks as it climbed the hill, until finally the trucks pulled up at the edge of what had once been the moat. Paco climbed out with the others. A temporary wooden bridge spanned the 10-meter-deep and 30-meter-wide chasm, and on the far side, a high arch opened in the gray limestone wall and led into a courtyard.

To the right, at the north end of the castle, the keep sat at the apex of the spear-point-shaped complex. It was a broad tower, two stories high, lower than the surrounding walls. The east wing, the wing that Paco faced, housed the resident workers who were digging out the moat and chipping away the plaster on the outer walls to reveal the original masonry. Their shadows moved behind small, square windows as they arose for their day's work.

Once inside, Paco saw that the renovation of the castle itself had barely begun. Paving stones were missing in the courtyard, and grass and weeds had pushed their way through the cracks where the existing stones had buckled and shifted. A great deal of the glass in the windows of the west and south walls was broken or missing, and loose roof tiles had shattered on the ground. A plywood ramp led up to the entrance to the keep, and Paco saw piles of rubble inside.

A junior officer assigned Paco to replace windows in the west wing. As Paco gathered his tools and materials, he roughed out a mental map of the first floor: a long conference room with a massive oak table and chairs, two bathrooms with chemical toilets, two fully furnished bedrooms, a working kitchen with kerosene stoves and an electric refrigerator, the latter powered by a generator in the west tower that also powered electric lights and outlets.

Paco quickly demonstrated his competence to the officer that supervised him. For two hours he worked hard, replacing glass and sections of the wooden sashes, freeing the ballasts and sanding the casings. Then he took a bathroom break and unwound 100 meters of fine insulated wire from around his belly and transferred it to the front of his pants. Wearing a purposeful expression, he climbed the circular staircase to the deserted second floor and hid the wire behind a large, flat limestone slab in an unrestored chamber above the conference room.

AT PRECISELY 8:37 on Monday morning, Gideon stormed into the Paderborn offices of the SS and demanded a car and driver. "Why was he not sent to my hotel?" he shouted at the desk officer, a boy barely old enough to shave.

"We...I...there are no orders, sir..."

"What? Who's in charge here?"

Within five minutes, through sheer bluster, Gideon found himself in the back seat of a Daimler-Benz G4 staff car with six wheels and a convertible top. The blood surged cold through his veins like a river through a mountain gorge.

At the castle, he ordered the driver to wait. Swatting the side of one knee-high boot with the new riding crop that he'd bought in town, he stomped across the wooden bridge and into the courtyard. He saw Paco working away in a first-floor window and was careful not to let the relief show on his face. "Hello?" he shouted.

An enlisted man peered out of a doorway.

"Heil Hitler!" Gideon said. "I am to report to the Reichsführer."

"I'm sorry, Herr Hauptsturmführer. Herr Himmler is in Munich today."

Gideon stretched his mouth into an icy smile. "Bureaucrats," he sneered. "Pencil pushers. They send us here, they send us there, with no idea of what they're doing. In my day, the Schutzstaffel were soldiers!" Gideon, all of 27, believed momentum to be more important than strict logic. "What's your name, Sturmmann?"

"I am only a private, sir. Private Zweig."

"Who is in charge here, Private Zweig?"

"Standartenführer Bartels is the senior officer today, sir. He's the architect in charge of—"

"I know who Hermann Bartels is, Private!" Gideon shouted. Keep them off balance, he told himself, and they can't turn on you. "I am not an idiot. Take me to him at once."

Bartels was in the North Tower, the keep, in the huge round room on the ground floor. He was in his mid-thirties, chipmunk-cheeked, with round glasses. He outranked Gideon, Colonel to Captain, but did not seem overly formal. He greeted Gideon with a casual salute, raising his right hand briefly as if taking an oath.

"Otto Mueller," Gideon said, and they shook hands.

"People need myths," Bartels said.

"Pardon?"

He beckoned Gideon toward a diazo print on the wall, still smelling faintly of ammonia. It was an architectural drawing of the room, labeled Obergruppenführersaal, Hall of the Generals. It pictured an inner circle of arches and columns, inset a meter or so from the outside walls, and a curious design inlaid at the exact center of the floor. The design was a bit like a 12-armed swastika, with the arms turning back into radials at the ends.

"The Black Sun," Bartels said as he pointed to the symbol. "The Reichsführer and I adapted it from Bavarian and Alemanni designs. It represents the spiritual light behind the material world. Verstehen Sie? This is the energy that invigorates the Aryan race. What we are building here is not merely a castle. It is a whole mythology, descended from Theosophy and sturdy enough to support our thousand-year Reich."

"I have read Blavatsky," Gideon said. In fact, what he had done was spend two exhausting days with a friend of Adler's, a Munich librarian who had coached him on the various bunko artists that Hitler and Himmler subscribed to, a lengthy catalog of anti-Semites and dubious, greedy spiritualists. "Also von List and von Liebenfels. I even travelled to Istanbul after university to meet Baron Sebottendorff."

"Really?" Gideon saw that he had Bartels' full attention, for the small price of having lost control and departed from his script. "I should very much like to hear the details of the conversation sometime."

"A remarkable man," Gideon said, trying to remember something more about him than his name. "Quite remarkable indeed."

"So. How can I help you, Herr Mueller?"

"I have been assigned here to assist in your research. I have my transfer papers here..." He showed them without actually offering them, and Bartels waved them away.

"You can give those to the Reichsführer tonight. He should be here in time for dinner. Perhaps you will join us?"

"I would be delighted," Gideon said.

ADLER WAS IN the local bierkeller when they came for him.

It was Tuesday night, 12 June, and he was sitting at a table with Kuefer and several of Kuefer's friends. News of the miracle on Saturday had spread through the region in what seemed like hours. Scores of the sick and deformed and injured had gathered in Adler's front yard, beseeching his help. The sight of them, the pain and desperation in their faces, the stained and odorous bandages, the harelip, the screaming child, the amputated foot, the improvised wheelchair, all tore at his heart.

"I want to help," he had told Kuefer, "but I can't possibly help them all. Besides, the artifact needs time to regain its power after you use it."

The Mayor obligingly sent his three local policemen to clear away the pilgrims. For Adler, dealing with his guilt was less easy. He reminded himself, repeatedly, of the importance of what he was trying to do.

To Kuefer and his friends, Adler was a hero. He had not paid for a meal or a drink in three days. He had remained steadfast in his refusal to take credit for Rudi's recovery, to show off the artifact, or to talk about the future.

When the ss burst into the beer hall, the room went instantly quiet. In the lead was a lieutenant in a peaked cap with an unholstered Luger, followed by a sergeant and three privates with leveled carbines. "Ernst Ackermann!" the officer barked. He had a long, narrow face with close-set eyes, as if he were wearing a mask from some primitive culture.

Adler slowly stood up. The lieutenant gestured toward the street with his pistol barrel. "Raus!" Adler moved toward the door, hands open and waist high, and the officer yelled, "Mach schnell!"

In the street, two of the enlisted men shoved him against the outside wall of the bierkeller to frisk him brutally and thoroughly.

"Nothing, Herr Obersturmführer," one of them said.

The lieutenant grabbed Adler by the back of the head. "Where is the Spear?"

"Spear?"

"The Spear, the Spear, you idiot, where have you hidden it?"

"If you mean the artifact, it's at my house—"

"You will take us to it, now!"

"Of course, of course."

The soldiers had left their truck blocking half the street. The lieutenant pushed Adler into the front, next to the driver, and the others climbed in the rear. They drove directly to his house without asking the way, and when they arrived, the front door was ajar and all the lights on. The interior had been ransacked: clothes everywhere, cushions from the sofa and chairs scattered across the floor, bed stripped and mattress leaning against one wall. The lieutenant's lack of reaction to the chaos told Adler that his men were responsible.

Adler picked up a screwdriver from the floor, where it had been dumped with the rest of the contents of the kitchen drawers. He pulled over a wooden chair and loosened the housing of the light fixture in the dining room. Reaching into the ceiling, he pressed the hidden button that would send a radio signal to Robert, and then he brought out the padded canvas bag.

The lieutenant grabbed the sergeant by the lapel, pointed to the hole in the ceiling, and backhanded him across the mouth. "Dummkopf!" he shouted, and shoved him away.

Adler meekly handed over the package. How long, he wondered, could any government sustain itself on an unvarying diet of violence, anger, and fear?

As if reading his mind, the lieutenant quickly checked to make sure the artifact was in the bag, then pointed to Adler and said, "Take him into the woods and shoot him."

IN HIS RENTED ROOM in Paderborn, Robert got the signal from Adler. The ss had taken the bait. Phase 3 had begun.

He changed into dark clothes and got out the rucksack that he'd hidden in the back of his closet. He tiptoed down the service stairs and out the rear of the building.

On a straight line, it was only ten blocks to the empty and shuttered synagogue that Adler had selected. Via the alleys and vacant lots that Robert used, it was at least twice as far. The pack was heavy and the night was warm, and Robert had begun to sweat by the time he arrived at the back door of the synagogue. He quickly opened the padlock and then the regular lock and slipped inside.

A wood-paneled passageway ran behind the sanctuary, ending in stairs to the basement. Using a small electric torch, he made his way to the bottom of the steps and oriented himself. The space had been divided into classrooms, with a hall down the middle. The building above was supported by three stone arches, evenly spaced down the length of it, like the ribs in a ship, only upside-down. Adler's experts had examined drawings of the building and assured him that sufficiently large explosions at the base of each arch, six points in all, would utterly collapse the structure.

Adler had gotten hold of a large quantity of a new explosive from the Nobel Company in Britain. It was called 808 and it was as malleable as modeling clay. Robert slipped on a pair of rubber gloves and opened a dun-colored paper cylinder. The material inside was pale green and smelled of almonds.

Standing atop a child's desk, he carefully molded ten packages of 808 around the bricks where the leg of the arch met the foundation. He hooked up a pair of detonators and ran electrical wire to the base of the stairs. Don't worry about using too much, Adler had told him. The bigger the explosion, the better.

He was ready to attach the second charge to the far side of the arch when a sound made him freeze.

It was the muffled cry of a child.

"WAIT," ADLER SAID. The sergeant, who had gripped his arm, hesitated.

"Make it quick," the lieutenant said.

Adler licked his lips. "I am a good German, a Party man. I want nothing more than for our Führer to use this weapon in his great struggle."

"So that is why you have kept it a secret all this time and hidden it away from us? You are not persuasive."

"If I had come to you and told you I had a magical artifact, you would not have believed me."

"I don't believe you now."

At last Adler met the lieutenant's gaze and said, "The Reichsführer, Herr Himmler, *he* believes. That's why he sent you to find me."

The mention of Himmler clearly made the lieutenant nervous.

"That is why," Adler said gently, pitching the words just so, "you must bring me to him. I must teach him how to use it or it will be worthless to him. And he will be terribly disappointed." Adler smiled. "You can always kill me later."

"Escort him to the truck," the lieutenant said angrily. "If he tries to escape, kill him instantly."

ROBERT FOUND three families, all Jews, living in the basement. Three women, two men, and seven children, all in dirty, ragged clothing, huddled together near the broken window they'd used to get inside. They were haggard and near starvation, yet defiance still blazed in the eyes of the men.

"You can't stay here," Robert told them. "The building is scheduled for demolition."

The men looked away as if they couldn't hear him. One of the women said, "Three days ago, a truck came to our building in the middle of the night to take everyone to a camp. We were the only ones who managed to get away. There is nowhere else for us to go. If they find us, they will shoot us down like dogs."

"You will be just as dead," Robert said, "if you stay here."

"Who are you?" one of the men said. He looked like an overexposed photograph, his skin deathly white, his wild hair and eyes completely black.

"I am a Jew, like you."

"How do you know the building is going to come down?" Robert hesitated, and the man stood up to confront him, looming over him. "You know because you are the one planting the explosives." His glance shifted to the rubber gloves, the roll of wire over Robert's shoulder.

"That doesn't matter," Robert said, sweating again now. "All that matters is that I know."

"It does matter," the man said, "because it means we have something to bargain with. If we took you to the police, maybe they would want to know what you're doing with those explosives."

"You already said you can't go to the police."

"Ah, but if we turn you in, perhaps there would be a reward. Perhaps the reward would be permission to leave the country."

"Is that what you want?" Robert asked. Possibilities sparked in his head. "To get out of the country? Because I can get you papers."

The refugees all looked at each other with sudden and pathetic hope.

"How?" the second man said. He was older, bearded, wearing a crocheted yarmulke.

Robert sighed. "We are going to have to trust each other. Yes, I am setting charges to blow up this building. I am part of a plot to depose Hitler, and I have access to money and resources. I have a man who can create any kind of document."

"How can we believe you?" the first man said.

"The explosive. It's English, experimental, unlike anything you have ever seen."

"Show us."

Both men followed him to the back of the basement, where Robert had left his pack. He opened one of the packets of 808 and rolled up a piece the size of a pinhead. He set it on the concrete floor and touched a match to it. It burned furiously, filling the hallway with poisonous fumes.

The first man nodded. "Let's talk."

They returned to the women and children, and in five minutes they struck a deal. Robert would provide them with papers and 250 marks in cash. He would also find them another place to hide.

"Until you deliver the money and the papers," the first man said, "I will be by your side, as close as your shadow."

"Dov, no," one of the women whispered. "It's too dangerous."

Dov gave her a severe look and she turned away. "First," he said to Robert, "we get the others to someplace safe. Then we make a telephone call to your document man, yes? Then you can finish your business here."

"You know this neighborhood," Robert said. "What other empty buildings are there?"

One of the women said, "There's the widow Schultz's house. It's been empty for months now."

Dov shook his head. "If we broke a window, it would be noticed, not like here. And no one could get in the doors without a whole ring full of keys."

"Perfect," Robert said. "Shall we go?"

SHORTLY BEFORE MIDNIGHT, they brought Adler into the castle in handcuffs and leg shackles. They marched him into a well-appointed room with an Oriental carpet and heavy furniture. Three men waited for him at the table: Himmler, his chief architect Hermann Bartels, and Gideon in his SS uniform. Adler did not recognize Gideon at first, so fully did he inhabit his Otto Mueller identity, and with that recognition came a powerful boost to his confidence. He had backup plans, all of them risky, and none of them an adequate substitute for Gideon's participation.

Himmler was already on his feet. "Obersturmführer Richter. Did you get it? Let me see." His beady eyes were feverish, his thin lips moist and trembling.

Richter gave a full, extended-arm salute, shouted, "Heil Hitler!" and took the cloth bag from under his left arm. He carefully set it on the table in front of Himmler, bowed, then stepped away and clicked his heels.

Himmler was bewitched. Without shifting his gaze from the bag, he reached to his belt and withdrew a pair of black kid gloves. He drew them on and gently slid both hands under the parcel, lifting it an inch or two from the table, testing its weight. Then, as delicately as if he were performing surgery, he loosened the strings and slipped the artifact, wrapped in cotton batting, out of the bag. He hesitated another long moment, his tongue flicking in and out just once, like a snake's. Slowly, carefully, he picked away the batting until the spear point was revealed.

Himmler, Bartels, and Gideon all sucked in their breath at once.

"Old man," Himmler said to Adler, "do you have any idea what you have here?"

"Some kind of artifact," Adler said. "That's all I know."

"It's the Spear," Himmler said. His voice dropped to a whisper. "The Spear of Destiny."

Adler did his best to look befuddled. "What kind of spear?"

"Also known as the Spear of Longinus," Gideon said. Bartels nodded, and Gideon puffed up with the acknowledgement. "Longinus was a Roman guard at the crucifixion of Jesus, the so-called Christ," Gideon went on. "He pierced Jesus's side with his spear, and blood and water ran out. Joseph of Arimathea caught the blood and water in a cup."

"Perhaps you have heard of this cup, old man?" Himmler said. "A cup called the Holy Grail?"

"These are legends...stories..."

"You have seen its power yourself, and you call it a legend?" Himmler said. "You are even more of a fool than I thought. Do you know what is under the gold sheath? A nail from the crucifixion. If you were not so stupid, you might begin to imagine the power this 'artifact' holds."

Bartels was suddenly troubled. "But...Herr Himmler...what of the lance at the Weltliche Schatzkammer?"

Himmler shrugged. "Either this fool has somehow robbed the Hofburg Palace without anyone noticing and activated an object that no one had activated before, or the lance in the museum is a forgery."

"Unless..." Gideon said.

"What?" Himmler snapped.

"Unless this is the fake. We have yet to see it do anything with our own eyes."

"True," Himmler said. "We must arrange a test."

"Understand," Adler said, "that it is like a battery. Or so the Indian I got it from told me. He said it absorbs energy from the lines of force that connect the ancient sites on the planet. After you use it, it must recharge itself."

"How long?" Himmler said.

"It should be charged now, I think," Adler said. "I'm sorry, there are so many things I don't know."

"What else can it do besides cure blindness in adolescent boys?" Gideon said.

Richter, the long-faced lieutenant, let out an inadvertent snort of laughter, earning himself a glare from Himmler.

"Again," Adler said, "I can only tell you what I was told." He hesitated a fraction of a second. This was the key moment in the entire operation. The pitch of his voice, the timing, everything had to be perfect. "Transmuting elements. Making a leader invincible. Igniting stone—"

"What," Gideon said. "You mean, blowing up buildings?"

"The Indian said the man he inherited it from once exploded a church."

"A church?" Gideon said. "Better a synagogue."

"Yes," Himmler said. "A synagogue filled with Jews. I like this idea."

"Begging your pardon," Adler said.

"Yes, yes, what is it, you tiresome old idiot?" Himmler said.

"This spear, you will be giving it to the Führer, yes?"

"Yes, of course."

"If your test draws too much attention, will it not detract from the Führer himself demonstrating his new power to the world?"

"Mmmm," Bartels said. "He has a point. That schwul Röhn and that peacock Göring are forever plotting against us. If we let the Führer take the glory on this, he will put you above all the others."

Reluctantly, Himmler nodded. "Perhaps an empty synagogue would be a better choice."

Bartels slapped the table. "Isn't there an old synagogue in Paderborn that we just shut down a couple of months ago? On

Höhenstrasse? We were planning to level it and build a new Party headquarters there."

"Perfect!" Himmler said.

"Remember, I make no promises," Adler said. "I only—"

"We don't care about your promises," Himmler said. "Either you show us how to demolish this synagogue with your Spear or we will kill you."

BEFORE THE PREVIOUS night's dinner with Himmler, Gideon had been literally sick with terror. He had vomited everything his stomach could find to spew out and had alternated between fever and chills. At last, sitting in a tub of hot water, smelling his own sour sweat, he confronted himself. What is it that you are so afraid of?

They will find me out, he answered himself. They will know who I am.

But how? he asked. How can they find you out if you are not Gideon any longer, and are only Otto Mueller?

At that moment everything changed. His fear melted away. He leapt to his feet, shot his right arm forward as if into Himmler's face, and shouted, "Heil Hitler! Sieg heil!"

He had washed the last of Gideon off of himself and dressed in his uniform as if it were the outer layer of his skin, his protection against the world.

In a former life, before he was Otto Mueller, he had learned that certain people seemed to exude a kind of odorless perfume that disabled the defenses of the people around them. It made little difference what lies these people told, because anything they said would be believed, at least as long as they were present. There were many names for these people: snake oil salesmen, grifters, con men, politicians. In his former life, Otto Mueller had that power, and he was pleased to discover that he had it still. He could feel Himmler's need for Mueller to like him, and Mueller reciprocated. This man with the accountant's face had a fierce and devious intellect, one that found connection after connection where Mueller had never

suspected them: between an early Christian sect called the Cathars—
who believed that Jehovah was evil and the Catholic Church sinfully
materialistic—and the Holy Grail; between the Cathars and the
Aryans; between the Aryans and the highly-advanced visitors from
outer space now living inside the hollow earth.

In the middle of the night, Gideon had awoken in a cold sweat
from a dream he could not remember. Nor could he remember many
details of the dinner beyond that fact that Himmler, as Adler had
warned, was truly a lunatic and that he himself, in the guise of Otto
Mueller, had said things that now made Gideon cringe in shame.

Yet, in order to get up in the morning and put on his uniform
and return to Wewelsburg, he once again had to surrender control
to Mueller.

Mueller spent the day with Himmler and Bartels, discussing
Bartels' plans for the Reichsführerschule ss, the Reich Leaders'
School, which was to consist of a walled circular complex 860 meters in diameter, with the North Tower as its center point. Looking
at Bartels' sketches, Himmler once more went into another world.

"The Indians were the first Aryans," he said. "They had incred-
ible knowledge, spiritual knowledge, that they have kept hidden for
centuries. You see how the outside wall of the complex makes a
shape like a human skull? This road rises into it like the spine. And
here, at the center, pointing upward, is the triangle of the castle, like
a spear point. And it's pointing to the pineal gland, yes? In yoga they
call this the ajna chakra, and they have exercises to make the spiritual energy rise through the spine and explode there. That area is
also called the Third Eye. Blavatsky called it 'the inner spiritual eye
of the seer.'"

"Yes," Mueller enthused. "Yes, I see!"

Himmler sat back happily in his chair. "And speaking of spears, I
have a surprise for you tonight."

It was not, of course, a surprise for Gideon when the soldiers
dragged Adler into the conference room. But Gideon was an
unwelcome voice in Mueller's head, an enemy of the Reich,

a traitor and a Jew. He kept asserting himself, nudging the conversation toward his own ends, tricking Himmler into selecting the very site that Robert was even now wiring with explosives.

Perhaps, Mueller thought, Robert has not finished his preparations yet. Would that not be a laugh on the intruder Gideon and the other traitors, to have the hoax exposed before the Führer was compromised? "What are we waiting for?" Mueller asked. "Why don't we have our test right now? Then we'll know."

"Good idea," Himmler said. "As the proverb says, 'What you can get in your hands tonight/Don't put off till morning light.'" He was rising from his chair when the telephone shrilled.

Richter answered. "It's for you, Herr Mueller," he said. "It's... a woman."

Mueller felt a flash of heat in his cheeks. "Excuse me," he muttered, and retreated to a corner with the apparatus. It could only be Cora, and the fact that she was calling at all meant something had gone wrong. "I told you never to call me here!" he whispered angrily.

"I am sorry, schatzi, but the doctor said the baby is due at six in the morning."

The code phrase meant that Robert had been delayed and gave an estimate of when he would be ready. Before Mueller could stop him, Gideon seized control long enough to turn toward the table and repeat, "Six AM?" It was for Adler's benefit, and he saw Adler register the news.

"Yes," Cora said. "I should go to the hospital now. You told me you wanted to be there..."

"No. No, it is simply not possible. Take a taxi or call an ambulance or something." He hung up and returned to the table. "My apologies," he said to Himmler. "We are about to bring forth a new Aryan superman."

"Wonderful!" Himmler said. One of Himmler's missions was to encourage unions—marital or otherwise—that would produce offspring from good Aryan breeding stock. "Do you need to be with the mother?"

"No, my place is here."

"Well, then. Shall we proceed?"

"A moment," Adler said. "My thoughts, as ever, are for my Führer. Should we not get motion picture cameras to record this, so that he can see for himself if it is successful?"

"You say that the Spear can recharge itself," Himmler said. "What's your hurry, old man? We can repeat this experiment as many times as we want."

"The Standartenführer," Adler gestured at Bartels, "has mentioned the rivalry among you who are the Führer's most trusted deputies. This is well known. People in the streets are losing their faith. They say the Führer's days are not long. Something must be done and done soon. The summer solstice is one week from tomorrow. If the Indian is right, the Spear will be at its greatest power then, and it only makes sense that this is the time when the Führer should reveal it to the world, nicht wahr? So we have time for only this demonstration, and one more for the Führer himself."

The summer solstice was central to the new pagan religion that Himmler and Bartels were cooking up. Mueller fumed at having to sit by and let Adler lead them around by their delusions. Even if Gideon let him, though, anything he said would expose his own complicity.

"Perhaps there is a reason," Bartels said, "that this old man came into possession of the Spear. The Spear of Destiny, yes? Maybe it's true that Destiny is working through him."

"It's two in the morning," Himmler said. "Where would I find a film crew at this hour?"

"We could call Berlin in the morning," Bartels said.

Himmler pouted like a petulant child. "I don't want to wait. Call Berlin now."

ROBERT'S NIGHT had been endless, and yet time was running out.

By the time that the family was safely installed in the widow Schultz's house, it was after midnight. Then he and Dov had walked to Robert's rooming house, where a wall-mounted tele-phone was available at the head of the first-floor stairs. A ledger sat on a table below where tenants were to note the time and desti-nation of their calls so that the landlady could add the charges to their weekly bills.

First he called Cora in Berlin. She was still awake and a little breathless. "You're lucky I came home early tonight," she said. Robert briefly wondered how it would feel to be touring the nightclubs of Berlin with Cora on his arm rather than rigging ex-plosives under a deadline, then pushed the thought away.

"The aeroplane," Robert said carefully, "is delayed."

"Oh dear," Cora said.

Dov was anxious, making as if to grab the earpiece. "Who are you talking to?"

Robert hushed him. "The new arrival time is six AM. Do you have that?"

"I'll make the call." He heard a hesitation in her voice, as if she were on the verge of asking how he was.

"Thanks," he said quietly, and hung up.

Next he woke the head of Adler's fabrication team and de-scribed what he needed. The man was surprisingly polite. "We can cover them with a single letter under the letterhead of the Jewish Department of the Ministry of Foreign Affairs. I can have one of my people bring it to you tomorrow morning. I'll just need all the names."

Robert turned to Dov. "You need to give this man all of your names."

Dov frowned. "I don't know. This could be a trick."

Robert's patience was fading. "If I were going to turn you in, I could have simply taken you to a police station. I could have left you in the synagogue to be blown up. Don't make me regret my decision."

Dov snatched the earpiece and bent to speak into the mouth-piece. "Why do you need this?" He listened briefly, then, with a

sigh, spelled out 12 names. After another pause he said, "Yes, I understand," and handed the earpiece back to Robert.

It was after two by the time they returned to the synagogue. "Can
you not trust me from here on out?" Robert said.

"Until I have the letter in my hands, I do not leave your side."

Robert worked as quickly as he could. He had no means of
knowing whether Cora had been able to get the message to Gideon,
whether Gideon was in a position to slow things down, whether
Adler had even been successful in forcing Himmler to choose the
right target, and, if he had, when they would arrive.

Gideon himself was another issue. Cora believed Gideon was
cracking up, and Robert trusted her judgment.

He set to work, finishing the most conspicuous and dangerous
chore first, that of running the detonation wire along the ground,
hidden by the grass and ivy, to a telephone pole, then shinnying
up the pole to anchor it. Down the pole, across Höhenstrasse,
up the pole on that side to pull the wire taut and anchor it
there. Down that pole and behind the empty house across from
the synagogue, which was the only logical place for the Nazis
to set up their observation post, again burying the wire in the
undergrowth. Finally, one last test of the drainpipe in back of
the house, making sure that it would support his weight, all
while Dov watched with patient, hooded eyes. These were all
actions he had planned days before, and rehearsed since then in
his imagination.

It was four AM when Robert finally began to set the remaining
charges in the synagogue basement. He had barely begun when he
heard the sound of heavy trucks in the street outside and he knew
that his time had run out.

To ADLER'S immense distress, Berlin informed them that a crew
was already stationed in Paderborn to film the opening of a new
motorway. He did what he could to drag his feet without arous-
ing suspicion. Despite his efforts, the film crew was awakened and

mobilized, and two truckloads of ss troops were dispatched to the synagogue by four AM.

By the time they arrived at 4:30, roadblocks had closed access to the street and generators were sputtering to life, powering massive banks of lights. Soldiers had evacuated the houses on either side of the synagogue and taken the inhabitants to a holding facility downtown. Other troops were going door to door, warning residents to stay indoors with their shutters closed on pain of death. Soldiers and civilians alike were told that a new explosive was being tested, with no mention of the occult nature of the experiment.

The heel-clicking Obersturmführer Richter had taken charge of the scene. "There is a deserted house directly across from the synagogue," he told Himmler. "It has a balcony facing the street."

Himmler turned to Adler. "How powerful will this explosion be?"

"I have no idea," Adler said. He was praying at that moment that there would be an explosion at all.

"Will we be safe on that balcony?" He pointed a black-gloved finger at the house. It was tall and narrow, built of granite blocks, the balcony supported by the ground floor.

"I would think so," Adler said. "Perhaps you could set up a command post in the attic?"

"I am not here to clean attics!" Himmler snapped. He turned to Richter. "Force the doors and make sure the house is truly empty. Be thorough but be quick."

Richter saluted and trotted toward the house, shouting orders.

Adler resisted a powerful need to look at his wristwatch. He knew that no more than five minutes had passed since the last time he'd checked.

He shivered in the early morning chill. Richter had not allowed him to bring a jacket from his house, and though the days were hot, the cloudless skies sucked the heat away overnight. Himmler snapped his fingers at his orderly, who ran to their staff car and returned with a Thermos bottle of coffee. The orderly poured a steaming cup and handed it to Himmler, who took a sip and nodded. He stared at

Adler over the rim and took another sip, then, to Adler's surprise, offered him the cup. "Be careful," he said. "It's very hot."

Adler drank it gratefully. He had not been prepared for how
physically demanding this enterprise would prove. He was exhausted and dispirited as well, afraid that he had committed an act of
colossal hubris. If in fact Robert had been unable to get the charges
ready, Adler knew that he was done for. If they didn't shoot him on
the spot, they would surely torture him, and he was unsure that he
could hold out long enough for the others to escape the country.

With a loud crackle, the floodlights illuminated the synagogue
like midday. Did everyone, he wondered, come to the end wishing
they'd done more? His wife, Greta, had miscarried twice, delivered
a stillborn daughter, and finally given birth to a son who died in
infancy. It had broken her and destroyed their marriage, and Adler
wondered, as he had many times before, how different his life might
have been if his children had lived.

He had seen the world, known many women, been cheered by
hundreds and sometimes thousands of voices at a time. If this last
work should be unfinished, well, the Americans had a saying: "...or
die trying."

Himmler reached for the cup and Adler returned it. "Come along,
old man," Himmler said. "Destiny calls."

DOV UNSPOOLED THE WIRE as Robert prepared the explosives,
sweat and exhaustion blurring his vision. Finally, at the rear of synagogue, he connected the last of the interior wires to the main outside
wire and they were done. He put the leftover wire and explosives in
his rucksack with the detonator and eased the back door open.

He had peered out at Höhenstrasse earlier and seen the light
panels and generators moving into place. Once those lights were on,
there would be no escape. Their only chance was to leave immediately, straight back from the synagogue, through the yard of the
house behind and into the street beyond.

"I'll go first," Robert said. "When I signal, run to me."

"Don't you have to be on the other side of the street?"

"I'll have to take the long way."

"I've got a better idea. Next time one of the soldiers comes around, we knock him out, tie him up, and put him in the basement. One of us puts on his uniform and marches the other one across the street, like he's a prisoner."

"No," Robert said.

"It's better than any idea you have."

"There's a hundred things wrong with it. The main one is that I'm not going to kill anyone. The man whose idea this was made us all promise. We're going to do this without violence."

"That's insane. You're going to overthrow Hitler with no violence at all?"

"That commitment is what saved you and your family. We can argue later. Right now we're going."

Robert crept quietly into the darkness. The grass had just sprouted a coating of dew. Ten meters, twenty. Suddenly lights swept across the house next door and Robert threw himself flat. They were headlights, from a Nazi staff car, and as it stopped, Robert glimpsed Adler and Himmler in the front seat, Gideon in the rear.

All the soldiers turned to the car and saluted. In that moment, Robert leapt to his feet, motioned to Dov, and together they raced across the yard, vaulted a low picket fence, and collapsed, breathless, in the street beyond.

Dov, grinning, said, "My heart is going to explode. I haven't run like that since I stole apples from the market as a boy."

Robert got to his feet and extended his hand. Dov took it and pulled himself up and Robert said, "We have to split up now. Don't speak, don't argue. You know it would be ten times the risk if both of us tried to get into that house across the street. It would only get both of us killed for nothing." Robert took out his room key. "Go back to my room, get some sleep. If I don't show up, you can take delivery of the document later this morning. You'll find money in my room, much more than we agreed to."

"I would be an idiot to trust you," Dov said. He looked into Robert's eyes for a long second, then shrugged and took the key.

As they climbed the stairs of the abandoned house, Adler checked his watch. Ten minutes to five. The coffee had warmed him, and at the same time, on top of his exhaustion and his empty stomach, it had also ratcheted up his nerves. Richter was in the lead, his oversized flashlight illuminating cobwebs and peeling paint. Adler followed, then Himmler, Gideon, Bartels, and a few enlisted men. Scurrying sounds in the walls spoke to the presence of a multitude of rats, large ones.

The stairs opened into a wide room at the front of the house, whose French doors opened onto the balcony. The massed lights outside were strong enough to reveal the dilapidation: peeling wallpaper, cracked plaster ceiling, a floor stained with rat droppings.

Himmler threw open the French doors and leaned out over the edge of the balcony. "Who is in charge of the film crew?"

A reply rose from the street. "I am, Herr Reichsführer."

"How much longer?"

"Only a few minutes, sir."

Adler heard a scraping sound, followed, a second or two later, by a creak.

Himmler turned, an anxious look on his face. "What was that noise?"

"I don't know, sir," Richter said.

Himmler stared at Adler, searching for signs of complicity. Adler let him see only a tired old man.

"Take these men," Himmler said to Richter, "check the attic, and have somebody walk around outside and make sure there's nobody on the roof."

"Jawohl!"

Adler tried to slow his racing thoughts. If the noise was Robert, it meant the explosives were set. But if they caught him, the game was up. If the noise wasn't Robert, at least Himmler was using up more time. But if Robert was not already in the building, then he was going to be too late.

"While we're waiting," Himmler said, "tell me what I'm supposed to do." He had the Spear out of the bag and held it tenderly in his gloved hands. "There were words you spoke over the boy. Some sort of gibberish, they said."

"He told me it was...Guju something..."

"Gujurati?" Bartels asked.

"That's it."

"It's an Indo-Aryan language," Bartels said. "From one of the western states of India."

Himmler was not to be distracted. "What are the words?"

"You have to be careful when saying them all together," Adler told him. "They are words of great power. First you say Jantar, and then Mantar, and then Jadu and Mantar again."

Bartels shook his head. "I don't know them."

Of course you don't, Adler thought. They were the Indian version of "Abracadabra." He watched Himmler's lips move as he silently rehearsed them.

Doors slammed and boots pounded up and down stairs. Eventually an out-of-breath Richter came back into the room and saluted. "Nothing, sir. Must have been an animal, maybe a cat."

"Very good," Himmler said, and beckoned to Adler to follow him onto the balcony. Bartels and Gideon quietly took positions behind them. If Gideon were going to help, Adler thought, this would be a good time. If Gideon had not, in fact, already crossed over to the other side.

"Film crew?" Himmler called.

"Ready, sir," responded the voice from below.

"Begin," Himmler said.

"Rolling," said the voice. "Speed."

Himmler turned to smile at Adler. "And now here we are, old man. The moment of truth."

Adler's mouth was dry, his palms damp. "You must focus your will power."

"Do I point the Spear at the building?"

"Yes, probably a good idea. However, it is not a gun. More like a magnifying glass, the way it focuses the sun's rays to burn—"

Himmler waved a gloved hand. "Spare me the analogies." He faced the synagogue, whose roof was at their eye level, 50 meters away. Holding the Spear in his cupped hands, he started to close his eyes.

"It's a very solid building," Adler said. "It will take immense will power to bring it down."

"It will be easier if you stop interrupting me."

"You must visualize the stone igniting, exploding—"

"Enough!" Himmler said. "Silence, old man. Focus your will too, as if your life depended on it. Which it does." He glanced at Gideon and Bartels. "Both of you, concentrate as well."

Adler had run out of ideas. Himmler faced the street and closed his eyes. "Jantar," he said dramatically. "Mantar. Jadu. Mantar!"

Silence.

I am a dead man, Adler thought.


ROBERT, FREE OF DOV at last, made a wide circle that crossed Höhenstrasse two blocks east of the barricades that now closed it off. He walked swiftly for another block before turning toward the synagogue and breaking into a jog. He was sweating profusely in his black turtleneck. It was already 4:45 AM and dawn would soon put an end to the covering darkness.

The focus of the action was obvious from blocks away. Lights blazed in the street outside the synagogue and voices called back and forth over the roaring generators. Robert hesitated in the front yard of the house behind the empty house where his wires awaited him. The whole area teemed with soldiers and the time for stealth was long over. His only hope was to brazen it out.

He shrugged out of the rucksack, removed a coil of wire, and carried both in his hands as he walked confidently to the back of the empty house. Kneeling, he quickly spliced the new roll onto the end of the wire he'd laid there an hour before.

The beam of a flashlight hit him in the face like a physical blow. "You! Put up your hands and get on your feet!" An ss private pointed a leftover Mauser carbine from the Great War at Robert's head.

Robert barely glanced at him. In gutter German he said, "Can't you stop interrupting me? Like I told the last guy, I'm with the film crew. If I don't get this finished, Himmler is going to have my ass."

"You have identification?"

"Hell no, I don't have identification. I'm a civilian. I got dragged out of bed at three in the fucking morning to do this. Go ask Himmler if you have any questions."

The soldier, confused, looked to the street and then at Robert. "You...you wait right here!"

As soon as the soldier disappeared around the corner, Robert put the rucksack on once more. With the wire looped over one forearm, he climbed the drainpipe straight up the back of the house. He pulled himself quietly onto the slate roof and unrolled the wire behind him as he made his way to the front of the house. A broad chimney interrupted the roof there, and the space behind it was invisible from the ground. As he attached the wires to the detonator and connected the battery, he heard someone shouting orders from the room below, the words borne out through the French doors.

He had made more noise than he realized in crossing the roof. He nestled the pack and the detonator in his lap, leaned against the chimney, and slowed his breathing. It seemed that he might yet be in time.

He felt the tension go out of the muscles across his stomach, and then the full weight of his exhaustion fell on him.

In less than a second he was fast asleep.

ADLER PUT BOTH HANDS on the low wall at the front of the balcony to keep them from shaking. "Try it again. Louder this time. Put your will into your voice."

Himmler raised one eyebrow. His face was soft, his jowls puffy, his chin weak, but the eyes, behind the round, wire-rimmed spectacles, were as cold and distant as the North Star.

"Go on," Adler said.

Himmler faced the synagogue once again. "Jantar!" he said loudly. "Mantar! Jadu! Mantar!"

There was no sound save the grinding of the generators and, somewhere in the distance, the frightened baying of a dog.

ROBERT WOKE with a start, completely disoriented. The sky was gray in the east. He was outdoors somewhere. A voice echoed in his ears. What had it said? Mantar? What did that mean?

He shook his head, fought to clear the fog from his brain.

"I HAD TO SAY IT three times," Adler said, fighting to keep the desperation out of his voice. "Maybe that's how it works."

"It doesn't seem to *work* at all," Himmler said.

"Perhaps we chose too big a target."

"The power of the Spear is immense," said Bartels.

"But it must be driven by will," Adler said.

"What are you saying, old man?" Himmler's voice had gone quiet and there was mayhem in his eyes. "Do you doubt my will?"

"Show me," Adler said. "Show me your will."

Himmler pointed the Spear at the synagogue, his stare fixed on Adler. "Jantar," he whispered. "Mantar," somewhat louder. "Jadu... Mantar!"

Adler felt the floor beneath him undulate a split-second before the explosion ripped the air. A shockwave knocked all four of them backward, Bartels crashing through the glass of the French doors, Gideon catching himself on the doorframe, Adler landing on his hands and buttocks. Himmler had gone down on one knee, the Spear still extended from his right hand, a broad smile cracking his dust-covered face.

Adler stood and leaned over the balcony, his heart hammering with relief and joy. The synagogue was gone. In its place was a huge, swirling dust cloud. Chunks of wood and stone still fell from where they had been thrown high into the sky. A truck had been overturned on the street below and one bank of lights had been completely demolished.

"Stupendous!" Himmler said. At least that was what Adler thought he said. He could hear only the muffled ghosts of sounds over the ringing in his ears.

In the street, soldiers cheered, the excitement of the moment overpowering their iron discipline. A cameraman panned across the devastation, then turned the lens toward the balcony. Adler backed away and let Barltels, shaking broken glass from his uniform, take his place. Himmler, forgetting himself in the moment, raised the Spear above his head in triumph.

Gideon looked like he might join them, and Adler caught his eye and gave a single, nearly imperceptible shake of his head. Gideon's first reaction was fury, then he stepped back, his face impassive.

Adler passed through the shattered French doors into the room beyond. The soldiers there seemed as excited as those on the street, laughing and pushing their palms against their ears to try to clear them, lighting cigarettes and gesticulating.

All but Richter. Richter looked out toward where the synagogue had been, then stared at Adler and narrowed his eyes.

Trouble, Adler thought.

As soon as the last of the rubble from the blast had clattered across the roof, Robert broke the detonator down and stowed it in his pack. So far so good, although it was too early for congratulations. He put on the pack and gathered up wire as he hurried to the drainpipe and climbed down to ground level. Then he casually rolled up the wire leading to the telephone pole, pulled it loose from where it was anchored, and continued to coil it as he crossed the street, nodding casually to the camera crew as they began to tear down their equipment. As still photographers converged on the ruins, Robert got there first and recovered the wire that led from the telephone pole to the basement and added that to his roll. In the street once more, he threw the mass of wire into the bed of one of the film trucks, then walked around to where the driver, dressed in khakis and a flat cap, leaned against his door.

"Hell of a way to start the day, eh?" Robert said.

The driver pointed to his ears and said, "Ask me again when I can hear."

They both laughed and Robert strolled away down Höhenstrasse, turned left at the barricades, and made sure he wasn't being followed before he returned to the rooming house.

Dov had left the door unlocked and fallen asleep sitting up in the armchair. Robert quietly stripped to the waist and washed in the basin, throwing the dirty water into the alley outside his window. When he was done, he put on a clean shirt and stretched out on the bed.

Now that he was in relative safety, sleep eluded him. His thoughts were of Houdini. For the second half of his life, Houdini had tirelessly exposed spiritualists, mediums, and psychics, anyone who claimed to have supernatural powers. Robert wondered whether Houdini would have participated in this affair of the Spear, whether he would have been willing to deceive for the sake of a higher goal. He was not a man who compromised, not even with the appendicitis that killed him. Like anyone, Robert wanted to believe that his hero would have liked and admired him. Yet he also knew that both of them were too driven, too sure of themselves, too inflexible to have ever been friends.

A knock at the door made Dov leap from his chair, eyes wide and mouth open.

"Be calm," Robert said. "It's only the courier."

To his relief, he was correct. The man was middle-aged and casually dressed in a white shirt and dark trousers, carrying a C4-sized envelope. Robert had him step into the room while he examined the letter, which seemed convincing enough. He turned to show it to Dov, but Dov had vanished. "Can you take something with you?" Robert asked. "You're not likely to be stopped or searched?"

"No," the man smiled. "We have all the permits anyone could desire."

Robert gave him the rucksack with the detonator and leftover wire and explosives. "Be careful with it," Robert said.

The man smiled again. "Always." He hesitated at the door. "I know a little of what you're doing. I...I wanted to say thank you. On behalf of all of us."

Accustomed as Robert was to inspiring amazement, gratitude was new to him. He was embarrassed and could only nod stiffly in response.

After the man was gone, Dov slid out from under the bed and stood, dusting his clothes. "Your landlady is not much for cleanliness."

Robert handed Dov the letter and got 250 marks from his dresser drawer. Dov read the letter over slowly, twice, then replaced it in the envelope. If Robert had been worried about dealing with more gratitude, he needn't have bothered. "This had better work," Dov said.

Robert handed him the money. "You have a much better chance now than when I found you. I wish you luck."

Dov counted the money and put it in the front pocket of his tattered trousers. "We will need it." He opened the door, looked in both directions, and was gone.

Robert sat in the armchair to get his breath. He was dizzy with fatigue. He would be able to sleep now, he was certain, but he dared not. This location was compromised, as both Dov and the courier could place him here. He splashed water on his face, packed his few belongings, and went downstairs to make excuses to the landlady, telling her he had been called to Dusseldorf for a job interview. He left her money to cover his telephone calls and was away within an hour of Dov.

A block later, in fear of passing out, he ducked into a café and ordered steak and eggs and coffee. "Keep the coffee coming," he said.

•

IN HIS FIRST WEEK on the job, Paco had lost ten pounds, gotten himself transferred to the resident work crew, and spent his nights installing the effects for Phase 4. When he saw Adler return from Paderborn on Wednesday morning, alive and caked with dust, with the equally dusty Himmler and Bartels all smiles, he knew that Phase 3 had, against all odds, succeeded.

Now it was up to him and Cora.

And the Führer.

ADLER'S ELATION wore off quickly. He had not stayed up all night in many years, and he nodded off more than once on the return trip to the castle. In the courtyard he stumbled and nearly fell. "Herr Himmler," he said, "I have done everything that you asked of me. Can I not go home now?"

Himmler laughed with what seemed genuine amusement. "As long as the Reich has need of you, this is your home." He snapped his fingers at Richter. "Find the old man a room in the east wing. One with a door that locks from the outside. And put a guard on it."

Adler hesitated. "Will...will the Führer be coming now?"

Himmler still had the Spear in his gloved hands, gently caressing it. "After what I saw today, I must say, one is tempted to have this power for oneself." Adler saw him glance at Bartels and Gideon, both of whom were clearly shocked and frightened. "Relax," Himmler said. "Naturally we will share it with the Führer." To Adler he said, "How long will it take to 'recharge' itself, or whatever it is that it must do?"

"Three days, I think. That will leave four days until the solstice."

"Saturday, then," Himmler said. "I suspect he'll want us to come to Munich."

"The power is greater here," Adler said, almost under his breath.

"What, the power of the Spear?"

"That too."

"Damn you and your enigmas and your insinuations and infernal hints! Speak clearly, man!"

"I just meant," Adler said carefully, "that you want to be sure that you get proper credit for the sacrifice you are making for his sake. Psychologically speaking, if he comes to *you...*"

"Now you are an expert on psychology? Like that Jew Freud?" Himmler turned to Richter and said, "Lock him up. And then we can all get some sleep."

BEING LOCKED IN his room gave Adler far too much time to think. At the same time, it kept him away from the Spear and any chance to intervene if a crisis should occur.

When he'd first come up with the plan, it had seemed crazy but possible. As hard as he'd tried to anticipate every conceivable problem, there were too many variables and eventually his imagination faltered in a future that had become nothing more than mirrors, endlessly reflecting each other. Now, in the midst of it, his mind conjured one scenario of doom after another. He was like a madman who could not stop injuring himself. How bitter it would be to come this close, only to fail.

In the long nights, he was so desperate for company that he barely resisted the temptation to open the flimsy lock on his door and find Paco and help with the preparations for Saturday. Instead he lay on his narrow cot and relived favorite performances from his past: vanishing an elephant at the Taj Mahal, levitating Greta above the clock in Grand Central Station. But the image he returned to most was that of a dying girl in a cancer hospital, whose eyes had widened with awe as he produced a doll for her out of empty air, giving her hope for a miracle for herself that, in the end, did not come. Because that was the essence of magic: the endless need of the audience to believe that the impossible could happen, that despite reason, despite science, the chaotic universe could be brought to heel, made to sit up and lick the master's hand.

Had he not fallen for his own illusion in believing that he had the power to change history?

The restless nights and endless days dragged by, and finally it was

Saturday. Adler sat at the window from first light, and shortly after eight AM he saw Himmler, Bartels, Gideon, and a driver climb into a staff car and drive away. Headed for Munich, he thought, and he felt the pull of despair. Why had Gideon not warned him?

He knew the answer to that, and it provided no comfort.

Thus he was giddy with relief when, an hour later, he heard the car's engine again. He rushed to the window and saw that they had returned with an additional passenger, a short man in a business suit with an unmistakable forelock and toothbrush mustache. Adler watched them get out of the car, laughing, and cross the wooden bridge into the castle.

After that he spent an hour sitting on his cot, staring at the second hand of his wrist watch, which moved as if through muci-lage. He imagined Hitler trying the Spear on his own and failing, Himmler baffled and apologetic, Hitler descending into one of his black rages.

At last the key turned in the door and it swung open to reveal Richter and two privates with carbines. "You are wanted down-stairs," Richter said. His narrow eyes radiated suspicion.

"Gladly," Adler said. He got up slowly, feeling an old ache in his left knee.

"Search him," Richter said to the soldiers. "Thoroughly."

The two men shoved him against the wall and made a rough job of it. "Nothing, Herr Obersturmführer."

Richter did not reply, merely pointed Adler toward the hall with the barrel of his Luger.

Hitler was in the conference room, Adler was relieved to see, though really it was the only suitable room that was in finished condition. With the shades drawn on the two windows that opened to the courtyard, the only light came from the fixtures overhead. Standing at the far end of the table as Adler entered were Hitler, Himmler, Bartels, and Gideon, with a handful of other officers, including Manfred von Knobbelsdorff, an older man with drooping jowls who was officially in charge of the castle in

Himmler's absence. The Spear lay on the table and the mood of the room was festive.

Adler waited for the conversation to die down and then bowed his head. "My Führer, this is the proudest moment of my life."

"So," Hitler said. "This is the man, eh?" His voice, somewhat high-pitched, had a restrained power that even here, in comparatively casual circumstances, split the room like the crack of a marching snare. "What's your name?"

"Ackermann, sir. Ernst Ackermann."

"Yesterday I saw the films," Hitler said. "A most impressive display."

"I never dreamed it was so powerful," Adler said. "I had no idea."

"Herr Himmler tells me that you are a good German, that when he interviewed you about the Spear, your first thought was for your Führer."

"It's true, sir. I surrendered it gladly, knowing that in your hands it can unite us all, make Germany strong again, make us invincible."

"And you don't fear the curse? That once it leaves your possession you will die?"

"I am not afraid to die for my country," Adler said, finding more emotion in the words than he expected.

"Good," Hitler said. "That is very good. So tell me, Herr Ackermann. You have used the Spear to cure the blind and to demolish buildings. What else can it do?"

"I only know what the Indian told me. Transmuting elements— lead into gold, or what have you. Making you invincible in battle." He tuned his voice to a precise, compelling frequency. "Raising the spirits of the dead..."

"What?" Hitler said. He looked stunned. "Spirits?"

"Perhaps. I don't know."

Himmler said, "Always he makes these evasions."

"You can speak to someone who has died?" Hitler said.

"The artifact operates through will power," Adler said. "It would have to be someone to whom you have a powerful emotional bond, and who feels that same bond to you, a bond that is literally stronger than death, stronger than time."

"Show me," Hitler said.

"You mean, right now?"

"Yes, now, you are not expected elsewhere, are you? Herr Himmler says it has rested from its exertions on Wednesday morning."

"There are words you must say..."

"Yes, yes, Himmler has trained me, as if I were his Alsatian." He wagged a finger as if there were a dog sitting up on its hind legs before him. "Speak, Adolf, good Adolf." There was a peculiar quality to Hitler's banter, as if he were both teasing and put upon at the same time. Himmler and Gideon laughed loudly at his antics, while Bartels and von Knobbelsdorff looked uneasy.

"So, I am to take the Spear in my hands, yes?" He picked it up delicately and held it in his lap. "I used to dream of holding it like this. When I lived in Vienna, I used to go to the Hofburg and stare at it. Well, at what I thought was the true Spear. And now? Should I close my eyes?"

"If it helps you to concentrate."

"And I say the words, as I have been taught?"

"Yes, my Führer. Three times."

"Jantar, Mantar, Jadu, Mantar," he said softly.

Adler said, "And you must picture someone. Someone very dear to you."

"Jantar, Mantar, Jadu, Mantar." The words came out more forcefully and more slowly.

"Someone you long to see again with all your heart. Someone whose feeling for you is so strong that it can bring him or her across the distance between the worlds of the living and the dead."

This time Hitler's voice was choked with emotion. "Jantar, Mantar, Jadu, Mantar!"

The overhead lights went out.

Adler heard gasps of surprise in the darkness. There came a distant keening, followed by a weird, shimmering, echoing chatter, like crickets. The sound danced around the room in circles, dizzying and disorienting.

The sound faded and was replaced by a woman's voice.

"Liebchen?"

The voice was distorted, as if coming over a wireless with poor reception. At the same time it seemed to speed up and slow down, like a gramophone record with its hole off center. Yet Hitler knew it. He inhaled as if he had been struck in the solar plexus.

"Mutti?" he whispered.

Of the various forces they had used, this had been by far the easiest. Hitler's devotion to his mother, who had died of breast cancer when he was only 18, was legendary, and he had never ceased to mourn her.

A form took shape at the opposite end of the room, ghostly, pale, and glowing, with tightly coifed light brown hair, large ears, and eyes so light that they seemed to have no color at all.

"Adolf, my wild boy, I am so proud of you. So proud of all you have done."

"Mutti, is it really you?" Tears ran untouched down Hitler's nose and chin.

"Yes, my son, it is really me. I cannot stay long, and I have much to tell you."

"First, you must tell me if you are in pain."

"No, no pain. All of that ended when I crossed over. I can barely remember those last terrible days and the iodoform. But listen to me, Liebchen. This power you have now, the power of the Spear, you must use it and use it quickly. There are those near to you who conspire against you. You must go to Berlin, where they are so willful, and you must show them and the people of Germany and the world, show them all that you now have the Spear, that you are invincible."

"Yes, Mutti, yes, I will."

"You can trust the man who brought the Spear to you. There are others who are loyal, but you must be careful." The last words echoed and her image began to fade. "I must go. I love you, my son."

"Wait! Wait, don't go!" Hitler sprang to his feet and reached for her, as if his arms could stretch across the room.

She was gone, leaving only darkness and a few seconds of eerie sound, diminishing to silence.

The overhead lights flickered and came on, revealing a devastated Hitler. He sat with his face in his hands, weeping openly, the Spear abandoned on the table. Himmler, clearly embarrassed, made shooing gestures with his hands and led everyone else out into the hall. As they filed out, Richter stayed close enough that Adler heard him breathing.

"Lock him away again," Himmler said to Richter. "Gently. I believe the Führer will soon ask for him."


AS WITH ALL THINGS that had interested his hero, Robert had studied spiritualism. In his twenties he had exposed a dozen or more fraudulent mediums across Europe and Great Britain, and along the way learned most of the tricks of the séance trade. With the help of the latest electrical devices that Adler's fabricators could lay their hands on, he had designed and choreographed Klara Hitler's apparition weeks before, working closely with Cora, and with Paco, who would install and operate the equipment. Cora had made quite an impression on him: smart, capable, uncomplaining, with a smile that hinted at some inner amusement with the whole undertaking. She was also quite beautiful, and very fit.

Robert's only part in Phase 4 had been to bring two crates to the castle in a rented truck. The first, on Wednesday night, had contained a pair of magic lanterns, a wire recorder, and a dozen tiny speakers. The second, before dawn on Saturday, contained Cora, folded up as in her early days when the Great Adonini had sawn her in half. Both times Paco was there to take delivery, each time in front of a different guard, each of which had grudgingly signed the paper on Robert's clipboard, directly below one of Dieter's signatures from the Hofburg Palace.

On Saturday evening he returned for her crate, trundled her into a rented warehouse in Paderborn, and quickly removed the lid.

"Why look," he said, in his heavily accented English. "Somebody threw away a perfectly good woman."

She raised her arms. "Help me up, my legs are asleep."

She was ecstatic, sweaty, speckled with wood shavings from the crate, her dirty hair tied in a knot, wearing only a loose cotton shirt and trousers. She wrapped her arms around Robert's neck and he felt the warmth of her breath in his ear. The danger of the moment, Cora's exhilaration, Robert's own feelings of power and invulnerability, the smell and the touch of her, all surged in his blood. He set her gently on the floor and stepped away. "How did it go?"

"It was *brilliant*," she said, massaging the backs of her knees. "If only you had been there. Hitler wanted to believe it so badly, we could have fooled him with a pasteboard marionette."

Their laughter lasted a moment too long. Then they were neither one laughing, and he saw his own desire reflected in her eyes.

Although the urge to go to her was strong, he could not stop thinking of Adler and the work ahead. He forced himself to look elsewhere. "It's dangerous for us to be together right now."

"Yes," she said. "Yes, I know."

He nodded, hesitated. "Good luck," he said.

"You too."

He left her there to change and make her own way to her hotel. He parked the truck at the garage where he'd rented it and left the keys on the floorboards. Then he caught a streetcar downtown, where he had two shots of apple schnapps to quiet the trembling in his hands. It had been a near thing with Cora, and only his discipline had saved him. He was still not sure he'd made the right choice.

Back in his own hotel room, he took off his shirt, opened the window, and stood hoping for a breeze that did not come. The night smelled of broiled concrete.

There was a gentle knock at the door. If it was Cora, would he have the resolve to send her away? He doubted it. He crossed the room in three strides and pulled the door open.

Four men stood in the hall. Three were sA Brownshirts: two foot soldiers and a Sturmhauptführer, a captain.

The fourth man was Dov.

His lip was split, one eye blackened and swollen shut, and he seemed unable to stand without the support of the soldiers.

"Well?" the officer said to Dov.

"Yes," Dov said. "Yes, that's him." He looked Robert in the eye. "You bastard, see what you've done?"

ADLER HAD BEEN in his room less than an hour before he was summoned back to the conference room. Hitler immediately dismissed the sullen Richter, and Adler found himself alone with Himmler and the Führer.

"At this moment," Hitler said, "you are the only two men in the world that I know I can trust." Hitler was only 45, although he might have passed for fifteen years older. He had the sad, wrinkled eyes of a basset hound, and the ends of his mouth sagged deeply.

"Heinrich, my good and loyal friend, for your part in this I will raise you to the second most powerful position in Germany. I will put the sA under you so that you will control the entirety of our national security. And to you I give the responsibility of liquidating the Jews and ending the Jewish problem forever."

And here, Adler thought, I had been on the verge of feeling a twinge of sympathy for him. How very foolish.

Himmler's eyes shone through his round glasses. "Thank you, my Führer."

Hitler took both of Adler's hands into both of his own. "And you, Herr Ackermann, you brave and simple man, I owe you more than I can ever repay. You will come to Berlin with me and help me plan how best to take advantage of this miracle that has come into our lives."

"Yes, my Führer."

"Soon, my mother said. I must act soon."

"Yes, sir," Adler said. "The summer solstice is this Wednesday. I believe the power of the Spear will be at its greatest then."

Himmler nodded along. "I agree. It makes perfect sense."

"Very well, then," Hitler said. "On Wednesday we will surprise the world."

THEY FLEW TO BERLIN on Hitler's personal aircraft, a big, squared-off monoplane with a propeller in the nose and one on each wing. In addition to Himmler and Adler, the passengers included Bartels and Gideon in his Otto Mueller identity. Richter, Adler was relieved to see, was left behind. The pilot, a humorless man named Baur, took off from a parched and bumpy field below the castle, and little acting was required for Adler to appear terrified by the experience.

Hitler, across the aisle, laughed with his head back and his mouth wide open. "Herr Ackermann, you have nothing to fear." He patted the breast pocket of his jacket, where the Spear made a conspicuous bulge. "I am invincible now, remember?"

"And I, my Führer, am under a curse."

Hitler leaned toward him. "You must learn to do as I do. Only believe the parts of the legends that serve you."

From Berlin's Templehof Aerodrome they drove directly to the Hotel Kaiserhof in Wilhelmstrasse, a grand hotel from the previous century that occupied an entire city block. Adler had often stayed there at the height of his fame, but never with such royal treatment as he received as Hitler's guest. By the time he finished a leisurely and long overdue bath, the concierge had personally delivered newly purchased clothes, toiletries, a dressing gown, and a hot meal, unasked and without charge.

He fell asleep the moment he stretched out on the luxurious feather mattress and slept for 12 hours, woken finally by a call from the hotel operator informing him that Herr Hitler had requested the pleasure of his company for breakfast in an hour's time. According to Adler's watch, that would make it 10:00 AM, typical for the notoriously late-rising Hitler.

Hitler was already at the table when Adler entered the dining room. Also at the table were two ss bodyguards, whom Hitler neglected to introduce, and his chauffeur from the day before, Erich Kempa, a smiling young man in his twenties wearing an ss lieutenant's uniform. Hitler was bursting with energy, jumping up to shake Adler's hand, pointing him to a chair directly across the table from himself, waving the waiter over with his whole arm.

Adler ordered the same breakfast as the vegetarian Hitler, oatmeal with fruit, and as soon as the waiter left, Hitler leaned forward. "Tell me," he said. "The Spear. Do you think we could make lightning shoot out of it?"

Adler scratched his chin. "I don't see why not. If you can see it clearly in your mind, I think the Spear can make it happen."

"Good, wonderful," Hitler said. "Let me tell you what I'm thinking of."

His plan was to have masons construct a massive wall at one end of the Pariser Platz, opposite the Brandenburg Gate. The wall would be painted with a huge red Communist star and a yellow Star of David. From a high stage facing it, Bartels would deliver a short lecture dealing with the history of the Grail and the Spear. Then Hitler himself would come forward and reveal the Spear, now mounted on a staff made of birch.

"You see, this refers to the Battle of the Birch Tree, which happened at Wewelsburg Castle, according to the legends." He winked at Adler. "This is one of the legends we like. In this battle the Army of the West, which is us, defeated the Army of the East, which is the Russians."

Adler nodded his approval, and Hitler went on to describe how he would rouse the crowd with tales of what the Spear could do, and then finish by summoning the lightning, through the Spear, to destroy the symbols of Communism and International Jewry.

"Brilliant," Adler said. "The lightning is perfect. The masterstroke. You will be like Thor, calling down the thunder and lightning and storms." He softened his voice. "Your mother will be so proud of you."

"Do you think so?"

"Absolutely," Adler said. "There will be an audience, of course."

"Yes, grandstands on both sides, but not too near the wall, nicht wahr, so that nobody will be hurt."

"An orchestra, to stir the audience with music?"

"Yes, good idea. On the stage behind me."

"You will broadcast over the wireless?"

"Naturally."

"And film?"

"Why not? There is a woman, Leni Riefenstahl, who has done work for me. She is devoted to the cause, a very accomplished cineaste. We will present this at night, and she can use all of her clever lighting tricks."

"It will be a night, my Führer," Adler said, "that no one will ever forget."

THEY TOOK ROBERT and Dov to the basement of the local SA headquarters, a bare concrete cube eight meters on a side. They handcuffed Dov to a heating pipe high up on one wall, his arms stretched straight above his head. Robert noted the rather ominous drain in the center of the unfinished floor.

When they finished with Dov, the two enlisted men beat Robert for ten minutes, until their arms hung limp with exhaustion. Robert had learned from Houdini how to tense himself so that blows to the stomach couldn't hurt him. Some of the same techniques that he used to expand and contract his body inside a strait jacket allowed him to soften or evade the worst of the blows to his head and kidneys for a time. In the end he could do little other than cover up and take the punishment. Through it all he worried about Cora. Did they have her too?

When the beating stopped, the Sturmhauptführer stood over him where he lay curled on the floor. The Sturmhauptführer was a big man, fleshy, with thick arms and a drooping gray mustache. "A neighbor reported hearing noises in an old lady's house that was supposed to be deserted," he said. "Then within minutes a synagogue blew up on that same street. When we came out for a look, we found this Jew—" He pointed to Dov. "—trying to sneak back into the house. So we arrested them all. The others are now in the Esterwegen KZ. We haven't decided what to do with this animal yet.

"Anyway, he led us directly to you, just as you were changing residences, it seems. We have been following you ever since. I only brought him along tonight for the pleasure of seeing him betray you in person, no thirty pieces of silver required. He tells us you were the one who set the charges that blew up the synagogue. Unless my nose deceives me, you are a Jew as well, so it doesn't make sense that you would destroy your own place of worship. And why this should happen at the very moment that the entire neighborhood was swarming with ss fanatics, and why you should be picking up and delivering crates at the ss stronghold in Wewelsburg, and how you should be able to come up with the paper the Jew was carrying, all of this is very puzzling."

He squatted down so that his face was less than a meter from Robert's and Robert could smell fried onions on his breath. "I don't like mysteries, and I intend to get to the bottom of this one. Maybe you have a good explanation, which you would care to share. If so, I will gladly listen now."

If they had Cora, Robert thought, he would have mentioned it. And it seemed that Dov had not given away anything about the plot against Hitler. In which case, Robert had nothing to say. Once you began talking, it became harder and harder to stop.

"You don't care to cooperate?" the Sturmhauptführer said. He straightened up and kicked Robert in the groin. The pain made him lose consciousness for a moment. "I assure you, you will."

CORA BOARDED A TRAIN in Paderborn on Sunday afternoon, alighting in Magdeborg long enough to make sure she wasn't being followed before catching the next express into Berlin.

Lulled by the rhythmic sway of the train, she recalled with some embarrassment the intensity of the desire that had swept over her in the warehouse with Robert. Two people, working closely together under conditions of high tension and emotion...it was not unreasonable that they would find themselves drawn to one another. Perhaps it was no more than that. Perhaps, when this was over, she would have the opportunity to find out.

On Monday the last pieces of the plan fell into place. She met Kurt at the Tiergarten lion cages, where he told her that Ernst Toller had returned to Berlin. Toller was in principle willing to head a provisional government, although he didn't understand how such a thing might be possible.

"Listen to the wireless," she told him. "Hitler will announce a major speech to take place the day after tomorrow. Wherever it is, whatever time it's scheduled for, make sure that Toller is there and ready to speak. And all the others must be there too, and ready."

"We will be," he said. "And you are still not going to tell me how this is going to happen?"

Cora smiled. "It's magic."

AFTER THAT FIRST BEATING, they clothed Robert in a gray striped prison uniform and locked him in a tiny, windowless cell in the basement where he could not distinguish day from night. They of course had taken his watch. Three walls of the cell were brick and the fourth was made up of steel bars at 15 centimeter intervals. A slops bucket stood in one corner. His bunk was a wooden plank suspended on chains and devoid of any padding. The Sturmhauptführer put a guard outside the cell and told him, "I do not trust this man. Do not take your eyes off him, even when he uses the toilet. If he approaches the bars, shoot him in the knees."

The guard changed regularly, and Robert made a surreptitious hash mark each time on the wall next to his bunk, using one of the several lock-picks he had smuggled in. Every fourth shift they brought him a small loaf of dark bread and a tin cup of water. How

like the Germans, he thought. In their very attempts to disorient
him, they could not repress their need for order.

Assuming the shifts were two hours long, which felt right, it was
Monday afternoon when the Sturmhauptführer came for him again.
In all that time Robert had taken no more than catnaps, so that he
could watch the guards. Not once had any of them fallen asleep or
been significantly distracted. Every time Robert changed position,
the barrel of the guard's carbine followed him.

Over and over he had asked himself what Houdini would have
done in his place. He felt certain the plot had not been exposed,
else the Nazis would have been exerting more pressure on him. Any
attempt to escape would carry tremendous risk, which he couldn't
justify at the moment.

Yet when they came for him and escorted him toward the room
where they had beaten him so badly on that first night, he found
himself cringing involuntarily.

The Sturmhauptführer ordered Robert chained to the wall
hand and foot and then, to Robert's surprise, sent the guards away,
leaving the two of them without witnesses. As far as Robert was
concerned, the chains were a mere formality, from which he could
free himself in seconds. The issue was the Walther service automatic
that the Sturmhauptführer kept trained carefully at the center of
Robert's chest.

"I have been asking many questions," the Sturmhauptführer
said. "It seems that Himmler was seen on the balcony overlooking
the synagogue that exploded. He was waving around some shiny
metal object and chanting meaningless words. It is well known
that Himmler is a superstitious fool, and so I am now thinking that
perhaps he does not know of your explosives. Perhaps he would be
very, very interested to learn."

Robert showed no reaction.

"Ordinarily I would be perfectly happy to discover that someone
was playing tricks on the Chicken Farmer. However, this is clearly
not some minor prank, and I intend to find out exactly who you

are, who else is involved, and what you are up to. If all you want is to bring Himmler down, perhaps I will stand aside and let you finish your work. Or perhaps I will go to him in his castle and earn his undying gratitude. It all depends on where my greatest self-interest lies."

Robert found it a hopeful sign that the guards were not there to overhear. As long as the Sturmhauptführer kept his knowledge to himself, Robert did not have to make a move.

"In any case," the Sturmhauptführer said, "it is now time for you to talk. If you are silent, you leave me no other choice than to go to Himmler."

"Please," Robert said. They were the first words he'd spoken in two days, and he let his voice reveal his desperation and fatigue. "I am exhausted and in pain. I cannot think clearly. I need a decent meal and some uninterrupted sleep."

The Sturmhauptführer looked at him oddly. "That voice. I know that voice." He clapped his hands together. "You are Hungarian, yes? The escape artist, the ersatz Houdini."

Robert, stung, said, "I am Robertini the Magnificent."

"I saw you many years ago in Hamburg. Most impressive. But please believe me when I say that I will not hesitate to kill you if necessary."

"I believe you, but I must have food and rest."

"Food and rest will only give you more time to invent lies. Tell me everything and I will see that you are fed."

"Can I at least have some water for my throat..."

"Do not test my patience any further."

"I dare not tell you," Robert cried. "The Führer would—"

"The Führer?"

"Already I have said too much. The Führer will kill me."

"Talk, or the Führer will never get the chance."

Robert sighed. "As you suspected, there is a plot against Himmler. It is the Führer behind it, testing his loyalty. He too knows of Himmler's crazy beliefs, and so he hired me—"

"You? A Jew?"

"He is willing to use Jews for his purposes, as you know, and there is nobody better for the job. He hired me to determine whether Himmler would choose a seemingly powerful magical object over his loyalty to his Führer."

"And you are working alone?"

If he agreed, Robert knew he would be caught in the lie. "There is one other. Inside Himmler's organization."

"How can you prove this outrageous story?"

"I do not know. Of course Herr Hitler would deny it if you asked him."

"Now that you are captured, surely your little plot has failed."

"We were moving very slowly. The next step is not until this coming weekend."

"You are telling me that Himmler believes this object destroyed the synagogue?"

"Yes."

The Sturmhauptführer smiled. "He is even more of a fool than I realized."

"Please," Robert said. "Let me eat and sleep."

"You had best think of a way to verify your story. And I will think about how to take advantage of this situation." He pounded on the door and two guards entered. "Gentlemen," he said, "allow me to present Robertini the Magnificent. In case you don't know the name, he is an escape artist. That means you must double the guard, and change one man every hour. I want two guns pointed at him at all times. Take no chances whatsoever. Do I make myself clear?"

"Jawohl, Herr Sturmhauptführer."

"Bring him dinner, and a mattress and a pillow." To Robert he said, "Bon appétit. Do not forget our discussion."

HITLER CONTINUED to treat Adler as his honored guest. On Monday morning, they drove together to the Pariser Platz to see work commence on the set for Wednesday's performance. The vast brick plaza was marked off by lead weights anchoring string that delineated the edges of the stage, the wall, and the grandstands. Lumber and concrete blocks were being unloaded from trucks as they watched.

By that afternoon, however, when they returned, Hitler was not pleased with the progress. It was as if a demon possessed him. His face flushed, his eyes focused on the foreman with manic intensity, and he began to scream and wave his arms. This was the most important project in the history of the Reich, he said, and the foreman was sabotaging it with his laziness and stupidity and incompetence. If he needed more men, then he was to get them. If he needed to work all night, then he was to do without sleep. The work was to be done exactly as ordered and finished ahead of the deadline or the consequences would be unthinkable.

The foreman looked at the ground, tears running from his eyes. "Yes, my Führer," he said, again and again, wringing his hands, clearly wanting nothing more in the world than for the tirade to end, and still it went on and on. Adler, standing with Kempa, the chauffeur, found himself unable to look away, as desperately as he wanted to.

At long last Hitler pivoted on one heel and stalked back to the car. Kempa ran to open the door for him, and Hitler got stiffly into the back seat and sat with his arms folded across his chest, glowering.

Kempa intercepted Adler and cautioned him, "Say nothing to him. The mood will pass in time."

Within half an hour Hitler's spirits began to gradually lighten, and by dinner he was smiling and joking. Adler, however, could not forget the all-consuming power of that anger and self-pity, lurking only one perceived slight away.

On Tuesday morning they revisited the site. After a full night of work under electric lights, the stage and basic shapes of the grandstands had been roughed out, and masons had begun the wall. Hitler was pleased and shook the terrified foreman's hand.

Adler was satisfied as well, with the construction and with Hitler's rage. He was counting on both.

Nothing, he thought, could stop them now.

•

SINCE HE'D ARRIVED in Berlin, Otto Mueller's nights had been
racked by nightmares. He saw himself beheading a live baby spar-
row on a kitchen cutting board, ramming his car into a bus full of
schoolchildren, strangling his own mother in her bed. Everywhere
he looked in those dreams, he saw the icon of the Black Sun, the
wheel of broken spokes. He saw it in the face of a clock, the steering wheel of the car, the dial of a telephone, the pattern on a china
plate, the lens of a camera, the pupils of his dying mother's eyes. He
had come to fear it as much as he had come to fear sleep itself.

Each time he woke in terror, he was Gideon again for a few moments, disoriented, searching for an urgent purpose he was unable
to remember, then Otto Mueller returned to drive the fear away
and he would stagger from the bed and cry, "Sieg heil!" in a fierce,
choked whisper, repeating it until the comfort of righteous anger
settled over him and drove the doubts away.

He spent Monday with Bartels, helping him prepare his introduction for Wednesday's unveiling of the Spear. "I must make the
audience understand the importance of our heritage," Bartels said,
"including the Spear, and yet I must not give away the Führer's surprise. I must tell a story, yet I must be brief. I must be technical, yet I
must be easily understood."

"And you will," Mueller told him. "I know you will."

On Tuesday Mueller accompanied Bartels as he and Hitler talked
through the program for the evening. First the orchestra would play
for half an hour, selections from Beethoven, Grieg, and Weber. Then
Bartels would speak for ten or twelve minutes.

They paused at this point so that Hitler could read through
the latest draft of Bartels' speech. He asked for a few changes,
mostly to make the references to the Spear less revealing of what
was to come.

Following Bartels' speech, the orchestra would perform Wagner's
"Ride of the Valkyries," then Hitler himself would take the stage. As
Hitler described each succeeding phase of the spectacle, his pride

and excitement grew more contagious. Mueller was thrilled to be a part of it and imagined telling his grandchildren about it in some distant Aryan Eden of a future. At the same time his guts churned with the knowledge that something was terribly wrong.

On Tuesday night he did not sleep at all.

ROBERT COULD NOT keep waking himself for hourly guard changes, and so lost track of the time. Still, when the Sturm-hauptführer sent for him, he felt sure it was Wednesday. Maybe, he thought, it's already happening, maybe Hitler is even now addressing the nation to tell them of his wondrous Spear.

Three soldiers escorted him to the same windowless concrete room, where the Sturmhauptführer awaited him with his Walther drawn. Dov hung once again from the pipe on the wall. The soldiers shackled Robert hand and foot to a wooden chair and then left the room on the Sturmhauptführer's orders. An unpleasant smile twisted his fleshy face.

"I have been quite busy since we last spoke," he said. "First I asked a few discreet questions of an acquaintance I have at the Wewelsburg Castle. Then I made an excursion to the Esterwegen camp and had the opportunity to speak to this man's wife."

Dov thrashed in fury. "You fucking bastard! I swear I will kill you!"

The Sturmhauptführer glanced at him. "You needn't worry. She required hardly any persuasion at all." Turning back to Robert, he said, "To get to the point, she quoted you as saying that you were part of a plot to depose the Führer. She said you bragged about hav-ing access to money and resources, which clearly must be true, as you managed to order up these forged papers in a matter of hours."

"I told them the story they were most likely to believe. Who could produce that document faster than the Party itself?"

"No. First of all, the document is a forgery. A good one, but still a fake. Secondly, if you were working for the Führer, you would have no reason to keep Jews alive. You would have killed them yourself or left them to die in the explosion."

"I am not a killer," Robert said. "And they might have tampered with the charges—"

"The man," Dov interrupted. "The courier who brought the papers. He was not a soldier, not with the Party. He thanked this man in advance for killing Hitler."

Not what I said, Robert thought, but it hardly mattered now.

"You see?" said the Sturmhauptführer. "Your lies are unraveling quickly now. Guards!"

The door flew open and the three soldiers rushed to attention.

"Get the car ready," the Sturmhauptführer said. "Does anyone know where the Führer is? Is he in Munich?"

"Berlin, sir," one soldier said. "You know, for the speech."

"What speech?"

"It's all over the wireless. He is giving a speech tonight, it's supposed to be very important. He says it will change the future of the world."

The Sturmhauptführer nodded at Robert. "I have it now. Very clever." He asked the soldier, "What time is the speech?"

"Nine tonight, sir."

He looked at his watch. "It's at least four hours to Berlin. We must hurry."

"What about me?" Dov said. "I have helped you in every way I could."

"Yes," the Sturmhauptführer said, with a bored expression. "The Party thanks you." He fired a single shot into Dov's chest, thunderously loud in the concrete room. Blood spattered the wall and floor, and Dov convulsed once before he slumped in his chains.

"Bring the car," the Sturmhauptführer said. "Now."

PACO ARRIVED IN BERLIN on Tuesday afternoon and found a transient's hotel near the Lehrter Bahnhof train station. He would have preferred the Adlon at the Tiergarten if anonymity had not been so much more important than comfort. With luck—a great deal of luck—everything would be over in slightly more than 24 hours. After that, if he was still alive, he promised himself all the cordon bleu meals and four star hotels his heart desired.

He collected the rental ambulance at noon on Wednesday and ran the final errands on his list. He began with a man's dark wig and glue-on mustache from a costume shop, followed by nurses' uniforms, two male and one female, a doctor's white coat, and a strait jacket, all from a medical supply house near the Charité University Hospital. He treated himself to a heavy lunch at a café across from the hospital, then changed into one of the nurse's uniforms in the bathroom.

From the hospital it was a short jaunt across the River Spree to the Pariser Platz, where he showed the appropriate passes to the guards and parked the ambulance behind the stage.

It was 3:30 on a hot summer afternoon. He put the second male nurse's uniform into a paper bag and locked the ambulance. His rendezvous with Robert was scheduled for 6:00 at the Zoo-Aquarium shark exhibit. He would pass the time until then calming himself by looking at fish.

THEY TRUSSED ROBERT in a dozen chains and carried him out to the open-topped Daimler staff car. He was again amazed at the doggedness of the German mind. They knew Robert could escape from any shackles they put on him, so their solution was more shackles. He picked the locks on all of them save the one around his legs even as the soldiers settled him face down on the floor of the back seat, leaving them loose around his arms and torso as if they were still fastened. Two Brownshirt soldiers sat with him, their feet resting on his back, while the Sturmhauptführer sat in front with the driver.

Despite the beating, despite the steady erosion of the plan, a part of Robert had believed himself to be in a chess match where he was the far superior player, observing move and countermove with detached confidence. That had changed the moment Dov was murdered.

He had clung to the idea that both of them would inevitably

escape from the basement. Escape was his art. He didn't blame Dov
for his repeated betrayals—Dov was a husband and a father, and
his priorities had nothing to do with Robert's. And Robert had
continued to believe in Adler's dream of non-violence, as foolish as
the words had sounded when he'd said them to Dov. Now that the
bloodshed had started, he knew that more would come.

He had run out of options. He had to overcome and disarm the
two men in the back seat before the Sturmhauptführer had time to
react. Then he had to somehow disable the Sturmhauptführer and
the driver and get control of the car. This would not be a matter of
intellect and planning, but rather of instinct and opportunity.

He gave them an hour to relax their vigilance. Based on the
sounds and smells in the air, Robert knew they were in open country, moving quickly, an occasional car whooshing past them in the
opposite lane. One of the soldiers was telling a tedious story about
his sister-in-law flirting with him, and Robert felt the man's weight
shift as he gestured.

Houdini had said, "My chief task has been to conquer fear."
Robert had thought he understood that, though he had never attempted Houdini's most dangerous feats—being buried alive, or the
upside down. He saw now that he had deceived himself. He wanted
badly to live. He wanted to smell the sea air from the deck of a ship,
to sleep under warm blankets on a winter night, to touch a woman's
lips with his fingers.

What would Houdini think of me, he wondered, lying here in a
paralysis of fear?

That thought, finally, spurred him to action. He pushed himself
onto his knees, the chains falling off him like raindrops from an
oilskin jacket. His nerves were so tightly wound that time stopped.
Both soldiers had pistols in their right hands. Robert grabbed the
arm of the one on the driver's side and slammed it backward, the pistol hitting the second soldier in the nose before it fell onto the seat.

The driver had seen him in his mirror and slammed on the brakes,
throwing everyone off balance. Robert did not hesitate. With his

immense upper body strength, he turned the first soldier sideways, grabbed him by the belt, and shoved him out of the moving car.

The second soldier waved his pistol in the air, disoriented and bleeding from the nose. Robert stood up on the floorboards, the deceleration pushing him against the front seat and giving him stability. He hit the second soldier on his broken nose, blinding him, and with two jerks of the man's right arm, threw him over the side of the car as well.

There was a chance, he told himself, both guards might survive.

He snatched the pistol from the seat and turned around. The Sturmhauptführer stared at him wide-eyed as the car fishtailed toward the verge of the motorway, the driver fighting the wheel. Robert put the pistol to the Sturmhauptführer's ear. "Both hands in the air!" he shouted over the screaming tires.

The Sturmhauptführer shouted back. "You are no killer." His right hand inched toward his holster. "I don't believe—"

Robert pulled the trigger. Blood and brains spattered the inside of the windscreen as the car lurched to a stop and the Sturmhauptführer's body pitched sideways across the driver's lap.

"Put your hands up!" Robert shouted, exhilarated, scarcely able to believe himself. Houdini, he thought, couldn't have done any better.

He must have heard a sound, because something made him turn and see, unbelievably, the second soldier charging down the motorway toward him, dragging his useless right leg after him, his face smeared with blood, his left shoulder scraped to the bone, somehow less than a dozen meters away, his pistol in front of him and flashing fire at the muzzle.

Robert felt the bullets punch into his chest and registered the last one, the killing shot through his left eye, as no more than a flash of white light and a split second of regret.

THE PERFORMANCE was scheduled for nine PM, so that the climax would come in full darkness. By 8:15, when Mueller, Bartels, and Himmler arrived, crowds already filled Pariser Platz to overflowing.

The air hummed with electricity, although Mueller could not feel it himself for the growing dread in his chest. Though he did not understand why, he carried a thin briefcase that contained pages of sheet music, two hypodermic syringes, and a pistol. He had no idea what they were for, only that he had been unable to leave them in his room.

As he walked toward the Brandenburg Gate, all that was visible of the bronze charioteer on top were her wings, as if the Angel of Death hovered overhead. He shuddered as he passed beneath her, and then he followed the others into the center of a plaza that had been completely transformed.

To his left, at the north end of the square, stood a three-meter-high stage large enough to hold an entire symphony orchestra. Huge swastika flags hung as backdrops. To one side of the stage a hundred SS troops milled about, and on the other side waited an equal number of Brownshirts. Beyond the soldiers on either side loomed ten-meter high grandstands, each of which was filled to its capacity of a thousand spectators. Thousands more wandered the plaza, many of them examining the wall that had been erected across the south side, blocking the view of the Hotel Adlon. The wall rose ten meters high and 15 meters long, built of concrete blocks and painted black, with a five-meter-tall red star and yellow six-pointed star in the center. Discreet signs on the pavement cautioned that the paint was still wet, and in fact the painters continued to work on the edges.

Motion picture cameras and banks of lights were positioned everywhere, and technicians had laid a track between the stage and the wall to permit a camera to travel back and forth. A severely beautiful woman in jodhpurs and a beret was apparently in charge of staging the ceremony. She moved from camera to camera to give instructions, pausing only to shake hands and chat with various high-level Nazis as they came to pay their respects. Here was Göring, even heavier than in any of the photos Mueller had seen, lumbering around in a fanciful powder-blue and white uniform of his own design. Here was Joseph Goebbels, propaganda minister, looking like an anti-Semitic cartoon with his big nose, thin lips, overbite, and dark complexion, limping on his club foot.

Mueller, Bartels, and Himmler slowly made their way to the curtain of swastika flags, where an affected little man in a monocle and pencil-line mustache identified himself as the assistant director and took them up on the stage. He pointed Mueller and Bartels to a row of folding chairs in front of the orchestra. Nearly at the front of the stage sat two chairs by themselves, behind and to the side of podium. Hitler already occupied one, and the little man led Himmler to the other.

Between them, on the plywood floor, lay a long, narrow object swathed in black velvet.

The Spear of Destiny.

The orchestra began to tune up. The background noise of the crowd slowly diminished in anticipation.

Mueller's place was one chair away from the end of the row. In the exact center sat Ernst Ackermann, the old man who had brought the Spear to Himmler.

Bartels, to Mueller's right, chattered away nervously, rolling and unrolling the typescript of his speech. Mueller had no idea what he was saying. Instead he kept looking from Ackermann to the Spear, listening to his own breathing as it came faster and faster. He wondered if he might be having a heart attack. Sweat ran down his face and underarms. He was dizzy and nauseated and his vision blurred.

Ackermann, he knew, had another name. A dangerous, terrifying name. As did Mueller himself. There was a conspiracy, a conspiracy against Hitler. He had to warn the Führer. But warn him of what?

He stood up, staggered, had to take hold of his chair.

"Mueller, are you all right?" Bartels asked.

Behind him, the conductor tapped his baton and the orchestra began the long, slow fade in to the first movement of Beethoven's Ninth. The music mesmerized him. Half a minute in, the violins

swelled, the horns blared, the tympani pounded. It seemed to drive
the madness from his brain for the moment. He sat down again,
weak and confused. He shook his head at Bartels. "All the excitement, I suppose."

His foot encountered the briefcase under his chair. The orchestra.
He had some task he was supposed to perform. Why couldn't he
remember? He opened the briefcase, hoping the sight of the music
might trigger his memory.

The syringes and the pistol had disappeared.

WHEN 6:00 CAME and went, then 6:15, and Robert had still not
appeared, Paco felt the first stirrings of panic.

This late in the game they had no contingency plans, no means
to contact each other. At 7:30 he walked to the ambulance, partly
to see if anyone had left a message, partly to give his restless body
something to do.

The ambulance was exactly as he'd left it, so he returned to the
aquarium, listing in his head all the possible things that might have
delayed Robert without putting the entire plan at risk. The list was
long but brought little comfort.

At 9:00 he gave up and headed toward Pariser Platz in the soften-
ing light of dusk. He was nearly on top of the ambulance before he
saw a man in an SS officer's uniform crouching beside the driver's
door, trying to see inside.

Paco's hesitation was brief, but fatal. The man had seen him.

"You!" the man said, and reached for his sidearm. "Halt!"

It was the last man in the entire world that Paco wanted to see:
long-faced Obersturmführer Richter from the Wewelsburg Castle.
The man who had arrested Adler. The man who did not believe.

Before Paco could think to run, Richter's pistol was pointing at
his belly. "Drop the package, then stand beside the ambulance and
face it. Spread your legs and lean forward on your hands."

Paco did as he was told. The man frisked him quickly and said,
"What are you doing here?"

Paco answered in a low growl. "I've never seen you before in my life. Who are you? Why are you searching me?"

Richter shoved the barrel of his gun into Paco's kidney, hard. "I have seen you at the castle, you are one of the workmen. The Spaniard. I knew Ackermann was a liar, but I couldn't figure out his game. Then a friend of mine, an SA Sturmhauptführer in Paderborn, called me yesterday. He asked me a lot of questions about the explosion at the synagogue, and they confirmed every suspicion I had."

"I have a brother in Paderborn," Paco said desperately. "Perhaps you—"

"Shut up!" Richer shouted. "You are perpetrating a hoax, and Himmler and the Führer have walked into it with their eyes closed. Now I will see to it that their eyes are open." He grabbed Paco by the collar, jerked him away from the ambulance, and shoved him toward the stage. "Schnell!"

THE ORCHESTRA CONCLUDED with "In the Hall of the Mountain King" from *Peer Gynt,* and the audience, their emotions fired by the music and the anticipation of watching their Führer speak, shouted and applauded wildly.

As the sun set, the stage lights had gradually taken over, and now Mueller sat in an island of blazing brightness. Wherever he turned his gaze he saw swastikas and black uniforms and shining boots.

Bartels said, "Wish me luck," and shook Mueller's hand as he stood and made his way to the front of the stage, where some local Party functionary was finishing his introduction. Bartels paused to salute both Hitler and Himmler, stepped up to the podium, adjusted his glasses, and began to read.

Behind the orchestra, at the rear of the stage, someone shouted.

Mueller began to sweat and hyperventilate again. He refused to look back, though he heard chairs shuffle behind him as members of the orchestra turned toward the disturbance.

The assistant director tugged at his sleeve. "Forgive me, Herr Hauptsturmführer. A man backstage insists that he must speak to the Führer. Obersturmführer Richter? He says that you can vouch for him."

Indeed he could, Mueller thought. His doubts melted away. He was Hauptsturmführer Otto Mueller, and he was going to put this conspiracy to an end right now.

CORA ARRIVED OUTSIDE the Brandenburg Gate at 6:30. Kurt was already waiting for her, with Michael and a mob of what looked to be two hundred young men and women. She thought her heart might stop at the sight of them.

She took Kurt's hands. "All of these people are yours?" she said.

He flashed an excited smile. "More will come later."

"And...Toller?"

"I haven't seen him. He said he would be here, but...if anyone recognized him and informed the Gestapo..."

She nodded. "We've done what we can. The fuse is lit."

It had been a long day. She had spent it in her hotel room, waiting for the telephone to ring. The code was simple and untraceable. The telephone would ring once, then the caller would hang up and dial again. The number of rings on the second call identified the caller and told her he was safe and in place: one for Adler, two for Gideon, three for Robert, four for Paco.

Only Adler and Paco had checked in.

Kurt's small army spread out through the crowd. They all knew what to do and awaited her signal.

Cora kept herself near the front of the stage. Leave it to the Nazis, she thought, to know how to put on a spectacle. The entire Pariser Platz had become a film set, the basic black and white theme set off by splashes of red from the flags, while the SA uniforms provided a hint of warm earth tones. She counted at least nine different cinema cameras and it occurred to her that if things miraculously went as they were supposed to, the resulting film would make motion picture history.

She watched the grandstands fill and felt her anxiety lessen somewhat when Gideon arrived in the company of Himmler and Bartels, followed shortly by the sight of Adler taking his place on the platform. Paco and, she hoped, Robert would be behind the curtain of flags somewhere, waiting in the ambulance. She fought the urge to look for them.

Nine o'clock finally arrived. Hitler and Himmler had their places up front, and behind them sat a row of dignitaries that included Goebbels, Göring, Adler, Bartels, and Gideon. The orchestra began to play with great precision, if not abundant warmth.

As she watched, Gideon began to come apart.

Instinct brought her closer to the platform, though there was nothing she could do. The crowd was packed so tightly that she scarcely had room to breathe. She pleaded with her eyes and smiled in gratitude as she squeezed herself between the ranks of SA troops and the grandstands on stage left.

The music dragged on interminably as she stood there, staring at Gideon, wishing she believed in the telepathy she had faked so many times on stage, so that she could send calming thoughts into Gideon's head. At last the orchestra finished and Bartels took the podium, regaling the crowd with legends of German great-ness, of Grails and Spears and the Black Sun that nurtured the Aryan spirit.

Then something went wrong. The musicians, hearing a sound inaudible to Cora, looked behind them, and the crowd near her be-gan to murmur. Cora climbed onto the first level of the grandstand so that she could see over the heads of the massed SA troops, and at that moment, an SS officer pushed his way through the hanging flags and onto the stage.

He was holding a gun to Paco's head.

MUELLER, AT THE VERY BACK of the stage, froze at the sight of the man in the white hospital uniform. A voice in his head urged him to help the man, said that the man was a friend. Mueller was tired of voices in his head, and he smothered it with his will.

Behind the male nurse was another face he knew, Obersturm-führer Richter, from Wewelsburg Castle. Mueller hurried to him. "What's the meaning of this?"

"I must speak to the Führer immediately. He must not take the podium! There is a conspiracy. I believe they mean to kill him."

Bartels finished his speech to applause and cheers, even as the orchestra's string section played the ascending, vibrato notes of the opening of "Ride of the Valkyries." Mueller felt his Aryan soul stir with pride and excitement at the sound.

"I knew it!" Mueller cried. "Those bastards! I never trusted them."

"You must take me to the Führer now. I don't know how much time we have left."

"Instantly!" Mueller said. He spun on his heel and started for the front of the stage.

That was when a woman's voice called his name. No, not his name. Gideon's name.

THOUGH CORA couldn't hear the words that passed between Gideon and the officer, the body language was clear: the officer insisting, Gideon consenting, the officer relaxing, the two of them moving forward with purpose.

It fulfilled every fear she had ever held about Gideon, and explained why he had never called to check in. He had been swallowed by his role.

The two men were still far enough to the rear of the stage that few in the audience saw them. Cora had no more than a second or two to think of something before Gideon betrayed them all. It was impossible for her to get to the stage in time to stop them physically. She surrendered to the first impulse that occurred to her.

"Gideon!" she called, using her stage voice, hands cupped around her mouth. She saw him stop, shake off his reaction, start forward again. "Gideon!"

He paused, looked out at the crowd. She waved her arms to get his attention. There was utter madness in his eyes.

"Gideon!" she shouted, and then called in English, "Do Hitler!"

He froze. People on both sides of Cora turned to look at her, edging away. We are lost, she thought. All is lost.

Then, slowly, Gideon rolled his eyes, hooked his left thumb awkwardly in the front of his pants, pushed his hair down over one eye, and gave a languid, bent-arm salute, fingers pointing upward.

The officer holding the gun on Paco stared, speechless.

"Gideon!" she shouted. "Do Cary Grant!"

The left hand dropped, then rose to the left hip. His eyes narrowed and a stiff grin spread across his face until his teeth sparkled in the electric lights.

"Gideon!" she shouted. "*Do Gideon!*"

LIKE MAGIC, GIDEON found himself back in control.

Richter stared at him open-mouthed. "Have you lost your mind?"

"Au contraire," Gideon said. Snapping the fingers of his left hand high in the air to distract Richter's eye, he took the gun out of Richter's right hand and tucked it into the waistband of his own pants. Otto Mueller didn't know what had happened to the hypodermics, but Gideon, who had taken advantage of his brief moments in command of their shared body, did. He pulled one out of the breast pocket of his uniform, flicked off the cork protector with his thumb, and before Richter knew what happened, reached around and jabbed it through several layers of uniform into Richter's buttocks and pressed home the plunger, injecting him with a massive dose of morphine diacetate.

"What have you done?" Richter said. "The Führer..."

Paco acted quickly, grabbing the tail of Richter's uniform jacket and stuffing it into Richter's mouth. "I think he's having an epileptic attack," Paco called to the assistant director, who stood at a distance, wringing his hands. "Get help!"

Already Richter's struggles were weakening. "You okay?" Gideon asked Paco, who nodded. "Good," Gideon said. "I have to see to the Führer."

The Valkyries were in full flight as Gideon approached Hitler, who had already risen from his chair. It felt wonderful, Gideon thought, to be on stage again. The stage was a magical place, the only safe place, the place where Gideon reigned supreme.

"My Führer," Gideon said, and clicked his heels.

Hitler looked mildly alarmed. "What was that commotion?"

"A crazy man," Gideon said. "He has been restrained. All is well."

"Only a few minutes now, eh?" Hitler said.

"Yes, sir. Good luck." Gideon shook Hitler's hand and, in the hidden space between his body and Hitler's, exchanged the pistol that had been his briefcase with the one in the holster at Hitler's side. Then he backed off two paces, threw a salute, and shouted, "Sieg heil!"

Hitler hooked his left thumb awkwardly in the front of his pants and gave a languid, bent-arm salute.

Gideon managed not to smile as he returned to his chair and took the sheet music parts out of the briefcase. The Valkyries completed their flight in a single explosive crescendo as Hitler reached the podium, sending the crowd into a frenzy. They cheered for two full minutes before Hitler finally began to speak. As always, he began in a slow, calm voice. "My German countrymen, men and women, you have heard tonight of the special destiny of the German people and the Aryan race."

The musicians laid down their instruments and wiped their faces. Between the lingering heat of the day and the heat of the lights, the temperature on stage was withering. Gideon walked up to the conductor and handed him the pages.

"The Führer has requested that you play this at the climax of his speech."

The conductor shook his head. "Impossible. We haven't rehearsed it, we have had no warning..."

"It doesn't have to be played well."

The conductor looked at the music. "The Führer wants us to play... *this?*"

Gideon gestured toward the black wall. "It will make sense when the time comes, I assure you."

The conductor nodded. "Well, it's not like it's difficult. We've all heard the tune. And I would not want to tell the Führer no."

"Good man," Gideon said.

He returned to his chair to wait.

CORA SAW GIDEON wink at her and she knew he was himself again. Moments later the ss officer's knees mysteriously buckled and Paco helped him lie down. Cora fought her way to her previous position, nearly at the front of the stage, only to be pushed back. The sa soldiers on one side and the ss soldiers on the other began to clear a corridor between the stage and the target wall, and when the passage was formed, they linked arms to form a human barricade on either side.

Hitler's speech heated up. "The Communists tried to stop us. The Jews tried to stop us. The inferior Slavic races tried to stop us. All of them failed. And now...now the enemies of the German people will not merely be defeated. They will be annihilated!"

Still staring straight ahead, he extended his right hand. Himmler rose, picked up the velvet-wrapped Spear, and unwrapped it in a slow, teasing pantomime that had the audience murmuring and straining to see. Finally he flung the cloth to one side. Some of the more astute members of the crowd gasped when the Spear point was revealed. The handle was freshly made, crudely planed with hand tools, rustic in the preferred style of the newly minted German traditions the Nazis were hawking. Himmler placed it into Hitler's waiting hand and Hitler held it over his head.

"Behold!" he said. His eyes burned and spittle flew from his lips. "The Spear of Destiny! The destiny it commands is not only that of the German people, but of the entire world. What you will see tonight is only a hint of what is to come. A hint...and a warning to all the enemies of the Reich!

"And now—stand away from the wall that bears the symbols of evil. Stand clear, because in the name of the German people I call down the lightning from the clear night sky, the lightning that will destroy our enemies utterly!"

Hitler waved the Spear in a slow circle above his head, chanting, "Jantar, Mantar, Jadu, Mantar," once, then twice. Then he pointed the Spear at the black wall and cried out, "Jantar! Mantar! Jadu! Mantar!"

She felt the collective breath of thousands of people held tight in their lungs. Long seconds passed.

Hitler, clearly surprised, shouted again, "Jantar! Mantar! Jadu! Mantar!"

Himmler was on his feet.

With desperate fury, Hitler shook the Spear and tried again. "Jantar! Mantar! Jadu! Mantar!"

Himmler grabbed for the Spear. Hitler, in incandescent rage, shoved him so hard that Himmler landed on his buttocks, a look of betrayal on his soft face. The crowd was muttering now, and Cora heard some laughter, immediately stifled.

Hitler drew his pistol and turned to Adler, who wore an expression of confusion and dismay. "Ackermann!" he shouted. "Make it work!"

Adler came forward and, with difficulty, pulled the spear point free from the staff, saying, "Perhaps the handle is interfering somehow." He pointed it at the wall and said, "Jantar, Mantar, Jadu, Mantar."

Hitler slapped him with his free hand, hard enough to put Adler on the floor of the stage. "Idiot!" Hitler shouted. He waved his gun in the air and looked like he might start shooting at any moment.

It was time.

Cora stood on tiptoe and shouted in German at the top of her lungs. "He's gone mad!"

Instantly Kurt and Michael and the others, stationed throughout the crowd, picked up the cry. "Verrückt!" "The Führer has lost his mind!" The words were followed by boos and catcalls and whistles.

Years of frustration and anger began to find release. Voices all over the square were shouting now, and the SA and SS waded into the crowd, looking for perpetrators and finally laying into anyone within reach of their truncheons and rifle butts. They were vastly outnumbered and the civilians bore them to the ground.

Cora's attention was on Hitler.

As he stood at the podium, watching the wreckage of his dream, the anger drained out of him. His face sagged and his eyes reflected only black despair.

He raised the pistol to his temple and pulled the trigger.

GIDEON WATCHED with elation as Hitler's triumph turned to chaos.

At the front of the stage, Himmler cradled the useless Spear in his lap, muttering the incantation over and over. Göring, Goebbels, and Bartels had all managed to disappear. The crowd had descended into hysteria. Fistfights broke out everywhere between the SA and the SS, between soldiers and civilians, between fascists and social democrats, between rich and poor.

Hitler, devastated, stood as if real lightning had in fact struck him. Then he brought his pistol to his own head and fired.

It was the pistol Gideon had traded for Hitler's, and instead of a bullet, a small black and red flag popped out of the barrel with the word BUMM! printed on it.

Hitler stared at the pistol as if willing himself to wake up. The crowd broke into laughter, great guffaws of it.

Gideon turned to the conductor and said, "Now would be good."

The conductor, apparently, was not a Hitler supporter. He smiled and said, "My pleasure."

He waved his baton and the orchestra, a bit hesitantly, began to play the socialist anthem, the Internationale. After a few seconds a third of the orchestra put down their instruments in disgust, but the rest simply played louder, and the crowd began to sing along.

*Stand up, damned of the Earth*
*Stand up, prisoners of starvation*
*Reason thunders in its volcano*
*This is the eruption of the end*


Gideon looked up and Paco was there, strait jacket in hand. "Ready?" Paco said.

Gideon nodded.

Hitler was trembling, nearly catatonic. Gideon didn't need the second hypodermic. They bundled him into the jacket, Gideon helped Adler to his feet, and the three of them carried the Führer down the rear stairs and into the ambulance.


AS CORA MADE her way to the ambulance, Kurt and the others began to chant Toller's name, and again the crowd picked it up. The ambulance's motor was running, the blue light turning on the roof. Paco had the wheel and Adler slumped, exhausted, on the passenger seat. Hitler lay stretched out in the back, and Gideon, sitting beside him, had changed his ss uniform for nurse's whites.

"Hurry," Paco said, "we need to get on the road."

"Has anyone heard from Robert?" Cora asked.

In the long, reluctant silence Paco finally shook his head, speaking for them all.

"I'm staying," Cora said.

Adler opened his eyes. "Cora, dear, are you sure?"

"Someone should be here for Robert, in case...well, just in case. And besides, I want to see this."

"We can't wait, you know," Gideon said.

"I know," Cora said. "You go on."

Adler said, "Thank you. I can never thank you enough."

Cora gestured toward Pariser Platz. "You already have."

She waited until the ambulance disappeared down the Unter den Linden, then made her way back into the rapidly thinning crowd.

Toller was on stage now, speaking into the microphones. He was a short man with a high forehead, intense eyes, and dark curly hair, combed straight back. The cameras that had survived the fighting all now pointed at him.

"I call upon President Hindenburg to declare martial law," he said, in a ringing, theatrical voice, "to ban the National Socialist Party, and to set a date for free elections, to be held no later than one month from tonight."

The audience was still cheering as Cora passed through the Brandenburg Gate and headed to her hotel, hoping the telephone would ring in the night: once, then three times more.

OUTSIDE HANNOVER, after they stopped for petrol, Gideon offered to take the wheel. Though he should have been exhausted, his energy felt limitless. Paco stretched out in the back and quickly fell into a deep sleep. Hitler, who had awoken in a fit of screaming rage an hour before, was sedated on morphine and snoring gently. Gideon had trimmed Hitler's hair nearly to the scalp and shaved his mustache before they left Berlin.

Adler, fragile and waxen-looking, claimed he could not sleep and sat up with Gideon while he drove.

"Are you able to talk about what happened to you?" Adler asked. Gideon struggled to find words and Adler said, "You don't have to answer that if you don't want to."

"No," Gideon said, "it's okay." He took another minute and then said, "You know the Black Sun that Bartels was talking about? That mystical light that's supposed to recharge the spirits of true Aryans everywhere? I think he's not entirely wrong."

"Don't tell me you've gone mystical."

"It's not mystical. I'm talking about the power of hatred. It's a force unto itself. It's everything that Bartels said about the Black Sun. It permeates the universe, and if you're lonely and sick and scared enough, it's there to comfort and nourish you. And then, before you know it, it controls your entire life."

Adler nodded and they were silent for a few kilometers. "Where do you go after this?" Adler asked at last.

"To the States, I think. Then maybe on tour. Something I know how to do. Something not frightening. What about you?"

"I hope I will be able to go back to Germany, back to my home town. I would like to be able to die there."

Gideon glanced at him. "You're not talking about the curse of the Spear, I hope."

Adler smiled weakly. "The curse of living too long."

THEY STOPPED FOR BREAKFAST at six AM, and Paco bought a copy of the *Vossische Zeitung,* Berlin's biggest daily. A banner headline read, "Hindenburg Declares Martial Law." Paco, always keeping one eye on the ambulance and its dozing passenger, read the story aloud as they waited for their food. Hitler, Röhm, Göring, and Goebbels were all missing and assumed to have carried out some longstanding escape plan, perhaps to South America. Himmler had been placed "in protective custody." Membership in the SA, the SS, or the Gestapo was now illegal. Hundreds had died overnight in riots, but the Reichswehr, the regular Army that Röhm had so badly wanted to supplant, was maintaining order.

When he finished reading, Paco, overwhelmed by a dozen different emotions, reached his hands across the table. Gideon gripped them, then Adler too.

Finally Adler said, "Hundreds dead."

"Instead of millions?" Gideon said. "Instead of a second Great War? It's a miracle."

Paco leafed through the rest of the newspaper and stopped at a photo of a bloodstained German staff car. A prisoner en route to Berlin, the story said, had killed a guard and an SA Sturmhauptführer before being shot to death himself.

Paco handed the newspaper to Adler, who scanned the story quickly and said, "Robert."

"Let me see," Gideon said, and took the newspaper.

Adler's eyes were red and tears rose in them. He excused himself and made his way toward the rear of the restaurant, where the public toilets were.

Paco stood up. Gideon put a hand on his arm and said, "Maybe you should give him a few minutes."

"I have to call Cora," Paco said. "She needs to know that she can stop waiting for the telephone to ring."

IN SO MANY WAYS, Adler thought, they had been lucky. Berlin had never loved Hitler, had only been bullied into accepting him. Hindenburg could have died at any point in the last two months. If the SA and SS had been able to act in concert instead of flying at each other's throats, they might have kept hold of the country for one of Hitler's lieutenants.

Still, it was the losses that weighed on him, Robert most heavily. He knew as well as anyone that when magic appeared effortless, it was always a hard-won illusion. Yet, like Himmler, like Hitler, he had wanted to achieve his dream without paying the inevitable price.

As they crossed the border into Belgium, he finally drifted into sleep and didn't awaken until they had arrived at the French seaside village of Saint-Valéry-en-Caux. Paco shook him gently and said, "Time to put on your white coat. Do you need a few minutes?"

"No," Adler said. "Let's finish it."

It was a beautiful summer Thursday morning. Adler could smell the sea. Some unshakable remnant of compassion had made him choose this place of natural beauty, of sand dunes and fishing boats, and now he was glad that he had.

Paco and Gideon each had one of Hitler's arms as they marched him through the doors of the asylum and up to the admitting desk. "I am Dr. Ackermann," Adler said. "I have the papers here to commit this man."

The orderly glanced over the paperwork. "Everything seems in order. What is this 'delusion' of his?"

Gideon said, "He thinks he's Adolph Hitler." If Gideon's French was not as good as Adler's, his accent was flawless, as always.

"Good timing," the orderly said. "I hear Germany is missing theirs." He looked Hitler up and down. "Not much of a resemblance, though."

Gideon placed the wig on Hitler's head and stuck on the false mustache. "He gets anxious without these."

"A little better," the orderly said. "He'd never fool anyone."

"Best not to take any chances," Gideon said. "Don't let him start any parties."

"In all seriousness," Adler said, "he has a high potential for violence, against both himself and others."

"Don't worry," the orderly said. "We'll keep him on enough Phenobarbital that he won't be able to raise his arm to salute."

PACO DROVE THEM to the Saint-Valéry-en-Caux train station and followed them inside. Adler bought a ticket for his home town of Quedlinburg in the Harz Mountains, and Gideon bought one for Marseille. Adler shook Gideon's hand, then embraced Paco, again overcome by emotion.

"What do you want me to do with the ambulance?" Paco said.

"You're a magician," Adler said, dabbing at his eyes. "Make it disappear."

ON THURSDAY AFTERNOON, Cora found herself drawn to Pariser Platz. The stage and grandstands had been carted away, and men with sledgehammers pounded at Hitler's black-painted wall.

Overnight the square had turned into a version of London's Hyde Park Corner, with people standing on stepladders or empty crates and declaiming to handfuls of listeners. She paused in front of one who risked arrest by wearing the newly forbidden brown shirt and Hakenkreuz. "The Jews brought down our Führer," he said, his face contorted with rage, "but he is only in hiding until we call for him to return. This martial law is no law at all, and we must resist it with all our Aryan might!"

Kurt appeared beside her. "It never ends, does it?" she asked.

"Look," Kurt said. The three other people who had been listening had all turned and walked away. "I don't think anyone is buying today. Let's us go too, shall we? No point in encouraging him."

Kurt took her arm and guided her toward the Brandenburg Gate. "Do you know," he said, "that the Eldorado has opened again? They are giving away free drinks all day. Everyone who is anyone will be there."

Cora stopped and faced him. "We lost someone," Cora said. "One of us who was part of the...the illusion. He was killed yesterday, and I only found out about it this morning."

Kurt drew her into a hug and at last she was able to cry, if only for a few seconds. Part of it was for Robert, part of it was relief at having survived, part of it was the terrible weight of knowing that whatever happened next to Germany was her responsibility.

"I am sorry for your friend," Kurt said, when her tears had stopped on their own. He slowly let her go. "But the time to mourn him is later. Right now you must come with me, and celebrate this wonderful new world you have given us, because who knows how long it will last?"

"All right," she said. "All right, I surrender. Will there be absinthe?"

Kurt smiled. "There will be everything."

He took her hand, and together they walked into the golden summer afternoon.

# THE

# NEXT

S HE'D HAD A LITTLE wine to get her courage up while she
dressed and did her makeup. Just a glass. Okay, two glasses. But
she'd promised herself she'd take it easy once she got to the bar.

She didn't go to the Valley much. Places like this, this Starr's, were
the reason. Cracked asphalt parking lot, a couple of Harleys, for
God's sake, parked near the entrance, some pimply biker making
obscene invitations as she passed. Beveled glass on the front door
and wood paneling inside, a fern bar gone to seed. The music loud
enough to be a physical assault. Eighties nostalgia, Pat Benatar, "Love
Is a Battlefield."

One drink, she told herself. Getting outside her comfort zone
was fine in theory. She didn't need to go deaf or get run over by a
drunken biker to prove a point.

The bartender couldn't hear her order and she had to point to
the overpriced Chardonnay on the drinks menu. This was crazy.
Conversation impossible, clientele unappealing, hopes circling the
drain. Chalk it up as a failed experiment. Finish the wine and cut
your losses.

Then, taking the stool next to her, the Sexy Stranger out of her
fantasies. Tall, casually elegant, movie-star looks and the confidence
that went with them, easy smile. A glance at her empty glass, an in-
quiring eyebrow. A gesture to the bartender, a 50-dollar bill materi-
alizing as if from thin air.

No more than a dozen words passed between them, breath warm
in her ear, an invitation to somewhere they could actually talk. The
wine had gone to her head—and her legs—but a strong, reassur-
ing arm slipped around her waist when she stumbled on the rough
pavement and it stayed there all the way to the dark gray Impala in
the farthest corner of the lot. The Avis sticker on the trunk struck

her as peculiar for no more than a second or two before she was overwhelmed by the wine, her nerves, her excitement, her amazement at her own daring.

The car door opening wide for her, her sliding in and fumbling with the seat belt. The engine throbbing to life, the warm smile again, suddenly changing, something in the eyes turning cold, predatory. Tires crying out as they spun against the asphalt, the car shooting in a backward arc, much too fast, then forward, pinning her to the seat, and the wine and the nerves and the excitement all burned away in the heat of her sheer, desperate, incredulous terror.

TOM CHECKED HIMSELF quickly in the hall mirror, less from vanity than fear of a strawberry seed caught in his teeth or a cowlick poking up from the edges of the ever-growing thin spot on the back of his head, a mustard stain on his tie. He sucked in his gut and grabbed his briefcase and went outside to confront his ungrateful children.

The morning was cool, bound for rotisserie temperatures. Tom didn't mind the occasional Southern California heat wave. The rustle of the queen palms, the faint salt tang in the air, the oranges and avocados he'd picked from the back yard an hour before, all were compensation enough. They even made up for the commute he was about to endure.

Jason, who had somehow turned 15 last month, though he couldn't have been more than four or five the year before, circled the driveway on his bike. He weaved complex patterns with his brother Brian, who had, with equal mystery, managed to turn 12 when Tom wasn't looking. Both were in baggy T-shirts, shorts, and overpriced sneakers. Brian, who was beefier than his older brother, had added a white Italian cycling cap to his ensemble. Both were bound for theater day camp at Jason's high school where they would be cruelly kept from video games until mid-afternoon.

"You ever think about getting married again, Dad?" Jason said.

"Seriously," Brian said. "I didn't think it was possible to screw up a Pop-Tart breakfast."

"Mom used to fix us bacon and eggs and stuff."

"A prophet," Tom said, "is not without honor save in his own country, and among his own kin." He supposed he'd done something right that they gave him such a hard time about Elaine and didn't resent him for being the parent that had survived.

Tom unlocked his high-mileage, sun-faded Corolla. As Brian pedaled away in the wake of his brother, he called over his shoulder, "Try not to get fired today, okay, Dad?"

The 5 Freeway was rolling, at one point as high as 40 miles an hour. Tom had his window down, trading a taste of monoxide for the pleasure of feeling the air move across his face. Periodically he switched the radio on, punched through the stations, and switched it off again. On one of his trips past KLOS he caught the news and lingered long enough to hear the latest on the "Devil Doll" murder, telling himself it was professional interest rather than rubbernecking.

"A twenty-five-year-old El Monte man was charged today in the brutal slaying of a UCLA medical administrator. A source at the LAPD told KLOS that the suspect is a member of a Satanic cult, which might explain some of the more bizarre aspects of the case. Meanwhile, the drought simmers on, with temperatures today expected to reach—"

Tom turned the radio off. Some high-dollar shyster would no doubt snap up the case for the publicity, run circles around the overworked DA's office, and with the right judge and a little luck put a psychopath back on the street.

DEEP DOWN, beneath the jealousy and the sniping, Tom supposed he had some genuine affection for Patrick, the fast-track kid out of UPenn. He did have one of those haircuts that failed to keep the blonde hair out of his eyes, yet cost more than Tom's best suit. He affected suspenders, a George Plimpton New England drawl, power ties and round, gold-rimmed glasses. He was funny, he was charming in his smug way, and he would make partner before he was thirty.

Tom remembered being thirty, barely. He would never make partner in this firm or any other.

"Let's settle this like professionals," Patrick said. He took a dart out of his desk drawer and threw it, without bothering to aim, at a dartboard on the far side of his office. He lifted his glasses, squinted, and said, "Guilty."

Half of the pie wedges on the board were papered over with the word GUILTY. The others were split among MOVE TO DISMISS, PLEA BARGAIN, PROBATION, and other popular outcomes. One thin triangle said NOT GUILTY.

"You're making racist assumptions," Tom said, "based on the fact that the guy is black and the old lady is white. She never saw the guy who allegedly—"

"I'm making assumptions based on the fact that your client— Collins, is that his name?"

"You know it's his name."

"—that your man Collins is a guilty piece of shit."

Emma, Roxanne's executive assistant, stuck her head in the door. "Ms. Vallence wants to see you, Tom."

"Now?" Tom said. He hated it when his voice broke.

"Now would be good." Emma disappeared again.

"Uh oh," Patrick said.

"Maybe it's not that bad."

"I'd ask for your office," Patrick said, "but I don't want your office."

"Thanks for the vote of confidence."

Tom paused outside Roxanne's door, raised his hand to knock, stopped, and wiped his hands on his pants leg. He tried again and made a noise about as loud as two acorns falling on a porch in a rainstorm.

"Come," Roxanne said. That was Roxanne all over. Her billing rate was so high, she wouldn't even give away an "in."

She had her back to Tom when he opened the door. In the same hopeless kind of way that he could admire the multi-million dollar houses that looked down on Laguna Beach, he could admire

Roxanne's shapely and well-toned glutes, covered this Monday morning by some sort of black stretch fabric that created the powerful impression that there was nothing between it and the skin underneath. Her three-inch heels, which brought her to an even six feet, had the intended effect on her calves and narrow ankles as well.

She spun around. Her own golden, expensively cut hair moved with a slight time delay, like heavy cream. Gold at her ears, around her fingers, hanging from her neck, and in the cuffs of her short-waisted, pristine white shirt set off her full red lips and colorless eyes.

"Tom," she said, with a tight smile, "do you know our DA, Matthew Clarke?"

The office was big enough to easily lose a couple of people in. One of them was Winston James, the firm's oldest partner, who was sprawled comfortably in one of Roxanne's Scandinavian designer chairs. The other was a good-looking man in his mid-thirties, deep brown skin, clean-shaven head, glasses, immediately recognizable from the evening news. He wore a suit that was not quite nice enough to suggest he was squandering the taxpayers' money, and he was headed for the door.

"I know of him, of course," Tom said.

"Matthew," Roxanne said, "this is Tom Davis."

"Ah," Clarke said, in a tone of voice that made it clear they'd been talking about him. That couldn't be good. On the other hand, it wasn't likely Roxanne had brought in witnesses to watch her fire him.

Tom shook Clarke's hand and got the expected firm grip. "Pleased to meet you, sir," Tom said.

"Likewise, I'm sure," Clarke said. "Roxanne, Winston, I'll see you tomorrow."

"Take care, Matthew," Roxanne said.

Clarke shut the door on his way out and Roxanne said, "Have a seat, Tom."

Tom sat on the edge of a vacant chair and leaned forward nervously. "About the Collins case..."

Winston, who was from North Carolina and liked to use words like "horse sense," said, "This isn't about the Collins case."

Roxanne said, "I assume you've heard of the so-called Devil Doll Killer?"

"On the radio this morning they said they'd arrested somebody?"

"A biker," Winston said, "by the name of Nathan Judd. A real piece of work. List of priors as long as my daughter's AmEx bill. Serious attitude problem."

"The judge ordered court appointed counsel," Roxanne said, "and I won the draw."

And a perfectly honest and above-board draw it was, Tom was sure.

"And," Winston said, "you'll love his personal hygiene."

It took a couple of seconds to sink in. "Wait. You're giving *me* the Devil Doll case?"

"I'll be out of town at the end the week at my retreat," Roxanne said. "I won't be available to handle it, so I'm assigning it to you."

"This is a cakewalk, Davis," Winston said. "You can do it with your eyes closed. You'll probably want to hold your nose while you're at it."

"Well," Tom said. "I don't know what to say. This is great." He saw he was in danger of babbling. "You won't regret this. I'll do it right."

"Davis?" Winston said. "We're not exactly looking for Alan Dershowitz on this one. A clean conviction with no reversible errors would pretty much sum up our expectations."

Roxanne sat down at her desk and peered at something on the monitor. Tom felt her attention leave him like the setting of the summer sun. "Thank you, Tom," she said. "Copy me on all your paperwork."

"Sure thing." He managed to get up and leave the room without tripping over his own feet. As soon as he was alone in the hallway, his knees buckled and he had to lean against the oak wainscoting to keep from going down. He closed his eyes and let the relief wash through him.

"Thank you, God," he said.

•

THE NEWSROOM, Susan thought for at least the one-millionth
time, was no place to get work done. The incessant sports talk. The
inescapable smells of microwave popcorn, or burritos, or leftovers
overdue for composting. The blur of someone brushing past her
desk just as her concentration had started to focus.

Then there was Ed Burlington's voice. The Foghorn, as it was
unaffectionately known. Even now, as he was kowtowing to Wallace
Arnette, one of the owners, his nasal tones were the aural equivalent
of sandpaper on a sunburn.

"Good to see you, as always, Wallace," Burlington said for the
entire newsroom to hear. The two of them were standing in the
doorway of Burlington's glass-walled office.

"I appreciate your hearing me out," Arnette said. He looked 35 at
most and had more houses than Susan had low-heeled, newsroom-
dress-code shoes.

"Hey," Burlington said, "it's your paper."

Arnette laughed in the same way he would have if Burlington
had actually said something funny. "Exactly!"

Arnette waved and headed for the elevators. As Burlington
turned around, Susan watched the artificial smile drop from his face
and give way to a sour and harried look. He scanned the news-
room and then walked over to Courtney's desk, across the aisle
from Susan's.

"I want you to take over the Devil Doll coverage," Burlington said.

Courtney's expertly made-up eyes went wide. "Me?"

Susan was likewise stunned. Courtney was two years out of J-
School and was on her way to a record for published corrections.
Cute, though, as male staffers inevitably pointed out.

"You think you can handle it?" Burlington said.

"Well, sure! But I thought it was Jim's story."

"I'm putting Jim on the homicide in Hawthorne."

Even Courtney could smell that rat. "The gang shooting?"

"Do you want the assignment or not?"

Arnette, Susan thought, must have thoroughly trampled Burlington's ego.

"Well, yeah, of course I do..."

"Get some background on the suspect, talk to his family, find out who the hell this guy is, where he went wrong. *People* magazine type of deal. Maybe fifteen inches for Sunday."

Susan watched Courtney's eagerness dry up. "I can't do anything in fifteen inches."

"That's the budget."

Holy shit, Susan thought. You're burying this.

"Um, okay," Courtney said.

"I'll edit this one myself," Burlington said.

"Yes, sir," Courtney said.

Burlington walked three desks over to where Jim sat with his feet propped up, keyboard in his lap, mouth open, having unavoidably picked up every word the Foghorn blared. "Any questions?"

Jim closed his mouth, opened it again, and said, "No."

Burlington jerked his head in an approximation of a nod, stomped back to his office, and slammed the door. Courtney grabbed her phone and hurried out of the room. Susan went over and perched on the edge of Jim's desk.

"What's going on?" she asked.

"You can't possibly know any less than I do." Jim was in his fifties, overweight from fast food, perpetually tired from the extra effort that nobody asked from him anymore, hanging on in hope that there would still be a pension fund when he retired.

"Fifteen inches for Sunday?" Susan said.

"Well, he didn't seem happy about it, if that counts for anything."

Jim's desk faced the opposite direction from hers. "Did you see that Arnette was here talking to him?"

"Ah. That would explain it. Remember when owners owned things and editors did the editing?"

"That was a long time ago."

"Wallace Arnette," Jim said. "Where did he come from, anyway?"

"I think he made it big with some kind of online legal agency."

"A lawyer. Figures."

"Why would Arnette want you off the story and Courtney on it?"

"The paranoid in me wonders if there was something he was afraid I would dig up."

"So they gave it to Courtney to screw up?"

"You said it, I didn't."

"It's really getting ugly around here."

"Don't forget the magic words. 'At Least I Have A Job.' You too could be experiencing life after unemployment runs out."

The job market was indeed glutted with ex-newspaper people. On the nights she lay awake worrying about it, she tried to tell herself that if she was going to quit, she should have done it years ago. If it was too late anyway, she might as well stay with the job she loved until the ship went down.

"So," she said, "what do you know about the case?"

"Are you sure you want to be seen talking to me about it? Might get you in trouble."

"C'mon, Jim, this is me."

"On the surface it seems pretty straightforward. Victim was Jennifer McKenna, mid-thirties, good-looking, hospital admin. Quiet, stay-at-home, well liked. The perp is a born loser, in and out of foster homes and juvenile hall as a kid, LAC as an adult. ADW, GTA, DUI, all the initials. Cops are satisfied that he did it."

"What about the Satanism angle?"

"Probably complete horseshit. I doubt this guy can read, let alone manage Anton LaVey. People do sick shit in this town every day without needing Satan for an excuse."

"So you're siding with the cops?"

"I do wish you wouldn't put it like that. But yeah, nobody gave me a reason to think differently until..."

"Until?"

"Until right now."

"Does this mean you're going to keep investigating this on your own?"

"While chasing my own tail on a dead-end gang killing? Not a chance. You used to do cops in Chicago. You could mentor our little Courtney, make sure she doesn't miss anything. I'm sure Burlington would appreciate that."

"Yeah," Susan said, "right."

TOM HATED THE SMELL of Men's Central Jail. Vomit and bleach, the one endlessly giving rise to the other. He sat at a scarred table in an interview room, his back to the big one-way mirror.

A clanking noise made him look up. A burly corrections officer stood in the doorway, his baton in one hand, the other gripping the arm of one of the sorriest looking prisoners Tom had ever seen: short, pale, acne-scarred, tattoos everywhere, wispy beard and mustache, long greasy hair in a ponytail, narrow eyes, and a long, twice-broken nose. The shackles on his hands and feet testified to his insubordination. He was smirking and the CO was fuming, a sure sign that Judd had been winding him up.

"You Davis?" the CO said.

"That's right."

The CO shoved Judd toward the chair on the other side of the table. "So you're defending this piece of shit?"

"Yeah, I am."

"Hope you never need a cop," the CO said.

Judd tilted his chair back, put his manacled hands behind his head, and dragged his feet up onto the table, no small accomplishment given the weight of the chains. The CO swept the feet off the table with his baton, cracking Judd's shin as he did it. The front legs of Judd's chair slammed into the linoleum and the CO said, "Feet on the floor, asswipe."

Judd's smirk got bigger and his eyes narrower. Tom smelled rotten teeth all the way across the table. The CO backed off a few paces and stood with arms folded, the baton still out and ready.

Tom didn't attempt to shake Judd's hand. "My name is Tom Davis. The court has appointed me to represent you. You don't know it yet, but you got lucky. One, because I'm with Brock, James and Vallence, one of the top criminal law firms in the city. Two, because I like my job and I'm going to get you a fair trial."

Judd's response was to pick his nose and examine the results before wiping them on his blue jumpsuit.

"I've got a list of questions here," Tom said. "I'm going to take it from the top and work my way down. Is that okay with you?"

"You're wasting your time," the CO said.

Tom nodded cordially and turned back to Judd. "Let's start with the night of the murder. Can you take me through where you went and what you did, starting around, oh, six or seven at night?"

Judd scratched his crotch, his gaze drifting idly past Tom to the mirror.

"He's not going to cooperate," the CO said. "With you or anybody else. He thinks he's a tough guy. He's got some surprises ahead of him."

"Is that right, Nathan? Are you really not going to talk to me?"

Judd sucked his teeth and let his eyes go out of focus.

Tom gathered up his papers and put them in his briefcase. He sat back and said, "I hear you ride, Nathan. My oldest boy wants a Harley more than anything in the world. He can't decide if he wants the Fatboy or the Heritage."

Judd settled deeper into his chair and closed his eyes as if he were going to sleep. In a second the CO was on him, slamming his baton into the back of the chair so hard that Judd was knocked forward and had to catch himself on the edge of the table. "Wake up, asshole. Show some manners to the shyster."

"Listen," Tom said, "do you think you could give us a moment in private?"

The CO said, "I don't think you want to be alone with this guy."

"I'll risk it."

"Your funeral." The CO walked out and slammed the door.

Tom wondered if he'd just done something terminally stupid. "Talk to me, Nathan. I can't help you if you—"

Judd didn't change anything more than the expression on his face, yet Tom suddenly saw a crude intelligence and self-awareness in his eyes. "Shut the fuck up," Judd said.

"Okay."

"You're not going to help me, okay? I'm already dead. The fix is in."

"What are you talking about?" Tom leaned forward, keeping his voice low. "What fix?"

The other Judd vanished, as if some alien creature had taken possession of his body for ten seconds and departed. Judd now stared mutely into space.

"Nathan?" Tom said. "Nathan?"

EVENTUALLY SUSAN REACHED a point in her day where coffee stopped working. She was grateful to see that that point had not quite arrived yet. She sat on a stool with her laptop open on the kitchen island, reading page 8 of the Google results for "Devil Doll Killer."

"Until that moment," Tom said, his back to her, chopping a leek, "I was thinking, 'This is one I'm not going to mind losing.' Now I don't know."

"Jim said he had priors out the wazoo."

Tom had taken six eggs out of the refrigerator earlier, and now he cracked them, one-handed, into a bowl. The effect was somewhat undercut by his stopping to pick out bits of shell. "Well, that's the thing," Tom said. "They're just biker stuff. The assault charges came out of a punch-up with another club. He stole a car, he gets drunk a lot, he got the indecent exposure beef for taking a leak in an alley. He's not a boy scout by any means, but no rape, no other violence against women, nothing that makes him look good for a murder like this one."

"Weird," Susan said. "The TV stations are trying to make him sound like the second coming of Charlie Manson."

"He's not even Manson Lite. And I don't like the fact that the District Attorney of LA County was in the office having a group hug with Roxanne and Winston when I came in."

"You're off and running again, aren't you?"

"You wouldn't, by any chance, be implying that I'm getting emotionally involved with a case I can't possibly win?" Susan watched him pour olive oil into the omelet pan and swirl it around.

"It's endearing, in a wonky kind of a way."

"I think I may have a chance on this one. And this could be big. Will you still love me when I'm on the cover of *Time?*"

"I guess we'll find out when it happens." Tom's optimism had been one of the things that first attracted her. She'd met him when she was covering a rally for hotel workers where he was fighting, on his own time, for their right to organize. He'd been quiet, self-effacing, determined, and inspiring.

"Do I detect some jealousy?" he asked. "Do you wish Burlington had given it to you?"

"First of all, there'd be a conflict of interest because of you. Secondly, no. I've interviewed enough guys like Nathan Judd to last me a lifetime. Still, I hate to see it go to somebody like Courtney." She considered whether she wanted to ruin her lovely caffeine buzz with a glass of wine.

"You really think they're trying to hide something?" He went after a red bell pepper with the big chopping knife.

"Things have gone downhill pretty fast since the new owners took over. And today one of the cronies they brought with them got caught stealing her movie reviews from an indie weekly in Cleveland. How could she imagine she'd get away with it?"

"I thought I was invulnerable when I was in my twenties."

"You weren't plagiarizing."

"No, just smoking a little dope and driving a little too fast."

"This is not laddish acting out. And she was so arrogant about it. Everybody does it, she said. She'd 'made it her own' by putting her 'stamp' on it."

"There have always been a few screwups who—"

"It's worse now. It's like lying is the new national pastime. And it's not just journalists, it's politicians who've proved that if you keep telling the same lie over and over, louder and louder, people will believe it. Then there's big business, if there's a difference anymore. Sociopaths are the perfect free market capitalists. No conscience to interfere with making a profit."

"Now who's off and running?"

"I know, I know," she said. She closed up her computer and went for the wine bottle after all. "I'm going to quit brooding before I ruin my appetite."

TOM DIDN'T SPEND a lot of time in El Monte. It lay east of East LA, its major attraction a 30-foot fiberglass replica of the Statue of Liberty. It was a town of strip centers and Laundromats and liquor stores with barred windows. And it was home to the Alameda Trailer Park, where Tom had a noon appointment with a biker named Sleazebag Steve.

Tom had dressed for the occasion in the jeans he wore for yard work, a black T-shirt, and an old flannel shirt hanging open in front. He was embarrassed at how well his Corolla fit into the neighborhood.

Steve was in full regalia—black leather vest with nothing under it, ripped jeans, boots, bandana tied pirate style to hold his long hair. He had his Harley under an awning attached to an antique Airstream knockoff, the engine covers lying on sheets of newspaper. "You're punctual," Steve said as Tom walked up. "I like that."

They shook hands, movement style, and Tom asked questions about the Harley, walking the fine line between sounding genuinely interested and revealing the depth of his ignorance. He let Steve work his way around to mentioning the case. "So what'd you think of Nathan?" he finally asked.

"Well," Tom said. "I don't think he picked up Jennifer McKenna in a bar."

"You got that right. I don't think Nathan's ever had any pussy that at least three or four guys haven't just had first."

"I don't make him for a Satanist either."

"Yeah, that's complete bullshit. There might be a hundred honest-to-Christ Satanists in LA, and Nathan ain't one of them."

"So why would somebody say he was?"

"People don't like to think. Give 'em a stereotype, like Satanist Biker? They'll go for it every time."

JUDD HAD WORKED at Chuy's Garage off and on for the last three years, the sincerity of his remorse repeatedly winning out over the drunkenness that got him fired.

The owner and namesake was about 40, well fed, sporting a neatly trimmed mustache and a silk shirt that was more expensive than his business seemed to justify. Tom suspected other business going in and out the back door, which was not relevant at the moment.

"Don't get me wrong," Chuy said. He sat behind his desk in an office whose cheap wood paneling held various framed certificates for advanced courses in auto mechanics. "Nathan is not what you would call a pillar of the community or anything. But he's no devil worshipper either. You've met him, right? He doesn't give a cacahuate. Not about God, not about the devil, and not about you or me."

FOR THE LAST 18 months, Jennifer McKenna had worked at the UCLA Medical Center in Santa Monica, where she was a Certified Medical Administrative Assistant in the Birthplace, their fancy maternity hospital. Her best friend at work was a woman named Cherie Baxter, an admin assistant in Surgery. She was pushing 50, compact and energetic, with short blonde hair brushed back like she was facing into a strong wind. They got Cokes from a machine and went outside.

Cherie's story matched the one from the case file: Jennifer was "nice," quiet, kept to herself. Cherie seemed withdrawn, uptight, like Tom could have bounced a basketball off of her and she wouldn't have felt it.

"I need something here," Tom said. "I don't think this guy Judd had anything to do with killing Jennifer. If they convict him, the real killer walks away free and clear. They won't even be looking anymore."

"I know," Cherie said. Her voice was so constricted that Tom barely heard her.

"What?" Tom asked gently. "What do you know?"

"If I tell you something, can it be off the record?"

Tom put down his legal pad and nodded.

"Cross your heart and hope to die?"

"I promise."

"They said in the papers that...that she let this biker guy pick her up at Starr's. On a Sunday night. When I saw that, I knew it was a lie."

"Why?"

"Because Sunday night at Starr's...it's ladies only. You know what I'm saying?"

"What, some kind of Chippendales thing? Male strippers?"

"The opposite. It's a pickup scene." She blushed. "You know. Girl on girl. No men allowed."

"Ah." He gave himself a moment to work through the implications. "Were you there that night?"

"Not...that night."

"You'd been there with her before?"

"Not with her. It was her first time. She said she didn't want me to come, that she would be even worse self-conscious. It was like an experiment for her. She was just starting to find herself as...you know." Tears came up in Cherie's eyes. "I told her about Starr's and now she's dead. One of those dykes killed her and it's my fault."

"It's not your fault," Tom said. "There's no way you could have known." He didn't know whether to put his arm around her to comfort her. Probably not. "Who else have to you told this to?"

"Nobody. And you have to keep this secret. If it comes out that I...that I, you know, go there. It could cost me my job."

"Seriously?"

"Yeah. Things are better than when I was a kid, but...we're not there yet. You know what I'm saying?"

Tom nodded. "All right."

"I must be crazy, telling secrets to a lawyer. It's just..."

"What?"

"You don't seem like a real lawyer. You're not slick enough."

"Thanks," Tom said. "I think."

THE DECAYING SUBURBS of Reseda were among Tom's least favorite parts of LA. By the time he got to the LAPD's West Valley Station it was 2:30, and the flat grid of two story strip malls made him feel like a crisp drop of batter on a waffle iron.

Worse yet, he had to talk to the police, and he never walked into a cop shop without the irrational fear of ending up in a holding cell.

Detective Beacham was in his forties, in shirtsleeves and khaki Dockers, tie loose and top shirt button undone. He was tall, muscular, had purplish-black skin, short, graying hair, and a trace of a Caribbean lilt when he yelled, "Hey, Oliver, get your ass in here." Mostly he looked tired.

Tom shook hands with Beacham while an even bigger guy, with the top-heavy look of a bodybuilder, filled up the doorway. Tom took a seat and they passed around a few half-hearted pleasantries about the heat wave. Finally Tom got down to work. "It says in your report that you arrested Judd on the basis of an anonymous phone tip?"

Beacham folded his arms. "We brought him in for questioning on that basis. Then we arrested him."

Oliver said, "We got forensics, we got eyeball witnesses putting him at the scene—"

"Forensics?" Tom said. "There was nothing in the report about forensics."

"One of the victim's hairs on his clothes," Oliver said. "We got the results this morning."

"He supposedly murdered her and drained her blood, and all you found was a single hair? He could have picked that up walking past her in the parking lot."

"Only he didn't," Beacham said. The pretense of politeness evaporated as Beacham leaned forward, openly menacing.

"And your witnesses," Tom said. "They're both members of the Comancheros. A rival motorcycle club."

"That's right," Beacham said.

"And they both saw him, *inside* Starr's, on Sunday night?"

"That's right," Beacham said. "Let me tell you something, Mr. Smartass Lawyer. Twenty-three years I been in this business." His accent got stronger as his voice grew more menacing. "You learn to tell a wrong guy when you see one. Judd's a wrong guy."

This was going nowhere. Tom stood up and said, "The problem is, he may be *the* wrong guy." It would have been a great exit line if Oliver was not still blocking the door. "Do you mind?" Tom said.

Oliver, grinning, stepped aside in slow motion. Tom had to brush against his cheap suit to get into the hall.

"Fuckin' lawyers," Beacham said. He was using his outdoor voice. "If you get this guy off on some bullshit technicality, I hope you remember it when he kills the next girl. It'll be the exact same as if you killed her yourself."

HE STOOD OUTSIDE Roxanne's office door at 3:45. The door opened before he could knock and Roxanne, carrying a handful of papers, nearly ran into him.

"Tom?" She didn't sound thrilled to see him.

"Can I talk to you for a second?"

"I'm trying to get out of here Thursday morning. I've got a million details to take care of."

"It's important. Nathan Judd was framed, and I can prove it."

Tom didn't get the reaction he'd been hoping for. Roxanne

looked at her watch and said, "I've got dinner free. My date can-
celled, but I've still got to eat. Spago at eight-thirty, take it or
leave it."

He hoped she was planning to pick up the check. "Uh, yeah, okay.
Do I—"

"Just meet me there, Tom, okay?" She fingered his flannel shirt.
"Jacket and tie would be nice."

Under five hours to make it to Orange County, shower and
change, and get back to Beverly Hills. It was possible, barely.

Roxanne pushed past him and Tom sprinted for his car.


THE GODS OF TRAFFIC blessed him, and Tom was tying his tie by
6:00. Jason stuck his head in the bedroom and said, "Hot date?"

"Your old man is eating at Spago tonight."

"If you can afford to take Susan to Spago, you can afford something better than that Little Caesar's junk you fed us."

"I'm meeting Roxanne there. This is for work."

Jason leaned in and sniffed. "You're wearing aftershave to work
now? Does Susan know?"

"Give me a break." Tom tightened up the tie, put the small end
through the label, checked his teeth.

"Hey, Bry," Jason shouted down the hall. "Looks like we're going
to the Gallaghers again tonight."

Brian's voice came from the vicinity of the kitchen. "Outstanding!"

Tom sat on the bed. "Jay, c'mere." Jason perched awkwardly at the
farthest corner from Tom. "I'm working on a pretty important case.
One that could make a difference to us. Make things a little easier
on us."

Jason was not at an age where sentimentality was to be tolerated.
"Roxanne's hot, Dad. I'd do her too if I had the chance."

"I'm serious. It's not like I enjoy driving a thrashed car and wearing second-hand suits. I mean, I didn't get into this business for the
money, but I didn't get into it to be poor, either."

"Why did you get into this business?"

Even if Jason had been serious—and Tom knew he was just putting the boot in wherever he saw an opening—Tom wasn't sure he knew the answer anymore.

ROXANNE POINTED to something near the top of the wine list and said, "Let's have a bottle of that."

"Fantastic choice," the waiter said. "I'll get that right out." He headed for the bar with a grace that looked choreographed.

Tom was in way over his head. It was all he could do not to stare at the woman two tables over who'd gotten multiple Emmy nominations for her show on AMC. Or at Roxanne herself, who had emphasized the "little" in the little black dress she wore. He forced himself to move slowly and be conscious of his extremities so that he didn't knock anything over.

The walls and furnishings were some kind of dark red wood, cherry or mahogany. Even with his reading glasses, the candle in the middle of the table, and what was left of the summer daylight, he could barely read the menu. He hoped he'd correctly made out the word "salmon" among the many entrees.

Roxanne, of course, was completely at home, and once Tom put his menu down, she gave him a smile unlike any he'd ever seen on her before, as if she'd mistaken him for her absent date.

"I've lived in LA my entire life," he said, "and this is my first time here."

"You should get out more, Tom."

"I've got two kids who think they're going to college someday, and just the one paycheck. We eat most of our meals at home."

"How long has it been now? Since..."

"Since Elaine died? Three years and change."

"You must miss her terribly."

"The truth is we weren't doing that well before the cancer was diagnosed, and it was a long couple of years afterward." I can't believe, he thought, I'm saying this to Roxanne.

"You stayed, though."

"I didn't want my kids to resent her for being sick, or me for running away. That would have screwed up their childhood a lot worse than her dying did."

"You're a good man, Tom. A lot of us count on that."

The compliment was so unexpected that it slipped past his guard and nearly made him tear up, right there in front of Roxanne and the actress and the ridiculously young and good-looking waiter, who had materialized with the wine.

By the time they'd gone through the ritual of the uncorking and the tasting of the wine, Tom had himself under control. Roxanne ordered the Prime New York Steak, "painfully rare," to which the waiter said, "I remember, Ms. Vallence." He then went on to extravagantly praise Tom's choice of the salmon before hurrying away again.

"So," Roxanne said. "Are you seeing anyone?" A faint smile flickered around her perfect mouth, as if she knew how flirtatious it sounded and didn't care.

Once again, Tom found himself blurting out the truth without thinking first. "I met her a couple of months ago. She's a reporter."

"Is it serious?"

"I hope so. I'm too old to be fooling around."

He was not imagining it. Another coy smile came and went, as if she were saying, "Oh, really?"

Tom felt seasick. Before he completely lost sight of land, he said, "About the Judd case..."

Roxanne let out a "must we?" sort of sigh.

"I talked to some of his associates today. They say the Satanism angle is bunk."

"Tom, Tom. He's not necessarily going to tell his friends something like that. I mean," and she paused for another quick flash of smile, "I'm sure there are all sorts of things you don't know about me."

Tom forced himself to look at the tablecloth. "I also talked to the victim's friends, and one of them told me Jennifer was—"

"Tom!"

It wasn't loud, but it cracked like a pistol shot. Tom closed his mouth.

"As a matter of fact," Roxanne said, "I talked with Judd on the phone this afternoon. He admitted the whole thing."

"You talked to my client? Why?"

"He'd called the office repeatedly since yesterday. He didn't believe you were really with the firm. He wouldn't take Emma's word for it, insisted on talking to me directly."

The story didn't sound credible, though Tom, still struggling for mental equilibrium, couldn't say why.

"Apparently," Roxanne said, "even a low-life like Judd can have a conscience. He seemed to be feeling pretty guilty, in fact."

"He told me he was framed."

She shook her head. "He's a pathological liar. You can't believe a word he says."

He remembered talking about liars with Susan and it gave him a moment of clarity. "Including his confession?"

"He knew she was wearing Hello Kitty underpants. He knew about a lumpectomy scar on her left breast."

"I thought they never found her underwear."

"I think they were in her purse or something. Trust me, Tom, the confession was real. I wouldn't be surprised if he copped a plea."

Tom watched his objectivity slip away again. He did trust Roxanne. He smiled sadly and said, "This was going to be my defining moment."

Roxanne laughed. It sounded like crystal wineglasses clinking together. "I'm sure you'll have plenty of other chances."

BY THE TIME Tom stepped into the hot Beverly Hills night, Roxanne's hand lightly on his arm, he felt like he had an idiot grin permanently stuck to his face.

"Are you okay to drive?" Roxanne asked. They were standing face to face, close enough that he smelled the perfume on her neck. She seemed to lean in toward him. "I could drop you somewhere."

"I'm fine," Tom said. In fact he'd reached the point where he no longer trusted himself, and not just about driving.

She looked disappointed. "Okay, if you're sure. I wouldn't want to have to bail out one of my own guys." She waved to a valet parking attendant and handed him her keys, wrapped with a ten-dollar bill. "It's the white z4."

"We remember, Ms. Vallence."

"I'm around the corner," Tom said. He paused, not knowing what he was waiting for. "I guess I'll see you in the office tomorrow."

"You probably won't see me. I've got a long day finishing things up."

Whatever flirtatious demon had possessed her had fled. Things would return to their normal chill, he realized, the next time he saw her. Unwilling to let go quite yet, he said, "Oh, yeah, that conference thing. Where is that?"

"Far, far away from the rest of the world."

"Is Winston going too?"

"I'm the only one from this office. This is a very big deal, Tom. They only invite the top attorneys from all over the country, and I mean attorneys in the broadest possible sense. The best of the best."

"Yeah, well," Tom said. Having overstayed, he was now unable to find his exit line. "I hope it goes well. Whatever it is."

"Me too." She glanced around impatiently for her car.

"Well, good night, then. And thanks again for the amazing dinner."

She had already dismissed him in her mind. Tom got 20 feet away before he realized he was walking in the wrong direction. He turned in time to see Roxanne step into the street.

Clearly she thought she was alone. An MTA bus had stopped at the curb and she stood directly behind it. Her eyes closed and she breathed deeply, as if she were inhaling a pine-scented alpine breeze, when the bus exhaust was so foul that Tom could smell it from where he stood.

He was sure there was a rational explanation. The sight made him deeply uncomfortable and a little afraid, and he turned away before

she caught him watching her. He decided to take the long way
around the block to his car.

ALTHOUGH THE WESTERN end of Ventura Boulevard was a
step up from El Monte and Reseda, it was not a big one. The strip
centers were in somewhat better repair, and the cars in their parking
lots were a few years newer. The ambience was the same. It was the
knowledge that you were no longer on the verge of anything. What
you saw was what you got.

Tom was on the phone with Susan as he drove. "I can't shake the
feeling that she was coming on to me. I know how ridiculous that
sounds, here in the daylight..."

"Not to me, it doesn't."

"You're sweet. And last night, as long as I was with her, I almost
believed it myself. That con man thing, you know, the pheromones
or whatever it is. Once I was alone in my car, the whole thing
turned to fairy dust. I'm supposed to believe she was chit-chatting
with my client when she was too busy to talk to me in the hall?
That Judd would break down and confess out of nowhere? To her?
And how in the hell did she know what kind of underwear Jennifer
was wearing? Unless..."

"Are you thinking what I think you're thinking?"

"It's crazy to think that. It's...unthinkable."

"But you're thinking it."

"It's easy enough to disprove. Then I can go back to thinking
thinkable things." He saw the sign for Starr's and turned in. "I'm
here. I'll call you tonight."

"Be careful."

"I will."

Tom had never been a drinker, never seen the appeal of places
like this one. Here in the middle of the afternoon it was empty
and quiet, a few dust motes floating in planes of sunlight from the
nearly-closed blinds. It could have been anywhere. The bartender, a
short 30-year-old with exaggerated curves named Dina, was filling a

cooler with longneck bottles of Bud Lite. She wore a Starr's T-shirt
that was a size or two too small, the logo stretched out of shape
across her overstuffed breasts. She noticed Tom and said, "It's Lawyer
Man! How you doing, Lawyer Man? How's the Devil Doll Killer?"
She flipped the blonde hair out of her eyes with a habitual half-circle
of the head.

"I expect he's still a completely obnoxious piece of human garbage, like the last time I saw him."

"I'll drink to that. What can I get you?"

"Club soda?"

Like Roxanne, Dina—a product of artifice from dyed crown to
painted toenails—was not the sort of woman he was attracted to.
He liked the strands of gray in Susan's auburn hair, the hard-earned
lines around her eyes, the soft curve of her stomach. But other men
wanted Dina, and they wanted Roxanne, and so by some transitive
property of attraction it mattered to Tom that, if they didn't outright
desire him, at least they didn't write him off.

Dina brought him his glass of soda and a saucer of lemon and
lime wedges. She waved away his attempt to reach for his wallet.
"We don't charge for this stuff."

Tom cleared his throat. "I feel like you haven't been completely
honest with me, Dina."

"Now what would make you say a thing like that?"

"How about the fact that this place is a lesbian pick-up joint on
Sunday nights?"

"Is it?"

"Come on, Dina. Give the old man some credit. I don't like Judd
any better than you do, but if he didn't do the murder, he doesn't
deserve to get sent up for it."

Dina straightened up and put her hands on her hips. "Every night
when I get off work, I have to have the bouncer walk me to my car.
Why? Because of creeps like Nathan Judd."

"He wasn't even in the club that night. No men allowed."

"He was in the parking lot, sitting on his hog. He harassed this

Jenifer woman on her way in. I had to call the cops to run him off. Guy like that, I figure he comes back, lurks in the shadows, waits for her to come out again, gets some payback for brushing him off."

"She brushed him off," Tom said, "among many other reasons, because she was looking for a different kind of action. She was looking for a woman."

Dina returned to her Bud Light. "Maybe."

"And she found one, didn't she?"

Dina didn't answer. Tom, his hands sweating, pulled a recent issue of *Los Angeles* magazine, folded lengthwise, out of his back pocket and put it on the bar. He took a deep breath and unfolded it. "Is this who she found?"

Dina walked over, read the cover copy that said, "Hot Defender: Roxanne Vallence," and then studied the photo for a few seconds. She shrugged. "She's hot looking, all right. But we get hot-looking women like her in here all the time. I couldn't say yes or no." She looked up at Tom. "Her name was on your business card. She's your boss. What's up with that?"

Tom ignored the question. "Jennifer *did* leave here with a woman the night she was killed. Yes?"

Reluctantly, Dina said, "Yeah."

"Who looked at least a little like her." He pointed to Roxanne's photo.

"Yeah."

Tom put the magazine in his pocket, took a five out of his wallet, and slapped it on the bar.

"Thanks for your help."

Dina's gaze frosted over as she turned away. "Don't mention it."

Tom was halfway to the door when his phone sounded. It was Susan's work number. "Hey, babe," he said.

"Have you heard?"

"Heard what?"

"One of our informants at Central Jail called. Judd's dead."

"What? How?"

"Suicide, they're saying."

"Son of a bitch. I'll call you back."

He turned halfway around. "Hey, Dina." She looked up. "You don't have to worry about Judd anymore. He's dead."

She raised her fist in silent celebration and Tom walked out into the heat.

TOM GOT A CO to escort him to Judd's cell. The entire block was on lockdown and three crime scene techs collected samples in the area of the bunk beds. A couple of EMTs wheeled a gurney toward the open cell door.

As if the cell wasn't already crowded enough, Detective Beacham was watching the techs, and the CO from the day before was now watching Tom.

"How'd he do it?" Tom asked the room, and the room did not answer. "So, what, nobody is going to talk to me?"

The CO from the day before said, "You wouldn't want to hear what I got to say to you. Your pal here got what he was begging for. So you can go find another ambulance to chase."

The EMTs tried to get past Tom, and he took the opportunity to lift a corner of the sheet.

He would be seeing that face in his nightmares, he knew. The skin was not merely pale but grayish-white, and the eyes were wide open in an expression of hopelessness, pain, and fear.

The nearest EMT said, "He cut his wrists and bled out."

Tom looked around the dry, dusty cell. A cobweb grew in one corner of the floor. "Where's the blood?"

It was none of the EMT's business. He nudged Tom aside with the gurney and wheeled the body away.

"Can I get some answers from somebody?" Tom said, knowing he should take the frustration down a couple of notches, unsure whether he was able to. "That guy is drained. That's a gallon and some of blood. It should be all over this cell!"

A voice behind him said, "Some of it went down the sink." Tom turned to see the DA, Matthew Clarke, his tie loose and his sleeves rolled up. "He used the rest to write a full confession."

Tom found himself unable to summon his previous awe of Matthew Clarke. "That's, uh, kind of hard to believe. Sir."

"Nevertheless..."

"I mean, you've got two people completely drained of blood within two weeks of each other."

"The Satanic cult—" Clarke started.

"He wasn't in a Satanic cult," Tom said. "Sir. I think you know that as well as I do."

"What was your name again?" Clarke's own frustrations were showing.

"Davis, sir. Tom Davis. Can I see this confession?"

"It's being transcribed."

"When *can* I see it?"

"You don't need to see the confession!" Clarke snapped. "Not now, not ever. Your former client is dead, the case is closed, and your involvement with it is over. Do I need to make myself any more clear than that, Mr. Davis?"

"No, sir." Whatever the "fix" was that Judd had been talking about, Clarke was part of it. Tom was not only endangering his career, he was risking his own gurney like Judd's. "I'm sorry, sir."

Clarke dismissed him with an abrupt nod. Tom backed up two steps and walked out of the cell.

THE BOYS WERE in the den, playing some kind of first-person shooter game. Eileen had bought them their first Xbox over Tom's objections and now it was years too late to take it away. When he tried to talk to them about the violence—people screaming as they were burned to death by flame-throwers, or driven through plate glass windows by machine gun fire that made them erupt in blood—they laughed at him and told him they weren't stupid, that they knew the difference between animation and reality.

"Can you guys turn that off a minute?" Tom asked. "I need to ask you something."

Jason said, "Is it important?"

"Compared to throwing hand grenades at Nazi werewolves? I'd say it was right up there."

Jason paused the game. "What's on your mind, Pops?"

"What do you guys know about..." Now that he'd come this far, he discovered he was too embarrassed to ask.

"This is not another sex talk, is it?" Brian asked.

"No," Tom said. "It's about...vampires."

It had been so long since he'd had their full and engaged attention that it felt like a miracle. "Is this about the Devil Doll murder?" Jason asked.

Tom had never told them he was working on the case. "What?"

"Her body was, like, totally drained of blood," Brian said. "It's so obvious."

"So how do you know if somebody is a vampire?" Tom asked.

"It was easier in the old days," Jason said. "The teeth, the cape. Nowadays it's harder. They can't stand direct sunlight. You may not be able to see them in a mirror."

"It's painful for them to see a cross," Brian said.

"Unless they're Jewish," Jason said.

Brian said, "'Oy, lady, have you got the wrong vampire!'" That sent both boys into convulsions of laughter.

"Go on," Tom said. "What else?"

"Garlic," Brian said.

"Yeah, garlic for sure," Jason said. "They can't cross running water. They can't come into your house unless you invite them."

"How do you..." Tom said. "You know."

"Kill them?" Jason said. "Stake through the heart. Then cut the head off and stuff it with garlic."

"Jesus. Where do you guys get this stuff?"

"I read *Dracula* for school," Jason said. "You're the one always talking about how great books are. I thought it pretty much sucked. Too slow. Anyway, there's also fire."

"Yeah, fire," Brian said.

"They burn really good," Jason said. "Like, whoooom!"

"Yeah, okay," Tom said. "Thanks, guys."

"Silver bullets," Brian said.

"That's werewolves," Jason said. "You imbecile."

"Okay, fine," Tom said. "That's all I need to know."

"Maybe not the bullet part," Brian said, "but vampires are allergic to silver, too."

"That's a myth," Jason said.

"No it's not," Brian said hotly. "They're corrupt, see? And they can't stand pure things. Pure silver. Pure sunlight. Pure running water."

Tom saw that he'd been forgotten. The boys loved to argue about things that had no bearing on reality and no solution. Who would win in a fight between the Thing and the Hulk? Who was better, the 1972 Oakland As or the 1955 Brooklyn Dodgers? Camaro or Mustang? Coke or Dr. Pepper?

As Tom walked away, he heard Jason say, "So what you're telling me is, a vampire can cross running water if it's got industrial sludge in it?"

In his bedroom, Tom got out the silver cross pendant his grandmother had left him and rummaged around the dresser until he found a jewelry box for it. A couple of bites of pesto from the fridge and a quick call to the Gallaghers next door to make sure they were around in case the kids had an emergency.

He kept moving so he wouldn't change his mind. The idea of vampires was ridiculous, impossible. So he would eliminate it from the discussion and move on.

ROXANNE STOOD at her desk, holding some kind of brochure. Tom reached in to knock on the open door. She looked up, her expression neutral. "It's open."

"Oh hey," Tom said. "You said you'd be working late and I..."

He hated the sound of his own voice, hated the patient look on Roxanne's face, as if she were counting down the seconds until she asked him to leave.

This whole charade depended on his playing it casual, and he seemed unable to. He waved a hand in the direction of the brochure. "Is that your, uh, thing?"

"Retreat," she said. She folded it, and Tom got a glimpse of the cover, showing an aerial view of a dome surrounded by trees. She put it into her into the top drawer of her desk and pushed the drawer closed. "What is it, Tom?"

Maybe, he thought, this was not such a great idea. "It's nothing," he said. "Never mind."

"Tell me, Tom."

Something in her voice made him feel like he could talk to her. He took the jewelry box out of his pocket and tried the words he'd rehearsed in the car. "I've always admired your taste, and I was wondering..."

He was squeezing the box so tightly that it popped open and the necklace spilled out onto the carpet. Tom knelt clumsily and gathered up the chain. When he looked up, Roxanne was standing over him. She was in some kind of high-end yoga wear, off-white, that hugged her body.

He got unsteadily to his feet and took a step backward. "I got this for my girlfriend. I can still return it if you think it's..."

She took back the step that Tom had moved away. She was well inside his personal space, beyond flirtation, all the way to dare. She took the cross out of his hand, not looking away from his eyes.

"...uh, tacky," Tom finished.

She took the chain in both hands and lowered the cross into the profound cleavage that her yoga top revealed. "I think it's lovely, Tom. Don't you?"

He imagined that his eyes were bulging like those of a cartoon mouse. A drop of sweat ran down his nose.

"And Tom?"

"Yes?" They were both whispering.

"The next time you have a lot of garlic in your spaghetti, you might try a Tic Tac or two. I'm sure your...girlfriend...would find you more kissable."

He was mesmerized by the movement of her full, sensuous lips. Her eyelids lowered halfway. She was waiting for him to kiss her. Tom felt himself lean toward her, against his will.

The elevator chimed in the lobby.

He stood up straight and blinked in surprise. He was suddenly aware of the open office door. "Is somebody else here?"

"Just security, making their rounds." Her tongue flicked quickly at her upper lip. "They never come in here...if the door's locked."

She took a small step toward the door, as if to lock it, giving Tom the chance to catch his breath. He had a sudden image of Nathan Judd on the gurney, and he saw that he'd made a terrible mistake.

"I have to go," he said.

Roxanne's mood shifted, as it had outside the restaurant. As if, having been turned down, she'd lost interest. "Suit yourself. I'm going too. I'll walk you out."

The lobby was in near darkness. Tom heard the guards trying the doors down the hall. Everything felt disjointed, dreamlike. He pushed the call button for the elevator and the doors opened immediately. He turned to Roxanne, who stood in the middle of the lobby, arms folded. "You go ahead," she said. "I have to make a phone call."

Tom got numbly on the elevator, turned, pressed the button for the ground floor. "Good night," he said.

She was still staring at him with her pale eyes as the elevator doors closed.

HE WASN'T SURE at first if he could drive. He sat in his car for a while, slowly coming out of his trance. As his intellect returned he began to sweat with fear and shame. What the hell had he been thinking? He'd not only made a fool of himself, he had as much as told Roxanne that he thought she was a vampire. The best-case scenario was that she would fire him for being an idiot. The worst case...

The worst-case scenario was that Roxanne really had killed Jennifer McKenna, and had either killed Judd as well, or ordered it done. Whether she was a supernatural being or not, she would now have to kill Tom.

Panic scrambled his brain. He took deep breaths, tried to think logically. He pictured himself going to Detective Beacham with wild accusations about Roxanne and no evidence. What had the CO said? "Hope you never need a cop."

The first thing he had to do was get the kids out of harm's way. He wasn't willing to risk their lives on the hope that Roxanne would leave them out of it.

That got him to crank the car and head for the 5 freeway.

He was southbound at a steady 65, still going over options in his head, when he glanced at the rearview mirror and saw a black SUV coming up on him fast. Much, much too fast. He waited half a second for some indication that it was going to pass, and then at the last possible moment he wrenched the wheel and got over into the right lane. The SUV nearly brushed him as it passed, doing well over 100 miles an hour.

"Jesus!" Tom yelled, and was about to lay on his horn, then decided that annoying a homicidal maniac might not be the best idea.

Up ahead, the SUV slammed on its brakes.

Tom braked too, unwilling to let the SUV behind him again, and the car following him honked and swung across two lanes to avoid them both. A stream of cars was coming up on them and Tom heard their tires scream as they braked. He braced himself for the impact, then went lightheaded with relief when it didn't come. The SUV had fallen back beside him. Tom looked over, unable to see in through the heavily tinted windows.

Suddenly the SUV swerved toward him. Tom swung the wheel

again and skidded onto the shoulder and lurched to a stop. He got
out his cell phone and punched up 911. When he looked up, the
SUV was also in the breakdown lane, stopped. The license plate was
covered in mud, illegible.

The SUV's reverse lights went on and it accelerated toward him.
Tom watched the rearview, saw a narrow gap in the traffic, and
floored it. He swung into the right lane barely in time to miss the
SUV. An 18-wheeler blasted his air horn as he passed Tom on the
left, and Tom, fighting the wheel, lost his grip on the cell phone. It
landed on the mat in front of the passenger seat.

He kept the gas pedal floored and reached for the cell phone with
one hand. No chance. He straightened up and checked his mirrors,
and there was the SUV, its gas-swilling V8 gaining on him as if Tom
were in a soapbox racer.

Time slowed as all of Tom's senses went hyper. He signaled right,
faked the lane change, then went for the left lane instead and hit the
brakes. The SUV fell for it and shifted right, caroming off a pickup
and spinning it sideways, where a Mustang plowed straight into it.
In a cacophony of squealing tires and tortured metal and thudding
impacts, all three lanes filled with wreckage as the SUV shot past
him once more.

A few cars pulled into the breakdown lane to call for help and
the rest of the survivors sped on into the night. Tom was alone on
the highway. He slowed to 45, pulled into the right lane, and fished
up his cell phone. It had disconnected. He dialed 911 and crested a
low rise.

The SUV was stopped dead in the right lane.

Tom swerved and the Corolla began to fishtail, narrowly missing
the concrete barrier between the north and southbound lanes. He
eased the slack out of the wheel and gentled the car down, weaving
across all three lanes. He was in the left lane, back in control, when
he saw the SUV come up on him again.

He hit the brakes, cut across the width of the freeway, and exited
into downtown.

He took one random turn after another, alternating lefts and rights, and finally darted into an alley. The Corolla's lights stayed on as long as the engine was running, so he killed it and sat in the darkness, soaked in sweat and shaking, watching the mouth of the alley in his rearview mirror.

He called 911 again. After a minute he got a live human voice, female and reassuringly middle-aged. "I'm on a cell phone somewhere near the convention center," Tom said. "Some maniac in an SUV is trying to kill me. Can you track my signal?"

"I can try. Works sometimes, other times not so much. Your name, please?"

"Tom Davis."

"Are you in immediate danger, Mr. Davis?"

"I don't know. I—"

In the mirror he saw the SUV—one window spider-webbed, gouge marks all down one side. It trolled past the mouth of the alley and then Tom heard it screech to a stop.

"Oh shit," he said. "It's back. Send help."

He put the phone, still connected, on the passenger seat. He started the car and bolted for the other end of the alley. It opened onto a broad one-way street, virtually empty of cars. Tom turned onto it and made three blocks before he hit a red light. He saw the SUV in the distance behind him and ran the light. He leaned on his horn, hoping to attract a cop, or to get anyone to notice and call for help.

The SUV went through the red light without slowing down.

Tom had no idea where he was. It was the anonymous gray heart of downtown, all office towers and parking garages, empty and shuttered for the night. He made a sudden turn and another, looked back to see the SUV still gaining on him, looked up to see a man in a hooded sweatshirt start across the street in front of him.

Tom kept working his horn and swerved to narrowly miss the man. In his mirror, he saw the man stop in the crosswalk and shake his fist at Tom.

The SUV hit him full on at 60 miles an hour. The man's body did a back flip over the roof of the SUV, flew ten feet, and landed in a wet pile on the sidewalk. The SUV's windshield washers came on and the wipers flicked a film of red into the halogen-lit night.

Tom had never watched anyone die before. He didn't feel anything beyond a certain primal understanding that it could have been him. And wasn't. Yet.

In the distance before him he saw a T intersection and overhead signs for right and left turns only. Beyond the intersection, concrete embankments dropped to the trickle of the LA River.

Tom had burned through his manic phase and only exhaustion was left. The SUV was three blocks behind him. Tom skidded up to the intersection, shifted to Park, and stepped into the street, hands up, the car door still open.

The SUV stopped a block away.

For a long moment, Tom stared into the high beams of the SUV. There were no other cars in sight. Then, slowly, the SUV began to rev its engine. Heat waves made it shimmer under the streetlights.

Then it was racing at him.

For an instant Tom was unable to move, thinking he'd cut it too close. Then he was in the car, ramming the gearshift into Drive, flooring it and spinning the wheel to the right.

The SUV clipped the rear end of the Corolla at 50 miles an hour and then went up on two wheels, trying too late to make the turn. Tom stopped and turned in his seat for a better look. The SUV rolled over the guardrail and disappeared.

Tom jumped out of the car and ran to the edge of the embankment. The SUV took a last bounce off the concrete slope, turned over again in mid-air, and flattened as it smashed roof-first into the dry grassland of the riverbed. Tom grabbed an intact section of the guardrail as the relief shot through him with a force that nearly made him pass out.

He closed his eyes and sucked in one breath after another, unable to believe he was still alive, exhilarated in his primate brain that he had defeated his enemy, wanting to piss on the driver's corpse and scream with joy.

When he opened his eyes, he saw the front driver's side window move. He tried to tell himself it was an illusion. Then the web of shattered glass bulged outward.

Something was alive in there.

The glass exploded in a shower of crystalline fragments and an arm emerged. The arm bled from a dozen cuts, and it was intermittently covered by the tattered remains of a suit coat. The hand clawed at the ground and slowly began to pull the remains of a body through the shattered window.

One eye dangled from the deformed skull. One arm was mashed flat. Broken bones protruded through the shredded clothes and one leg was bent sideways at an impossible angle.

Tom told himself to run and found that he couldn't move.

By the time the body had dragged itself completely out of the wreckage, it had literally begun to pull itself together, like a time-lapse video of decomposition in reverse. The thing got to its knees and then its feet, stumbled, and then began to shamble forward.

It was coming for Tom.

Within five halting steps it was recognizable as a handsome young man in the ruins of an expensive suit. It stopped and smiled and pointed at Tom.

At that moment the hood of the suv dropped open and piece of smoking shrapnel landed in the dry grass behind where the creature stood. The thing paid no attention and took another step. The grass smoldered and melted into flame. The creature felt something then, and it turned to look as a tongue of fire touched its pants leg.

In an instant the thing was blazing, as if it had been doused in gasoline. The flames roared and the thing burned to a cloud of ash in seconds.

Finally Tom was able to move, and he ran for his car as sirens began to wail in the distance.

•

Tom pulled the car into the garage and closed the overhead door. He went to the den where the boys were gaming and switched off the TV. "Oh, man," Jason said, and then he got a look at Tom and closed his mouth.

Tom imagined he looked like a crazy man from central casting. "We are in deep shit," he said. "This case I'm working on has gotten dangerous. There are some seriously bad people involved and I'm afraid they might try to come after you."

"This is the case that was going so well?" Jason said. Making Tom flinch was a skill he'd inherited from his mother.

"Is it the mob?" Brian said. "Are we going into witness protection?"

"It's like that. I need you to go pack what you need to spend a few days at your grandmother's."

"We're got a dress rehearsal tomorrow," Brian said.

"The understudy will have to take over," Tom said. "Now hop to it, you guys have a bus to catch."

"I think," Jason said, "in the interests of my own safety, you should let me carry some heat. A nine millimeter would be nice."

"Another time. You've got fifteen minutes. Get a move on."

He'd looked up a dozen different destination cities on his phone as he drove home, in case they were monitoring him. He was too late for any of the flights to Phoenix, but with luck he could still make the midnight bus out of the downtown Greyhound station, only a few blocks away from where the SUV had driven off the embankment.

He packed his own bag and wrote a note to Elaine's mother, who loved the boys and was already planning to take them for a couple of weeks in August. He kept the details vague in hopes that she, too, would assume mob trouble. He carried the note and his suitcase out to the darkened garage. By the time he had the back seats folded down, the boys were ready. He stowed them on their backs, legs extended into the trunk, a blue nylon tarp over their bodies. His fear had infected them and they didn't argue.

He cruised around the neighborhood a few times to make sure

nobody was following him, and once he was northbound on the 5 he got off twice, circled the block, and got on again.

As he drove he rehearsed them. They were to keep posting to Facebook, pretending they were in North Carolina at the beach with their cousins. They were not to leave their grandmother's house under any conditions. If there was a life or death emergency, they were to call Susan's cell. They were not to answer their own phones or their grandmother's phone.

He got to the bus station and walked the boys onto the bus himself. It was all he could do not to cling to them. The odds were that he would be dead before this was over, that this was the last time he would ever see them. He did his best to act like it was no big deal. After he watched the bus pull out, he drove to the Valley and paid for a motel room with cash and there, with the door shut and double-locked, he finally let himself break down.

SUSAN WAS SO DEEPLY asleep that she didn't understand what the ringing noise was, and once she had the phone in her hand and switched on, she forgot what it was you were supposed to say. She looked at the clock. One thirteen in the morning.

"Susan?"

"Tom?" She was awake now. "Where are you? What's happened?"

"I'm in trouble. I'll have to tell you the details later. I tried telling them to myself before I called you and I sounded like a lunatic."

If he didn't sound crazy, he did sound exhausted, and in despair. "Are you hurt?"

"So far, no. Look, I need you to do some things. Can you get your hands on some cash, maybe five hundred dollars? More if you can? I'll write you a check to cover it. I can't risk using my credit cards."

"Yes."

"And I want to borrow your good camera, the one with the telephoto lens, and a couple of extra memory cards. And I want to borrow your camping stuff."

"Where do I bring them to you?"

"Meet me at noon at the place I kissed you for the first time. Don't say it over the phone."

"Can't you tell me anything? I'm scared for you."

"You remember that conversation we had about sociopaths? It's worse than that."

"What's worse?"

"You don't want to refuse to accept what's right in front of you, no matter how crazy it sounds."

"How crazy *what* sounds?"

"It's not just Roxanne, either. There's...there's a conspiracy of them."

In the few months she'd known him, she'd never heard him like this. When he'd been up and down with his job, it was always with a sense of humor, and he was always grounded in his love for his boys. "Conspiracy of what?"

She heard him gather himself on the other end of the phone. "Vampires," he said.

"Wow."

"I warned you. I saw something tonight that I can't explain." And he proceeded to tell her about being pursued and nearly killed by some kind of anthropomorphic, indestructible monster.

"Were you not going to tell me about this?"

"I didn't want to scare you."

"And now you do?"

"I need you to believe me."

"I never said I didn't."

"Roxanne is headed to some kind of convocation of these... things. Big dog vampires from all over the country. From what she said, we're talking about names everybody would know. If I can find where this place is, I'm going to hide out, get photos of everybody who goes in and out."

"Um...should we be talking about this on the phone?"

Tom sighed. "Probably not. I don't know. I'm not cut out for this. If they're tapping your phone, then it's probably all over anyway."

"If they catch you..."

"Going public with this is my only chance. If I try to run, they'll find me sooner or later."

"What about the boys?"

"They're safe. As safe as I can make them."

"Then I'm coming with you."

"I can't let you do that."

"I'm an investigative reporter. I have exactly the skills for this. And you need somebody with some common sense to watch your back."

When Tom finally spoke again, his voice was tight with emotion. "Thank you."

"You sound like you need some sleep."

"I'm going to try. Probably not a lot of hope for it."

"I miss you," Susan said.

"I miss you too. I have to go. I'll see you tomorrow." The phone went dead and she slowly put it in the cradle.

She didn't have much hope for sleep either. She moved to the couch and got onto the Factiva database with her laptop. She had an itch in the back of her brain, and it turned out that searching for news stories that contained "vampire" and "los angeles" was what it took to scratch it.

AT TEN BEFORE SIX in the morning, Tom rang the buzzer for Patrick's apartment. On the third try, Patrick's voice came over the speaker. "Do you have any idea what time it is?"

"It's Tom. I need a favor."

"This is a hell of a time to ask."

"It'll only take a minute. Can I come up?"

Patrick let a long silence convey his annoyance, then the door buzzed open.

Tom had been to a party in Patrick's apartment a year or so before, where he'd felt like a gatecrasher. Aside from the members of the firm, the other guests were all young, rich, and beautiful, and their gazes passed over Tom as if he'd been wearing a starched white uniform and carrying a tray. The apartment was enormous, with linen wallpaper and white Persian carpets over oak floors, Art Deco sculptures on pedestals, furniture carved from birds-eye maple. When Tom had bluntly asked how he paid for it, Patrick had said, "I have some money of my own."

Patrick answered the door in a silk robe, his hair stylishly disarrayed. He stood aside to let Tom in, but didn't offer him a chair. It occurred to Tom that this might be another in a long line of poor decisions. He'd assumed there was some genuine affection behind their banter. He wasn't seeing affection now.

"Roxanne laid me off," Tom said. "She called security to escort me out and didn't let me pack up my office."

"Did it have anything to do with the fact that your last client slashed his wrists? I don't think the LexRex software even lists that as an outcome."

"They deactivated my keycard. I've got a prescription in my desk for one of my kids, and I can't get to it." Tom was reasonably certain his keycard would still work, at least long enough to alert security. Or more likely deliver him to another homicidal maniac like the one in the SUV.

"Did you explain that to Roxanne?"

"By the time I remembered it, she was on her way to her retreat. Winston's not answering his phone. I need to get in the office for five minutes."

"Using my keycard, I assume?"

"That was my hope."

"You're a decent guy, Tom. You're just not a very good lawyer. And you could be poison for anyone who tried to help you."

Tom reached for the fancy gold lever-type handle on the front door. "I don't need insults, Patrick."

"Hang on, hang on," Patrick said. His eyes lost their focus as he thought it over. "I suppose you should be able to get your stuff."

"The prescription. That's all I care about. I'll have the key back to you in under an hour."

"Wait here." Patrick shuffled down the hall to his bedroom and came out a moment later with the plain white plastic card. "Leave it in the mailbox. On the off chance that I do manage to get back to sleep."

"I really appreciate this."

"And don't forget to bring it back," Patrick said. "I wouldn't want to end up like you."

"Not much chance of that," Tom said.

TOM PARKED in the deserted garage and opened his trunk. Though the sun was well up, lack of sleep had left him weak, and he shivered in the cool morning air. He saw that his back seats were still folded down, and he missed his sons with an intensity that threatened to undo him.

He forced himself to concentrate. He went through his toolbox and got out his biggest screwdriver. He stuck it in his back pocket and pulled his sweatshirt down to cover it. He was about to close the trunk when he saw the zip bag for his jumper cables and re-membered the emergency flares that he kept inside. He put one of them in the pocket with the screwdriver for luck.

He swiped Patrick's keycard over the metal plate outside the rear entrance to the building, half-expecting alarms to go off. Instead the LED flashed green and the lock released with an audible click. He stepped into the rear of the lobby and pushed the button for the el-evator. It chimed immediately and the doors flew open, unnaturally loud in that empty space of marble and glass, making Tom jump. He looked both ways, got in, and pressed 19.

By the time the doors opened in the Brock, James and Vallence lobby, Tom was sweating. He got off the elevator and saw, to his im-mense relief, that the ever-punctual cleaning crew was at work. He'd been here at six on enough mornings, either staying late or coming in early, to know their routines. First they opened all the offices that were locked, as Roxanne's surely had been, what with her being out of town. They dusted and emptied the trash, then they vacuumed and locked everything up again at six-thirty. A short, middle-aged Latina was coming out of Roxanne's office as Tom looked in. "Buen día," he said.

The woman, unimpressed, gave him a curt nod and pushed her metal cart into Winston's office, at the end of the corridor. Tom slipped into Roxanne's office and closed the door.

The blinds were open and the overhead fluorescents blazed. Tom tried the center drawer of Roxanne's desk. Locked, as he expected. He went to work with the screwdriver. It was clear in seconds that he was not going to get in without destroying the lock. What the hell, he thought. Nothing left to lose. He pried the drawer open, bending the cheap metal beyond repair, sweat dripping off his forehead.

The brochure was where she'd left it the night before. "The Pleasure Dome," the cover said. "A luxury retreat in the Northern California wilderness." He turned it over and verified that there was a map. He folded it lengthwise and put it in his back pocket with the screwdriver.

He was halfway to the elevator when the bell sounded and the down arrow flashed red. Before Tom could sprint for his own office, the elevator doors opened. Frank, one of the building security guards, stepped out and nodded to Tom.

"Oh, it's you, Mr. Davis. I saw somebody on the security camera, and I couldn't make out who it was."

"Morning, Frank. I was just on my way out." Frank's level gaze made Tom nervous. "I left a, uh, prescription in my desk. For one of my boys."

"You find it okay?"

"Actually it wasn't there after all. Must be in my car or something." Frank nodded. "Uh huh."

They got on the elevator together and Frank touched the 1 button. He seemed nervous too. Tom, desperate for conversation, said, "You were going to go for your Realtor's license, weren't you?"

"That was a year ago," Frank said.

"How'd that work out?"

Frank didn't answer. So many noises, Tom thought, that you could hear in the early morning that were drowned out during the day. The groan of the cables as they moved through the pulleys on the elevator car. The hiss of the air conditioning. Frank's rapid, shallow breathing.

The elevator bell rang again and the doors opened on the lobby. Patrick and a second security guard were waiting.

"Okay," Patrick said, "thank you gentlemen. I can take it from here."

Frank looked at the other guard. "Are you sure? Because the book says we should call the cops in this type of a situation."

"I don't think Tom did any real harm up there. I'll give him a talking to and then let him...disappear."

Tom panicked. "On second thought," he said to Frank, "maybe you *should* call the cops."

"Shut up, Tom," Patrick said. It was like it had been with Roxanne. Tom felt a desire to make Patrick happy, so he didn't say anything.

Frank looked at Patrick and Patrick nodded slightly. Frank laughed without conviction. "We'll, if you say so." He and the second guard started toward the security office. Patrick grabbed Tom by the upper arm and propelled him through the door to the garage.

The first thing Tom saw was a can of black spray paint lying near the door. He looked up at the security camera and saw that it had been sprayed over. This was it, then. Patrick planned to kill him on the spot. Tom felt oddly indifferent to the idea.

"Keycard?" Patrick said.

Tom handed it over.

"Now," Patrick said. "Show me what you really went up there for."

Tom was no longer in control of his own body. He reached for his back pocket and his hand found the flare.

"That's right," Patrick said. "Show me what you've got there."

Tom watched himself pull out the flare and show it to Patrick. Patrick stared at it in disbelief. "What the..."

Show him what it is, Tom told himself. Show him how it works. He pulled off the plastic cap and scratched it across the igniter. Flames shot out of the end.

Patrick instinctively threw up his arms. "No! Don't—"

Tom felt Patrick's mental hold on him release. He threw the flare at Patrick's raised arms, and Patrick lit up like a pile of wadded newspaper. The blast of heat sent Tom staggering back, covering his face. He watched for a second or two, fists clenched, and then he ran for his car. He backed out without looking and then burned rubber out of the garage, taking out the wooden barricade at the exit and rocketing onto Sunset Boulevard.

SUSAN MADE IT to the Metropolitan State Hospital in Norwalk by 9:30 AM. She was running on four hours of sleep and three cups of coffee, and she'd already been by the bank to withdraw a thousand dollars in small bills. "Pretty cheap for a ransom," the teller joked. "The kidnappers still in middle school?" Susan's smile, she saw from the teller's face, was not convincing. From there she'd called Vicki Chiang in Norwalk, who'd worked with her on a story about a sex-abuse case there a few years ago.

Dr. Chiang had called ahead and Susan found a pass waiting for her. She showed her driver's license and signed a register and a burly orderly took her into the ward. The hospital was clean and modern as such places went, though nothing could hide the mood of institutionalized despair or the lingering aroma of uncontrolled bodily discharge.

Jonas Fielder was in the common room, staring out the window, a novel from the hospital library open on his lap. The skull and crossbones sticker on the spine indicated that it was a mystery, and Susan knew she was overreacting in letting the image disturb her. Fielder looked to be in his late thirties, his dark hair only slightly longer than his five o'clock shadow. Like the others in the room, he wore a short-sleeved khaki uniform. The other patients quietly amused themselves, one with a jigsaw puzzle, another with an electronic keyboard and headphones, another nodding off next to a potted fern.

"Dr. Fielder?" the orderly said gently. "You have a visitor."

Fielder roused himself and got to his feet. Susan shook his hand and said, "My name is Susan Altman. I'm with the paper."

"I know the name," Fielder said. "I'm pleased to meet you. Care to sit down?"

Susan pulled up a gray plastic chair and the orderly moved discreetly out of earshot. Susan didn't anticipate any problems. Despite her first impression of a certain intensity held in pharmaceutical check, Fielder was alert and pleasant enough.

"I assume you're working on a story," Fielder said. "Is there something I can help you with?"

"I remembered reading about you a few months ago. You claimed there were vampires living in LA."

"Not just in LA," Fielder said. His tone was quiet and reasonable. "Though they are particularly common here. And the term 'vampire' is rather sensationalistic and distracting. May I ask what your interest is?"

"This is in the way of background research so far. Do you mind if I take some notes, and possibly quote you in a future story?"

"Be my guest. I've read some of your pieces. They seemed well researched. It would be interesting to be quoted accurately for a change."

Susan got out one of the steno pads that she bought by the case. She had her own shorthand that she'd developed over the years, and she used it to make a few notes. "I'll do my best. You said, 'the term "vampire" is rather sensationalistic and distracting.' Can you elaborate? Is there another term you prefer?"

"First let's back up a little. How much do you know about evolution?"

"The usual, I suppose. That was your field, wasn't it? Evolutionary biology?"

"Indeed. Evolution is like anything else. It tends to work in fits and starts. If you have some kind of major environmental stress, you'll see more mutations crop up. If the mutation provides an advantage, and it breeds true, you can have a new species in comparatively short order."

"Our environment is pretty stressed right now," Susan said. "Especially in LA."

"Precisely. And I had DNA evidence that a new species has split off from Homo sapiens, which I call Homo praedatorias."

"As in predatory?"

"I'm afraid so. They're the wolves and we're the sheep."

"And they live on human blood?"

"Not exactly. I'll get to that in a minute. You're of course familiar with the term 'sociopath'."

Nerves and surprise made her let out a short laugh. "My boyfriend and I were talking about the subject the other night."

"The technical term is Antisocial Personality Disorder. Symptoms include failure to form emotional attachments, lack of guilt, inability to take responsibility for one's actions. They're typically liars, con men—"

"Heads of major corporations?"

"Frankly, yes. Our economic and political climate increasingly favors ruthlessness, opportunism, lack of personal investment."

"How do you get from that to a separate species?"

"It's not only the socio-economic environment that these creatures are adapted for. They can metabolize carbon monoxide and dioxide. They can inhale toxic exhaust and their exhalations will be richer in oxygen than what they breathed in. It's like nature evolved them to help clean up the environment."

"You said you have genetic evidence?"

"Had, past tense. I was doing a study on sociopathology at UCLA. I discovered that a small but significant number of my subjects had only 42 chromosomes. Normal humans have 46. And all of my subjects with 42 chromosomes were sterile—male and female alike."

"I don't get it," Susan said.

"Neither did I. How was this mutation being passed on? Then, in the middle of the study, there was a murder on campus. The victim was some sort of sports person, so there was a lot of publicity."

"Oh my god," Susan said, remembering the furor in the news-room. "Tyrone Johnson, the quarterback."

"That's right. He was—"

Susan finished his sentence. "—drained of blood."

"You remember the case. Six weeks later, one of my 42-chromo-some women turned up pregnant. Her conception date was consis-tent with the night of the murder. I did a DNA test on the amniotic fluid and identified the father. It turned out that he was also in the study. Sterile, of course.

"So I set a trap. I left a unit of whole blood in the lab refrigerator and made sure he knew about it. The next day the blood was gone and he had live sperm cells."

"So they have to drink human blood—"

"Or semen," Fielder interrupted, "which is not that different, biologically."

"—to reproduce?"

"That's about the size of it. They crave both blood and semen, which makes them potential sexual predators, at least on male hu-mans, as well."

Roxanne's flirtation with Tom suddenly made more sense. "So one or both of your vampires killed Tyrone Johnson. Did you call the cops?"

"That's how I ended up here."

"What about your evidence?"

"It seems my students had not been known to the...let's call it the network of other members of their species. Once I outed them, their more experienced relatives moved in. A virus was introduced into my computer and wiped out all of my backups. Both subjects agreed to DNA tests and got help faking the results."

"Couldn't your lawyer do anything?"

"My lawyer," Fielder said sadly, "was one of them, as it turned out.

I didn't figure it out until afterward, when I had a colleague test one of her hairs."

"Do you mind telling me...who your lawyer was?"

"No, not at all. Roxanne Vallence, of Brock, James and Vallence. I see you've heard of them."

"My boyfriend works for them."

"Ah."

"Don't worry, he's not one of them. He's quite human. And from what you say, they can't change a normal human into one of them."

"No. We're stuck with the genes we have. These things are born, not made."

She had trouble focusing on her notes. Everything Fielder said confirmed everything Tom had told her. Yet part of her still resisted belief, balking at the sheer horror of it. "Go on," she said. "About Roxanne."

"She offered to take my case for free, and who was I to turn down a firm with that reputation? I suppose I was lucky they let me live."

"I was wondering about that." She tried to soften the words with a laugh, which came out brittle and unconvincing.

"The way I figure it, I'm worth more to them alive. I sound so crazy that I discredit my own story. Roxanne said as much, when she and my soon-to-be-ex-wife had me committed here."

"You don't sound that crazy to me," Susan said, and Fielder shrugged, showing the sad smile again. "Tell me," she went on, "how we fight them."

"Don't even think about it. They're no stronger than humans, and they generally avoid physical confrontation. But they can be incredibly persuasive. And they're nearly invulnerable. They can recover from just about any kind of injury, short of decapitation or something lodged in the heart, in a matter of minutes. On top of which, they're cunning, and they have no scruples at all. They've taken us right out of the top of the food chain."

"Don't they have any weaknesses?"

"There is one thing. They produce ethyl alcohol as a by-product of their metabolism. It's in their sweat, and it helps disseminate the pheromones that make people trust them. It makes them highly flammable. Another reason they don't like oxygen-rich environments."

Susan checked her watch. She didn't want to be late to her meeting with Tom. "Thank you for seeing me, Dr. Fielder. You've been a huge help. Can I come talk to you another time?"

"I would enjoy the company. And I'm not going anywhere."

Susan shook his hand and Fielder held on, gently, insistently. "Listen," he said. "Do you have a way to get hold of President Gore?"

A chill shot down to the ends of her fingers. "President Gore?"

Fielder's tone was exactly the same as before, calm, reasonable. "Yes, yes, the real president. He's got powerful friends, friends who could get me out of here. They're in his headquarters, north of the Arctic Circle."

In her peripheral vision, she saw the orderly moving in. "Dr. Fielder," she said, "are you feeling all right?"

"If you can't help," he said, "you can't. It's just that I don't know how to reach him. The headquarters is near the entrance to the hollow Earth. There are saucers coming in and out of there all day long..."

The orderly put one large hand on Fielder's shoulder and with the other he stroked the stubble on Fielder's head, as if soothing an agitated child. "The lady has to go now, Dr. Fielder."

"Okay," Fielder said.

"You go on, now, ma'am," the orderly said. "We'll be fine here."

" 'Bye now," Fielder said.

Susan backed away. Fielder continued to smile sadly as the light slowly died in his eyes.

TOM LEFT THE COROLLA in Corral Canyon State Park, knowing it would be towed eventually. If he lived long enough, he would deal with the consequences. He felt a certain manic satisfaction in letting go of his responsibilities.

He hiked to the Malibu Seafood Restaurant. It was after 11 in the morning and people were already lined up. He paid cash for fish and chips and ate them at a bright red painted table with an umbrella. He had a good view of the beach. Everything was intense—the salt and vinegar, the primal funk of the ocean, the swooping gulls, the heat of the sun, the tug of the wind.

When he finished, he cleared off his trash and moved to the other side of the restaurant, facing the Pacific Coast Highway. He tried to let the distant sound of the waves take the place of everything else in his head. When he saw Susan's silver Honda hatchback pull into the parking lot, a flood of pure joy lifted him to his feet.

SUSAN DROVE NORTH on PCH as far as Oxnard to make sure they weren't being followed, then cut over to the 101. While she drove, she reconstructed her conversation with Fielder, glancing at her notes a few times to get the wording exactly right.

Tom mostly listened in silence. He seemed to vacillate between denial, despair, and grim determination. In a world full of arrested adolescents with their macho posturing and self-regard, Tom was boyish in a different way. Despite twenty years in the legal business, he had maintained a kind of innocence, a readiness to trust, an ability to get hurt. She loved him in the way she loved a beautiful spring morning, a way that she didn't worry that she'd regret later.

If she'd cut him loose when this trouble started, she could have saved herself, at the expense of everything she believed in. It hadn't seemed like a choice then, and now that they were driving into the heart of the madness, if a part of her wanted to run away and hide, she supposed that was to be expected.

"And then," she said, "at the end, he completely loses it and starts talking about flying saucers and the hollow Earth—"

"Which is why nobody has ever believed the other stuff."

"The vampire stuff."

"The stuff that's actually true."

"Listen to us," Susan said.

"We sound like Brian and Jason arguing about comics," Tom said. "Except..."

"Yeah. This is really happening."

Susan listened to the silence for a while, then she couldn't take it any longer. "There's one more thing. Fielder said it's not just blood they crave, but...a certain other male bodily fluid."

"Ah, of course. So that's what Roxanne was up to. It wasn't my ineluctable masculine charm."

It should have been enough, yet it wasn't, quite. "He said they're very persuasive."

"When I was alone with her in her office, it was like I was hypnotized. Then she got distracted, and that was the end of it. I don't think she was that intent on me in the first place."

"So nothing happened."

"No. If I'd let her do that to me...I don't think I'd be alive now."

Her affection for him blossomed inside her, filling her up. Without taking her eyes off the road, she caught her fingers in the hair at the back of his head. "I know, sweetie, I believe you."

"About Roxanne, or about the vampire business?"

"Both," Susan said. "All of it."

"Why? I mean, how can you?"

"I couldn't do my job without a good bullshit detector. You're not lying, and neither was Fielder."

"What about the flying saucers?"

"His voice was the same, but his eyes were different. He didn't see me anymore."

"Well," Tom said. "I appreciate the vote of confidence."

She heard a rustling noise, and looked over to see him with a slick 8 1/2 by 11 brochure.

"I stole this out of Roxanne's desk this morning," he said. "From the photos, it looks like pretty dense forest all around. It should be possible to spy on them without being seen..." His voice changed and the brochure rattled to the floorboards. "I can't read this now, it makes me carsick."

He did look sick. "Tom? Are you okay? Do you want me to pull over?"

"I killed a man this morning."

"What? What are you talking about?"

He told her about using Patrick's keycard, and about setting him on fire in the parking garage.

"That wasn't a human being," Susan said. "That was some kind of...*thing*. A monster." She sounded like she was trying to convince herself as much as Tom.

"I used to make fun of his haircut," Tom said. "I hated it that he got all the high-profile cases. But when I lit him up, it was like this total caveman feeling of joy. Of triumph. I can still feel it, and it makes me a little sick. I don't want to be like that."

Susan slowed and pulled onto the shoulder. She shrugged out of her seatbelt and gathered Tom up in her arms. "We like a little caveman once in a while," she said. "As long as you don't make a habit of it."

"I wanted to be like him. I wanted the big cases, the money, the BMWs."

"That's not you."

"No. No, I don't really have what it takes."

"What it takes to be a sociopath? To be Homo praedatorias? Do you think I would want a man like that?"

"We have to find a way to get clear of this. I can't live the rest of my life like this."

"We can turn the car around," Susan said. "We can be in Mexico by sundown."

"And then how long until they find us? Or find my kids?" He eased away from her, kissed her on the forehead. "No. We have to find something, some kind of leverage to use against them. A little more caveman will be required."

THEY SPENT THE NIGHT north of San Francisco, in Santa Rosa. The first motel they tried wouldn't let them rent without a credit card, which struck Susan first as absurd, and then as frightening. One more way in which the world was being remade on the predators' terms, requiring their prey to leave an electronic trail wherever they went.

By the time they checked into the second motel, they were too exhausted to do anything other than fall into bed and sleep. But in the early morning hours she woke to Tom's hands on her, and his urgency triggered her own desire. Afterward, as they held each other, she thought about the way that sex told you, in the strongest possible terms, that you were still alive.

They got on the road early and were in Eureka by mid-morning. They ran a few errands, ate lunch, and then headed north and east into the Shasta-Trinity National Forest.

Tom drove and Susan navigated, using the topographical map that Tom had liberated from the Eureka Public Library. The scenery was spectacular—blue mountains in the distance, dusted with white at the very peaks; black oaks in the foothills that gradually gave way to 200-foot-tall redwoods and white firs like giant, conical Christmas trees; running water everywhere. The road rose now more than it fell, as they made their way deeper into the wilderness. With the windows down, the car filled with clean, cool air and verdant smells.

When she wasn't actively navigating, she studied the pages Tom had found on the web for the Pleasure Dome, hearing Coleridge in her head, Xanadu and Kubla Khan.

"What's with the interior layout?" she asked. "You're not thinking about trying to get inside?"

"Christ, no. I printed everything I could find. I didn't stop to ask how useful it was. I mean, you never know, right?"

"It says here they've got hotel facilities for 200 on premises, plus support staff, plus banquet facilities, all in a hermetically sealed environment."

"They'll like that. They can pump in their own monoxide."

"Isn't that going to make them tough to photograph, if they're not coming and going?"

"There's a deck that opens off the dining room. For cocktails and breakfast and all that. Worst case, we can shoot them as they leave on Sunday."

She shuffled through more paper. "Menu from a Microsoft retreat they had last year?"

"Like I said, I wasn't discriminating."

"And what's this, some kind of structural drawing?"

Tom glanced over. "Yeah, this is pretty amazing. The whole place is suspended over the gorge on steel cables."

"So we could cut the cables..."

"The cables are three feet in diameter and there are ten of them. Don't even kid about it. We take some pictures, hopefully catch some big fish hobnobbing with other big fish they are not supposed to be hobnobbing with, and then we get out."

"And then? We haven't really talked about what happens next."

"You use your contacts to spread the story. We have to assume Fielder was right about the chromosome stuff. After what I've seen, I have no doubt that they're not human. So there has to be a simple genetic test to show that, to count chromosomes. We get somebody big, like the New York *Times* or Washington *Post* to ask questions, the kind of questions that'll put pressure on these predators to get tested. Once this gets going, there'll be a lot of unsolved murders that suddenly link up, a lot of cover ups that get uncovered."

"It's not going to be easy, you know."

"You have friends at both those papers."

"They'll want sources. Sources that I'm not sleeping with and that are not in a mental institution."

"They can get a DNA sample, from Roxanne, or from Patrick's apartment. All we have to do is get the ball rolling."

"I'm not disagreeing. And we need the photos. But I should be the one to do it. I'm more likely to recognize political figures than you are. I'm a better photographer. And they don't know me. I can pass for a hiker if I get caught."

"Your logic is flawless. But there's no way in hell I'm letting you do this alone."

She leaned over and touched his lips with two fingers. "Okay, caveman."

"Okay, then."

They passed an old man walking by the roadside with a fishing rod and a backpack. He watched them with a closed expression as they drove by. This close to the Pleasure Dome, Susan thought, he was probably used to seeing stretch limos and town cars, not a ten-year-old Honda Civic.

Less than a mile later they passed the entrance to the Pleasure Dome, a wrought iron gate in a ten-foot wall built from native stone. The wall continued for a hundred yards, then turned into a hurricane fence topped with coils of razor wire.

Tom had seen the razor wire too, and they looked at each other for a second, neither of them asking the obvious question of how they were going to get to the other side of it. The fence went on and on, then finally made a sharp angle away from the road.

Susan went back to the map. "It looks like there should be a turn-off coming up on the right. An old logging road or something."

A moment later Tom said, "There it is."

They followed the dirt road into a mixed forest of fir and red-wood. For a while it ran directly perpendicular to the main road, then it began to curve to the left. "Anywhere along here," she said.

Tom pulled between two trees. As soon as he turned off the engine, Susan heard running water. Birds squabbled in the distance and the air was full of the spicy scent of the firs. They looked at each other then, as if giving each other one last chance to back down. Then Tom got out and walked around to open the hatchback.

They loaded her tent and sleeping bag and the rest of the supplies into two backpacks and helped each other into them. Susan slung her camera bag over one shoulder and looked at her compass. "That way," she said.

·

WHEN THEY CAME OUT of the forest, they were on the lip of the gorge. Susan saw the razor wire fence off to her right. They left their backpacks under the trees and crept up to the edge of the cliff on hands and knees.

The view made her forget to breathe. It was a sixty-foot drop to the Trinity River, which was running high and fast, surrounded by steep basalt walls. The rocks had been sheared off in a succession of intersecting planes and then weathered to a matte finish. Clumps of tenacious greenery hung on to cracks in the slope.

The river curved as it flowed, blocking any view of the Dome. Susan's impatience overcame her awe and she backed away and went for a look at the fence. It ran up to the very lip of the gorge, a final metal post set in concrete only a couple of inches from a sheer drop.

"Is it electrified?" Tom said.

She hadn't heard him come up behind her. "No," she said. "No insulators." She brushed the pole with a fingertip, then grabbed it with her whole hand. She leaned her weight into it, shook it, and felt no give at all. She stripped off her camera bag and binoculars and set them at Tom's feet.

"What are you doing?" he said.

"Trying an experiment."

She faced away from the drop, planted one foot next to the pole, then swung herself around it and onto the other side.

"Nothing to it," she said, her heart beating hard in delayed reaction. "Hand me the stuff, will you?"

He passed the binoculars and camera bag around the edge of the fence. "Okay," he said. "Here I come."

Susan hovered as he set himself up for it, and he said, "No offence, can you give me a little room? I don't like heights and other people make it worse."

"Okay," she said.

Once he was across he nodded stiffly, breathing hard. "If it had been on level ground it wouldn't have been anything at all. But knowing the drop was there..."

They moved under the cover of the trees and worked their way downstream. Susan estimated that they traveled a mile or more to make their way around the curve of the gorge. When they stepped into the open again, Susan saw the Dome.

It seemed to float above the river, the suspension cables invisible at this distance. It was shaped like two shallow bowls glued lip to lip, making Susan think of Fielder's flying saucers. The off-white reflective glass that covered it had no visible seams, adding to the otherworldly effect. A wooden walkway led from Susan's side of the gorge to the Dome, and on the opposite side a wooden deck stretched nearly to the far canyon wall. A couple of dozen widely scattered tables with umbrellas gave her an appreciation of how large the deck, and by extension the dome, really was.

"Almost funny, isn't it?" she said. "That they would have their retreat in all this clean air and natural beauty. It's everything they're trying to destroy."

"I don't think a sense of irony is one of their strong points."

She froze. "Do you hear something?"

Tom started to shake his head, then listened intently. "Helicopter."

They ran for the cover of the trees. A few seconds later a helicopter glided overhead, circled the dome, and then landed on a concrete pad on solid ground on the near side of the ravine. Susan watched through binoculars as a squad of security guards in paramilitary getup—black caps and shirts and trousers, Kevlar vests, automatic weapons—ran across the footbridge to the landing pad. Meanwhile men in white pants and T-shirts began unloading refrigerated containers from the helicopter.

"Bringing in some kind of supplies," Susan said, and passed the binoculars to Tom.

"This is good," Tom said. "We can see everything from here. Whether they leave by chopper or by car."

"I don't like the AR-15s and the full military gear," Susan said. "It's too much for a quiet corporate retreat."

Tom shrugged. "They're not just guarding a bunch of computer geeks this time."

"I guess." Tom handed her the binoculars and she unpacked the camera. "I'm going to get some shots of the people on the deck," she said. "Why don't you go on back, get the tent set up, get some shuteye? I'll meet you there in a couple of hours, well before dark."

"I don't know..."

"You're worn out. And you'll need to be awake later so you can take a shift, in case there's something happening out there tonight."

"Yeah, okay."

"And remember what we agreed to."

"Never give you a live animal as a present?"

"I'm serious, Tom. If something happens and they only get one of us..."

"Yeah, yeah. No heroics, go for help."

The moment was thick with unspoken emotion. She kissed him quickly and said, "Go."

Once the sound of his footsteps faded, she regretted sending him away. She tried to concentrate on the camera, picking out the faces that were turned toward her, bringing each one into tight focus, getting the shot, moving on. Hard as she fought against it, a hopeless gloom began to settle on her. What if she and Tom did get away? Once she tried to make the story public, the predators would be looking for her too. From the early days of a promising relationship, she and Tom had gone, in a matter of hours, to losing everything. Their jobs, their homes, their life savings. The turquoise necklace her mother had given her on her 12th birthday, her high school yearbooks, her great-aunt's china that had been in the family for 150 years. She was on the brink of tears, as much from the injustice of it as from the loss itself.

She shook it off and raised the camera again. Giving up was literal suicide. The only way to fight back was to keep on with what she was doing, to get the photos out into the world.

She scanned the crowd again through the telephoto lens, stopped

on a hatchet-faced man in his 40s, and recognized the junior sena-
tor who had been a serious contender in the last Republican
Presidential primary. She steadied her hands and clicked the shutter.
A moment later he was joined by a flamboyant Hollywood agent
who had been on the cover of last week's *People* magazine, and
Susan clicked the shutter again.

TOM HAD PICKED a spot inside the tree line where the tent
wouldn't be visible from the air. It was igloo-shaped, no poles inside,
flexible rods outside that the thing was supposed to hang from.
Staking out the bottom was easy enough. Getting it to stand up
required a Zen vision that Tom had yet to master.

He was threading one of the rods through the loops for the
seventh time, completely focused on the job, when he heard a twig
snap behind him. The rod sprang off into the leafy undergrowth and
Tom spun around to find five automatic rifles pointing at him. They
were in the hands of security guards wearing the same gear as the
ones at the helicopter pad, spread in a semicircle around him.

The one closest to Tom turned his head and said, "Secure the
perimeter, see if there's anybody else here."

Tom slowly raised his hands. He saw, too late, that he had been
naïve again, maybe for the last time. He was less afraid of being shot,
he realized, than of being tortured and humiliating himself. He was
afraid that Susan would suddenly show up and be captured too. He
was afraid for his kids.

They searched him and then made him lie on his face in the rough
grass while they searched the tent and the backpacks. "Hey, Sarge,"
one of them said. "There's some panties and bras and stuff in this one."

The sergeant had already been through Tom's wallet. "Davis, your
name is? Okay, Davis, start talking."

"It's my girlfriend's stuff. She's coming up to meet me tomorrow."

"Bullshit. She'd bring her own stuff with her. Either you're a
cross-dresser or she's around here somewhere. Royce, Suresh, check
the other side of the fence."

"Look," Tom said. "This is all a misunderstanding. I didn't see any no trespassing signs. I just wanted a quiet weekend in the woods."

"Sure you did," the sergeant said. "Don't worry. We'll get the truth out of you."

EVENTUALLY THE SERGEANT got tired of waiting and took him along the fence line to the road, where two Jeeps sat parked on the shoulder. They'd bound his hands in front of him with a zip tie and they'd left two men at the canyon to keep looking for Susan. The sergeant had called somebody at the Dome on his phone and gotten instructions that Tom couldn't hear. He was physically sick with fear—nausea, blurred vision, dizziness, his heartbeat skittering around. The sergeant sat in the back seat with Tom, and one of the other guards hot-rodded the jeep to a parking lot next to the heliport.

The sergeant ordered Tom to get out of the jeep and lie prone on the asphalt, bound hands resting on top of his head. "Hold him until I get back," the sergeant said to the other two. "If he tries anything, do whatever you have to do."

Tom had his head toward the canyon and he saw the sergeant go into a covered walkway that led to the Dome, a utilitarian service entrance, not the fancy wooden one that the guests used. As soon as he was gone, the younger of the guards fished out a pack of cigarettes and lit up. He had short, curly hair and a mustache with ends that trailed down the sides of his mouth. "I can't breathe in that fucking place," he said.

The older one said, "Like you can breathe with that shit in your lungs? The irony is compelling." He shook his head. "The clients turned the oh-two down inside, that's all."

"The what?"

"The oh-two. The oxygen, you moron. They got it down around eighteen percent instead of twenty-one, where it ought to be. One of their tech people told me."

"What the hell they do that for? That's fucking weird."

Because the more oxygen there is, Tom thought, the more easily things catch fire.

The older man shrugged. "Clients do what they want."

"They don't seem that weird. They seem nice."

"Yeah, they're okay for a bunch of lawyers. They want low oh-two they can have low oh-two."

"Did you see some of who's in there? This morning I swear I saw—"

"Hey," the older one said, nodding at Tom. "Shut the fuck up, okay?"

"Oh, yeah. Right."

The sergeant reappeared and the younger guard hastily threw his cigarette on the ground and stepped on it. The sergeant pointed at him and said, "You, Wasserman, you're with me." He pointed to the other one. "Stay with the jeep, keep tabs on the guys in the field." Finally he looked at Tom. "On your feet, asshole."

The miniscule sway in the covered walkway was enough to trigger Tom's acrophobia. To make it worse, windows lined both sides of the passage, and a pair of red-tailed hawks swooped and glided a few yards away. Tom could see the cliffs on the far side of the ravine and the river, wide and deep, directly underneath him. He thought he might lose it if he didn't get his hands free soon.

The sergeant typed a code on a keypad at the entry to the main body of the Dome. On the other side of the door was a walkway that curved gently in both directions around the circumference. The outside wall was glass from floor to 12-foot ceiling, making Tom's calves ache with muscle contractions. He edged toward the inside wall.

"Don't like heights, eh?" the sergeant said. "Good to know."

They came to a door labeled SECURITY and the sergeant used what looked like the same code to unlock it. A burst of laughter came out of the main dining hall a few yards further along.

The sergeant held the door open and the other man, Wasserman, gave him a shove to propel him inside. The space was no bigger than Tom's former office at Brock, James and Vallence, and they'd managed to squeeze two desks into it, each with a keyboard and flat screen monitor. A guard in a black T-shirt sat behind one of them, watching the screen with no particular interest and repeatedly pressing the Enter key. The other was occupied by LA County District Attorney Matthew Clarke.

Before he could stop himself, Tom said, "What are you doing here?"

"I'm in charge of security for this event," Clarke said, with mild amusement. "I think the more interesting question is, what are *you* doing here?"

The sergeant looked from Clarke to Tom and back. "You know this guy?"

"We've crossed paths," Clarke said.

"So," Tom said. "You're one of them."

Clarke blinked. "Thanks," he said to the sergeant. "I'll take it from here." He looked at the guard at the other desk. "I'll have to ask you to leave as well."

The guard said, "Who's going to watch the cameras?"

"Use the business office," Clarke said.

Tom held out his zip-tied hands to the sergeant. "Can you take this off before you go? My hands are going numb."

The sergeant looked to Clarke, who said, "Go ahead. He's harmless."

The sergeant cut the tie with a folding knife from his utility belt. "If he gives you any trouble..."

Tom massaged his wrists, gently, avoiding the places where the skin was rubbed raw.

"Don't worry," Clarke said, opening his jacket to show a shoulder holster. He took out a revolver and laid it on his desk. "I'm not expecting trouble."

The sergeant laughed and motioned Wasserman and the other guard in front of him. Once they were gone, Clarke said, "Have a seat, Davis. I have some questions for you."

"Do you really drink human blood?" Tom said.

"Well, that answers most of them right there. Not that there was a lot of doubt, but you are definitely a dead man now."

"I left the complete story with somebody before I left LA. About the forty-two chromosomes and everything. If anything happens to me..."

"Oh, please," Clarke said. "I assume you're talking about Susan Altman. She's not in LA, she's wandering around somewhere near your campsite. Once we find her, we'll kill her too."

Somebody knocked crisply at the door. Clarke pressed a buzzer on his desk and the door flew open. Roxanne walked in, already talking. "What's the holdup, Matthew? It's time for the ceremony and...oh."

"Roxanne," Tom said, with a nod.

"He set off one of the perimeter alarms," Clarke said. "The security guys found him trying to set up a tent in the forest, about a mile upstream from a great view of the Dome."

"Alone?"

"We think the Altman woman is here too, we just haven't found her yet."

"Tom, Tom, Tom," Roxanne said.

"He knows," Clarke said.

"The truth? Not some Bela Lugosi fantasy?"

"Sounds like he talked to Fielder."

Roxanne sighed. "That's what I get for leaving him alive. Can you actually manage to kill Davis this time? And maybe make it look like an accident?"

Clarke looked like Roxanne had hurt his feelings. "Do you want his blood?"

"Given the Judd business, it might be one too many drained corpses following us around. A fall into the river should do it. It could account for a crushed skull, for instance."

"I was there the day you joined the firm," Tom said. "I showed you how to use the copier."

She flashed him an empty smile. "I'm in a bit of a hurry just now,

Tom." As she opened the door, Tom saw past her to a crowd of predators milling around, dressed in their corporate finery. Roxanne turned to Clarke. "Wait half an hour before you take him. I don't want people to see him in the hallway and be alarmed. It might spoil the big event." She closed the door firmly as she left.

"Big event?" Tom asked. "What are you doing, giving out awards?"

"Something like that. Make yourself comfortable. Once everybody's settled in, I'll take you out and kill you."

"Do you really not feel anything?"

"I feel lots of things. I just don't feel upset at the thought of killing you. All these empathic emotions of yours, there's nothing real about them. They're a trick your genes played on you. Like religion."

"Empathy is like religion?"

"It's a fluke of the genes whether you're a believer or not. I mean, some old white guy with a beard who gives babies AIDS and lets his priests screw their altar boys? How could you worship that without some kind of weird genetic disposition for it?"

"So what *do* you feel?"

"At the moment I feel great. I like winning. Ever see a cheetah bring down a gazelle?"

SUSAN'S SENSES WERE ALREADY in overdrive when she heard the clank of military gear in the distance. She rolled onto her feet and was moving silently for the trees before she consciously registered what she'd heard.

As she watched from behind a pile of fallen brush, two of the black-clad security guards from the Dome walked past her. They kept close to the edge of the ravine, where the going was easiest. They had their weapons out and were making no more than a token effort at stealth or at looking into the woods.

As soon as they were out of sight, she headed for the campsite. She tried to balance her fear for Tom with caution. Let him not be

dead, she thought, over and over, drowning the other voices in
her head.

She crept up to the fence in time to see three soldiers marching
Tom in the direction of the highway. He was alive, then, at least. She
swung around the fence and headed for her car at a lope, her feet
silent on the dry, hard packed trail. She got in and started the engine
and drove back to the highway as fast as the rutted road allowed.
Then she floored it, away from the Dome and toward the nearest
town, Clearwater, five miles away.

According to her phone, the sheriff's office was located in a strip
mall on Highway 96. She pulled up to the front door with her tires
screaming.

The front half of the office consisted of a worn linoleum floor,
a few plastic chairs, and a Coke machine. An older man sat at a
high desk, partially surrounded by glass. He had a massive radio-
telephone set at one elbow and a flat screen computer monitor at
the other. Behind him, visible through the glass partition, a younger
man and woman sat at their own, smaller desks.

"Is the sheriff in?" Susan said, losing the battle to keep her voice
calm. "It's an emergency!"

"He's in court. Deputy Kinkaid is available." He made a vague
gesture toward the woman behind him. "Now get you a couple of
deep breaths and tell me what's going on."

"It's my boyfriend. We were camping in the woods and these
armed men came and took him away."

"Like cops, or military, or what?"

"I think they were security guards from the Pleasure Dome."

The younger man, without looking up, made a noise that could
have been indigestion, but sounded more like a snort of derision.

"Hang on," the older man said. "Why'd they take him and
not you?"

"I was taking a walk, and when I came back I saw them holding
guns on him, and I...I hid."

"Did you ask at the Dome?"

"You can't just drive in there. There's a guardhouse, and...I was afraid."

The younger man made a throat-clearing noise. The older man turned in his chair and adjusted his glasses and squinted at the monitor. He moved the mouse around and clicked it a couple of times and said, "Name of the missing person?"

"He's not a missing person! He's in that dome, and they're holding him illegally, and I want somebody to go up there with me and get him out!"

"We have to fill out a report before—"

"You can fill out the report later. This is an emergency!"

She and the old man stared at each other, then, finally, a chair scraped against the linoleum and the woman got up from her desk. She was six feet tall, with dark hair pulled straight back from her face and tied in a short ponytail. She was broad in the shoulders and her khaki uniform was crisply pressed. "I'll handle this," she said to the old man, and he let her take his place at the desk. "I'm Deputy Kinkaid. What were you two doing in the woods?"

"Camping, I told you—"

"This was at the State Park?"

"No, up by the Dome."

"On the Dome's private property?"

The younger man made another noise. Kinkaid turned on him. "You got something to say, Litton?"

"Got a frog in my throat."

"Maybe you need to step outside."

Susan interrupted. "There weren't any signs. We didn't cross any fences." Not setting up the tent, anyway, she thought.

"They're incorporated as their own city up there," Kinkaid said. "Got their own police force. Got to. They get heads of state."

Susan teetered between rage and panic. "Are you going to help me or not?"

"You got to take it up with the folks at the Dome. We got no jurisdiction." Susan felt an abyss of paranoia open in front of her. This woman, she had to remind herself, poorly educated, poorly paid, was not part of some predator conspiracy, tempting as it was to believe it. She was simply an offensive jerk of a bureaucrat, passing along her personal bitterness.

Susan started for the door, and Kinkaid called after her, "They got themselves a business office over to Eureka, be open tomorrow morning—"

By the time she was out the door, Susan was running. She jumped in the car and roared out of the parking lot. She drove up and down the streets of Clearwater, leaning forward, pounding her fist on the wheel in frustration, searching the signs on the buildings she passed for a courthouse or a police station or highway patrol office or anyone who could possibly help. She didn't notice the squad car behind her until she heard the whoop of the siren and saw the strobing lights. She considered trying to run for it, letting them chase her to the Dome. The fantasy ended badly, with bullets in her tires and herself in jail while Tom was tortured and killed.

She pulled over and watched in the rearview as the cruiser sat motionless for a long minute, then Litton, the younger deputy, got out, billed cap over his dark hair, mirrorshades in place. He strode up to her window and tapped on the glass. Susan reluctantly rolled it down.

"Ma'am, that dome is in Humboldt County. That's jurisdiction enough for me."

Susan let out a long, noisy breath.

Litton smiled and said, "There's a friendly judge around the corner that I've already talked to on the phone. If you'll step into my vehicle, we'll pick up a warrant and go find your boyfriend."

TOM QUICKLY RAN OUT of things to say to Clarke. Clarke, for his part, was apparently monitoring the banquet hall on his computer. At one point he chuckled and said, "If you knew who all was in that room, you'd go out of your mind."

"Tell me," Tom said.

Clarke laughed again. "Why?"

Tom sat as the last minutes of his life slipped away. He knew that Clarke's pheromones were working to subvert his natural emotions. Still he couldn't manage to break through the haze, even when Wasserman came in, AR-15 at the ready. "They're all inside," he said.

"Finally," Clarke said. He put the pistol in his shoulder holster. "Let's go, Davis."

Tom got unsteadily to his feet.

Clarke said, "We'll take him through Maintenance and out to the south landing."

"The landing?" Wasserman said. "What happens there?"

"Don't worry about it. Help me get him there and I'll take care of the rest."

Clarke led the way out of the office and Wasserman fell in a step or two behind Tom. They passed the closed doors of the banquet hall, where an amplified voice said, "—and our deepest gratitude to all of the volunteers who gave of themselves so selflessly to make this evening possible—" Harsh laughter buried the end of the sentence.

Past the entrance to the kitchen, they stopped at another door with a keypad and Clarke, relaxed and sure of himself, didn't bother to screen his hand as he typed in the numbers. Tom picked up the first three of the four, for whatever good they might do him.

Behind the door was a huge space full of humming fans, compressors, elevator cables, water heaters, generators. The curved top of the dome was 30 feet over their heads and the metal grid they stood on was another 12 feet above a solid floor. The space was crisscrossed with catwalks, bundled electrical and fiber optic wires, HVAC ducts, and PVC pipe. To Tom's right was a four-foot-high metal gate with a sign that said CLIMATE CONTROL / AUTHORIZED PERSONNEL ONLY. He vaguely remembered seeing it in the schematics he'd found at the Eureka library that morning.

They walked across the width of the structure, not seeing another person. Everything was automated and computerized, monitored from somewhere else. The outer wall they approached, like the rest

of the Dome, was covered in one-way glass, and Tom could see out
to the canyon and the river and the trees.

Clarke stopped at a door with another keypad and a sign that
said OUTSIDE ACCESS / CAUTION. Tom focused his attention and
this time got all four numbers. He looked up to see that Wasserman
had noticed.

"What difference does it make?" Tom said. "Five minutes from
now, I'll be floating dead in the river."

"I didn't hear that," Wasserman said.

"What's the matter?" Tom said. "Don't have the stomach for
this job?"

Clarke said, "Shut up, Davis. I'll shoot you right here if I have to,
and find somebody to clean up the mess afterward."

Clarke opened the door and pushed Tom out onto another gridded platform, this one in the open air on the side of the dome,
following its curvature in both directions. A set of handholds led up
and down so that workers had access to the skin of the structure.
The wind was strong and the temperature was dropping as the sun
neared the horizon. Tom gripped the railing to steady himself, trying not to look at the eddying water 60 feet below.

"Give me your baton," Clarke said to Wasserman, holding out one
hand. Wasserman hesitated and Clarke wiggled his fingers. "I can't
be sure the fall alone will kill him."

Wasserman put one hand on the baton without taking it out of
his belt. "Look, I'm not sure about this. You're talking about cold-
blooded murder here."

"Fine. Go inside. Just hand over the baton first."

Wasserman slowly took out the baton and put it in Clarke's hand.
Tom realized that Wasserman, too, was at the mercy of Clarke's
pheromones. Wasserman was reaching for the door handle when his
shoulder radio squawked.

"Wasserman?" Tom recognized the sergeant's voice. "You got DA
Clarke there?"

"Yeah, what's up?" Clarke said.

"We got a situation at the front gate."

"I'll be there in a few minutes," Clarke said.

"All due respect, sir," the sergeant said, "we need you immediately. I'll explain when you get here."

Clarke took a few long strides along the platform, far enough that the front entrance would be visible. Whatever he saw there make him say, "Oh, shit."

He returned to the door and gave Wasserman the baton. "Keep him here until I get back," he said irritably. "Do you think you can do that?"

"Yes, sir, I—"

"I can't risk getting his blood on me right now. If he tries to escape, shoot him. Are we clear?"

"Yes, sir, I—"

"Good."

Clarke went in the service door. Wasserman took a step back and pointed the AR-15 at Tom's stomach.

LITTON HAD GOTTEN them as far as the main entrance of the Dome, and Susan didn't know if they were going to get any further. A squad leader from the security team and two of his thugs blocked the door. Susan was sure they were the same men who had taken Tom away.

"There's nothing to discuss," Litton said. "It's a legal search warrant. It means I get to go in there and look around."

The squad leader achieved the appearance of politeness without any genuine deference. "I don't make the rules, sir. My orders say there are issues of national security here and nobody goes inside without approval from our head of operations."

"If you don't let me in there..." Litton said.

The squad leader seemed to smell the bluff. "Yes?"

Before Litton could answer, the door opened and Matthew Clarke stepped out.

"DA Clarke," Susan said. "This is a surprise." Except that it wasn't, now that she thought about it. She'd interviewed him more than once and always found him arrogant and deceptive—but only afterward, when listening to her tapes or reviewing her notes.

"Ms. Altman," he said. "What are you doing here?"

"I'm looking for a friend. A lawyer named Tom Davis."

"I'm acquainted with Mr. Davis. I feel certain he's not on our guest list."

She saw that Clarke knew everything. Where Tom was, how much Susan knew, how hopeless her quest was going to prove. He was making conversation purely for the sake of the witnesses.

"Your hired goons," she said, "kidnapped him from our camp site less than an hour ago."

"That statement is so riddled with false assumptions that I hardly know how to answer it."

Litton took half a step forward, forcing the squad leader to back up. "Are you holding Tom Davis on these premises?"

"No," Clarke said.

"Are you willing to let us search the place to verify that?"

"No," Clarke said.

"We have a warrant—"

"This is a matter of national security, Deputy—" He squinted at the tag on Litton's shirt. "—Litton. This is bigger than Humboldt County and you are in way, way over your head. Now turn around and go back to Jerkwater, or wherever the hell you came from."

"Clearwater. They named it that because the water there used to be clear, before a bunch of rich lawyers let the highest bidders come in and pollute it. You just pissed me off, mister. Now either you let me in for a nice, quiet look around, or I call up the State Police and the State Militia and we'll come in there by force and take this place apart."

She watched Clarke weigh his options. In the long run, Clarke had the connections to make Litton disappear. In the short run, it was possible that Litton could stir up more trouble than Clarke was willing to deal with.

Clarke stepped aside.

Litton gestured for Susan to go first and Clarke, with not much conviction, said, "Not her. No reporters."

"Sorry," Litton said. "I need her to identify Davis. After you, ma'am."

"Wasserman," Tom said. "That's your name, right?" His head had started to clear the second Clarke went inside.

"I'm not talking to you. I'm not listening. I'm just waiting for Mr. Clarke to get back."

"We could go inside. You could call the sheriff or the State Police, and you could walk away from this."

"What do you mean, walk away?"

"I'm a lawyer too, you know. If you let Clarke go through with this, you're an accessory to murder. You could get life. At the very least, your career is over."

"That's enough," Wasserman said. "No more talking."

"Whatever you say. I'm only trying to help."

"You can help me by shutting up."

"You're not going to shoot me for talking, are you?"

"I'm warning you..."

"Because now we're getting into Murder One."

"I don't have to kill you to shut you up," Wasserman said. He slung the AR-15 over his shoulder and reached for his baton. "One more word..."

Now or never, Tom thought. I'm dead anyway.

He slipped between the bars of the guardrail and swung down into the metal structure below the deck.

Wasserman went berserk, trying to smash Tom's hands with the baton, screaming, "You fucker! You fucker! I'll kill you!" The metal platform rang with the blows. Tom was completely under the deck now, terror and rage pumping him up with manic energy. He grabbed a strut with both hands and let his legs swing free, not looking down, staring instead at his distorted reflection as he swung back and then slammed both boots into the glass.

The impact nearly tore his hands loose. The glass was reinforced, strong enough to resist a hundred kicks, far more than Tom had in him.

He looked up. Wasserman had unslung his AR-15 and was on his knees, poking the barrel through the bars of the guardrail, trying to bend himself double so he could aim. When he couldn't manage it, he held the rifle upside down and fired blind. As Tom saw the glass wall of the Dome crack, he felt something like an electric shock along the right side of his ribcage. His right arm lost its grip on the metal supports and he lunged to get it back, inflaming the wound in his side. He looked down, saw a rip in his shirt and blood oozing from the exposed skin.

"Fuck!" Wasserman yelled. "Shit!" He stuck the rifle under again and Tom, in desperation, swung himself around and kicked out with both legs. He caught the rifle barrel a solid blow and something crunched in Wasserman's hand. Wasserman yelled in pain and the rifle came loose, bouncing off the metal supports and falling toward the river.

Tom turned himself around again. His arm muscles burned as hotly as the graze in his side and he knew he only had seconds left before he lost his grip. Wasserman's bullets had turned the glass into a mosaic. Tom pumped once and hurled himself, with the last of his strength, into the shattered window.

SUSAN WAS AWARE, dimly, of the spectacular view, the clean lines of the metalwork, the subtle earth tones of the carpet, the extravagant amounts of money that the Dome put on display for its customers. Yet the further they went into the building, the more numb and demoralized she felt. She remembered the finality with which Clarke had told them that Tom was not there.

"Is that running water I hear?" Litton said. He was looking around as if he'd just arrived at the State Fair.

"It's a recording," the squad leader said disdainfully. "The dome is completely soundproof. But the clients want to hear water."

Litton stopped in front of a set of double doors with windows, where another security guard stood in at-ease position. "What's in here?"

"Banquet hall," Clarke said. "Where I'm supposed to be right now. You can bring the Mongol Hordes, but you are *not* going in there."

"Take a look," Litton said to Susan.

"No," Clarke said.

Litton finally succumbed to the same inertia that had taken hold of Susan. "Well," he said at last. "I can't see why you'd be holding Mr. Davis in the middle of a banquet hall, anyway."

"That is correct," Clarke said. He looked at Susan then. It was a look of pure contempt. The look said, it doesn't matter what you see in here because you're dead anyway. It left Susan drained and unsteady.

"Have you seen enough?" Clarke said.

Susan looked at Litton. "This is hopeless. I don't think we're going to find him. They could have him hidden anywhere, in one of the guest rooms, in some utility closet. They could move him around while we're searching."

"You're the boss," Litton said. "Tell me what you want to do."

Clarke had sapped her will and the last of her hope. "Let's go," she said.

THE WINDOW EXPLODED into nuggets of glass as Tom hurtled through it. He fell and rolled, his skin tingling from a dozen tiny cuts.

He had only seconds before Wasserman came after him. In the fading light of the floor-to-ceiling windows, Tom saw a closet-sized space that said FIRE PANEL, the door standing open. He locked himself inside as he heard Wasserman slam open the access door and run across the gridded floor. "Davis!" he yelled. "Show yourself, you fuck, or you're a dead man!"

The logic, Tom thought, was not impressive. He was a dead man in any case.

He heard Wasserman on his shoulder radio. "This is Wasserman. Davis is loose. Somewhere in the maintenance area. And I need another rifle."

"Wasserman," said a crackly voice on the other end, "you jackass, how did you manage to so completely fuck this up? You might consider offing yourself before Clarke does it for you."

"Shut the fuck up and get me a weapon and some backup, will you?"

"Backup is not available at the moment. We've got visitors. Hold your position."

"Shit!" Wasserman said, and his footsteps pounded away.

Tom eased the door open. No sign of Wasserman. He found a set of steps that took him to the second level, and he made his way as quietly as he could to the climate control station. He clambered over the locked gate and sat in front of darkened monitor. He moved the mouse and a screen saver appeared, showing an animated ten-key pad.

Tom blinked the sweat out of his eyes and tried the combination Clarke had used for the door. After an agonizing moment, the screen refreshed, revealing a complex dashboard. He took a couple of deep breaths and blinked again, trying to get his eyes to focus and his panicked brain to function.

The number 72 in big orange letters in the upper right had to be the temperature. Link to vent locations. Heat or cool, air pressure in the main vent, humidity, pollen count, toxins.

Air composition.

He clicked the link popup. A window showed two stacked bar graphs, the one on the left labeled CURRENT and the one on the right TARGET, with plus and minus signs next to each element. He began to click the plus sign next to OXYGEN. Once he passed 25 percent, a warning message popped up.

"This mixture is highly combustible. Continue?"

Tom clicked Y and ran the oxygen level up to 50 percent before another warning message appeared.

"Extreme combustion risk. Enter override code to continue."

Tom tried the same passcode, this time with no luck. Fifty percent would have to do. He stood up and fought off a moment of dizziness. The first graph showed the actual oxygen content had already climbed from 18 to 20 percent.

Go, Tom thought. Go, you bastard, go.

He climbed over the gate again, this time feeling it in his injured side, and hurried for the door that Clarke had originally brought him in by. He was thirty yards away when the door suddenly slid open to reveal Wasserman, silhouetted by the lights in the corridor, carrying a replacement AR-15. As Tom skidded to a stop, Wasserman swung the rifle around and brought the stock to his shoulder.

Tom saw a doorway marked KITCHEN. He flung himself headlong through it, landing on hands and knees.

He took in the scene in an instant. He was on the tile floor of a huge, ultramodern kitchen, with solid elements on the stove so there were no flames or glowing coils. A massive walk-in refrigerator stood next to a long row of stainless steel sinks. Waiters filled short-stemmed wine glasses with red fluid from an iced keg and carried them out on trays. The air reeked like a butcher's shop. Tom felt his stomach lurch.

He saw the hunger in the waiters' eyes as they handled the glasses, saw the hostility as they looked down at him, and understood that they were all apprentice predators, Roxannes and Clarkes in the making. He scrambled to his feet and ran past them for the only available exit, straight across the kitchen and through the double doors into the dining room.

He froze as the room slowly went silent and eyes began to turn toward him. He felt like half a mackerel, oozing blood, that had been dropped into a shark tank.

The room was wedge-shaped, two stories high, the narrow end filled by a stage, the rear wall made up of windows and sliding glass doors that opened onto the deck. Tables dotted the tiered floor space, each on its own level, each holding a dozen predators. They were all between 30 and 50, all fit and expensively dressed, and Tom realized with a jolt that they were seated in perfect alternation, male and female, at all of the tables. Tom saw Roxanne, high up near the windows, and at a table nearby, Wallace Vandermeer, the owner of Susan's paper. Waiters had been placing glasses at every setting, and now they too had stopped and were turning to stare at Tom.

He edged along a side wall, making for the glass patio doors. Some of the predators were getting to their feet, unsure exactly what they should do, when a sudden, shrill alarm went off. At the same instant, Wasserman kicked open the kitchen doors and ran out with his rifle extended.

Tom dodged between two of the tables so that Wasserman couldn't get an unobstructed shot. The predators were confused, some with their hands over their ears, others covering their goblets protectively. A low hiss of conversation began to build under the shriek of the alarm.

DA Clarke pushed his way in through the main doors, saw Tom, and shot him a look of unadulterated hatred. He pulled out his phone, said something into it, and the alarm shut off.

In the sudden silence, Tom heard Roxanne say, quietly and clearly, "Unbelievable."

"I apologize for this incident," Clarke said. "If all of you will please take your seats, we'll have things under control in a moment."

More armed guards came in the main door behind Clarke, and he waved at them to spread out around the room. "Set your weapons for single shot. Wait until you have him in the clear. There will be *no* accidents, is that understood?"

"No *more* accidents, you mean?" Roxanne said. She had ignored his order to sit.

Tom tasted the difference in the air, the sweetness of the oxygen. Things were looking up. If he could only avoid getting shot by half a dozen heavily armed men and get out of the dome past 200 inde-structible predators, he might have a faint chance of living through the night.

He grabbed one of the goblets from the nearest table and sniffed. Yes, definitely blood.

"Put that back," said the man he'd taken it from.

Tom grabbed another goblet and held them both up, in hopes it might discourage them from tackling him. His right arm wouldn't go as high as his left.

He looked at Roxanne. "So this is the best of the best? All gathered together for your bloodthirsty little orgy. To make new little monsters."

"The human race is washed up, Tom," she said. "We're what's next."

"Roxanne, please," Clarke said. "Sit down. Let me handle this."

Tom moved slowly toward the glass doors again, weaving between tables to use the predators for cover, holding up the goblets as feeble hostages.

"Shut up, Matthew," Roxanne said. She looked at Tom again. "You're washed up because you got greedy."

"You're calling *me* greedy?"

"You made the world that we've adapted to. You plundered the environment. You made money the measure of everything. Now you get to see who's *really* bad."

"Okay, Roxanne," Tom said. "Let's see."

He threw both goblets high in the air. While all the predators stared at them, he jerked the curtain from the glass doors and fumbled with the latch. A noise came from behind him, like a stifled mechanical sneeze, and a starred hole appeared in the window an inch from his head.

He ducked, tugged, and the door slid open as another shot hummed past his ear.

SUSAN, HALFWAY ACROSS the parking lot, said, "What was that?"

"Sounded like a gunshot," Litton said. He was half-turned, hesitant, listening.

Two more shots followed, then a third.

She and Litton stared at each other and then turned and ran toward the Dome.

•

TOM DOVE THROUGH the door and rolled as more shots pinged through the metal and glass. He ran to the edge of the deck and looked over the railing in the near darkness. The river was the only thing below him and he had nowhere left to run.

He looked toward the dome in time to see sparks fly as a bullet ricocheted off a metal girder. A pair of them landed on one of the curtains, turning into brown dots. And then, in the oxygen-rich atmosphere, the dots grew into flames. The curtain flicked out in the breeze from the open door and Tom saw the flames leap from the curtain to the lace shawl around one of the predator's necks. She erupted in fire and it spread instantly to the predators on either side of her.

Tom, his body moving in thoughtless reflex, wrenched one of the giant umbrellas loose from its table and climbed over the railing as the entire Dome exploded.

AS SUSAN BEGAN to run, the Dome vanished in a gigantic ball of fire.

A wall of boiling air lifted her off her feet and hurled her onto the asphalt, tearing the back of her sweatshirt and leaving her stunned. For a few heartbeats she couldn't remember where she was, and then she struggled onto her hands and knees, looking for Tom.

No. Tom wasn't there. Tom was in the Dome.

FOR AN INSTANT, the umbrella checked Tom's fall, and then the fabric inverted and the struts tore themselves to pieces. He hit the water feet first and kept going, deeper and deeper, until he bounced off the moss-covered rocks at the bottom and the current swept him away.

THE FIRE ROARED ON, black smoke pouring into the sky, so hot that she had to retreat. A hand grabbed her arm and she turned to see Litton, his face blackened by smoke.

"Come on," he said.

"Tom..." she said.

"There's nobody left alive in there. Come away."

"Where...?"

"Somebody blew that place up. If it was your boyfriend, and he got out, he's going to wash up downstream."

Susan looked back at the ruins of the Dome. One of the steel cables that tied it to the rim of the canyon was anchored a hundred feet away. As she watched, it darkened and reddened and began to stretch and melt. The blazing, smoking infrastructure of the Dome tilted, rocked, and tore free, plummeting into the river below.

TOM CAME TO with his head underwater and his lungs empty of air. He managed to roll his head sidewise and spit and take a huge, shuddering breath.

He saw that he'd hung up on a boulder at the edge of the river. Steaming debris rushed past him on the current, the remains of the wooden deck, followed by charred sheets and pillows and scraps of carpet. Tom reached out and snagged an orange as it floated by. It was warm to the touch. He tore it apart and stuffed the pieces in his mouth. After believing himself dead for so long, he was suddenly all appetite.

He crawled onto the riverbank on hands and knees. He hurt in so many places that he didn't dare take inventory. His clothes were in shreds and he'd lost his shoes somewhere along the line.

In the last rays of the sunset, a haze of smoke still lingered at the top of the hill where the Dome had been. In front of him was a narrow bridge that he remembered crossing early that afternoon. An old man stood with his fishing rod leaning against the concrete railing as he stared up at the fire.

Holding the wound in his side, which was seeping blood, limping on both legs, Tom managed to climb the embankment. "Hey!" he shouted to the old man.

The old man glanced at him, then looked away.

"Hey!" Tom shouted. "You need to go for help. There's a fire up at the Dome!"

The old man looked down at the debris in the river and shook his head.

LITTON HAD THE SIREN on as they raced downhill. The sun was almost down, the forest submerged in twilight. Susan's thoughts were chaotic—shock from the explosion, joy that the predators were dead, fear that sooner or later the ones who hadn't been in the Dome would come after her. And above all, the edge of a pain too bitter to bear, the thought that Tom too had died in the fire. She would not give in to that one until Litton had played out his far-fetched hope that Tom had washed up downstream.

"Those people up there," Litton said. "There was something not right about them. Other than, you know, them being lawyers."

"Yes," Susan said.

"Are you going to tell me?"

First she shook her head, then she changed her mind. "I'll tell you one thing. There won't be anything left of their bodies, but if they can find any traces—toothbrushes, sheets they slept in, plates they ate off of—you need to test the DNA. Tell them to count the chromosomes."

"Count the chromosomes?"

"That's it," Susan said.

They came around a sharp turn and Litton slowed. An old man was packing up his fishing tackle on a bridge. Litton said, "This is where I—"

Susan saw something move in the trees on the other side of the river. "Stop the car!"

She didn't dare hope. The cruiser lurched to a stop and Susan jumped out. "Tom?" she called. She ran across the bridge toward the shadow moving out of the underbrush. "Tom?"

He stepped into the headlights of the cruiser. He was battered and bleeding but walking under his own power. Susan ran to him and threw her arms around him. They stood that way until the love and relief and gratitude had finished battering her and she thought she might be able to speak.

"How bad is it?" she whispered.

"You could maybe...squeeze a little more gently."

Laughing and crying, Susan let him go. She put one of his arms around her neck and Litton ran up to take the other one.

"You must be Tom," Litton said.

"I guess I must be," Tom said.

"We'll get you to the hospital in Eureka."

"No," Susan said. "Got any doctors who owe you a favor? We're going to have to make ourselves very scarce for a while."

Litton nodded. "I expect that can be arranged."

They were crossing the bridge when Tom lurched to a stop. The old man, head down, carrying his rod and tackle box, was about to pass them on the other side of the road.

"Hey, mister," Tom said. "How come you wouldn't go for help?"

The old man stopped, looked Tom up and down. "Wasn't nobody up there but a bunch of bloodsuckers."

"What?" Susan said.

"Lawyers!" the old man said. "Nothing but bloodsuckers. Let 'em burn."

Tom began to laugh. His voice had an edge of hysteria. Susan touched his cheek and helped him into the cruiser. She got in beside him and cradled his head against her shoulder.

As the cruiser began to move, a fire truck screamed by, headed toward the top of the mountain, where the last tendrils of smoke dissolved into the coming night.

# DOGLANDIA

I N THE FIRST LIGHT of morning, the dogs came down from the bluffs above the river to forage for leftovers in the dump. Once it had been Toby's favorite time of day—the grass damp and cool under his paws, the air a jumble of smells from the old and new garbage, always exciting, always different.

Lately those days of abundant garbage were a distant dream. People used the new dump on the other side of town more and more, and all eight of the dogs were thinner and hungrier than they'd ever been. Sometimes Toby didn't even bother to pick his way downhill only to struggle to climb back up again.

Toby was small, and more and more often the big dogs would take away his best finds. Every now and then, though, he'd gulp down a mouthful or two and then sprint with the rest to a narrow cleft between two rocks where the big dogs couldn't follow. On this particular morning he counted himself lucky to polish off a few rotting cabbage leaves that he would have walked right by in the old days.

He didn't see the new dog approach. One minute Toby was sitting, licking his chops, wondering if the cabbage had been a mistake, and the next he was looking up at a huge black Rottweiler that loomed over him. Humans had clipped the Rottweiler's ears and cut off his tail the way they did sometimes, the entire purpose of which, as far as Toby could tell, was to put them into a permanently bad mood. That certainly was the case with this one.

"Find something?" the Rottweiler said, in a deep, ominous voice.

"Some old cabbage," Toby said, and burped. "It wasn't very good."

The Rottweiler leaned down to smell Toby's breath and Toby instinctively took a step back. "Oh," the Rottweiler said. His gaze shifted away when Toby looked at him.

"It's all gone anyway," Toby said nervously.

"Oh," the Rottweiler said again.

Then he, too, was gone.

KEVIN HAD NEVER been that sick before. He missed two weeks of school and his fever got all the way to 105. He was so sick, he didn't feel like watching TV. He just lay in bed with Doug, his big stuffed blue dog, and half-slept all day long.

Kevin had wanted a real dog as long as he could remember, more than anything. His mom had explained that it was not possible. Ever since Kevin's dad had left, when Kevin was only a baby, they'd had to move a lot. The kind of apartments they stayed in—cheap ones— mostly didn't allow dogs.

On the first day that he'd felt well enough to go back to school, after supper and homework and a shower, Kevin went to bed early. It was then that he discovered that Doug was gone.

He looked under the bed and in the closet and in the dirty clothes hamper. The search started to get frantic and noisy, and that was when his mother came in. She was wearing the Bad News look that Kevin hated.

"Honey, I had to get rid of Doug. And all the sheets and your toothbrush and even your pillows. You were really sick and I didn't want to take the chance that you'd get infected again."

"What do you mean 'get rid of'? What are you talking about? Doug wouldn't make me sick again, that's just crazy."

"Kevin, you know I don't like that word. I had to throw all those things away."

"Throw Doug away? Like a piece of garbage?"

"Now calm down, honey. You're too old to be playing with stuffed animals anyway."

Kevin saw that she wasn't going to change her mind. The deed was done, as she liked to say. And then she did say it, to put an end to the discussion.

All that night Kevin thought about Doug being thrown on some

garbage dump somewhere, and it made him so sad he could hardly
stand it.

SOMETIMES THERE WERE as many as 15 of them, and then, cats
being cats, some would get restless and move on and there might
be only as many as nine or ten. Rita, a small black-and-gray tabby,
had been at the dump more than a year now, living on the mice and
roaches and other creatures that thrived in the garbage.

The life was not without its dangers. The city would sometimes
put out traps and poison to keep the animal population down. And
a pack of wild dogs lived on the bluff above the river. The dogs
mostly roamed by day, when the cats had retreated to the woods to
sleep, and as long as they stayed out of each other's way, they were
able to maintain an uneasy peace.

So it gave Rita a bad moment the night that she came upon a
dog's face staring at her from a pile of trash. She did a backward
somersault and landed with all four legs spread on a flattened cardboard box, facing the wrong way, with the breath startled out of her.
She was struggling to get her legs under her so that she could run
away when she realized that something was not right about the dog.

She turned slowly. The dog hadn't moved from where it lay,
mostly buried under a pile of cloth and paper. Its fur, she saw now,
was blue, and its eyes oversized and shiny and unnatural. She arched
her back and hissed at it, and it didn't react at all.

She crept up to it, sniffing. It smelled of humans and not like
a dog at all. She bumped her nose against the dog's nose and got
no reaction, so she grabbed the nape of its neck in her mouth and
pulled it free from the pile. It appeared to be some kind of toy,
larger than Rita, stuffed with something white and fuzzy that leaked
out of a slit in its belly.

Rita knew what toys were. Long ago, when she'd been a kitten,
she'd lived with humans. They used to fill small furry toys with
catnip and let her play with them. They also fed her and petted her
and talked to her in voices she couldn't understand. One day she'd

wandered away and been unable to find her way back, and she'd
been living on her own ever since.

Rita looked around. No one else had seen the toy dog. Without
knowing why, Rita covered it back up with the pieces of cloth and
marked the place in her mind so that she could find it again.

FALL HAD COME. The nights felt chilly now, and the dogs slept
together in a big pile in the Hollow at the top of the Bluffs. Oak
and pine trees and sticker bushes and clumps of dried pine needles
made a natural windbreak around the Hollow and on even the
coldest nights Toby was comforted by the heat and tangy smells of
the other dogs.

The sun had been down for a while and the heat of the day
had leached out into a clear sky. Toby was dozing at the edge of
the dogpile when Fang, an old part-Husky mutt who claimed her
mother was a wolf, sat up and took a couple of tentative yips at
the moon. Ilse, a Shepherd mix lying next to Toby, barked at her to
knock it off. "If you're a wolf," Ilse said, "I'm an iguana."

Fang was quiet for a while, then she said, "What's an iguana?"

Ilse was not in the mood. "It doesn't matter because I'm not one,
I'm a dog, and so are you, so be quiet and go to sleep."

Toby yawned. Sleep sounded good. He closed his eyes and was
starting to drift off when he felt something cold and wet on his muzzle. He opened his eyes to see the Rottweiler's face filling his vision.

"Yipe!" Toby said.

"Hush," the Rottweiler said. "Come over here, I want to talk
to you."

Toby had a policy that applied to this situation. The policy
was, don't argue with big dogs. He followed the Rottweiler to a
rocky outcropping near the Cliff, where a straight vertical rock
face dropped all the way to the river far below. Max, a skinny little
Dachshund, waited there with shining eyes and a wagging tail. They
sniffed each other quickly in greeting and then the Rottweiler said,
"My name is Bruno. Do you want to be in our club?"

"Club?" Toby said. "What kind of club?"

"It's going to be cool," Max said.

Bruno said, "It's a kind of a mutual protection society."

"Whatever that is," Max said.

"Protection from what?" Toby said. "Nobody bothers us much. Being cold or being hungry, that's about all we have to worry about."

Bruno showed him a thin, superior smile. "You're fooling your-self—what's your name?"

"Toby."

"You're fooling yourself, Toby. You have plenty to be afraid of."

"I do?"

"You're a purebred, aren't you?"

"I don't know. I never knew my parents. I've been here at the dump as long as I can remember."

"I've got a good eye for these things, and I think you're a pure-bred Corgi."

"I am?"

"A very distinguished breed, from the old country. Herding dog. Natural leader."

"Wow."

"And I bet some of those big mixed-breed dogs take food away from you sometimes."

"Well, yeah, but that's what big dogs do."

Bruno leaned toward him with a fixed stare. "The mixed breeds have no pride. We must tolerate them because they are fellow Dogs, but they can only serve in inferior ways. They have no nobility."

"I hadn't noticed that."

"You have to pay attention. The worst danger is the danger you don't see. Then there's raccoons. Thieves, all of them. And buzzards. Hawks."

"Gosh, none of them ever bothered me."

"Consider yourself lucky, then. But the worst of all, the absolute bottom rung of the evolutionary ladder..."

"Yeah!" Max said. "Tell him, Boss!"

"What?" Toby said. He'd always been a happy and easy-going dog. This whole conversation made him very nervous. "What is it?"

Bruno bent down until his muzzle was next to Toby's ear. He growled a single word: "Cats."

"Cats?" Toby said.

"Cats!" Max yelped, and started to run around in a circle. "Cats! Cats!"

"What about them?" Toby said. "I mean, I don't like cats any better than the next dog, but why should I be afraid?"

"Because they're out to get us," Bruno said. "They're sneaky, they're mean, and their poop smells really, really bad. There's not enough food for all of us, so why should we have to share with a bunch of stinking cats?"

"They catch mice and eat bugs," Toby said. "Who wants to share that?"

"You don't have to believe me," Bruno said. "Once push comes to shove, you'll see."

Toby thought that for a big dog, Bruno seemed awfully scared and lonely. It sounded like he just wanted to have some friends and didn't know how to go about it. "Who's in the club so far?"

"Max and myself. It's very exclusive at the moment. We're only allowing purebreds in as founding members. You would be our third. If you wanted to, that is."

"Does the club have a name?"

Bruno looked embarrassed. "Right now it's called The We Hate Cats Club. We're working on something better."

What could it hurt? Toby thought. It would be nice to have a big dog for a friend. He might even get to eat a little better.

"Okay," he said. "Count me in."

RITA LOVED MICE. They were funny looking, they gave her exercise and thrills, and they tasted good besides. Once you got used to them, anyway.

She'd been on the trail of one particular mouse for a long time now, well into the darkest part of the night. In the old days, there'd been so many mice that the hunt never lasted long. Lately there were not only fewer of them, they were quicker and skinnier and had better hiding places.

This one had led Rita to the edge of the dump, where the land began to rise to the Bluffs where the dogs lived. With no more garbage to hide under, the mouse finally darted out onto open ground, the way Rita had pictured it. Rita pounced, too tired and hungry to play any more with her food. Clamping her dinner in her jaws, she was about to turn back toward the woods when a deep-voiced dog barked, "Halt!"

Rita froze, then, annoyed with herself for obeying a dog, she looked over her shoulder. A big Rottweiler, his eyes reflecting the moonlight in a spooky way, glared at her from a short distance away on the hillside. Beside him stood a Dachshund, a little dog that might be part Corgi, and one of those Chihuahua dogs with the pointy faces. Rita couldn't talk with the mouse in her mouth, so she merely glared back.

"Hand it over," the Rottweiler said.

"Yeah, yeah, hand it over," said the Dachshund.

Rita spat the mouse out and put one paw on its tail to keep it from getting away. "What are you doing down here at night?" She heard the nervousness in her own voice. "This is cat time."

"We're Dogs," the Rottweiler said. "We can do whatever we want."

"Suit yourselves, but this is *my* mouse. I've been chasing it forever. What do you want it for, anyway? Dogs don't eat mice."

"None of your business," the Rottweiler said. "Your job is to do what you're told. Now give me the mouse."

Rita's legs were trembling. "No way."

"Then we'll take it anyway," the Rottweiler said. "Come on!" he yelled to the other dogs, and suddenly they all rushed at her, the Rottweiler's huge teeth flashing bright white against the darkness of his coat. Rita had no time to think. She abandoned the mouse and ran for the nearest tree, fifty yards away.

The dogs were all baying now, which was a good thing, because they were using up their breath that way instead of putting it into their running. Just the same, it was a terrifying sound, and Rita couldn't tell if they were getting closer. She was fear on four legs. She leapt for the tree as soon as it was in range and ran up the side of it. The dogs, unable to stop, skidded past her tree and into the woods, where there was a terrible crashing sound and a startled yip.

Rita was still trying to catch her breath when the dogs tramped back into the clearing. The Rottweiler stopped every few steps to put one paw to his head. "It was a feline trick," he said. "That cat ran me into that tree on purpose."

"They're tricky all right," the Dachshund said. "You always say that, Boss. How tricky they are."

Rita, from a high branch, saw them clearly in the moonlight as they formed a circle around her mouse.

"Now what?" the Corgi mix said. "I'm not going to eat that."

"Maybe not," the Rottweiler said, "but neither is that cat." He picked it up in his jaws and made a disgusted face. The other dogs followed him up the hill.

Once she was sure they were gone, Rita went looking for Spike, the toughest cat in the dump. She found him by the river, chasing a fish through the shallows. The fish laughed at him as it flopped out of Spike's grasp and shot away into deep water.

"I hate fish," Spike said. He was a big, muscular black cat with white socks and stomach.

"Until you catch one," Rita said. "Listen, I think we have a problem."

"No kidding. I haven't eaten since yesterday."

"I mean a new problem. With the dogs. A pack of them just now came down and took a mouse away from me."

"At night? And took a mouse? That's weird."

"They're up to something. I don't like it."

"Like it or not," Spike said, "there's nothing we can do about it. They're dogs. We can't fight them."

"We can't let them come down here and take what little food there is."

"Face it, Rita. They can if they want. If the dogs decide to run us out of here, that's it. We're gone."

BRUNO AND MAX talked up their night-time adventure, the story getting more dramatic every time they told it, until Toby no longer remembered exactly how many cats they'd faced down, or how badly they'd been scratched in the fight. Bruno was the only one with obvious injuries, which he claimed he'd gotten when three, no, four huge toms had caught him alone by some big rocks.

Toby wondered whether this was before or after Bruno ran into the tree, because he didn't remember Bruno ever being by himself. He decided, however, that he would keep quiet for now.

In any case, the adventure got them two more members. With the addition of Pierre, the oversized poodle, they had their first big dog besides Bruno. Then Fang wanted to join, and Bruno made a speech about how membership was now open to wolves as well as dogs.

"Fang," Toby said, when Bruno finally began to wind down, "is *not* a wolf."

"Part wolf," Fang said.

"I've got a good eye for these things," Bruno said, "and I say she's a wolf."

If Bruno could be so wrong about Fang, Toby wondered, what did that say for his belief that Toby was a purebred Corgi?

"What difference does it make?" Toby said. "I don't care whether she's a wolf or not. She's our friend, and that's all that matters."

Bruno had been sitting on his haunches. He quickly stood up to his full height and flexed his front legs so that the muscles stood out on his massive neck and shoulders. "Are you questioning my authority?"

"Who, me?" Toby said, squatting involuntarily and releasing a little pee into the dirt. "No, no, not at all."

"Good," Bruno said. He sat down again and said, "Fang's wolf heritage will be very important to us later in the struggle."

It was getting late, and Toby had been up most of the night before. All he really wanted was to crawl into the Hollow and get some sleep. Unlike Bruno, who was always full of energy and whose eyes always had a fierce, yellow-green glow. Some of the other dogs had wandered over to the Hollow, thinking the same thing as Toby. They began to settle in with a lot of scratching and snuffling and yawning.

Suddenly Bruno marched into the middle of them and said, "I have an announcement. From now on, the Hollow is reserved for club members only."

At that moment a cold wind came up out of the north, ruffling the dogs' fur and making Toby shiver.

"What?" Ilse barked. "You're telling *me* where I can and can't sleep?"

Ilse was most definitely not in the club. Toby had been there when Bruno invited her and she'd laughed in his face. "I wouldn't be in any club," she'd said, "that would have *you* in it."

"Fang?" Bruno said. "Pierre?" Fang and Pierre trotted over and stood on either side of Bruno. Now it was three big dogs against one. Toby saw the first flicker of doubt in Ilse's eyes.

Bruno saw it too. "Get out," he said, baring his teeth at her. Max pranced back and forth behind Bruno on his tiny legs, barking and letting out threatening yips.

Ilse looked to King for support. King was the oldest of them, a big yellow dog with intelligent eyes. All the younger dogs respected him, even though the fur on his muzzle had gone gray and his hips had gotten so stiff that he could hardly walk.

"If you let them do this," Ilse said to him, "they'll come after you next."

King looked at her with his sad brown eyes, then stared at the ground in front of him.

Ilse got to her feet. The hair on the back of her neck stood up and Toby found himself wishing she would go after Bruno. This business with the Hollow wasn't right. Toby was too small to do anything about it himself, but he was sure that Bruno would back down if Ilse attacked.

Ilse must have thought otherwise. She growled one more time and then her tail went down between her legs and she slunk away. At the edge of the clearing she stopped to look back—not at Bruno or King, but at Toby. The look was full of disappointment.

Bruno turned to King. "I'm going to give you a choice. As a mixed breed, you can become an honorary member of the club and stay where you are. Or you can leave with Ilse."

King licked his chops noisily, something he'd been doing a lot of lately. "What do honorary members have to do?"

"Nothing at all. They can just lie here in the Hollow and sleep if they want."

"Can I think about it?"

"Yes. But if you sleep in Hollow, that means you've made your decision, and you're one of us."

"Okay," King said. "I'll think about it." He closed his eyes and was asleep in seconds.

Bruno assigned Max to guard duty. His job was to tell any of the other dogs who showed up that they had to become honorary members too, or get out. If there was a problem, he was to come find Bruno. Since the only dog left who wasn't in the club was Tippy, a wire-haired terrier who was not too sharp, Max wagged his tail excitedly and began to march back and forth in front of the entrance to the Hollow, ears cocked forward.

Toby sat by himself for a long time. He kept remembering the way Ilse had looked at him. But the night was cold, and before too long he crept silently down into the Hollow, curled up next to King, and went to sleep.

A WEEK OR SO after the dogs took her mouse away, Rita woke up in the middle of the day to a sound she'd never heard before. First the Rottweiler would call out something, then what sounded like all of the other dogs would answer back, "Bark *bark!*" in perfect unison.

At first Rita thought it was a bad dream. She had them sometimes, especially one where a giant mouse held her down and tickled her paws. This particular nightmare, with the dogs shouting, was going on entirely too long, until Rita thought she might start barking too. She went down to the river to get away from the noise and found some of the other cats there.

"We really have to do something," Rita said.

Spike shrugged and licked one paw. "Maybe the humans will notice the dogs have gone crazy and take them all away to the Shelter."

"We can't just wait and hope," Rita said.

Hooky, a gray male tabby, said, "Maybe we should go away, find another place to live."

Male cats didn't like to be called cowards, so instead Rita said, "We have every bit as much of a right to be here as they do."

Chiang, an old Siamese, said, "Those dogs are so stupid, they're more likely to hurt themselves than anybody else."

"Maybe somebody could reason with them," Rita said.

"Reason?" Spike said. "With a dog?"

"Try it if you want," Hooky said. "I don't want to be around to watch what happens next."

Rita shook her head. "I don't know. Maybe there's a way."

She walked into the dump, not thinking about where she was going. She found herself in the place where she'd discovered the big blue toy dog, and she got an itchy feeling in the back of her brain. She pawed at the papers on top of it in a random way, and then she pulled it free of the nest of used tissues and other trash and laid it out on the piece of cardboard where she could look at it. She walked around it a couple of times, and then she poked and prodded it until it slumped over on its side and the slit in its belly was exposed.

Still in the grip of a mental picture she didn't fully understand, she pulled at the broken seam with her claws and teeth. It was hard work not to tear the fabric, and once she got the seam open and started pulling out the stuffing, it left a nasty, chemical taste in her mouth. Still, she got it all out, and spat a few times to clean off her tongue, and then she sat and stared at it for a long time with her head tilted to one side.

IN THE OLD DAYS, Toby had been bored a lot. The only things to do had been to sleep and to look for food. Now Bruno had them doing things all the time. He said it was part of running things like a business, to which Max had said, "Whatever that is." Now everyone was on a team, and everyone had a job to do, and if you didn't do your job, you didn't eat. A lot of times they didn't eat anyway, though Toby didn't point that out.

Tonight, instead of sleeping, his job was reconnaissance, which turned out to be a lot like spying. He had Max for his partner. At first thought, Max seemed like a poor choice for a spy, seeing as how he was unable to hold still or to stop talking. He seemed like a bad choice at second and third thought too.

Nevertheless, down the hill they climbed, Toby creeping quietly, low to the ground, and Max doing the best he could, yelling "Yikes!" and then "Sorry!" every time something startled him and made him jump or run around in circles.

That was when they ran into the strange blue dog.

Toby had never seen a dog that color before. Or, for that matter, a dog that clumsy. He would take three or four steps and then one of his legs would bend at an impossible angle, and down he would go, only to get back up, biting and clawing at himself.

Toby wondered if the strange dog might have rabies. He'd seen a rabid raccoon once, and the memory of it still frightened him. This blue dog was different, though. He didn't have any foam around his mouth, and wasn't stiff in his back legs—more like the opposite. Still, it was probably a good idea to give him lots of room, maybe follow him from a distance. He was about to whisper that suggestion to Max, but Max had already jumped onto the path and yelled, "Halt! Who goes there? Friend or foe?"

These were the special words Bruno had taught Max to say when he was on guard duty. Apparently Max had gotten too excited to remember that his job at the moment was spying. In fact, he'd gotten so excited that he was unable to control himself and was running in circles around the blue dog.

The blue dog had looked at first like he wanted to run away. His legs had gotten tangled and he sat down instead, then slumped oddly to one side.

Toby sighed and stepped out from behind the rock that had been protecting him. "Forgive my overexcited friend," he said. "We're curious because we haven't seen you around here before."

"I'm new," the blue dog said, in a voice as strange as his behavior, low in the throat and strained. "My name is, uh, Fred."

"Listen," Toby said, "I don't mean to sound rude, but you're not sick are you? You don't seem too steady on your feet."

"Fleas," Fred said, promptly falling on his chin. He then raised one hind leg and thrashed at the air in the rough vicinity of his neck. He looked like a broken wind-up toy winding down. "They're driving me crazy, see?"

Toby was anything but reassured. He was trying to think of a good exit line when Max cut in. "Are you going to join the club? Are you? Are you?"

"What club is that?"

"The *club*," Max said. "There's only one. Everybody's in it. Except Ilse, and she doesn't count. It's Bruno's club. Bruno is the Big Boss."

"Is Bruno the big Rottweiler?"

"Yep, yep, yep!" Max said. "We're his most trusted lieutenants, he says. Whatever that is."

"What does this club do?"

"We hate cats!" Max said.

"Well," Fred said. "I sure hate cats, all right. Yes sir, I hate cats like poison."

"Mostly," Toby said, "we do whatever Bruno tells us to do."

"Interesting," Fred said. He was looking at Toby and ignoring

Max, who was so excited now that he was springing completely off the ground with all four legs at once. "Sure," Fred said, "I'll join your club."

Reluctantly, Toby introduced himself and Max and they all sniffed each other's rear ends.

"Max?" Toby said. "Why don't you go on with the mission while I take Fred to meet Bruno?"

"Okay!" Max said, and pranced down the hillside, starting small avalanches of dirt and rocks.

"Max!" Toby said. Max turned and galloped back up to where they were. "Stealth," Toby said. "Don't let them hear you."

"Yep, yep! Stealth! Right!" He charged down the hill again.

Fred and Toby made their way toward the Bluffs. "You smell kind of like humans," Toby said.

"I only ran away yesterday."

"Did they have cats? Because, no offense, you kind of smell like a cat too."

"That's why I ran away. Too many cats, always crawling all over me. I hate cats. I sure do."

Fred was walking better with each step, as if he were just learning how. By the time they got to the top, he was moving almost normally.

They found Bruno in the Hollow, eyes open, staring off into the distance.

"Bruno, this is Fred. He wants to join the club."

Bruno lifted his head and looked Fred up and down. "What kind of a Dog are you?"

"Um, Australian Blue Heeler?"

"I've heard of that," Bruno said. "And you're certainly blue enough."

"Yes, sir. Whatever you say, sir."

"Hmmmm. I like your attitude. You'll do well here." He looked at Toby. "Good job—what was your name again?"

"Toby."

"Ah, yes. Good job, Toby. Now get on with your reconnaissance, and I'll explain to Fred here what we're up against."

Toby looked back once before he started downhill. Bruno and Fred were deep in conversation.

Bruno had never explained anything to Toby. He couldn't even remember Toby's name, even though Toby was only the second dog to join the club.

It wasn't fair.

In a way, Rita liked being in the dog suit. Like most cats, she liked being touched all over, and she was cozy and warm when the wind blew. She'd used pine sap to glue together the edges of the slit in the toy dog's belly, and that was working well. The holes she'd made above the dog's glass eyes were less successful, and she had trouble seeing out of them at first. She was falling all over herself when Toby and the Dachshund found her, and she still didn't believe she'd managed to fool them. Good thing dogs weren't very bright.

As for Bruno, a little phony respect and he was eating out of her hand. He claimed to base his philosophy on pure logic, then turned around and used logic to justify being at the mercy of his emotions. Once Rita got him talking about his past, the story came tumbling out.

"What does it mean, anyway, 'cat person'?" Bruno asked her. "I think that's the stupidest thing I ever heard. Are you not a *real* person if you're a 'cat person'?"

"Tell me what happened," Rita said.

"My mistress got a new boyfriend who was a 'cat person.' He was always complaining about me barking and sleeping in the bed and chewing up his shoes. And, you know, needing to go outside. Not like a cat, who does his business in the house and smells the place up. How disgusting is that? So then he moves in and brings his cat with him, and the cat is always starting fights with me, which I get blamed for. The next thing I know, she gives me away to some total strangers."

Rita had trouble focusing on Bruno's story because she was remembering her own long-lost home.

Bruno sighed and lay down with his head on his paws. "The new people made me live in the back yard. And I didn't even have a doghouse to get out of the rain. They used to put me in the bed of their pickup truck and drive around. One day we were stopped at a light and I saw a cat that looked like the boyfriend's cat. I got a little crazy and jumped out to chase it. I don't think they even noticed I was gone."

"Did you catch the cat?"

"No," Bruno said. "It tricked me."

"Cats," Rita said. "They'll do that. They're the worst."

She'd had this vague idea that if she looked like a dog, she could argue the cats' point of view and the dogs would listen. Now she saw that Bruno was so full of rage and blame that there was no room for understanding. He'd focused all his disappointment on the feline species and Rita had no hope of reasoning with that.

"Yes," Bruno said. "They're evil. They're down there right now, plotting against us. I don't know what their plan is, but it's going to be bad news for us Dogs unless we stop them."

"Stop them how?"

Bruno sat up tall. "We will drive them into the sea!"

Rita stared at him. "Seriously? How are we going to do that? There's no sea within a thousand miles of us. Sir."

Bruno jumped to his feet and barked, "To the sea! We will drive them into the sea!"

Rita jumped, got tangled in the dog suit, and ended up unable to move. When she got her breath back, she said, "Drive them in cars? How do you think you're going to get them there?"

Bruno sat down again, suddenly calm. "It's good that you're not afraid. I was just testing you. 'Drive them into the sea' is only a, a..."

"Figure of speech?" Rita suggested.

"Right. One of those."

Rita knew it hadn't been a test. Bruno was seriously crazy, and he went in and out of his mind like Rita used to go in and out of her cat door.

"If we drive them into the river," Bruno said, "it comes to the same thing. You have to put things in a big, dramatic way sometimes to get your point across."

"I get your point," Rita said. "Believe me, I get it."

"What are you sneaking around for?" a voice said.

Toby froze. The voice came from the night sky directly above him, and what's more, it was a cat's voice, a kind of mush-mouthed yowl. He looked slowly upward and finally made out a large tuxedo cat lying on a branch of a twisted old oak tree.

"Uh, nothing," Toby said.

"There's no food for you in the woods. This is where we sleep during the day. Speaking of which, you're supposed to be asleep now. What do you want?"

"I'm, uh, just looking around." Bruno hadn't told him what to do if he got caught. "I didn't mean any harm."

"What's your name?"

"Toby."

"I'm Spike."

Toby bobbed his head. He couldn't truthfully say that he was pleased to meet a cat.

"Listen, Toby, what do you know about what's going on up there on the Bluffs?"

"On the Bluffs?" Toby said.

"All the barking and carrying on."

"Barking?"

Spike sighed. "I suppose this means you're part of it. Are you going to tell me what it's all about?"

Toby scratched at some pine needles, circled around a couple of times, lay down, then got up again. He scratched one ear and then said, "It's this big dog, Bruno."

"Big Rottweiler?"

"Yeah. He's got this club, see."

"What kind of a club?"

He stopped himself from saying the name of the club just in time. He ducked his head and put his tail between his legs and started to walk away, looking mournfully over one shoulder.

"Wait!" Spike said. "It's something to do with us cats, isn't it?"

Toby bobbed his head again.

"Good thing I can see in the dark," Spike said. "He's planning something bad, isn't he?"

Toby, utterly miserable, nodded again.

"What is it? What's he planning?"

"I don't know!" Toby cried. "He doesn't talk to me!"

"But you're in this club, aren't you? *Aren't you?*"

Toby couldn't help himself. The guilt and the anxiety were too overwhelming. His bladder let go and he peed in the middle of the path.

"That really smells awful," Spike said. "Do we come up and pee where you guys sleep?"

"Sometimes," Toby said.

"Yeah, okay, maybe we do, but that's a territorial thing, it's not because we can't control ourselves. I can't believe you're part of this club. You don't seem all that bad, for a dog. Aside from the peeing thing."

"I didn't think he was serious about the cat-hating stuff at first. I thought he just wanted us to like him."

"One of my friends is missing," Spike said. "A gray tabby named Rita. Do you know anything about it?"

"No."

"How come you look so guilty?"

"Because I'm a dog! It's that tone of voice."

"Okay, okay. What about this Bruno? Would he have done something to Rita?"

"No," Toby said. "He doesn't do anything himself, he gets others dogs to do everything for him." The words sounded disloyal once he'd said them, so now he felt guilty about that, too.

"So now that you know Bruno is up to no good," Spike said, "what are you going to do about it?"

Toby was still thinking that over when Max came running up. "Hey, Toby, who you talking to? Are you doing reconnaissance? Am I interrupting? What's going on?"

Spike made a skittering sound as he climbed farther up the tree, startling Max, who began to bark furiously.

Toby lay on his belly and closed his eyes and put his front paws over his ears.

THE NEXT DAY, Rita listened in her dog suit while Bruno led an All Dogs Meeting. He announced that the area formerly called the Bluffs would henceforth be known as the Independent Nation of Doglandia. Cats were no longer permitted within its borders. Where exactly those borders were was not entirely clear.

Bruno also revealed that military training was now mandatory, and he ordered all Dogs to report to the training field at noon. It turned out that the training field was the big clearing at the very top of the Bluffs, next to the Hollow, and bounded on the one end by the Cliff, a sheer drop to the river below.

The training itself consisted of everyone chasing sticks that they were supposed to pretend were cats. Bruno had figured out a way to throw them by holding them in his mouth and then snapping his head sharply to one side. The sticks didn't go terribly far, and with all the dogs chasing them at once, chaos ruled. The dogs ran into each other, knocked each other down, rolled each other into the bushes, and snapped and growled at each other.

Rita didn't participate. She'd fed Bruno a tale about having a delicate constitution and having to make constant trips to the vet in her earlier life, all because she wasn't big and strong and rugged like Bruno was. The more flattery she piled on, the more sympathetic he became, until he eventually allowed her to sit on the sidelines.

The dogs enjoyed the play at first, then quickly tired of it.

"Maybe," Rita suggested, "you might want to take it easy on them the first day, sir. Build them up gradually."

"Oh, all right," Bruno said. "At ease!"

The other dogs flopped down in the dirt, and Bruno began to pace back and forth, lecturing them. If there was logic to the speech, Rita missed it, though she would be the first to admit she was not paying a lot of attention. The general idea was that Dogs had a special destiny to rule over all other animals, which was why they were Shepherds and Cow Dogs and Hunting Dogs.

Whereas cats were a cosmic mistake that needed to be corrected.

He droned on and on, and the exhausted and underfed dogs one by one fell asleep. As soon as their eyes closed, Max rushed at them, yelling, "Wake up, up, up, up!" The glass eyes on Rita's dog suit never closed, so she was able to nap a bit between Max's assaults.

Finally it was over. Some of the dogs went down to the river to drink, and Rita tagged along. She hung back from the others and finally slipped away and got out of the dog suit long enough to catch and eat a vole. The river ran high and fast because of the fall rains upstream, and Rita watched it for a while, thinking how you never appreciated how good you had things until they changed on you, first when she'd had a house and humans to wait on her, and then at the dump before Bruno came along and spoiled everything.

Toby liked the first day of training well enough. The second day left him less than enthusiastic. He snuck away during the speech afterward without Max noticing and stole partway down the hill, moving into the wind. He was looking for a good place to curl up and nap when he picked up a familiar scent.

"Ilse?" Toby said.

"Who's there?" Her voice came from the far side of a pile of boulders.

"Just me, Toby."

"Nobody else is with you? Not that yappy little Dachshund or anybody?"

"No."

Ilse came out slowly from behind the rocks. She'd lost weight and her eyes flicked from side to side nervously. "What was all the yelling up there the last two days?"

Toby explained about Doglandia and the training and the speeches. "I don't like being in this club anymore," he said.

"Yes, well," Ilse said. "Maybe you should have thought about that before you joined. How does everybody else feel?"

"Except for the yappy little Dachshund, I don't think anybody is especially happy about it."

"If you all stood up to him at once..."

"You've seen him. At least one or two of us would get killed. And we'd have to be prepared to kill him. I don't know about the others, but me, I don't have the instinct for it."

Ilse sighed. "I suppose we could all go live somewhere else."

"Bruno's crazy. He'd probably follow us and attack us."

"Well, you should think it over. I'm ashamed that I ran away the other day. If you decide to make a move, I'll be close by. Just call my name."

ON THE THIRD day of training, Rita saw the first signs of resistance. Paco, the Chihuahua, and Tippy, the dim terrier, were grumbling from the start. Bruno barked at them and nipped at their legs, but as soon as he chased one, the other sat down. Then King sauntered over under a tree and went to sleep.

Bruno refused to give up, and with Max egging him on, he kept after them. He grabbed Paco by the neck and shook him hard, and he drew blood when he bit King in the tail. Grudgingly, growlingly, the dogs went through the motions of chasing the sticks. Bruno, his eyes glowing yellow-green, looked on with a mixture of pride and madness.

In the end, Bruno chose not to push his luck. He cut the exercise short, and he kept his speech brief and to the point. "Tomorrow," he said, "is the day we have prepared for. Tomorrow we attack! Tomorrow we drive the cats into the sea!"

"Uh, sir," Rita said. "I think you mean the river."

"Whatever," Bruno said, under his breath, and then he began to bark again. "By tomorrow night our cat problems will be over forever!"

This is it, Rita thought. Time's up. I'd better think of something fast.

TOBY PRETENDED to chase the sticks with the other dogs. Many of them passed looks back and forth as they trotted around, and Toby knew they felt the same way he did, sad and tired and disillusioned.

After his speech, Bruno retreated to the Hollow to make his battle plans for the next day. The rest of the dogs lay down wherever they'd been standing and looked at each other. As soon as Toby's glance connected with that of another dog, the other dog looked away. They were all, Toby realized, waiting for somebody else to speak up first.

Fred, the weird blue dog who had become best friends with Bruno by sucking up to him, walked over and lay down next to Toby. Toby scooted a few inches away to show his disapproval.

"We have to do something," Fred said in his strange, gravelly voice.

Toby shot him a quick, reproachful look and put another inch of distance between them.

"I've been watching you," Fred said, "and I think you're not happy with the way things have been going."

"Oh no," Toby said. "I'm incredibly happy." He thumped his tail in the dirt to prove it. "Bruno is the greatest."

"You don't have to lie to me. I've only been pretending to get on Bruno's good side. I came up here in the first place to find a way to stop him."

"Sure you did," Toby said.

Fred thought a minute, then he got up and repositioned himself so he was facing away from all the other dogs. Then something really strange happened. It looked like there was another animal inside Fred's skin, clawing at Fred's neck from the inside. Then it got even stranger because Fred's head leaned way, way back and a cat's head poked through a slash in Fred's belly.

The cat's head took a deep breath and whispered, in a cat voice, "My real name is Rita and I'm a cat."

Toby could not make sense of what his eyes saw. All four of his paws twitched and he began to whine involuntarily. "This can't be happening."

"Keep your voice down, please," the cat head said. "Or there's going to be a riot."

Fred—Rita—moved the dog head back where it had been before. "We have to talk to the other dogs," he—she—said.

"I already went through this with Ilse."

"Who's Ilse?"

"A German Shepherd that Bruno ran off. There's nothing we can do. If we try anything, dogs could get killed."

"If we *don't* try something, cats will die for sure."

Toby stopped himself from saying the first thing that came into his mind.

"Look," Fred/Rita said. "At least we can get some other dogs on our side. Maybe one of them will know what to do."

Reluctantly, Toby agreed. The obvious first choice was Paco, given the way he'd resisted the day's exercise. Toby made sure Max wasn't around, then casually sauntered over to where Paco lay and stretched out beside him. Despite his casual posture, Toby was tense and scared. A minute or two later, Fred/Rita lay down on his other side. Paco looked from one to the other. "Uh oh," he said. "Am I in trouble?"

Fred/Rita explained, using her dog voice, that they were tired of being in the club and were looking for support. And for ideas about how to get out of it.

"Count me in," Paco said. "Only, I don't know how you're going to get Bruno to give up."

"We'll think of something," Fred/Rita said.

"How about your pal Tippy?" Toby asked.

"He'll go along with anything I tell him to," Paco said. "But if you're looking for ideas, he's not your dog. Let me talk to Pierre. I think he's pretty fed up."

"Okay," Fred/Rita said. "But we need to come up with something fast."

Paco got up, looked both ways, and then crossed the clearing to where Pierre lay.

"King's not going to take a stand," Toby said.

"No," Fred/Rita said. "That leaves Fang."

Talking to Fang struck Toby as a bad idea, though he couldn't say why. "Maybe we should wait, see what Pierre says."

"I'm going," Fred/Rita said. "You can stay here if you want."

Toby thought about Ilse again, and the way she'd looked at him when Bruno ran her off. He thought about the kind of courage it took for a cat to put on a dog suit and walk into the heart of enemy territory. He thought about the harsh things that the cat Spike had said to him. He thought about how he'd spent his whole life doing what big dogs told him to do.

"No," he said. "I'm coming."

Fang was sound asleep, and she jumped when Toby gently nuzzled her neck. "What?" she said. "What happened?"

"Shhhh," Rita said. "Don't get excited. We just want to talk to you."

"Talk?" Fang said. She was sitting up now, practically barking. "Talk about what?"

"Please," Toby said, suddenly afraid. It was all going wrong. "Please keep it down."

"Why should I?" Fang said. "What are you up to? Why are you whispering?"

"If Bruno hears..." Toby said.

Suddenly Max leapt out from behind a bush, his short little Dachshund hairs bristling, a snarl on his rat-like face. "What?" he yelped. "If Bruno hears what?"

"Nothing," Rita said, but it was too late.

Max rushed back and forth, barking at the top of his high-pitched little voice. "Treason!" He darted toward the Hollow, shouting, "Boss! Boss, come see! Treason! Traitors!"

"Run for it," Rita said.

Before Toby could get his feet under him, a black cloud rose into the sky from the general direction of the Hollow. Except that it wasn't smoke, it was solid muscle and black fur and white gnashing teeth. Bruno landed in the middle of the clearing, so hard that he skidded halfway to the edge of the Cliff. His back legs dug into the dirt and he launched himself toward Toby.

Toby stared up in a paralysis of fear as Bruno's immense shadow fell on him. Goodbye, everything, he thought. Then a ball of blue fur hit him in the chest and knocked him out of the way. An instant later, Bruno landed where Toby had been, skidding again in the loose dirt and knocking a birch sapling to the ground.

"Help!" Toby shouted, as soon as there was air in his lungs to do it. "Help, Ilse!"

The other dogs started to run around in a panic, barking incoherently.

Bruno shook himself and turned slowly to face the other dogs. His eyes burned yellow-green and his face twisted in uncontrollable rage. His gaze passed over Toby and came to rest on Rita.

"You!" Bruno shouted. "You tricked me! I trusted you! And now you're plotting against me?"

"Help!" Toby called again, looking around frantically. Where was she? "Help, Ilse!"

Bruno glared at Toby. "Shut up."

Toby shut up.

"I," Bruno said to Rita, "am going to tear you into little pieces."

He charged at Rita and somehow Rita moved just enough, at just the last second, so that Bruno shot past her and slid head-first into the big oak tree next to the Hollow. He shook his head a couple of times, spun around, and charged again. Rita sprinted for the sticker bushes with Bruno gaining on her, but before he could catch her, a streak of yellow-brown roared through the clearing and knocked Bruno off his feet.

"Ilse!" Toby shouted.

Ilse and Bruno rolled on the ground, raising a huge ball of dust. Snarling and snapping sounds came from inside the dust cloud, and the other dogs stood frozen, looking on.

Then, as quickly as it had started, it was over. The dust settled to reveal Bruno with his jaws clamped around Ilse's throat. He hurled her through the air like one of his training sticks, and Ilse flew half the length of the clearing. She landed hard and she didn't get up.

"Fred!" Bruno roared. "You're next!"

He bounded into the bushes in the direction Rita had taken, and a moment later Rita scurried out a few yards away, with Bruno right behind her. She ran straight between Pierre's legs, which didn't deter Bruno at all. Instead he smashed into Pierre's legs so hard that Pierre flipped over in mid-air before crashing into the Hollow. All the while, Max ran in circles as fast as his tiny legs would move him, yelping furiously.

Rita got the big oak between her and Bruno, and for a little while she kept him dancing one way and then the other. Toby knew it was hopeless. Rita couldn't have more than a few breaths left to take.

Not letting himself think, Toby hurled himself across the clearing and sank his teeth into Bruno's rear leg.

Bruno didn't even turn. He simply kicked out, and Toby was knocked backward into the dirt, stunned. From where he lay, he saw Rita running for her life and Bruno chasing her.

"No!" Toby tried to call out. "Not that way!" But he didn't have enough air to breathe, let alone to talk.

Rita ran straight off the Cliff, and Bruno, insane with rage, ran after her.

And then they were both gone and the clearing fell eerily silent.

•

RITA KNEW she was done for. Any direction she ran, Bruno would catch her. She was exhausted and the power of Bruno's hate was endless. Better, she thought, to fall to her death than to be gutted by a monster.

Maybe, she thought, the dog suit would help her glide, the way she'd seen flying squirrels do.

She had no time left to change her mind. She ran to the edge of the Cliff and threw herself into the air with the last of her strength, hoping that Bruno was still behind her.

The autumn wind was strong above the river. She spread her arms and legs as wide as she could, and she felt the breeze lift her up. Something brushed past her, and then she saw Bruno falling beneath her, legs thrashing. The river below was the highest Rita had ever seen it, reflecting the blue of the sky. For a moment she felt completely at peace.

And then she realized that she was falling after all, and falling hard. Almost as hard as Bruno, who hit the water with a giant splash and went under, only to surface downstream, all four legs pumping, his body spinning helplessly as he was swept away.

Then the water rushed at Rita and slammed into her and took her into itself.

TOBY GOT SLOWLY to his feet. He joined the other dogs at the edge of the Cliff, though there was nothing to see. Bruno and Rita, whatever was left of them, had been washed downstream.

Toby turned and saw Ilse struggling to get to her feet. He went over to her and licked her muzzle in sympathy. "Take it easy," he said. "It's all over."

"What happened?" Ilse said, sinking back onto her belly. Her voice was scratchy and strained from the damage to her throat. Toby told her about Rita's sacrifice.

"And she was a cat?" Ilse said. "You've got to be kidding me."

Growling from the direction of the Cliff interrupted them. The

other dogs had Max backed up to the edge. "I think maybe you
need to take the same trip your pal Bruno did," Paco said.

Toby trotted over. "Leave him alone."

Fang turned on him. "Who made you boss?"

"No more bosses," Toby said. "And no punishment for what happened. Everybody here was a Bad Dog in one way or another." At
those words, they all looked down and their tails drooped in spite of
themselves. Toby said, "Let's see if maybe we learned something and
we can all get along now."

Pierre, though shaky, was standing on his own four feet. He nodded. "The little guy is right." He looked at Max. "But you need to
take it down some, buddy. Try to shut up and not get on everybody's nerves."

Max wagged his tail furiously. "You bet. Yep, yep, I will be so
quiet—"

"Shut up!" King roared, and everybody was so surprised that
they all stopped talking, and after that they all wandered away and
lay down to rest for a while before they went downhill to look
for food.


KEVIN HAD KEPT at his mother until she finally agreed to drive
him to the dump and let him look for Doug.

"One hour," she said. "And you have to wear leather gloves and
be really careful what you touch. And you have to take a hot shower
as soon as we come home."

But once they arrived at the dump, it seemed hopeless. The dump
smelled sour and the air was cold and there were bags of trash
everywhere that animals had torn into. After a while, Kevin gave
up kicking at the broken bags and let himself wander. His feet took
him down to the river, and there, suddenly, he saw it.

"Mom!" he cried out. "Mom, look! It's Doug!"

Doug had lost most of his stuffing, and he had washed up on
a rock on the downstream end of the dump. Kevin, overjoyed,
splashed into the shallow water and reached for Doug, then

jerked his hand away at the last minute. Doug's belly had been torn open and there was a real animal's black and gray leg sticking out.

Kevin's mom stood on the shore and shaded her eyes. "What on earth?" she said. "How did a dead cat get inside a stuffed dog?" Then her voice changed and she said, "Don't touch it, Kevin. It could be full of diseases."

Kevin shook with frustration. To have come this far, and to have actually found Doug, and not be able to touch him, was unbearable. "Mom? Mom, you have to do something. I'm not leaving him."

His mom let out a long sigh and waded into the river. "Let me see." She had gloves on too, and she cautiously picked Doug up off the rock and carried him to shore, where she put him down on a patch of sand. Kevin stood behind her as she delicately pulled Doug's blue fabric away from the cat's body and laid the cat out on the ground. She took Doug to the river and rinsed him repeatedly, saying, "We can wash him properly when we get home, and I can put new stuffing in him. He won't be entirely as good as new, but close."

Kevin barely heard her. He knelt in the sand and looked at the cat. Its chest was moving up and down.

"Mom?" Kevin whispered.

The cat opened its eyes and looked at Kevin. And Kevin felt an instantaneous rush of love, stronger than anything he'd ever felt before. Without thinking, he gathered the cat up and held it to his chest. The cat seemed to smile. It shut its eyes and began to purr.

"Kevin!" his mother screamed. "Put that thing down!"

Kevin looked up at her. "It's alive, Mom. Something terrible must have happened for it to end up in the river like that, but now it's found us and it needs a home and we have to keep it. Please, mom? Please?"

The cat opened its eyes again, and blinked at Kevin's mom, and purred even louder. Kevin saw his mom weaken.

"I thought you wanted a dog," she said.

"We can't have a dog because of the apartment," Kevin said. "But we *can* have a cat. And Doug found this one for us. Please, mom? Please?"

"We have to take it to the vet and make sure it's not sick. And get it bathed and dipped and get it its shots. And get it fixed. And you'll have to learn to clean its litterbox. Twice a day, do you hear me?"

Kevin stroked the cat's head with his thumb. "It's okay, kitty," he said. "You're going to live with us now."

The cat smiled again and closed its eyes and purred.

THAT NIGHT, Toby came down from the Bluffs and walked into the forest.

"Spike?" he said.

High in the trees, a shadow moved. "What do you want?"

"I came to tell you," Toby said. "I saw your friend Rita. There was a big fight, and we all turned on Bruno, and it was Rita that saved us. She tricked Bruno into jumping off a cliff. She saved us, but...I don't think she could have lived through it."

"She did, though," Spike said. "One of the other cats saw her this afternoon. Some humans came and took her away."

"They did?" The thought made Toby happy and his tail started to wag. Then he said, "Oh. If Rita survived...that means maybe Bruno did too."

"If all of you really did turn on him like you said, he won't be back. And if he does come back, or another dog like him, you'll have to run him off again. That's the way it is. You can't give in to that kind of a dog."

"Yeah. I guess you're right."

Toby was walking away when Spike said, "Hey, Toby?"

"Yeah?"

"Thanks for coming to tell me. And...good luck."

"Thanks, Spike. You too."

For once, the climb uphill was easier than the climb down. The moon was bright and the night was still and Toby was eager to get back to the Hollow so that he could lie down in the warmth of all of his friends.

# DOCTOR

# HELIOS

*Cairo, September 1963*

T HROUGH THE WINDOW of the Boeing 707, he watched the
Nile as it flowed toward the distant Mediterranean. It glinted
silver in the noonday sun, then turned greenish-brown as the air-
liner banked over the pyramids at Giza and descended toward the
brand-new Cairo International Airport northeast of the city.

"Mr. York?"

He turned to see the petite, auburn-haired BOAC stewardess
reaching toward him. John York was the name on his entirely legitimate US passport, though he was still learning to respond to it.

"I shall have to take that coffee cup now," she said. "We'll be on
the ground in a few minutes."

"So soon?" he said, handing her the mug. "I hate to see our
relationship end before it's properly begun." His smile transformed
his face, and he knew that people would go some lengths to see
it happen.

"First time in Cairo?" she asked. Melody, her name was.

"That's right."

"Well..." She put her index finger to her chin in a pantomime of
serious thought. "I've been known to provide a brief orientation
tour, in exchange for dinner."

"Lovely. I'm at the Nile Hilton." He glanced at his watch.
Seven minutes past noon, Cairo time. "I could meet you in the
lobby at, say, eight o'clock?" He'd flown overnight from Dulles to
Heathrow, then immediately caught this direct flight. His body no
longer had any idea what time it was, and he desperately needed a
bath and a shave.

"Done." She smiled and moved on to tourist class.

He turned back to the window, but the Nile, the longest river in the world, the life blood of Egypt, had disappeared.

THE METAL RAILING on the rolling stairs was too hot to touch, and the broiling air smelled of dust and garlic and, faintly, raw sewage. York trudged toward the gate, watching mirages form and disappear in the heat waves reflected off the tarmac, trying not to reveal how conscious he was of the briefcase in his left hand.

The ceiling fans inside the terminal stirred the languid air to no effect. The chaos of mingled voices had a distinctive lilt and throat-clearing rasp that reminded him on a visceral level that he was far from home.

A boy pushed his way through the crowd. He looked to be no older than 15 and was dressed in a bright yellow shirt open at the throat and pin-striped trousers. He held up a square of corrugated cardboard with the word YORK in elaborate calligraphy, the K spouting serifs and a flourish.

"I'm York," he said to the boy. "You speak English?"

"Passably," the boy said. "I'm Zakkaria. I'll be your driver. Let me take your bags."

York hesitated. "Who sent you?"

"Don't worry," the boy said. "I work for Mr. Giles." He produced a glassine envelope from his shirt pocket that contained an index card bearing the typed words, "This is my employee Zakkaria, in whom I am well pleased." There was a passport-style photo of the boy, over which Giles had scrawled his signature.

The godlike tone was consistent with that of the dispatches York had been reviewing for the last two weeks. He handed over his garment bag, but kept the briefcase. Zakkaria led him through passport control and then to customs, where he beckoned York to the head of the line and called out something to the officer, who laughed and waved them both through.

York, who was not sure the false bottom of the briefcase could withstand rigorous inspection, was nearly done in by feelings of relief on top of two days' worth of fatigue. He yawned and kept walking, through glass doors back into the sun-scorched afternoon.

Parked at the curb was a cream-colored 1960 Cadillac Series 62, complete with modest tail fins and four doors. It was a few years out of date and a bit scratched, but clean and polished to a dazzling shine. A boy of 8 or 9 in a galabiya squatted barefoot on the hood, holding ragged sandals in one hand. His brown face, brown peppercorn hair, and off-white robe were all coated in a layer of yellowish dust. Zakkaria tossed him a pair of coins and said, "Imshi!," flicking his hand imperiously. The boy grinned and sprinted off, still barefoot.

Zakkaria slid the garment bag across the rear seat and then stepped back, holding the door. "Best to keep the luggage next to you, sir, if you've no objection."

As they eased into traffic, Zakkaria tilted the rearview mirror until he made eye contact. "To Mr. Giles' office, then, sir?"

"We need to make a stop first. I need a bank where I can rent a safe deposit box. Someplace reasonably large and anonymous."

"There's a Barclays branch near your hotel, sir."

"Perfect."

They passed a row of palm trees at the airport entrance and then they were in open desert. "There's air conditioning, sir, if you wish it."

"No, Zakkaria, thanks, I'm all right." The air was dry, and once they built up speed, it was not unpleasant. The land was less flat than he'd imagined, the sand more of a reddish brown, the landscape more rocky. Periodically the road intersected wide, flat depressions that looked like dried river beds.

"I would have thought you'd drive on the left here," York said. "What with the British and all."

"Napoleon was here first, sir. So we stubbornly follow the French model."

York studied the cars behind them on the two-lane blacktop. Zakkaria held to a steady 95 kilometers per hour, slow enough that one car after another shot past them as the opportunity presented itself. One car, however, a new red-and-white Buick sedan, matched their speed and kept exactly one other car between them.

Within five minutes, the first signs of civilization appeared and the traffic slowed. York leaned forward and described the Buick to Zakkaria. "Once we get into the city, I want to make sure he is in fact following us. And if he is, we need to lose him." With some reluctance, he added, "I can take over if you want."

"Have you driven in Cairo before, sir?"

"No."

"Best leave it to me, sir."

Zakkaria turned off the highway, the Buick following at a distance. They passed a series of cheap apartment buildings, then made their way down badly paved streets lined with older homes in brick and stucco. It was not that different from neighborhoods York had seen in East Los Angeles, down to the palm trees and elaborate window gardens. The main difference was the mosques every few blocks, even the poorest of them decorated with onion domes and minarets that sprouted loudspeakers like metal mushrooms. The richest were spectacular palaces out of the *Arabian Nights,* ornate with tile and arches and bas-relief.

Within a kilometer the vegetation dried up entirely and York saw thick-walled houses built of mud brick and plaster, many of them two stories, with shops on the ground floor. The windows had wooden shutters in place of glass. The narrow streets of hard-packed clay elicited groans from the Cadillac's suspension. Still, no matter where York looked, the minarets and domes of one mosque or another were always in view.

"Best roll up the windows now, sir," Zakkaria said. York leaned across the seat to take care of the window on the front passenger side, then got the rear windows as the boy turned on the air conditioning. Dust had already lightly coated the upholstery.

There were more people on the streets now. The adults were all male, most of them in white galabiyas and turbans rather than Western clothes. Mongrel dogs threaded their way between them, skinny and rheumy-eyed. The other cars were older and missing vital parts, and donkeys and pushcarts shared the road. The smells were stronger too, despite the closed windows: rotting fruit and dung and dust.

The Buick had abandoned any pretense of innocence. It was only a few car lengths behind, and York could make out the man behind the wheel, an Arab in a fedora too small for his head, with another business-suited Arab next to him.

Zakkaria threw the car into a hard left and it skidded on loose gravel, then shook itself back on course. They barreled into an open square occupied by a souk. Two enormous sides of beef hung from a wooden frame, completely black with flies; mangoes, oranges, and peaches were stacked in pyramids; bolts of striped cloth covered tables next to cages of chickens. Men leaned out to shake their fists and curse as the Caddy roared by, then pelted the Buick in its wake with onions and tomatoes.

"Listen," York said, "this is not worth killing somebody over."

"Don't worry, sir, we drive like this here all the time."

Zakkaria took another sharp turn, throwing York back in his seat. They accelerated for two blocks, braked, slid, turned again.

"This isn't working," York said.

"Fear not, sir, I have a plan."

Zakkaria took a hard right into an alley that appeared to be a dead end. A pushcart full of melons meandered down the left side of the road. York was not sure there was room to pass it.

"Ah," Zakkaria said. "There he is."

He slammed on the brakes and rolled down his window. The boy pushing the cart looked to be Zakkaria's age. He wore a galabiya and a few loops of plastic ribbon around his neck, apparently as ornament. Zakkaria leaned out and shouted something as they passed. The boy raised one hand in acknowledgement.

The end of the alley was coming up fast. At the last second, Zakkaria braked and turned left into a kind of underpass, an enclosed space where the ground floor of the building should have been. York heard the front bumper of the Buick scrape the wall as it made the turn behind them.

Zakkaria circled the block, this time coming down the alley at higher speed. "You watch your friends now, sir," he said.

York swiveled around as they passed the melon vendor and so was able to see the entire thing unfold: The boy was already starting to turn his pushcart as the Cadillac passed, then he sent it flying into the street in front of the Buick.

The driver of the Buick had no choice. He hit the cart at more than 50 kilometers per hour and the melons arced into the air like green and white balloons, paused at their apogee, then fell back to explode over the Buick, covering it in red, green, and orange pulp.

As York watched, the boy in the galabiya carefully stretched out in the road behind his shattered cart and began to writhe and scream in simulated pain.

As they entered the tunnel again, the alley had already begun to fill with outraged locals.

Zakkaria struggled to hold back laughter as he said, "I assure you, sir, they will not extricate themselves for many agonizing hours."

"Who's going to pay for that poor boy's cart?"

"Not to worry, sir. He's on the payroll. He will file an expense report."

AS THEY APPROACHED the center of the city, York had Zakkaria circle a few blocks to make sure there were no further tails. When he was satisfied, he had the boy drop him in front of Barclays with instructions to return in half an hour.

Standing in the street, York dusted off his sport coat and slacks, marveling that he was only a couple of miles from where they'd left the Buick. Other than the Arabic calligraphy on the signs and the relative absence of women, he could have been in any large European city. The shops were elegant, the cars new, the pedestrians dressed in jackets and ties, albeit with the occasional fez. As he stepped into the lobby he felt the welcome chill of conditioned air and heard the same carpeted hush he would have expected in London or Geneva. Men in expensive suits moved in and out of glass walled offices, making York feel shabby in comparison.

The stunning dark-eyed woman at the information desk addressed him in English and summoned one of the suited men to arrange his safe deposit box. With the paperwork complete, they inserted their keys together and York took his box and briefcase to a private viewing room. There he removed the false bottom of the briefcase and transferred 100,000 Egyptian pounds to the box. The notes, all slightly used and untraceable, were worth over $300,000 US.

Again the fatigue hit him hard, leaving him momentarily dizzy. He closed his eyes, let himself drift off for exactly one minute, then rang for the clerk.

GILES' OFFICE was east of the city center, in a cluster of buildings from the 1930s and '40s. York climbed three flights of concrete stairs and found a pebbled glass door that read ATLANTIC IMPORT- EXPORT. Inside was a disused reception desk fronting three offices. Two appeared to be empty. The third, lit by harsh fluorescents, was occupied by a man in his sixties with brush-cut white hair. His long white shirtsleeves were rolled past the elbow, his tie loose, a cigarette burning in his nicotine-stained right hand while the other made its way down a typed list of numbers. A box fan sat in the open window and blew hot air across the surface of the desk, which contained an overflowing ashtray and various piles of papers held down with chunks of dark brown volcanic rock.

Giles stood up as York entered, still not looking away from the list. He parked the cigarette in the corner of his mouth and extended his hand. "York, I assume."

"Yes, sir."

"We're informal here. Call me Giles." The hand waved toward a cracked leather armchair and recovered its cigarette. Giles sat down again, still reading. "Damn, damn, damn." He circled one of the figures with a number 2 wooden pencil that bore his tooth marks and then finally looked up. "So. How do you like Cairo?"

"We were followed from the airport. Your boy Zakkaria lost them, but we incurred some expenses."

Giles shrugged. "We have money. Even more now, thanks to you."

"Speaking of which," York said, "there's a duplicate key to the safe deposit box—"

Giles held up his cigarette. "Don't want to know about it. I assume the bank won't let anyone else into it, so there's no point." He pushed his chair back from the desk. "I've got you set up for a lunch meeting tomorrow at the Gezira Sporting Club with the Under Assistant Secretary of Fly Swatting or some such. You'll discreetly slip him a hundred pounds and he'll hand you a letter that says you're a beloved friend of Nasser's government. They've got their own chartered airplane that runs between here and Aswan, and, among other things, that letter will get you a seat, and one for your translator."

He plucked an 8 x 10 black and white photo from the middle of one of the piles. "You'll meet him at lunch too. Older wallah, name of Mahmoud. Quite sound. He's been fully briefed on your mission and he'll be able to help you with the fine points."

Giles' accent was east-coast US private school, but his slang was strictly British Colonial. York had seen the same affectation among the Americans stationed in India two years before.

The photo showed a lean-faced, light-skinned Arab with a turban and a gray mustache. The camera had caught him looking away, pensive, even a bit sad. York nodded and handed back the photo.

"There's one other thing," Giles said. "The chap you were supposed to meet in Aswan is not going to make the rendezvous. They found him early this morning at the foot of a cliff with his neck broken."

GILES SAID, "Too early to know what it means, of course. I suppose it might even have been an accident."

"No," York said. His exhaustion delayed his recovery from the shock. He couldn't stop picturing the shattered body.

"No, I suppose not. One of the security people might have found him hanging about where he wasn't supposed to be and decided to handle it ex cathedra. But the most likely possibility is the worst, which is that somebody in his organization figured out he was working for us."

"Even though we're on their side."

"It's never that simple here. There are more sides than there are players on the pitch."

"So we're back to square one, with no contact."

"Or worse. The entire mission may be blown." Giles dropped his voice, making it hard to hear over the roaring fan. "Now look here, I was never keen on this mission in the first place. We might be destroying something we might do better to leave alone."

York shook his head. "I don't write my own orders. The mission goes ahead unless I hear otherwise from Washington."

"If they're onto us, it could put you in physical danger."

"I'm not concerned about that."

"You should be. I'm not sure I entirely trust a man with no sense of self preservation."

"Tell me what you know about this organization."

Giles sighed. "They call themselves Al-Mashiah Ra, the Cattle of Ra. Ra was supposedly the father of the Egyptian race. Their symbol looks like a sketch of a doughnut." He reached across the desk to draw two concentric circles on a random piece of paper near York. "Some sort of hieroglyph representing the solar disk, I'm told."

"What is it they want?"

"Nasser out, the Yanks and Ruskies out, a return to the good old days, which according to them would be somewhere around twelve or thirteen hundred BC."

"Do we take them seriously?"

"The part about wanting the Ruskies out, anyway. Look, if you're going to insist on going forward with this, I suppose you could pop down to Aswan, take a shufti, ask a few questions via Mahmoud, put a stick in the anthill, as it were. Mahmoud is a sharp djundi, he can sort out the black tarbooshes from the white."

"Fair enough." York hesitated, then said, "Can I ask a favor? I have a date this evening with a stewardess from my flight over here."

"You're living up to your reputation, I see."

"Her name is Melody. She seems like a very nice girl. Still, I'd feel more secure if the London office did a quick background check."

"It might take a bit."

"That's fine. I don't need the information until, say, a quarter of eight." Giles shook his head in mild disbelief and made a note on a scrap of paper. "So tell me," York said. "What do you make of this guy Nasser?"

"The fellahin love him. Al Rayyes, they call him. The Chief. He could have been the King of Araby. Still could, I daresay."

"That's the problem, isn't it? I mean, that's why I'm here, to make sure that doesn't happen."

"Oh, we've done our best to put the kibosh on it. Cutting off his handouts. Giving aid and comfort to his enemies, from Prince Faisal and the Saudis to Hussein in Jordan to the Moslem Brotherhood here at home. Not to mention Israel."

"He's a Red, Giles. He's buying guns from the Soviets and taking their rubles to build his dam. Nationalizing Suez and all the European companies in Egypt. Redistributing land."

Giles leaned across the desk, his weight on his forearms. "When I was a lad, everybody was a Communist. Including some of the people who are yelling the loudest now about the Red Menace."

"Including you?"

"I never cared for parties. The thing is, Nasser's no Commie. He throws them in jail every chance he gets. All he wants is a secular Arab state. And he's right, too, by God. You want real trouble, put a religious nutcase in charge. I don't care if he's a Hindoo, Musulman, Jew, or Southern Baptist. You don't want people in charge of armed forces who think they're getting orders from God."

"So you're against this mission."

Giles retreated into his chair. "I don't make policy. I do what I'm told except in the most extreme cases. No, I don't like this mission or the harm it would do a lot of ordinary working joes in this country. But I've been in this station a long time, and I intend to be here another five years and collect my piss-ant little pension and retire to someplace where it snows in the winter.

"So in other words, yes, I will help you blow up the Aswan Dam."

YORK WAS IN DANGER of dozing off in his overstuffed chair in the cavernous lobby of the Nile Hilton. He sat in front of a reproduction of an ancient bas relief, lulled by the sound of running water, possibly piped in via hidden speakers in the ceiling.

Before wrinkles had a chance to set in his tropical-weight suit, he was roused by the sound of high heels on the marble floor. It was Melody, precisely on time. She wore a dark skirt that reached her ankles, a loose-fitting, long-sleeved black blouse that buttoned to the throat, and a black beret that hid most of her hair. As he got to his feet, she kissed his cheek and said, "Not the outfit you had envisioned, I expect."

"You look lovely."

"I prefer something sexier, myself, but it's simply not worth the stares and the hostile remarks."

"I admire your respect for the local culture."

She laughed. "A respect born of fear."

They walked out to the parking lot, on the opposite side of the hotel from the Nile. Zakkaria brought the Cadillac around; it had been freshly washed, inside and out. The boy had been adamant about driving, telling York that his life might be in danger otherwise.

York paused for a moment before getting in back next to Melody. The night was still and finally beginning to cool. The brightly lit façade of the Hilton, with its two-story mosaic of ancient symbols, pushed the darkness back into the surrounding trees. Reflections glimmered on the Nile on the far side of the hotel, and beyond it shone the lights of Gezira Island, where he was booked for lunch the next day. The beauty of the city had a fantastical quality, so green and lush in the midst of such a lifeless waste that it might have been no more than another mirage.

He got in the car. "Melody, this is my associate, Zakkaria. I tried to give him the night off, but he insisted on meeting you."

Zakkaria turned sideways in the seat and kissed the hand that Melody had extended. "I am enchanted, miss."

"I don't wish to make you uncomfortable," she said, "but if you could bring yourself to call me Melody at some point during the evening, I would be most pleased."

"Yes, miss."

"Would you mind driving us around for a bit before dinner? I thought we might take Mr. York through Garden City, then to dinner on Gezira. I have reservations for nine-thirty at the Cairo Tower."

"Excellent choice, miss. The view should be spectacular tonight."

As they settled into the leather seats, York caught a whiff of spice and vanilla. "Shalimar?" he asked.

"I'm impressed, Mr. York. Yes, it's my Oriental scent. In London I wear Joy, when I can afford it."

"I have something of a keen nose. It can be a nuisance in some quarters, but I'm grateful for it tonight."

Zakkaria pulled out of the hotel into a traffic circle a hundred meters in diameter, filled with cars that barely moved.

"Do you know the local history?" Melody asked.

York shook his head. What little he did know he didn't mind hearing again from her.

"A hundred years ago this was all part of the Ottoman Empire, until our lot put the boot in around 1882. Before that, Johnny Turk's man was Ismail Pasha, and Ismail was seduced by the Paris Exhibition of 1867. He decided to build a Paris on the Nile with Egypt's cotton export money. And that's where all of this came from." She pointed to the palatial pink granite building that occupied an entire city block downstream from the Hilton. "The Egyptian museum, where there's so much stuff they've got King Tut in a glass case in a corner with odds and sods piled on top of him. This square here was originally named for Ismail. After they threw our lot out in 1919, people started calling it Tahrir, Liberation. It's only officially had that name since Nasser tossed King Farouk out in fifty-two. Then there's the Abdeen Palace, a few blocks east of here. Unbelievably luxurious and ornate. It's supposed to be the presidential residence, but it's too rich for the blood of Al Rayyes. There's a revolutionary for you."

"We passed it today. It's amazing, really. All this beauty, all these trees and lily ponds and huge buildings, more or less imagined into existence by sheer force of will."

"That's it exactly. Aswan and Khartoum are much the same. It's like walking into a run-down, overcrowded opium dream. It's one of the things I love about it."

They finally escaped at the far end of the circle, though the traffic remained heavy. "This next bit is Garden City," Melody said, "another neighborhood dreamed up out of nothing, or at least nothing more than some orchards and farm land, this time by a big real estate company and a French agricultural engineer. All the streets curve back on themselves and change names. One of the stories they tell is that this was somebody's brilliant idea to keep mobs from marching on the British embassy, which is in there somewhere, God knows where."

Zakkaria turned right for a block, then right again, and suddenly they were surrounded by trees: towering ornamental palms, flowering flame trees and jacarandas. Black wrought-iron gates blocked long driveways that led to Italianate villas buried deep in the vegetation. They flashed in and out of visibility in the car's headlights.

"It's very posh here, obviously," Melody said. "Yet affordable, by London standards. When I'm rich and famous, this is where I shall come to retreat from the world."

Zakkaria, with help from Melody and only a couple of wrong turns, managed to extricate them from Garden City, get them through the Tahrir traffic circle, and onto a short, flat bridge whose supports rested on small concrete islands in the Nile.

Gezira was large enough to not feel like an island once York was on it. It was the brightest part of the city and traffic there was worse than ever, crawling past the glowing facades of restaurants and night clubs. Above it all rose a huge minaret, 200 meters tall, lit by purple floodlights, with floor-to-ceiling windows that opened into the rotating restaurant at the apex. It was to this tower that Zakkaria brought them at 9:29.

York and Melody tried in vain to get Zakkaria to come to dinner with them. "My place is with the car," he said firmly. "You must go now, sir, or you will lose your reservation."

The view was indeed magnificent. York looked past Melody's right shoulder to see the pyramids and Sphinx on the west bank of the Nile, lit up like a Hollywood premiere. Over her left shoulder were the scattered lights of the new housing development in progress to the north of Giza.

"It must be disorienting to travel so constantly," York said. "I travel a good deal myself, but nothing like you do."

"There's no continuity," Melody said. "My life is in episodes, like a television program, not a great sweeping novel like *War and Peace*. Therefore I try to make each episode count for something. One good way is to cast interesting guest stars. Like you, for instance. What is it that makes you travel so much?"

York slowly rotated his glass on the white tablecloth, counter-clockwise, opposite to the direction the restaurant was turning beneath him. The glass was half-full of the local beer, Stella, at Melody's suggestion. He'd drunk very little for fear of intensifying his fatigue.

He didn't feel up to the usual pat answers to her question. "I don't want to lie to you. And I'm not allowed to tell you the truth about my job. I can say that what I do involves a great deal of other people's money." It was true enough, if more misleading than helpful.

Melody smiled with obvious pleasure. "I do love a good mystery.

Now I shall be forced to piece together the various clues you let slip. Do you have family, Mr. York? Are you allowed to talk about that?"

"I've never been married, not involved with anyone, no children. Both parents are still living, and quite well off, though we don't have a lot of contact. They wanted me to pursue the family business."

"I don't suppose you can tell me what that business is?"

York shook his head and smiled. "We'll do better talking about you, I'm afraid. You really seem to love it here. It's quite remarkable the way you've made yourself at home."

"Well," she said. "Yes and no. There are ways in which I shall always be at a distance."

"How so?"

"It's the women, you see. They're not just second class citizens as they are most everywhere. There's a huge number of women in this country who are essentially prisoners. They're not allowed an education, let alone a profession. They're sequestered in their parents' house from birth until they're married, which is supposed to somehow happen without the prospective groom ever seeing his bride before the wedding. Then they're shut in the husband's house, cooking and cleaning and having children, and if they go outside they have to be wrapped up from head to foot.

"There's a certain sort of religious zealot here who believes that women are carnal monsters, and men are their weak, helpless prey. Even the sight of a lock of a woman's hair in public can so inflame the passions of these poor creatures as to make them lose all control of themselves. And if they were to attack such a woman, it would be her fault, for having tempted them beyond all reason."

"Thus your conservative clothes."

"Yes. I still get some hostile stares, but far fewer than I used to. And things are changing, slowly, in part thanks to Al Rayyes. More and more women are refusing to go along with the traditions."

She was smiling, though clearly it was an uncomfortable subject. York tried a different tack. "You mentioned being rich and famous one day. What is it you're going to be famous for?"

She visibly relaxed. "I haven't quite decided that yet. I assume that if I keep placing myself in the way of adventure, my destiny will eventually reveal itself. Do you believe in destiny, Mr. York?"

"Only in the ones we create for ourselves."

"That sounds a frightfully heavy responsibility."

"It has its rewards."

Dinner arrived. Though the menu relied heavily on European dishes, Melody had pushed him toward the local cuisine, which was largely vegetarian. York had settled on koshari, an odd-looking combination of rice, chickpeas, lentils, and macaroni in tomato sauce that proved quite delicious. She showed him how to eat it using the local flatbread instead of silverware and shared her ful madamas, a dish made with fava beans. She had a mixture of innocence and lack of inhibition that York found utterly charming.

Even so, once the plates were cleared away, he found that his reserves were gone. He reached across the table and took both of her hands. "This has been a completely lovely evening, in every way. But I'm done in, and I really should be in bed."

"What a capital idea," she said. "Let's."

It was 11 the next morning before York was able to drag himself from bed. He'd slept deeply, although with several interruptions from Melody, whose eagerness to please was exceeded only by the intensity of her own desire. He sponged off a few critical areas with a washcloth and put his trousers on. As he shaved, he watched Melody in the mirror as she slowly turned over in the thoroughly rumpled bed, reached out one arm to find him gone, then sat up and stretched. He felt a pang as the sheet fell away from her.

"Well, my goodness, Mr. York," she said in mid-yawn, meeting his reflected gaze. "You certainly know your way around a woman's body."

"And a magnificent body it is," he said. "Where is it going to be later this evening?"

"On its way to London, unfortunately." She got out of bed and stretched again, knowing he was watching, then snatched a terrycloth robe from an armchair and threw it on. She ran across the room to open the sliding glass door to the balcony. "Oh, you must come look. You can see Giza from here, the pyramids and the Sphinx and everything."

He went to her and embraced her from behind. The view, as he'd noted the previous afternoon, was indeed stunning, almost enough to distract him from the woman in his arms. "Will you be back?" he asked.

"Someday. Don't fret, love. I assure you this has been an absolutely smashing episode, and if the stars align, perhaps we'll make the sequel." She turned, kissed him lightly, and said, "But you have your luncheon and I have my flight, and right now I desperately need the loo."

THE MAIN CLUBHOUSE of the Al Gezira Sporting Club was two stories of pink stucco surrounded by acacia trees. According to Zakkaria, the trees were a legacy from its days as a botanical garden, before the British built their polo fields and tennis courts and 18-hole golf course. The golf course was only nine holes now, thanks to Nasser's addition of a youth club.

York walked into the high-ceilinged lobby, looking for Mahmoud, his translator. A tall woman in a stylish black business suit approached him and said, "Mr. York?"

She appeared to be Egyptian, her thick black hair falling to her shoulders, loosely secured with black silk Hermes scarf. She wore heavy, black-framed glasses that distracted attention from her eyes, which were large, dark, and outlined in kohl. What he could see of her figure beneath the suit was lush and shapely. She had a clean, talcum powder scent that was more child than woman.

"I'm afraid," she said, "Mahmoud was taken ill last night and may not be available for several days." Her English was crisp and fluent. The British flavor reminded him of Melody, a thought that stung him unexpectedly. "My name is Nadya Moustafa. The Embassy arranged for me to take his place." York accepted the hand she offered, which was cool and dry. She pressed his fingers gently and let go. "I've arranged an outdoor table, if that's acceptable. It's cooler in the open air, and there is shade."

"Quite acceptable," York said.

"The Minister will be late, of course. A matter of demonstrating his importance. You can order a drink if you like."

"No, thanks. If we do have a few minutes, there is a phone call I need to make."

"There are telephones around the corner, just there."

He called Giles. "There's a woman here named Nadya Moustafa. Five eight or nine, black hair, late twenties, attractive. Claims Mahmoud is indisposed and she's a substitute."

"Christ. Hold on, I'll check."

It took less than a minute.

"The Embassy vouches for her," Giles said. "Worked there for a couple of years. Utterly dependable, they said. And she's been briefed."

"That's all well and good, but she's a woman."

"Yes," Giles said. "The second one I've had to vet for you in less than twenty-four hours."

"Humor aside, this is an Arab country. There are places I need to go where she won't be allowed."

"They assure me it's a temporary situation. We can arrange to have Mahmoud meet you in Aswan once he's recovered. And I think you'll find that things have changed significantly under Nasser. Some don't like it, but women have made significant strides on his watch."

York found his way out to the patio. There were twenty or so oblong granite-topped tables and rattan armchairs in the intermittent shade of the acacias, half of them occupied. Nadya had managed to secure one under a large turquoise-and-white umbrella. In the near distance, York heard the irregular clop of tennis balls being struck.

Nadya ordered a tonic water and York did the same. In ten minutes of idle conversation, he learned that she had been born and raised in Cairo, educated at the London School of Economics,

and saw translating for the Embassy as a stepping stone to a government position.

"Anything specific in mind?" York asked.

"President," Nadya said. She smiled. "I realize that may be a bit
of a non-starter. I intend to try, nonetheless." She looked up. "Ah.
Here's Minister Fayed now."

Previous assignments in the USSR had prepared York for thuggish
low-level ministers barely distinguishable from gangsters. Fayed was
instead slight, balding, and nervous, with dandruff flakes on his suit
coat and smudges on his wire-rimmed glasses. York stood and Fayed
gave his hand a single sharp squeeze.

Fayed summoned a waiter to ask for coffee and, through Nadya,
exchanged a few pro-forma pleasantries with York. They ordered
lunch, with York opting for an omelet and fresh orange juice, Fayed
for lamb, and Nadya for a salad. When the conversation finally
lagged, York said, "I understand you might be able to accept a small
contribution toward President Nasser's efforts to build the High
Dam." He placed the envelope of cash on the table and slid it a
cautious two inches toward the minister's cup. The envelope disappeared as if by sleight of hand and another envelope replaced it.
Fayed relaxed minutely.

"And he understands," Nadya translated, "that you are perhaps
interested in seeing the progress that's been made."

"Very much so," York said, slipping the new envelope into his
jacket pocket.

"There is a flight to Aswan this evening at six. We are to be at
Gate 1, Almaza Airport, by 5:30. Your name will be on the manifest
for two seats. He regrets that he cannot provide accommodations
for us in Aswan. He does recommend the Cataract Hotel. Very his-
torical, very luxurious. So he hears."

The food arrived. York could not conceal his surprise at the flavor
of the omelet. Through Nadya, Fayed said, "Yesterday those eggs
were still inside the chicken. The cheese was made here in Cairo
and is no older than the eggs. Neither have ever been refrigerated.

One of the pleasures of a backward country is that we don't put a lot of technology between ourselves and our food."

"I would hardly call this a backward country," York said.

"You have not been outside Cairo yet."

York was mopping up his plate with a slice of rich, dark bread when a man appeared beside him. The other diners were in European clothes while this man wore an off-white embroidered tunic over loose matching trousers. An off-white skullcap sat atop long dark hair. He was York's height, six feet, and appeared to be in his early twenties and quite fit.

"I apologize profusely for interrupting," he said in English, though he did not appear to be sorry at all. "At your convenience, my employer would like you to join him."

"Your employer?"

"Dr. Helios."

He clearly expected York to know the name. Minister Fayed certainly recognized it; his expression changed first to one of pure fear, then to nervousness raised to an even higher pitch.

"And the rest of my party?" York asked. "It would be rude to leave them."

Fayed blurted something to Nadya, stood abruptly, tossed his napkin on his unfinished plate, and hurried away. "Minister Fayed has another engagement," she said. "Quite pressing, it seems."

"Dr. Helios's English is quite accomplished," the stranger said, "so no translation will be required."

York glanced an inquiry at Nadya, who whispered, "Go. Go now."

York drained his orange juice and followed the stranger across the patio. "Am I the only one here who is not familiar with Dr. Helios?"

"Quite possibly," said the stranger, ignoring the hint.

They arrived at a large table on the far side of the patio, a good five meters from the nearest of the other diners. A gnarled and stately banyan tree put the table in complete shade.

"Dr. Helios," the stranger said.

A mountain of a man in a blazing orange caftan rose from the far side of the table and extended a gigantic arm. He was at least six foot seven and three hundred pounds, built like a lineman in American football who had begun to go to seed. His head was shaved beneath a black fez, his eyes equally black.

"Pleased to make your acquaintance, Mr. York." His English was mellifluous and seasoned with Mediterranean accents. "Can you join us?"

York inclined his head.

Helios gestured toward a young Oriental, who stood and offered a curt bow. He had longish hair, penetrating eyes, and a hint of a superior smile. He wore a loose black cotton robe, black pants, and sandals. "This is Mr. Chang, originally of Peking," Helios said. "Now my head of security."

York bowed in return, certain that Chang was sizing him up as a possible opponent. He was close enough to smell cigarette smoke in Chang's clothes, of a peculiar flavor that he couldn't immediately place.

Helios said, "And you've met my secretary, Mr. Kamal," pointing to the young man who had brought York to the table. "Please take a seat."

York sat. Chang was to his left, Kamal to his right, and Helios returned to the chair facing him. For a big man, Helios moved lightly, as if unaware of his size.

In front of Helios lay a platter containing the remains of an entire roasted chicken: rib cage, leg bones, a few scraps of skin. Three grains of couscous and a bit of melted butter were all that were left on his plate. An empty liter bottle of mineral water sat upside-down in an ice bucket. Both Chang and Kamal had half-finished meals of their own.

"Can I offer you refreshment?" Helios asked. "We were about to order coffee."

"Coffee would be fine."

"I find hot coffee in the heat of the day to be paradoxically refreshing." He raised his hand and snapped his fingers. Immediately three waiters set about clearing the debris, one of whom quickly returned with four glasses of thick Turkish-style coffee.

Helios commented on the weather while York nodded and maintained a pleasant expression. He then inquired whether York's flight had been smooth and his hotel comfortable. The performance satisfied the minimum requirements for small talk while letting York know that he was under observation.

Eventually Helios said, "You are no doubt wondering why I sought you out. I believe we share an interest in al-Saad al-Aali. The Aswan High Dam."

John York, the character he was portraying, had nothing to hide, no reason to be anything other than eager to discuss his mission. "That's correct. I'm hoping to do some business with President Nasser's government."

"I am a businessman myself. Might I ask what sort of business you're in?"

"Heavy construction equipment. I represent a consortium of American manufacturers—Allis-Chalmers, John Deere, Caterpillar, all major names. We know the Russian equipment is no good. The Ulanshev excavators are clumsy at best, and the BelAz dump trucks spend more time in the shop than on the job." He happened to glance at Chang as he finished the sentence and felt a chill at the intensity with which the man was staring at him. "Anyway," he recovered, "I believe there are mutual interests that can be served here."

"Is this legal?" Helios asked. "I thought your government was opposed to Nasser."

"President Kennedy feels more warmly toward him than Eisenhower did." York didn't mention that the Director of the Agency did not share those sentiments. "And the US government tends to see reason when there's money to be made."

Chang spoke for the first time. "I thought the Russian aid was contingent upon using Russian equipment." He had an intriguing accent, his liquid consonants muffled, his cadences not quite Chinese or European.

"They've had to back down," York said. "Even the Russians finally admitted that they couldn't make their timetables without better tools."

"You'll be traveling to Aswan, then," Helios said.

"Yes, I need to see the work in progress. Maybe I'll get a chance to see Abu Simbel while I'm there."

"Alas," Helios said, "the government has closed access to Abu Simbel because of the dam project." York tried to remember if he'd ever heard anyone use the word "alas" in conversation before. "You know that if they do finish the dam, they're going to have to dismantle Abu Simbel and rebuild it on higher ground."

"'If?'" York said. "I didn't think there was any question about it at this point."

"Ah, you are correct, sir. They have indeed accelerated the work sufficiently that, barring some sort of disaster, they will in fact complete the dam. It was a near thing, though. A very near thing. As you know, they have inflexible deadlines imposed by the annual rise and fall of the Nile. It was only in the last few weeks that legitimate predictions began to bear out the optimism that the government has been disseminating."

"May I ask what your interest in all this is?"

"My business is shipping. Import and export. Oil. I have business up and down the Nile, and obstacles to that business concern me greatly."

"You see the High Dam as an obstacle?"

"At one time, plans for the dam included locks. Sadly, that is no longer the case. It could prove expensive for me. As Nasser has shown little concern for international business in the past, I doubt he will have much sympathy for my troubles."

"We may be on opposite sides of this issue," York said. "I'm here to help the dam get built, and you oppose it."

"Don't misunderstand me, sir. The dam is good for the economy, and I am a firm believer in economic growth. Is creates all manner of opportunities. It gives you the opportunity to sell your heavy equipment, and provides me opportunities of my own."

Helios stood again, signaling that the audience was over. "Thank you for being so generous with your time," he said. "Perhaps our paths will cross again."

HE CALLED GILES again from the same phone in the lobby. "What do you know about a guy that calls himself Dr. Helios?"

"I know there's a dossier on him at Langley. Top Secret clearance required. I know he's got a Get Out of Jail Free card straight from the Director. We keep nothing on him here, do not surveil, do not ask questions."

"What's he a doctor of?"

"I believe it's an honorary degree. PhD in economics, Harvard Business School. He is considered friendly and not to be disturbed. Why the sudden interest?"

"I just had lunch with him. I didn't find him that friendly."

"Don't worry about it," Giles said. "He's not relevant."

THE PLANE TO ASWAN was a DC-3, the workhorse of the third world—reliable, easy to maintain, able to take off and land on short runways or even, on one occasion York would not soon forget, on a strip of beach as the tide was going out.

As they taxied into the setting sun, Nadya said, "Bismillahi rahmani rahim." When York gave her a questioning look she said, "The opening words of the Koran. 'In the name of God, the Compassionate, the Merciful.' A suitable thing to say when beginning something. A journey, a meal, a business venture."

"I'd wondered if you were religious. The veil isn't mandatory, I take it?"

"The Koran says we should not display our charms beyond what is acceptable, which allows rather wide interpretation, don't you think? I believe it's pretty clear what God had in mind. Devout women should not dress as if they were advertising their sexuality, according to contemporary standards."

"And yet..."

"And yet, indeed. What a different world it would be if people followed the clear intent of their sacred texts instead of using them to excuse bad behavior. And you? Are you religious?"

"In my country, religion has so little impact on daily life that most people have stopped going through the motions."

"Yes, you have declared God dead there, haven't you?"

"I think Nietzsche was the first, but yes, you hear that more and more."

"You don't see the hand of God, then."

"I'm afraid not. And I see far too much of the hand of man."

"Talking of the hand of man, I'm afraid I'm not terribly comfortable with flying. At least the taking off and landing bits. Would you mind terribly if I held your hand, only until we're in the air?"

"Of course not," York said. She was intelligent, ambitious, and brave enough to defy custom in her dress. This show of weakness was out of character, and rather unconvincing. Still, she was a beautiful woman, and York was happy to take her hand, which was more lean and powerful than he had noticed that morning.

The engines revved to a piercing scream and Nadya gripped his hand fiercely. Her eyes squeezed shut and she leaned back in the seat, mouthing what York assumed was a prayer. The plane bounced twice on the runway and lifted off. It banked steeply over the city, giving a brief glimpse of tan buildings and clumps of green along the river, then leveled off. As the pilot throttled back the propellers, Nadya gently pressed his hand once more and let go.

There were eight other passengers on the plane, all Arab men in suits. They sat in ones and twos throughout the cabin, none of them within hearing range. Below, the Nile was a glittering thread in a darkening khaki fabric. Across the aisle, York saw the setting sun, and from his own window, the rising moon. The moon appeared to be gigantic, as if it were hurtling toward the Earth to shatter it with a single blow.

Nadya took a worn leather-bound book out of her purse, opened it in the middle, and began to read. York glanced at the page; it was printed in Arabic. "The Koran," she said. "It's very soothing to read, when you're afraid."

"I'll remember that," York said, though the times he'd been most afraid had not permitted any reading.

He closed his eyes and fell into a deep sleep.

"THE NILE HAS six cataracts," Nadya said, "numbered in reverse order." They stood on the terrace of the Cataract Hotel, listening to the rush of water in the darkness forty feet below. Islands shone white in the moonlight, ranging in size from a few feet in diameter to those, like the one directly across from them, that held entire neighborhoods. "You would call them white-water rapids in America, I think. This is the First Cataract here, actually the last before the Nile flows into the sea. The Second is across the border in Sudan, at Wadi Halfa. Wadi Halfa will be under water when the High Dam is finished."

"The Sudanese can't be too happy about that."

"Reparations are being paid, and a whole new city is being built for them, Khashm al-Girba, in a part of the country where there is rain and they can farm more successfully."

"There's not much room for sentiment in that point of view."

"The world is changing," Nadya said. "The Arab countries are coming out of the darkness into the light. Literally, with the new hydroelectric station producing enough electricity to light half the country. That's worth some sacrifices."

"Spoken like a true socialist," York said.

"You know, socialism is not a curse word anywhere except your country. I wonder why you are all so afraid of it."

"We're very attached to our freedoms."

"Freedom to be poor, to be hungry, to have no medical care?"

"Yes, I suppose so, if necessary."

"I think perhaps your country is more religious than you give it credit for. Enterprise is your God, and Communism your Satan."

It was one of the mildest arguments York had ever had. They were both smiling, neither of them with serious emotions engaged. Part of the reason was the tranquility of the setting. While Aswan was not as European as Cairo, it was nonetheless green and civilized, even if temporarily overrun with Russian engineers. The Cataract Hotel itself was magnificent, three stories of red brick and granite, with interiors out of a Busby Berkeley Old Kingdom spectacular: huge circular archways decorated in red and white stripes, shining parquet and marble floors, giant clay urns, potted palms, Persian carpets, awnings, oiled wood cabinetry.

"Tell me," York said, "what do you know about this man Helios?"

"You're changing the subject."

"Yes, I am. I don't enjoy talking about politics."

"Or thinking about it?"

"Not really."

"You of all people should be thinking about it."

"Does the foot soldier question foreign policy?"

"If he did, there might be fewer wars."

"Or greater losses on both sides. Tell me about Helios."

Nadya sighed. "Talking of enterprise, he's ludicrously rich. Half Greek, half Egyptian. Lives in Abu Dhabi, one of the emirates on the Arabian Gulf. He owns the Helios oil company, which sells crude oil to all the major refiners—Esso, Shell, British Petroleum. You've heard of it, I'm sure."

York nodded. "I hadn't made the connection."

"He owns a fleet of tankers to transport it, refineries to produce it, wells to pull it out of the ground. Some say he also owns the politicians he needs for everything to flow smoothly."

"Why would he be interested in the High Dam?"

"That's a fair question. Certainly he hates socialism too, but that hardly seems sufficient motive." She ducked her head and held one hand in front of a yawn. "Sorry. But if you're not even going to argue with me, I don't know how I'm meant to stay awake."

"Forgive me," York said. "It's been a long day for both of us." He walked her to her room, wondering idly if she were flirting with him, but too exhausted to press the question.

•

THE ROAD OUT of the city took them south, past dusty neighborhoods that bordered on the green farmland along the Nile. The houses were adobe and plaster, one story, with flat roofs that needed to withstand sun, but never rain. They were much like, York imagined, the houses in Wadi Halfa that would dissolve into lumps of mud when the floodwaters began to surge against their walls.

Nadya had spent close to an hour on the hotel phone that morning as she worked her way through the hierarchy of engineers to get York an appointment with the first assistant to Sidki Suleiman, the Minister of the High Dam. Shortly after 10:00 a Land Rover had arrived to pick them up. The vehicle's original paint job appeared to be the same shade of beige as the dust that covered it from canvas top to balding tires.

York and Nadya had both crowded into the bench seat next to the driver. The Rover was British-made, putting the driver on the right; Nadya sat in the middle to facilitate translation. She wore khaki jodhpurs and long sleeved shirt, her thick black hair pinned up beneath a long-billed cap. She clearly made the driver, who was wearing virtually the same outfit, uncomfortable. York, in gray slacks and a white shirt, had broken into a sweat the moment he'd stepped outside the hotel.

As the houses dwindled into the desert, the original Aswan Dam, built by the British at the turn of the century, came into view ahead, its buttressed masonry walls standing a hundred feet high. The Rover turned onto the top of the dam, putting a sky-blue lake two kilometers wide on York's left, and a tumbled landscape of granite outcroppings, grass, and acacia trees on his right. The humbled Nile lay in a deep channel to the west. York looked past the driver toward the First Cataract, a landscape of blue water and white islands where triangular felucca sails tacked back and forth like slow, pale butterflies. The sunlight was so powerful that it bleached the panorama like an old photograph.

The scene had a timelessness, an immunity to change, that carried a powerful emotional resonance. Those feluccas, those rocks, those fishermen had been there since the days of the pharaohs, and they conjured a defiance, a sense that they would outlast the Aswan High Dam and the civilization that built it. They gave York a much-needed moment of perspective.

On the far side of the old dam lay the west bank, an expanse of dusty, broiling, hard packed desert that ran uninterrupted to the Libyan border. The Rover turned south again for five or six kilometers on a narrow strip of asphalt that drew a black line down an otherwise blank sheet of manila paper. The whine of the engine and the creak of the Rover's stiff suspension were loud enough to discourage small talk.

Eventually they passed a turnoff with a sign in half a dozen languages; the English portion read "Workers Estate." The driver said that many of the 30,000 workers employed on the dam project were quartered there. York glimpsed military barracks tents and improvised shelters made of cardboard, cloth, or jerry cans as the road curved toward the river again. Two minutes later they pulled up to the plain but modern cinderblock complex where the construction offices overlooked the dam site far below.

As York got out of the Rover, small explosions erupted in the valley like distant mortar fire, none of them sizeable enough to shake the high ground where he stood. He walked around to the front of the building and the spectacle of the excavation opened up before him. The work was concentrated on the east bank, where a thin wall of rock separated the riverbed from a vast trench that had been hacked and dynamited and chiseled from the granite bedrock. The mile-long trench ended at a solid granite wall, where two of the six tunnels in that wall were visible, 50 feet in diameter and 800 feet long. Those tunnels would eventually contain the turbines for the hydroelectric plant that was already taking shape high above, a broad, flat foundation of concrete that had sprouted a few low walls. By May of the next year, the Nile would be diverted through that channel and work on the main dam would begin.

At the moment the trench was a vision of hell. Smoke from the blasting trickled from the mouths of the tunnels as excavators lurched back and forth, striking sparks off the rock with their huge metal claws, and dump trucks crawled into position to receive their cargos of dust and rock. White-robed workmen climbed slowly over the uneven ground in the stupefying heat, only visible against the white granite when they were in motion.

Nadya touched his elbow. "The Assistant Minister is back from the site. We should go in now."

The blockhouse was air-conditioned to the low eighties, enough of a contrast to give York a brief chill. Their somewhat surly driver led them up a flight of metal stairs to a white-walled office that looked out on the site. A plain gray steel desk was buried in maps, blueprints, invoices, reports, and correspondence. Sorting through the layers of paper was a good-looking man with salt-and-pepper hair and mustache, both neatly trimmed, wearing a sweat-stained white shirt and khaki pants.

"Minister Rashid," the driver said, and excused himself.

Through Nadya, Rashid said, "Mornings are for explosions here. We go out after daybreak and begin planting the charges for the day's work. You heard some of them going off, I'm sure. The idea is to create enough of a mess that, with God's help, it will take all day and night to clean it up."

"You're working around the clock, then," York said.

"Three shifts, yes, though we don't get much accomplished in daylight because of the heat."

York found himself distracted by a cross section of the projected dam that was pinned to the wall. Rashid noticed and walked around the desk. "You are familiar with rock-fill dams?"

"In principle, yes," York said, "though I've never worked on one."

"You are used to the vertical dam. Hoover Dam, Grand Coulee Dam, Fontana Dam." It was strange to hear the English words in the midst of his rapid-fire Arabic, then to have to wait for Nadya to provide the context. "Those are only good when you have solid rock to build upon. Here the bed of the river is shifting sands. So you must make a gradual slope up and then down again."

In fact the cross section showed a flattened pyramid.

"Al Rayyes's pyramid, some call it," Rashid quipped. "His bid for immortality. And I expect he'll get it, too, God willing. To give you an idea, the amount of material in the dam will be fifteen times as much as in the Great Pyramid at Giza."

"I'd like to take a closer look at the work," York said. "Is that possible?"

"Yes, very possible. The sooner the better, however. It's already forty degrees out there." Nadya's voice changed as she interpolated, "That's well over a hundred degrees Fahrenheit."

York smiled. "That's all right, I speak Centigrade."

They walked downstairs to the frying pan of the parking lot. "We only use locals during the heat of the day," Rashid said. "The Cairenes can't tolerate it." As if summoned by telepathy, their driver pulled up next to them in the Rover. York and Nadya got in the back seat and they roared down to the edge of the lake, where a World War II landing craft had lowered its ramp onto the makeshift wooden dock. The boat was 50 feet long, painted in flaking silver, and wide enough for them to open the doors of the Rover and get out onto the metal deck. As they looked over the shoulder-high sides, York felt a cool, somewhat fetid breeze skim the gray-brown water.

"The river is at its highest now," Rashid said. He and Nadya both had to shout over the roar of the massive diesel engine. "You can see the silt that's washed down all the way from Uganda and Ethiopia. That is God's gift of life to Egypt, fertilizing her crops every year since time began."

"If you dam the river, doesn't the silt settle out?" York asked.

"Much of it, yes. But we are building a fertilizer factory that will be powered by the hydroelectric plant, and that will more than make up for the deficit."

It took only five minutes to cross the river, which was passing through a deep and narrow channel on its way to the old dam and the cataract. The Rover backed off the landing craft and got on a blacktop road that was crumbling at the edges; it took them to the edge of the pit. As they got out, Rashid got down on one knee and beckoned York over. "This is what we're dealing with." He pointed to a lighter spot in the blacktop. "There is only granite here. We had to blast the roadway out of solid rock. When we poured the asphalt, there were sharp bits of granite poking through everywhere. They tore the truck tires to ribbons. We had to send crews with hammers and chisels to clean the spikes of granite out of the road."

As they stood up, a bulbous Russian BelAz dump truck strained uphill toward them, engine screaming, two workmen hanging off of the back. It was filled to overflowing with chunks of pale granite.

"On its way to the holding area," Rashid said. "Next year we begin dumping it upstream to build a temporary coffer dam. As soon as that is finished, we blow up the wall here and divert the Nile through those six tunnels."

"What if that wall broke before you were ready?" York asked.

"We would be ruined. We would never meet our deadlines or our budget, the dam would never be finished, the government would probably fall, and Egypt would never be able to repay the money we borrowed to build it." Rashid smiled. "But do not worry. The wall is strong and nothing will happen to it."

AT THE HOTEL, York found the heat had exhausted him. He took two salt pills, drank a liter of water, showered, and slept for two hours. At four that afternoon he met Nadya in the lobby, where they picked up the keys to the car the hotel had hired for them.

York drove them over the same route they'd taken that morning, this time turning off into the workers' estate. The worst of the shanties were at the edges; as they approached the center York saw block after block of single-story unfinished plywood sheds, windowless, utilitarian, with deadbolts and screen-door handles. They were sturdy enough for their purpose and reasonably clean.

A stub-nosed blue Russian minibus, filled to capacity, passed them as it headed toward the work site. A constant stream of pedestrians, working men in twos or threes, trudged purposefully down the dusty side streets.

At the center was the Arab Contractors' Club, a great squared-off mass of concrete that occupied most of a city block, not counting the improbably blue swimming pool visible through a chain link fence. A middle-aged man in Western clothes was leaving the building, and York pulled up to the curb to ask him, "Do you speak English?"

The man smiled. "La, ana assif."

To Nadya, York said, "Can you ask him about this place?"

It was a private club, Nadya translated, for workers hired by the Arab Contractors construction and engineering company, who had built the workers' village and was one of several contractors on the dam. Guests had access to a movie theater, restaurant, game rooms, TV—luxuries many of them had never seen before.

"Shokran," York said.

As they pulled away, Nadya said, "I thought you didn't speak any Arabic."

"A half dozen words. Please and thank you are the first to learn in any language, yes?"

He drove around to the back of the complex, where a concrete wall separated a row of garbage cans from the grounds. Someone had drawn two concentric circles on the wall in thin white paint. At that size, two meters high, it looked ominously like a target.

He parked on a side street. There were not many private vehicles in the estate and thus not many parking spaces. Like the construction offices, the club was lightly air-conditioned. Nadya talked to the uniformed security guard inside the front door, who smiled at York and swept his hand toward the lobby. "Welcome," he said in English.

Nadya read the handwritten poster boards on the wall and said, "There's meant to be a bar over there."

York nodded and followed her into a small, dimly lit room. Despite stools lined up at a long wooden bar and a few tables with candles, the floor was linoleum tile and the only available drinks were non-alcoholic. The place was half full, the clientele of course all male, most of them dressed in western cast-offs—shabby pants and T-shirts or faded long-sleeved dress shirts.

Though they were out of earshot of the nearest customer as they stood in the doorway, York kept his voice low. "This is hopeless," he said. "There must be at least, what, ten thousand workmen in this village? We know that some of them are part of this Al-Mashiah Ra outfit—we saw their handiwork on the wall. But my only contact is dead, I don't speak the language, and they won't talk to you because you're a woman. I've got no way to even stir up trouble."

Nadya patted his hand. "Leave it to me."

"No disrespect, but what can you do?"

"More, perhaps, than you think. I'll need the car later tonight. For now, let's go back to the hotel and have an early dinner."

"You intend to go out alone after dark?"

She smiled gently, reminding York of their "argument" the night before. "You're not responsible for me. I'm employed by the Embassy, and I know my job. And God is wise and compassionate and I will be safe in his hands."


THEY HAD DINNER on the patio of the hotel, with the rushing river and the drifting feluccas already in twilight as the sun touched the western hills.

"Tell me, Mr. York," Nadya said, "if I may be so bold, how did you end up in this line of work? The other men I've met in your profession generally resembled bureaucrats or salesmen."

"I've never fit in," he said at last. "My parents are quite well off, and even as a kid I disliked that feeling of privilege. I wanted to do something useful with my life, and they fought me at every turn. I think I might have been happy if I could have been an auto mechanic or a carpenter or something."

"Why didn't you? Once you were on your own, surely you could have taken up a trade?"

"There's an entire culture that goes with that sort of work, and I don't fit into that either."

"I barely know you, yet I have a strong feeling that you're at war with yourself. A war of self-determination, if you will."

York shrugged uncomfortably.

"This job," she went on, "lets you be many people, none of whom are really you. Perhaps this is part of why women find you so attractive. There's the mystery, and there's the sense that you need to be saved from yourself."

York seized the chance to change the subject. "Are you speaking for yourself, here?"

"What do you mean?"

"When you say women find me attractive."

After a pause, she said, "Theoretically, I suppose."

"Only in theory?"

"Mr. York, you are pressing me for answers that I am perfectly willing to give, but that you might find uncomfortable."

"If it's that you prefer women, you won't find me that easily shocked."

"Do you really want the truth?"

"I care very much about the truth. Whatever other motives you may ascribe to me, the search for truth is one of the fundamental aspects of what I do. Breaking codes, discovering secrets."

"And you wish to break my codes?"

"I would like to know your secrets, yes."

"Very well then. If at some point this becomes too unpleasant for you, raise your hand or something and I'll stop."

"Now I really am intrigued."

"Do you know what female circumcision is?"

"I expect I've heard of it."

"It's a deceptive term. It implies a minor cosmetic operation, a harmless religious ritual, like circumcision for males. In fact it is female castration. It is the complete removal of the clitoris, often with a rusty razor blade. From your expression I take it you are familiar

with the clitoris. Cultures across Africa and the Middle East practice it. It is supposed to keep us from having lustful thoughts, and
while it is not completely effective at that, it does make the notion
of sexual fulfillment rather abstract. In the baldest terms, Mr. York,
no orgasms. Over three quarters of the women in this country were
subjected to this, usually as small children. Myself included. None of
us will ever have an orgasm."

York's face was cold. His hands were cold. He set his knife and
fork carefully on the table.

"I'm sorry," Nadya said. "I should have waited until you finished
eating."

"It looks like I *am* finished." He drank the last of his beer, which
spread the chill to his stomach and groin. "How can you...how can
you continue to be a Moslem when..."

"This has nothing do with Islam, Mr. York. This is an Arab phe-
nomenon. They did this to women in the time of the pharaohs.
Herodotus wrote about it in the fifth century BC. And, frankly,
though I resent this being done to me against my will, I have a good
life. I find sex pleasurable enough. I enjoy the intimacy. It's possible
to have other things to live for than sexual gratification."

York found himself, for once, without words.

Nadya patted his hand. "Please don't dwell on this. It's simply the
way things are here, and have been for thousands of years. Though I
do hope for a future where things are different." She looked at her
watch. "Now, if I might have the car keys, I must go. I'll call your
room in the morning, hopefully with news."

York handed her the keys. "And you won't tell me where
you're going?"

"In the morning," Nadya said, pushing back her chair, "all will
be revealed."

YORK SPENT a restless night, obsessively searching for a way to
regain control of the mission. It was hardly fair; feelings of his life
being out of control had led him to the Company in the first place.

When the phone woke him at 9:30, he had been dreaming of Russia, of a dacha in winter where the air was thick with smoke of Balkan Sobranie cigarettes, and as he came out of the dream he realized he had identified the heavy, sweet odor that he'd smelled on Chang's clothes. The antidote to helplessness, it seemed, was to keep processing the available data, even in his sleep.

It was Nadya on the phone. He agreed to meet her at 10 at the hotel restaurant.

When he got there, the sun shades were down on the covered patio and the thrumming of the ceiling fans blended into a jittery rhythm. York ordered three eggs and a small steak to make up for his lost appetite from the night before.

"I have a contact," Nadya said. She wore loose off-white cotton trousers, a matching long-sleeved top and scarf, and sunglasses. "His name is Bisri al-Hakim."

"Who is he?"

"He's in charge of a work crew that's finishing the insides of the tunnels on the two to ten PM shift. Over the last six months he has manipulated things such that his entire crew are now members of Al-Mashiah Ra."

"How did you find him?"

She took off her sunglasses. Her eyes were bloodshot and puffy. She rubbed them wearily with the back of her hand. "I haven't met Bisri himself yet. I spent the night talking to prostitutes. I shall need considerable reimbursement from petty cash."

That many men, far from home, with more money than they'd ever seen before—naturally there would be prostitutes. And hashish, and gambling, no doubt. "We didn't see any women at all yesterday."

"The government is being realistic about it. The women have their own village on the far side of the workers' estate. There are soldiers stationed there to keep things peaceful, which is apparently not that hard, as they are strict about the prohibition of spirits. There are doctors who are attempting to keep the women free of venereal disease and give them some basic education as to hygiene and birth control."

"How did you figure all this out?"

"It wasn't that difficult. I showed up at the estate dressed for the part and was quickly directed to where I needed to be."

She showed him her mocking smile again, daring him to imagine her lush body in scant and tight fitting clothes. York felt an odd stab of jealousy. "You're a remarkable woman," he said, grudgingly. "Do you know how to find this Bisri?"

"If my new friend Hasnah is successful, we'll meet him tonight at midnight."

YORK ASKED HER to call and cancel their lunch appointment with Minister Rashid, then get some sleep. She reluctantly agreed.

With the rest of the day before him, York wandered down to the river. A man in his early twenties called out to him, "English, you want sailboat ride? I take you cheap." He had a blue and white striped galabiya and wore his turban at a jaunty angle.

York liked the gleam in his eye. On impulse he asked, "Can you take me upstream to the dam?"

"Old dam, yes." They settled on a price of five pounds. The man, whose name was Yusef, pushed the nose of his felucca into the river and held the stern while York climbed aboard, then pushed off and scrambled in after him. He fitted a rudder onto the rear of the boat and raised the sail, steering with one hand and handling the lines with the other.

The boat was fifteen feet long, made of unpainted wood that shone along the gunwales from the friction of many hands. It was crudely made and rode low in the water, but was sturdy and dry for all of that. The Nile smelled of silt and fish and the sunlight dazzled York's eyes. The creak of the rudder and the sloshing of the water against the sides and the sigh of the mast as the sail filled against it brought him his first real peace in days.

Yusef recognized the quality of York's attention. "You know how to sail, yes, English?"

"Yes."

"You want to sail the boat? Five pounds more, I let you."

"You want me to do the work and you get paid extra for it? If I do the sailing, you should pay me."

Yusef laughed and luffed the sail. "No extra charge," he said, and stood up. York carefully traded places with him and raised the sail again. It took him a minute to find the wind, and when he did, the felucca was slow to respond, wallowing heavily in the water. He got the hang of it quickly enough, though, and Yusef pointed him toward the channel that would take them upstream.

Sailing had been his method of choice to escape his parents. It had also given him an outlet for the recklessness that would take him like a black mood and send him into foul weather or into the shipping lanes to play hide and seek with freighters headed into Chesapeake Bay. Then, as now, it gave him something he had power over.

As they approached the dam, York said, "There's no way to get upstream from here?"

"No, is as far as I go."

"No portage, no locks, no way to get past the dam?"

"No, not since they build it, not for sixty years now. Nobody gets through."

Later, in the deep water near the dam, Yusef pointed out something brown and conical, at its thickest the diameter of a car tire. As they closed on it, York smelled the decay.

"Catfish," Yusef said. "Nile cat."

Only the head remained, and it was three feet long. "My God," York said. "How big was that when it was alive?"

"How big," Yusef said, "is the fish that bite that head off?"


HASNAH WAS NOT PERMITTED in the men's housing estate, so the meet was set for a public square in the village of the prostitutes, a kind of souk for female flesh. Crude park benches lined the sides of the square, in pairs, back to back, so that prospective clients could walk around an inner circle and an outer circle before making a selection. At each corner, a uniformed policeman with an M-1 rifle slouched and bantered listlessly with the women nearest him. A string of bare, low-wattage bulbs hung above each row of benches. Fewer than 30 women were on offer as York and Nadya drove up. York parked in the shadow of an apartment block next to the square.

Like most of the working-class prostitutes that York had encountered, these women were not romantic figures. Many were in a fog of hashish, opium, or worse. As each new man approached, some attempted a weary smile or a mildly provocative pose. Most took for granted that they would be chosen eventually. As York watched, a steady stream of customers arrived, made quick selections, and disappeared again into the darkness. A roughly equivalent stream of women arrived to replace the ones chosen.

Midnight came and went. At 12:20 a man and woman entered the square together and Nadya, suddenly tense, said, "That's Hasnah."

Hasnah was short, dark skinned, and fashionably plump. She wore a flowered shift with sweat stains under the arms and a low neckline that advertised her best features. The man with her was nothing like what York had imagined. He was Nubian rather than Arab, very dark skinned, with a large, flat nose and generous lips. He wore a galabiya, a brightly colored skull cap, and leather sandals. He was five foot ten, stocky in an athletic way, and radiated good cheer.

Nadya got out and walked toward them as Bisri looked her over appreciatively, head to toe. York couldn't hear their voices, only read their body language. Bisri was reluctant, Hasnah nervous. After a minute of conversation, Nadya gave Hasnah a folded banknote and she walked quickly away. Bisri followed Nadya to the car and sat in the passenger seat while Nadya got in the back.

"Good evening," York said. "Thank you for talking with me."

As Nadya started to translate, Bisri waved one large hand. "I have some English. I was cook for a British regiment for many years." He was turned sideways in the seat, his attention directed out the windshield.

"How did you end up in construction?"

"I had a change in my heart." He patted his chest. "The English, begging your pardon, are the enemy. Egypt should be for the Egyptians."

"Isn't the High Dam for Egyptians too?"

"It is for the glory of Gamal Abdul Nasser. It makes us owing the Soviets, like before we were owing the British."

"But you're helping to build it."

"A man has to eat."

"It also puts you in a position to do harm."

"Why would I want to do that?"

Bisri had neatly put him on the defensive. York attempted to regroup. "There are a lot of people who would like to see the dam fail. For a lot of reasons."

"Including you?"

"Yes."

"Why? Are you CIA?" The big man's smile did not hide the light of cunning in his eyes.

"I represent a group of businessmen who don't want to see the Soviets get a foothold in the Middle East."

"Businessmen with money?"

At last, York thought, we come to the point. "That's right."

"Money to see, as you say, the dam to fail."

"Yes."

"So why do you come to me?"

"Because I think maybe you don't like Nasser any more than we do."

"Who tell you that? Did Hasnah tell you that?" York didn't answer. "Hasnah is a whore. You shouldn't listen to whores." He glanced over his shoulder at Nadya.

York felt him slipping away. "Do you know anything about a group called Al-Mashiah Ra?"

He saw his mistake as soon as the words were out. Bisri looked him directly in the eyes for the first time and his smile fell away.

"No," he said. He got out of the car, then leaned in the open window to say, "I think you have the wrong man."

As he walked away, Nadya said, "That went well."

"I'm out of my depth," York said.

"Yes, I think you are. And I fear we have cost Hasnah a beating."

"Damn."

Nadya got in the passenger seat. "There's nothing more to be done tonight. We might as well go back to the hotel."

HALF A KILOMETER from the square, the headlights picked up a crude sawhorse blocking the street. A teenage boy in a galabiya sat on top of it, waving them toward an alley.

"I don't like the look of this," York said, slowing. "Ask him what's the matter."

York stopped a few meters short of the boy and Nadya stuck her head out the window and called to him. The boy, instead of answering, slipped off the sawhorse and ran away.

"Something's fishy," York said. Before he could put the car in reverse, someone rushed out of the darkness with a length of two-by-four and smashed the windshield. York's door flew open and hands dragged him onto the pavement.

They were amateurs, fortunately, all of them trying to throw kicks and punches at once. York bent over, partly to shield himself, mostly to get his feet under him. Once he was grounded, he threw a side kick that took out the knee of the man closest to him. The man went down with a scream and York turned, grabbed an arm, and threw a second man over his back and onto the ground. With space now to get his bearings, he saw three more men on his side of the car, including the one with the two-by-four. York took the board away and hit him in the solar plexus with one end. The other two ran away.

A gunshot echoed off the plywood walls. York spun around to see Nadya pointing a small caliber automatic at the sky as two men fled from her.

The shot would bring the Army in moments. "Get in the car," he ordered. He threw the sawhorse aside and climbed in as Nadya was closing her door. He still had the two-by-four and he used it to clear a hole big enough to navigate by in the shattered windshield. As he put the car in gear, bits of safety glass scattered across the seat and floor.

"That was very impressive," Nadya said.

"You shouldn't have used the gun," York said. "Now when they come back, they'll have guns too."

"You're not armed?"

"I avoid it if I can. Guns are usually more trouble than they're worth. I'm surprised you carry one."

"Are you really? With the way women are treated in this country?" She was being facile, but York lacked the patience to pursue it.

After a long pause, Nadya said, "What do we do now?"

"This man Bisri is our only lead. I'm going to have to shadow him."

"How are you even going to find him again?"

"I'll find him," York said.

THEY RODE TO THE HOTEL in uncomfortable silence, York brooding over the many ways the mission was spiraling toward failure. He had to keep his speed below 50 KPH to prevent the surprisingly cool wind that came through the hole in the windshield from blinding him.

He left the car keys with Nadya along with instructions to call the car hire agency for a replacement in the morning. Their mutual fault-finding had left them wary of each other and their farewells were curt.

York took a hot shower and inventoried his bruises, all of which were minor. It was 2:30 by the time he was in bed, and he had to resort to one of the mantras he'd learned in Burma in order to relax enough to fall asleep.

He came instantly awake again before dawn when he heard a click at his door. With no hesitation, he rolled out of the far side of the bed and lay on the floor, hidden by the trailing edge of the duvet. The door clicked again and made a brushing noise on the carpet as it swung open. A second later the bed shook as the intruders pounded on it with some sort of clubs.

There was silence, then muffled cursing in Arabic. When the overhead lights came on, the duvet shielded his eyes enough to keep him from being blinded. When he was sure that he could see clearly, he rolled away from the bed and sprang to his feet.

There were only two men this time. They wore dark pants and T-shirts and zip jackets, and they carried lengths of bamboo. One of them took a cricket batter's swing at York that he easily sidestepped, then he moved in quickly and punched the man in his large gut and his throat. As the other man turned to run, York tackled him, driving his head into the door frame.

With both men incapacitated, York started toward the phone to call the front desk, then changed his mind. He took a pen knife from his trousers where they lay over a chair and used it to rip one of the sheets into wide strips. He quickly bound and gagged both men, then made a quick search of their pockets that revealed, as he expected, nothing at all.

He called Nadya's room. She answered groggily on the third ring.

"Are you all right?" he asked.

"Yes, why?"

"I've had visitors. Is your gun handy?"

"It's beside the bed."

"Get dressed and wait to hear from me. If anyone tries to come through your door without knocking, shoot them."

His second call was to his emergency contact in Aswan. Then he put on clean clothes, packed his garment bag, and made a half-hearted effort to straighten the room, keeping one eye on his guests.

By the time the discreet knock came at the door, the sky had turned a tentative shade of gray and the dawn call to prayer was echoing across the city. York stood to one side of the door, holding a bamboo staff. "Who is it?"

"Carlson."

York opened the door. A fresh-faced young man in round glasses and white coveralls pushed a rolling laundry hamper into the room. "Where's the dirty clothes?" he asked.

Together they loaded the two struggling bodies into the hamper and threw the remains of York's top sheet over them.

"What should I do with them?"

"Take them a mile or two into the desert and dump them. I expect they'll be able to untie each other eventually."

"Do you need a lift anywhere?"

"We'll chance it later, once we've got a new hired car."

"Right. Here's the binoculars you wanted and a map to the safe house. You'll have your translator along to help with the addresses?"

York nodded. "Thanks."

"Good luck. Call if you need anything."

Carlson, whistling softly to himself, wheeled the hamper into the hall. York called Nadya's room again and told her to start packing.

THAT AFTERNOON, York spread a dozen full-color brochures across Minister Rashid's desk. Bright red and silver Kenworth T800 dump trucks, phosphorescent yellow John Deere excavators and Link Belt HTC-series cranes. Rashid and four of his top-level supervisors stood around the table with longing in their eyes. If York had brought pinup photos of American starlets, he could not have more fully engaged their attention.

He was exhausted, as Nadya must have been. After getting the car exchanged and moving house, they'd found a flea market where York had bought shabby, locally made work clothes, sandals, a bandana, and a turban, which Nadya had reluctantly agreed to tie for him. Though the clothes had been washed, the perfume of the detergent barely masked the odor of years of sweat and corrosive sunlight. York hid them under the front seat of the car and then they bolted down a meal from a market stall before driving to the dam site.

"With an expedited order," York said, "we could deliver them in Alexandria in three weeks."

One of the supervisors actually licked his lips.

"And now," York said, "if I may, I'd like to leave these with you and do some more investigating on the site."

Nadya stifled a yawn as she translated Rashid's reply. "Of course. Let me call my driver."

"Is it all right if we take our own car?" York said. "I don't want to be a bother."

"It is no bother."

York offered his best smile. "I really would prefer to drive myself."

Rashid inclined his head. "Mind your tires," he said. "The roads are treacherous."

THEY TOOK THE FERRY and then York drove to the edge of the pit, and then past it, onto a ridge where massive boulders hid them from the view of the offices on the west bank and the workers on the East.

At one point Nadya said, "Please be careful. I don't want to have to explain a second wrecked car." Other than that she was silent. The fatigue that dragged at both of them only added to the strain.

York parked and handed Nadya the keys. "Go to the safe house and get some sleep. I won't have an easy way to call you, so let's set a rendezvous at the Arab Contractor's Club at midnight. If I'm not there, try again at six AM. If I miss that one too, get back to Cairo somehow and give Giles a full report."

He climbed over the seat and began to change into the work clothes.

"You're being quite ridiculous," Nadya said. "What do you hope to accomplish by this, other than blowing your cover at the very least, and most likely getting yourself killed? You don't speak the language, you can't pass for Egyptian. This is a complete fool's errand."

"I've never claimed it was anything else," York said. "Bisri is our only lead. You can't follow him. I can at least try."

"Samson in the temple. If a man can't get his way, he must pull everything down around him."

"What would you have me do?"

"Admit defeat. Retire from the battlefield with your life."

"Politics is a good career choice for you," York said. "Can you help me with this turban?"

She sighed. "Lean forward."

York was sure she tied it more tightly than was strictly necessary. He would probably end up with a headache before the night was out, if his head was still attached to his body.

He took a long drink from a canteen of filtered water, then got out and squatted in the sand, legs spread, knees high, and began to rub dirt on his face.

Nadya watched him from the car. "Remarkable. Where did you learn to sit like that? I could have mistaken you for an Arab."

"I pay attention," York said. "How do you say 'deaf' in Arabic?"

" 'Atrash," she said. "Why?"

"Thinking ahead. You should go now."

"Listen," she said. "I'm sorry for...I'm sorry this hasn't gone well."

"It rarely does. It's not your fault. You've done really well, and I apologize for underestimating you."

"Listen to us," she said with false heartiness. "Talking as if we'll never see each other again. I'll see you at midnight."

"Insha'Allah," York said. He raised his hand as she drove away.


HE GOT OUT the binoculars and walked downhill to a position he'd noted earlier. It was out of the sight lines of the construction offices, partly shaded, and had a view down into the pit. He checked his watch, a cheap Timex with a plain leather band. Twelve past four. The temperature had to be at least 120, and it was three hours until nightfall, six hours until the end of Bisri's shift.

He focused the binoculars on the area in front of the tunnels. For a long time the movements of the workers appeared random, like the crowds at a Macy's Thanksgiving Sale. Then, gradually, he began to make sense of it. These men directed the fleets of machinery, and these shoveled the sharp-edged rock fragments out of the roadway where they had spilled on their way from the excavator to the back of the dump truck. These refilled the barrels of drinking water and these tended the machines, changing tires and fan belts, adding oil to crankcases and water to the radiators. A few in sunglasses and billed caps carried a roll of blueprints or a stadia rod or a walkie-talkie.

The noise was incessant, a physical assault. The whine of diesel motors that constantly rose and fell in pitch, the grinding of gears, the crash of metal against rock, the thud of rock on metal, the screaming voices, the clatter of jackhammers, the warning klaxons and truck horns. It was muted somewhat where York lay, doubtless deafening in the enclosed walls of the pit.

As York watched, a cement mixer waddled down the uneven road into the thick of it, the asphalt under its tires rutted and buckled from the relentless heat and constant use. It parked in front of the second tunnel from the left. A man emerged from the depths of the tunnel with a wheelbarrow and filled it with wet concrete from the spout. It was not Bisri, but it was almost certainly one of his crew.

York hid the binoculars under some rubble and put his head on his folded arms. He pushed the noise away with an effort of will and instructed himself to sleep until 7:00.

HE AWOKE HUNGRY, thirsty, and depressed. In the twilight, the whole venture seemed both impossible and pointless. The noise, if anything, was louder than before, and the glare of the sun had been replaced by stark white light emanating from banks of mercury vapor lamps, like the ones at baseball games in the States.

On assignment in Benares, York had listened to a Hindu sannyasi explain the mortification of the flesh, and he had understood the concept immediately on an emotional level. He thought of that now as he got to his feet, welcoming the hollow pain in his stomach and the ache in his stiffened muscles, defying them to slow him down.

He worked his way downward, at first hiding when trucks appeared, then, as the traffic increased, walking alongside them. Sometimes voices called to him and he ignored them.

In the pit, the clanging and roaring was a Pentacostal's soundtrack of Hell. The sweetish, metallic stink of poorly combusted diesel blanketed the smells of sweat and cologne and burning rubber. The faces of the men around him looked like death masks, white powdery dust clinging to the sheen of perspiration. He tied his bandana over the lower half of his face as some of the other man had, and for a minute or two his breathing came more easily.

He moved slowly toward the tunnels, pausing from time to time to join in the work, lending his weight to three or four other men pulling on a line, spelling a man on a jackhammer. Once some sort of supervisor grabbed him by the arm and shouted at him angrily, pointing him in the direction of a stalled tractor, and York nodded and pretended to understand.

At ten o'clock a steam whistle blew and work came to an abrupt halt. Men climbed out of truck cabs or threw down their shovels where they stood and began to move along the road toward the open air, as the long column of their replacements passed them on their left.

York squatted near the entrance of the second tunnel and held his head in his hands. The heat alone had been enough to exhaust him within minutes. He had forced himself to dip tin cups of water from the barrels, despite its oily smell and texture, and drink it down. His intestines would probably pay, eventually; the alternative was worse in the short term.

He heard voices in the tunnel behind him and then a loud, heartfelt laugh that he recognized as Bisri's. He kept his head down as the crew passed and then slowly got to his feet and followed at a few meters' distance. By the time they were climbing the road, other men had filled the space between them and York had confirmed, from a glimpse of his profile, Bisri's presence. As he watched, Bisri put a hand to his stomach, as if he felt a pang of indigestion.

Hunger, thirst, and fatigue had left York light-headed. He was taking too much pleasure, he knew, in this minor success. For the moment, though, he was in control, with a clear, defined task in front of him, and grateful for it.

At the river they stood in docile formation, waiting for a landing craft to ferry them across. One boat docked as soon as the previous boat left, taking a hundred or so workers at a time. York was impressed by their patience and lack of aggression.

As the crowd ahead of him dwindled, he shuffled closer to Bisri for fear of being left behind. He kept his eyes unfocused, and when the man next to him tried to engage him in conversation, he pointed to his ear, shook his head, and said, " 'Atrash."

Mosquitoes swarmed at the edge of the water. The workers around him were indifferent to them, so York resisted the urge to swat, casually wiping his face when he felt one bite his cheek. He tried not to think about malaria or, worse, dengue. Bonebreak fever, they called it at the Benares station, because of the ache in the joints and the severity of the chills.

Finally they surged onto a boat. For as long as it took to get on board, he stayed within arm's reach of Bisri, then slowly edged away. Luck put him near the railing. Once they were moving, his sweat turned cool in the breeze and the mosquitoes dissipated.

The stars were so thick in the sky that they seemed to be in layers. The voices of the men and the throbbing of the engines and the splashing of the wake were curiously soothing as they echoed across the water. They were the sounds of completion, of imminent food and rest, the furthest point from the next day's work. For a moment York wished he were one of them, that the rest of his night were going to be that simple.

A flatbed truck waited for them on the far side. The only thing that kept the men from falling out was a rough sisal rope wound through stakes along the sides. York allowed himself to be pushed into the center, surrounded by the reek and body heat of the men. He breathed through his mouth and let his body sway with

the motion as the truck ground its way uphill toward the housing estate.

The truck made three stops inside the compound, and Bisri got
off at the last one, along with York and the thirty-odd remaining
men. They moved as one toward a nearby souk where crude food
stalls faced into a courtyard with tables and chairs. York got on line
at a stall some distance from the one where Bisri stood, and he saw
Bisri touch his stomach again, apparently unconsciously.

York decided that ordering food was less risky than sitting at
a table without eating. He was also starved. When his turn came
he said, "Falafel," and laid down a pound note. The man asked
him something and York said, "Aiwa," yes, which satisfied him. He
slapped down a few piasters in change and handed York a small
newspaper-wrapped bundle and a bottle of Pepsi.

In the darkest corner of the square, he found a chair that faced
into the courtyard. He was in operations mode. He was a set of
receptors and alarms, scanning his surroundings, reviewing data,
absorbing everything and emitting nothing. Some of those receptors
noted that the falafel was hot and delicious. The passage of time was
irrelevant as long as he had his target in view and he himself was
not attracting attention.

With three shifts working around the clock, time had little meaning in any case. Here in the middle of the night, men roamed the
streets, arguing and laughing, and an impromptu soccer game had
started in the next block. The lines at the food stalls stayed constant
and the streets were brightly lit throughout the night.

Someone brought another round of Pepsis to Bisri's table. The
crew had settled in, so York risked a quick trip to the row of public toilets on the other side of the square. Each stall contained a
plywood seat with a hole and a bucket underneath. Nadya had
explained the system to him. Several times a day a truck, euphe-
mistically called the "honey wagon," came around to a trapdoor in
the back to empty the bucket and pour a layer of disinfectant in the
bottom. The honey wagon workers were the untouchables of the

Arab world, and every village had its legend of the day the train collided with the honey wagon. This particular honey bucket had not
been emptied recently and the sharp chemical tang of the disinfectant was losing the battle with the reek of human waste and the
swarming flies.

When he opened the door of the stall, Bisri was no longer at
his table.

Fighting panic, York glanced to his right. There were twenty or
thirty men walking away, several of whom might have been Bisri.
He turned to his left and nearly stumbled into Bisri himself as he
emerged from the next stall.

York looked down and mumbled, "Ana assif."

"Malesh," Bisri said.

York returned to his table. Bisri had looked him directly in the
face for some fraction of a second. Even if he hadn't recognized
York from the night before—and the car had been dark, their
contact brief, the circumstances entirely different—he might have
sensed something off in York's disguise. At the very least, he had
now imprinted York's appearance and would be more likely to notice him in a crowd.

With more resources, York would have pulled out and put another operative in play. He had only Nadya, who was useless in the
village. The assignment teetered on the edge of failure and York was
not yet ready to let it go.

He considered losing the turban, but his American haircut would
stand out a mile away. Although he had enough of a tan to go shirt-
less, he'd noticed none of the other men did, no matter how high
the temperature, and he suspected some sort of cultural prohibition.

So when Bisri's crew at last stood up, York gave them a head start
and then followed.

The object was to be inconspicuous, which meant not hurrying,
attaching himself to first one clump of strangers and then another,
always keeping people between himself and Bisri. One by one, other
members of the group broke off, sometimes embracing one or two

of the others before unlocking a plywood apartment door. Occasionally one of the doors would be open as York passed, and he saw that the insides were all the same—bare plywood floor, four metal cots along one wall, a single light bulb in the ceiling, an enameled pitcher and basin for washing up.

Finally Bisri, after several hugs and handshakes, went into one of the rooms. York immediately turned into a side street and squatted down with his back against a wall. Bisri's door was just visible past the corner of the building across the street.

He glanced at his watch. It was one-thirty, long past his rendezvous with Nadya. He had kept his sense of direction, if little else. He knew that turning left onto the street that had brought him here would eventually take him to the main paved road, where a right would get him to the Arab Contractor's Club. The streets were marked with stenciled icons—a camel, a palm tree, a pyramid, a dog's head—on the corners of the buildings, with numbers below for the more literate workers. The colors of the spray paint changed every ten blocks. Bisri's building was at the corner of a green cobra and a black shepherd's crook.

The challenge at this point was to stay awake. Soldiers patrolled the streets regularly, and York would not survive an interrogation with his fifteen words of Arabic. He took one sandal off and saw that it had worn a raw patch on top of his foot. Sooner or later that was going to be painful.

He pretended to tinker with the sandal for a few minutes, then a wave of fatigue hit him. He had accomplished enough for one day. He had tracked Bisri to his lair and could find him again if he needed to. Clearly nothing else was going to happen tonight.

He put the sandal on and got to his feet. The muscles in his legs tightened in pain. He had to brace himself against the plywood behind him and stretch. When he looked up, two men were standing outside Bisri's door.

York froze.

Bisri opened the door and glanced down the street in both

directions. If he registered York's presence, he didn't show it. He locked up his room, put his arms over the shoulders of the two men, and they walked away together.

Now that York had seen the raw wound on his foot, it cried out for attention. He tried to conjure the image of an unselfconscious walk, focusing on the mechanics of moving among the other men on the street. The crowds thinned, and then, abruptly, the official mass-produced order of the estate gave out and the ad-hoc shanties began. There were no more floodlights on poles, only campfires and moonlight. Dogs with patchy fur and prominent ribs roamed purposefully between the huts. A scrawny old man and two black-swaddled older women, one of them with a baby in her arms, sat in the dirt with outstretched hands. A six-year-old boy with one eye leaking pus tugged at York's clothing, crying, "Baksheesh, baksheesh!"

Even as he felt exposed and vulnerable, York's excitement was rising. Bisri had to be close to his destination, if only because the possibilities were nearly exhausted. Time slowed as York's sympathetic nervous system went into overdrive. He heard the sand crunch under the feet of the man next to him and smelled the goat meat roasting a hundred meters away. The colors and shapes around him became vectors and he tracked the subtle changes in their trajectories without conscious thought.

Bisri and the two others turned between two of the huts. York stopped, pretended to adjust his shoe again, then slowly walked past where they'd turned and glanced casually after them.

They had vanished.

York doubled back. The hut on his right was built from empty fruit crates and roofed with a sheet of clear plastic. On his left was an improvised pup tent made of bedsheets. He passed a refrigerator-sized cardboard box lying on its side, a lean-to made of scrap wood, another of corrugated aluminum. The inhabitants had no obvious reason to be there other than proximity to the comparative wealth of the workers. There was no sight or sound of Bisri or his men.

The alley abruptly emptied into desert and York realized, too late, that he had been deceived. He spun around to see Bisri standing in front of him with folded arms.

"Hello, CIA," Bisri said.

In the flickering light of a burning torch, York saw one of Bisri's men a few meters to his left, the other closing on his right. The flames made a rattling noise in the desert wind.

"You must think us very stupid," Bisri said. "With your sad costume and your dirty face. Did you think I would not know you as soon as I came out of the tunnel and saw you sitting there in your pale skin and foolish turban?"

"I'm here to help you," York said calmly. "We're on the same side."

"We don't want your help," Bisri said. "Do you think us children? Savages? Trained monkeys, perhaps. We are quite capable, you see."

York turned again as another shape moved toward him out of the darkness. It was a small man, dressed completely in black. Still in the shadows, the man stopped, crouched slightly, and pulled his arms into his chest. York couldn't see his face, but he knew the art that underlay the movement.

It was Chang, head of security for Dr. Helios.

YORK KICKED OFF his sandals and felt the sand warm his feet. He pulled off his turban and tossed it after the sandals. Then he loosened his shoulders and began to circle to his left. Chang shadowed him, maintaining his distance, edging into the light. He moved with the grace and restraint and lethal threat of the tiger York had once encountered in the Burmese jungle. The tiger had stalked away into the undergrowth; he would not be so lucky with Chang. He could read nothing in Chang's expression, no curiosity or amusement or swagger.

York knew he was no match for Chang, and the longer he hesitated, the more advantage he gave up. He moved closer and Chang did the same, leaving them four meters apart, still circling. This was no time, York, decided, for fair play. He kicked sand directly at

Chang's eyes with his right foot and pushed himself forward with the other, taking two running steps and throwing a flying kick at the side of Chang's knee.

What happened next came so fast that he never saw it. Something hit him in the solar plexus, in the jaw below his left ear, in the throat, in the right temple, and in the upper chest, with no perceptible interval between the blows. One moment he was in the air, the next he lay battered on the ground, unable to breathe, half-blind and paralyzed by pain.

It took all his strength to suck air into his collapsed lungs, and he paid an agonizing price for every cubic centimeter. His brain was trying to shut down and he fought to stay conscious, to focus his eyes. He blinked tears away and dimly saw Chang with a hand on Bisri's shoulder, giving him what looked like a sheaf of bills.

After that he blacked out briefly, and came to as he felt himself lifted by the arms and legs and dragged across the sand. The weight of his own body, hanging from his shoulders and hips, seemed to tear fresh wounds in his chest and groin. Then they were swinging him, and he was weightless for a long second before he landed hard in the back of a Land Rover, his head bouncing off the metal floor and the darkness closing in again.

He would have remained unconscious if he could, but the Rover was moving fast, hitting rocks and potholes that lifted him off the floor and then flung him into it again and again. Every breath was a difficult choice between asphyxiation and agony. The inside of his head was trying to push its way out through his skull and his stomach lurched with every bump.

When the Rover finally skidded to a stop, he smelled water and knew they were close to the river. Sparks winked on and off like fireflies and a dark fog filled the back of the Rover. He suspected that neither the fog nor the fireflies were real. He quickly lost all sense of how long the Rover had been stopped.

Suddenly the tailgate flew open and hands reached for him. The hallucinations, he was sure, were intensifying, because the men who

dragged him out and tied him to a stretcher wore the white linen
robes of ancient Egyptians. They had headbands made of gold fabric
and they had lined their eyes with kohl and drawn two concentric
circles around their right eyes. The eyes themselves were glazed,
as if they were drugged. Some of them carried metal rods with a
glowing crystal in one end. He couldn't tell how many there were
because they all looked the same.

The Rover was parked at some sort of secondary dock. There was
a wooden shack and there were at least two other Rovers standing
nearby, but no other people except the weird costumed men. They
carried York onto a motor launch by the light of their rods and laid
his stretcher lengthwise across the center seats. The engine, which
had been gurgling quietly, roared to life and they began to race
across the water. York's stomach heaved. He kept from vomiting, less
out of concern for his dignity than from fear that he might strangle.

As soon as they hit full speed they slowed again, and the launch
made a sharp turn that brought them to rest against the hull of a
larger ship. Hands reached down and the men in the launch passed
him up. York found himself dragged onto a teak deck and left there,
staring up at the night sky. He tried to get up on one elbow and his
arm did no more than flop twice, like a drowning fish.

A man towered over him. Helios. He was in costume as well, a
long white robe and a white pharaoh's headdress that fanned out to
his shoulders. Barking mad, York thought.

"Take him below," Helios said in English. "Put him in the stateroom next to the foreign girl."

So they have Nadya too, he thought. He was puzzled that Helios
would call her foreign, but it was no crazier than his costume, or
his speaking English, or anything else York had witnessed in the last
few minutes.

They picked up his stretcher and carried him head first down a
companionway. He cried out involuntarily as the blood rushed to
his head, lighting it up with explosions of pain. The corridor had
a high ceiling and bright crystal-shaped light fixtures like the ones

that the men on the launch carried. The stateroom doors were marked with gold hieroglyphs. A door marked with the eye of Horus opened and they took him inside and dumped him onto a bunk. Even as they left the room and turned the key in the lock, the engines engaged and the ship began to move.

HE DRIFTED OFF for a while and was more lucid when he returned. He had a concussion, he realized, and as he took a slow and painful inventory, he added two cracked ribs, a swollen larynx, and a bad bruise along his jaw line. Nothing disabling.

He sat up and held on to the wall until the vertigo largely receded. Extrapolating from the size of his stateroom, he guessed that it was a big ship, probably 60 feet or more. Still holding the wall, he got to his feet and had to wait again for his vision to clear. He saw an empty closet, a sink with hot and cold water, and the bed. The walls were mahogany panels finished with a pale wash. At the foot of the bed was a porthole that he was able to open. It was barely big enough to put his hand through, and there was nothing to see but the darkness of the night and the water and the desert. Still, the fresh air helped his head.

Something thumped next door, in what he assumed was Nadya's cabin. He closed the porthole to hear better, and made out voices, low and indistinct. He put his ear against the wall and recognized a deep, rumbling cadence that could only belong to Helios, though he couldn't distinguish the words.

There was a scream and a woman's voice said, "You bastard! Don't—"

The sound of a blow cut her off.

It wasn't Nadya's voice.

It was Melody's.

SOUNDS OF A STRUGGLE ended in another strangled cry, followed by the sickening rhythm of the bed pounding against the cabin wall.

York tried to cry out, but his throat was too damaged to do more than croak. He pounded on the wall with both fists, then backed away and threw himself against it with what strength he had. The room went dim and his head throbbed, but he was demented with rage and barely noticed. He hurled himself at the wall again, and as he staggered back, the stateroom door slid back and Chang stepped inside. York attacked him with wild fury and Chang, almost tenderly, tapped him on the point of his chin with the heel of his hand. York's legs melted and he was unconscious before he hit the floor.

WHEN HE CAME TO again, his left hand was cuffed to the bed frame. Bright sunlight drilled through the porthole. His head seemed to swell and collapse with each hammer stroke of his pulse, but otherwise he didn't feel significantly worse than before. Not physically, anyway.

It was obvious, in retrospect, what had happened. Helios's men had been in the Buick that followed him from the airport. They'd watched his hotel and seen him with Melody that night. They must have taken her as soon as she left the next morning.

Of all the failures that had plagued this wretched mission from the start, this was the one he could not forgive. Everything that had happened to Melody since she was captured was his fault.

When he tried to turn onto his left side, his cracked ribs objected. He managed to get onto his other side and rest his head on his hand.

And what was the mission? The destruction of something that would benefit millions of people, for no other reason than the politics of those who were footing the bill.

Stop it, he told himself. It was a train of thought he had scrupulously avoided for years. It led to questions he was not willing to ask and answers he might not be able to live with.

Eventually he dozed for an hour or two, and then a change in the drumming of the engines woke him. He felt the ship come about and heard the splash of an anchor as the engines shut down.

The door slid open and five men in golden headbands came in. Four of them held his arms and legs as the fifth unlocked the handcuff from the bed and attached it to York's free hand. They shackled his ankles and pulled him onto his feet. He didn't want to give voice to his pain, and he did it anyway.

They walked him up the companionway ladder and he stopped on the deck, stunned by what loomed in front of him. Less than 50 meters from where he stood, at the end of a narrow, sandy beach, three massive, perpendicular walls had been carved out of the yellow mountainside of the west bank. In the space they defined sat four stone giants, 60 feet tall, the second one missing his upper torso. The three remaining heads showed the pharaoh Ramses II at three stages of his life, from teenage prince to a mature king with jutting oblong beard and long, flowing headdress.

York had seen photographs of the Abu Simbel temple, but nothing had prepared him for the sheer strangeness of it, dozens of miles from anywhere, stark and majestic, a towering monument to one man's unrestrained egotism.

A hundred and fifty meters downstream stood a second, smaller complex, partly obscured by a crane and piles of steel girders. Why would Helios bring him here, where the government was working to salvage the temples? The site was supposed to be off limits. And yet the white-robed crewmen were prodding and pulling him toward the starboard rail, clearly intending to put ashore.

They held him by the armpits as he climbed down toward the launch, his hands useless in the cuffs behind his back. As he stepped into the boat, he saw Nadya already settled in the middle row of seats, hands also cuffed behind her, one of the crewmen with a protective grip on her shoulder.

York sat opposite her and felt a heavy hand on his own shoulder. "So they got you, too," he said.

"The safe house, it appears, was not so safe."

"Did they hurt you?"

"Only my dignity."

He couldn't stop thinking about Melody. She was not on the launch, nor was Helios, and apparently neither of them was coming. One of the crewmen fired up the engine and they began to ease away from the yacht. He wondered if Helios had killed her, wondered if it would be better for her if he had.

He forced himself to think of something else, to keep the anger from taking him over. "I thought," York said, "this place was closed down."

"The company that has the contract to move the temples," Nadya said, "is owned by Helios Oil."

Something was off in Nadya's voice. "How did you know that?"

Before she could answer, the man with his hand on York's shoulder said, in accented English, "No talking."

They covered the distance to shore in moments, and the crewmen hustled them over the bow onto dry land. The morning sun had already heated the sand to the point that it burned York's bare feet.

The crewmen, he noticed, were armed only with wooden crooks. He counted five of them and was wondering how far a surprise attack might get him when the man behind him, as if reading his thoughts, shoved him hard enough to make him lose his balance and fall on his face in the dirt.

"No tricks," the man said, yanking York onto his feet by his armpits and giving him another, less violent shove. "Just walk." The accent, York thought, might be Greek.

Around the legs of the seated pharaohs were smaller carved figures of women and children. The broken pieces of the ruined statue lay in the dirt by its feet, presided over by a long-billed stone bird. Heavy-duty power cables, covered with a thin layer of sand, snaked in front of the temple and through the 20-foot high rectangular opening that led inside. From somewhere upstream came the distant hum of a generator.

The high ceiling of the first chamber was supported by eight more statues of Ramses, four on each side. Helios had trained spotlights on each of them, and laid Oriental carpet on the floor. The ancient and modern were so thoroughly mixed that they could have been in the lobby of the Nile Hilton.

The chamber was 60 feet long and nearly that wide. At the far end were three doorways. Through the center opening York glimpsed a second, smaller chamber with square pillars. Helios's men pushed him through the third of the doors into a long, narrow room with four animal cages of wide steel mesh along one wall. The cages were cubical, two meters on a side, and each held a thin, bare mattress and a honey bucket. A single floodlight on the low ceiling added to the stark effect.

They led York to the farthest cage, and he fought back then, hopelessly. They pinned him to the dank floor of the chamber, removed his handcuffs and shackles, and threw him headfirst into the cage like a sack of grain. The cage door was bolted and padlocked before he could get to his hands and knees. He fell onto the mattress and watched as they unshackled Nadya and shoved her into the cage nearest the door and farthest from York. One of the men sat on a wooden bench against the opposite wall and the other four left.

"Nadya?" York said. "Are you all right?"

"No talking," the guard said, and got up to poke York viciously in the kidney with the end of his crook. York curled in a fetal position, eyes running with pain, and lay still until the man moved away.

THE ROOM SMELLED of damp and the sweet, ancient musk of decay. And, of course, the disinfectant in the buckets. He was getting a bit ripe himself, he noticed. His bare feet were cold to the point of discomfort, the air was motionless and oppressive. His muscles tensed as he fought off a moment of claustrophobia.

He distracted himself by examining the cage. He spent thirty minutes searching for a weak spot, any kind of loophole that Helios might have left open, and found nothing. The cages were designed to hold wild dogs, chimpanzees, animals vastly stronger and more stubborn than humans. He would not get out that way.

The fact that he and Nadya were still alive meant that Helios wanted something from him, information most likely. Once Helios had it, or determined that he wasn't going to get it, they would both be disposable. As to Melody, he couldn't bear to think about her.

Funny, York thought, that at the end of the worst debacle of his career he should suddenly decide that he wanted to live after all. If only to get revenge on Helios.

HE WOKE TO the shaking of his cage. Three men, indistinguishable from the others, had arrived with food. While two of them prodded him toward the back of the cage with their crooks, another unlocked the door long enough to set down a piece of flatbread and an enameled cup of beer. They delivered the same thing to Nadya, changed the guard, and left.

The beer was thick and cloudy, unlike any he'd seen before. The bread had coriander seeds and bits of date in it. York guessed that the food, like the costumes and the setting, was some kind of throwback to ancient times. He saw no point in not eating and drinking; if they wanted to poison or drug him, they had plenty of other ways to do it.

Afterward he used the bucket and slept again.

THE NEXT TIME they woke him, he felt stronger, more alert. One of the guards ordered him, again in accented English, to face away from the cage door while they cuffed his hands. They pulled him out and shackled his legs again. The only opportunity York saw was for another beating, so he remained passive as they sent him stumbling toward the exit.

As he approached Nadya's cage, he gave her a wink that he hoped did not look like a nervous tic. They'd taken her scarf and glasses and shoes. She looked exhausted and dirty, but no worse than that. She offered York a vague smile of encouragement.

From the outer chamber they took him deeper into the mountainside. The second chamber was smaller than the first and less ornate. York had read somewhere that this was the standard design of Egyptian tombs; like the inside of a pyramid, everything became smaller as you approached the inner chamber.

A narrow hallway after the second chamber led to more rooms. Along a straight line from the doorway to the outside was the entrance to the final chamber. The guards pushed him through and then immediately beat him to the floor with their crooks.

As he went down, York saw a low-ceilinged room five meters square. A stone bench ran along the back wall with four figures seated on it. Three of them were stone representations of either pharaohs or gods, if there was a difference. The fourth was Helios.

York peered carefully to his left. Two of the guards had folded themselves into a position of supplication, sitting on their heels with their foreheads to the Oriental carpet on the floor, arms stretched in front of them like Moslems at prayer. Two more were prostrated on the other side. The fifth man accounted for himself by whacking York with his crook and snarling, "Avert your eyes, dog."

Defiance would gain him nothing at this point. York assumed the same position as the guards, except that his cuffed arms had to remain behind his back. He stared into the wine-colored carpet.

"This much we know," Helios said. "Your name is not John York. You work for the CIA. You brought a briefcase into this country that we believe contains a great deal of cash."

"You want to destroy the High Dam," York said. His voice was hoarse but functional. "We want the same thing." The word "we" tasted like ashes in his mouth. In fact he was no longer certain that he did want the destruction of the dam, and he was positive that he did not want the same things that Helios did.

"How much money was in the briefcase?"

"One hundred thousand Egyptian pounds."

Helios let out a small, contemptuous grunt. "And where is it?"

"In a safe deposit box in Cairo."

Helios sighed. "So we would have to bring you along to get at it. Not worth the trouble."

"The United States could be a powerful friend to you." Again, his stomach turned at his own words. He pressed on from sheer inertia. "Why do you refuse our help?"

"Oh, I have taken a good deal of money from your government over the years. It's your friendship that I don't want. If the Cattle of Ra were known to be the Dogs of the CIA, we would lose all our standing in the Arab world. That's how the man you sent to infiltrate us got his neck broken."

"Our friendship can be discreet."

"Discreet? *Discreet?* Do you know who Abdel Karim Kassem was?"

"He was the Communist strongman in Iraq. His own army overthrew him back in February."

"He was not a Communist. He was dearly loved by his people. The CIA planned and executed the coup because he wouldn't do their bidding. You dare talk to me of discretion? They put on a show trial and shot him on Iraqi national television. Do you call that discreet?"

"The CIA had nothing to do with that." The response was automatic. York had heard rumors; there were always rumors.

"I don't know if you're merely a liar, or truly are as naïve as you claim. Did you then have nothing to do with the Bay of Pigs? With the overthrow of Árbenz in Guatemala? With the coup in Iran in fifty-three? With the violence in the Congo right now?"

York didn't know how to respond. Despite the source, they were reasonable questions. Did he really believe the denials that the agency routinely made? And if not, what about the acts themselves? Were these, in fact, the actions of a civilized nation?

"At least let Nadya go," he said. "She works for the embassy, she has nothing to do with the CIA."

"The audience is concluded," Helios said.

"Wait. Will you tell me why? Why do you want to destroy the dam? What is it that you want?"

"Why should I tell a dead man? Take him away."

•

WHEN THEY THREW York in his cage, they left the cuffs and shackles on. He suspected it was not a good sign. He had come down to the last few minutes of his life.

It was a life he had tried for years to throw away. He saw then where so much of his risk-taking had come from, how deeply his contempt for his own mortality ran, and how inextricable that was from the work he'd been doing.

Too little, he thought. Too late.

When Chang appeared, wearing a holstered pistol and trailing five guards, it was almost a relief.

Almost.

Standing in front of York's cage, Chang said, "I respect your bravery, if not your skill. For this reason I will kill you quickly, with a single bullet to the skull. The same for the woman."

"What about Melody?" York said.

"When Helios is done with her, I will see that she also dies quickly."

Chang gestured, and a guard unlocked Nadya's cage. She came out meekly, then, as the guard reached for her hands, she bolted for the door. Apparently someone was waiting on the other side, because she immediately flew backwards into the room, where the first guard threw her to the floor, knelt on her back, and cuffed her wrists. A second guard chained her feet.

York left his cage quietly and they walked out in single file, Chang leading, York and Nadya buffered by guards. As they came into the main chamber, York saw dust motes dancing in the spotlights above the statues and felt the shifting textures in the rug under his feet. It was as if he had never noticed before what an infinity of detail the world contained.

They walked out into the dying day, the long shadow of the temple coving the beach and half of the river. York had lost all track of time.

"What will you do with our bodies?" he asked Chang.

Chang slowed and turned his head halfway toward York. "The men will slit you open and put you in the river. The Nile catfish will take care of the rest."

The walked to the edge of the beach. A puff of breeze came off the water, cool enough to make York shiver. Absurdly, he was embarrassed that Chang might think he was trembling in fear. Then he saw that Chang's hands, held at waist level, had a slight tremor as well.

And then the breeze brought him something else, the faintest aroma of Balkan Sobranie cigarettes.

York looked at Chang and said, "Uzkoglaziy."

Chang's head snapped around, anger flickering and then dying in his eyes. "Very clever," he said.

"No offense," York said. It was a racial slur the ethnic Russian bigots used when they referred to Asians. "You're KGB, aren't you? You're not even Chinese. Some sort of half-breed from the eastern provinces."

Chang didn't react.

"You're not really working for Helios at all," York said. "You're a mole, supposed to keep an eye on Helios, maybe take him out if he gets too dangerous."

Chang pulled out the pistol and said, "You have a very weird idea of how to keep from getting shot." For an instant York thought Chang would use it right then, before any more damaging revelations could come out. Instead he waved it at the guards. "Back inside, now!"

The guards hesitated, looking at each other in confusion and fear.

"Imshi!" Chang shouted, and York saw how close the man was to coming apart.

The guards scrambled toward the temple.

"Where's Helios?" York asked.

"He took the helicopter to Aswan. They're going to blow up the retaining wall tonight."

York flinched.

Nadya looked at Chang. "And you're going to let him do it? Are you mad?"

"Whose side are *you* on?" York asked her.

"I might ask you the same thing," Nadya said. "But first I want to hear from Chang."

Chang looked embarrassed. "My superiors can't decide. If I let Helios wreck the dam, it will prove my loyalty and I can get even closer to him. He has worse things planned, you see. They argued about it until it was too late."

"Committees," Nadya said.

"Helios's guards all speak English," York said. "Your cover is blown now."

"Thanks to you."

"Obviously you can kill me if you want. Or we can work together."

Chang shook his head. "You really must think I'm crazy."

"Nadya," York said, "if that's your name, why don't you start by telling us who you work for?"

"How long have you known?" she said.

"I began to suspect something when you pulled that gun in the workers' estate. But I don't know what your loyalties are."

"Egyptian secret service," she said. "I report to Al Rayyes personally."

"So you were going to stop me if I got close to succeeding," York said.

"In that unlikely event, yes," Nadya said coolly.

"What did you do to Mahmoud?"

"Oh, he was genuinely ill. Thanks to something we put in his food."

"And you?" Chang said to York. "What do you bring to this? The last I heard, you were here to sabotage the dam yourself."

"I had a change of heart." The words made him think of his first meeting with Bisri.

"Because of the girl?" Chang asked.

"Partly. Helios is a monster."

"He's a monster that your country helped create."

"After today I don't know that I'll still have a country. Where is she?"

"The girl? She's here."

"Is there another helicopter?"

"No," Chang said. Then, reluctantly, he added, "There's the boat."

"How long will it take?" Nadya asked.

"Four hours, at top speed. If we're lucky."

"Get Melody," York said, "and let's get on the water."

Chang looked at him curiously.

"You can kill me halfway to Aswan and throw me overboard," York said. "But we'll never get back the time we're losing now. We can finish arguing once we're underway."

Chang shook his head, more in disbelief than disagreement.

"And bring the keys to these shackles," York said, "in case you decide not to kill us."

THE FIRST DOORWAY off the main chamber led to another long room, this one fitted out with a European-style door. Chang unlocked it to reveal a facsimile of a hotel room with a double bed, nightstand, carpet, and lamp. Melody lay across the bed, drugged or asleep. She wore a cotton shift with bloodstains around the groin. Her hands were tied with a silken cord and her feet were chained. One eye was severely blackened. Her lips were swollen and split in two places. The room stank of sperm and blood.

"My God," Nadya said.

Chang had removed York's handcuffs, leaving the leg shackles in place. York knelt beside the bed and gently touched Melody's shoulder. She jerked away without opening her eyes.

"Melody," he said. "It's York."

She opened one eye. "You," she said, with loathing. "What did you do to me?"

"I'm taking you out of here."

"Bastard!" she yelled. "Don't touch me!" She tried to strike him with her bound hands.

"Please," he said. "We have to go. Everything is falling apart."

She fought him when he tried to pick her up. "I can walk," she said. She pushed herself to the edge of the bed, tried to stand, and fell on her knees. She began to cry. York scooped her up, looping her bound arms around his head. "Don't!" she said.

"I'm not leaving you," York said.

"Hurry," Chang said. "These servants of his are brainwashed, but they're starting to panic."

They ran out to the beach, a shambling, painful motion for York and Nadya. Near the launch, a small knot of Helios's servants had gathered, moving their crooks nervously. Chang waded into them, throwing them to the left and right as if emptying clothes out of a closet. In a few seconds the rest had lost their nerve and retreated to the temple.

York sat Melody in the center of the boat and then, as Chang and Nadya settled themselves, pushed the launch out into the river. Chang was fumbling with the controls and York took his place. The engine coughed and roared and York sent them skimming across the fifty meters of water to Helios's yacht.

York got on board first and Chang handed Melody up to him. He started to carry her toward the companionway and she fought him, saying, "No! Don't take me to that room again!"

"Okay," York said. "Relax, it's okay now."

"No," she said. "It's not."

He took her to the saloon and laid her on one of the leather-covered sofas. He tucked an afghan around her and untied her hands. The room was spectacular, with windows along both sides and a stunning view of Abu Simbel backlit by the setting sun. Cream-colored industrial carpet covered the floor and the cabinets and paneling were burnished teak. A bowl of green apples sat on the black marble dining table and a cabinet in the forward bulkhead held an expensive marine VHF radio.

"There's blood on your robe," he said. "He didn't...cut you, did he?"

"No. He was just...brutal."

Nadya stuck her head in. "I think Chang needs help."

"Can you stay with Melody?"

She nodded and York ducked outside. He showed Chang how to winch the launch out of the water and secure it to the transom, where he noticed the name of the ship for the first time: *Amon Ra.* Sun god of the ancient Egyptians.

"I hope this means you can drive this thing," Chang said.

"There's nothing to it. Even millionaires can do it. But first, we need to get Nadya on the radio to the authorities."

Chang considered briefly, then nodded. "Go ahead."

"It would be a lot easier with these chains off."

Chang tossed York a set of keys. "I'm not sure why I trust you. Maybe I think you're a good man who ended up in the wrong job."

York sat on the deck to strip off the leg irons. "I could say the same for you. Somehow I don't quite feature you walking the Communist Party line." He threw the chains over the side.

"Nor you working for the Colonial Imperialist Assassins." Chang showed him a tight smile, then looked away. "I was relieved that I didn't have to kill you. I've never executed anyone before."

"But you've killed."

"A few times. To protect my life. You?"

"Once. Like you, in self-defense."

"Was he Russian?"

"Burmese."

"Ah. Well, that's all right, then."

In the saloon, York gave Nadya the keys and she removed Melody's chains first. York pointed to the radio. "Can you work a VHF unit?"

"Yes."

"Are you all right without your glasses?"

"I'm nearsighted. I'll be fine."

"Get hold of your people and the engineers at the dam, let them know there's going to be a sabotage attempt tonight. But leave me out of it. I don't want to attract any more attention to myself than absolutely necessary."

"Yes," she said. "I understand."

York showed Chang how to work the anchor winch and then climbed the ladder to the bridge. He fired up the twin engines, slacked off the anchor chain, and shouted down to Chang to hoist it. As soon as the anchor was loose he headed downstream at full throttle.

Chang joined him and York explained the basics of the instruments. He gave Chang the wheel and moved to the hard plastic couch at the forward point of the bridge, feeling the night wind in his hair. York was a sailor, not a lover of motor yachts; still it was still a pleasure to be moving swiftly over water when he hadn't expected to be alive at all.

He looked at Chang. "Earlier you said Helios had worse things planned. What's his game? What's he after?"

"Profit. After that, more profit. After that, still more profit. Some men want to rule the world. Helios wants to own it."

"What does that have to do with the High Dam? The line he was spouting at al Gezira about obstructing his free passage on the Nile was nonsense. The original Aswan Dam did that sixty years ago."

"The dam is only a means to an end, the same end your masters want. To ruin Nasser. Nasser and the Moslem Brotherhood have been at each other's throats since the Revolution in fifty-two, and if the dam fails, the Brotherhood will take over."

"How does that help Helios?"

"The Brotherhood hates Communism as much as you do. They believe in free enterprise as devoutly as they believe in Allah. They would be willing to take certain assets that Nasser nationalized and put them back in private hands."

"Specifically?"

"Specifically the Suez Canal."

"Are you serious?"

"Completely. There was nearly a world war over the canal in fifty-six when Nasser took it over. If Helios bought the canal from

Egypt—and there's every reason to believe the Brotherhood would sell it to him—he would control shipping between Asia and Europe. He would basically become a world power unto himself."

"Isn't that against the Brotherhood's own self-interest?"

"This is why in the Soviet Union we abolished religion."

Nadya appeared at the top of the ladder. "I got hold of security at the dam. They are evacuating the channel and bringing in the Army."

"Good," York said, and then felt a sudden chill in his stomach. "You left Melody alone," he said.

"She was asleep. I'm sure she's..."

"We never searched the ship," he said, realizing it only as the words came out of his mouth.

He pushed past her and scrambled down the ladder. He couldn't see in the tinted windows of the saloon. He ran to the door and threw it open.

A white robed figure, one of Helios's men, looked up in surprise from the middle of the floor. He had barely raised his crook to defend himself when York charged him. All of his suppressed rage burst out and he straddled the man, throwing punch after punch until Melody screamed, "Stop it!"

He froze. Some measure of sanity gradually returned. The man was hurt, but not critically. York lifted him in a fireman's carry, took him onto the deck, and threw him over the side. The man floundered, then began to swim, his head above water as he disappeared into the darkness. And if he hadn't? York asked himself. If he'd started to drown, would you have gone back for him?

He stood at the railing and gripped it as if he meant to tear it loose. What was happening to him? Less than an hour ago he'd abandoned his career and thrown in with a pair of Communists. He'd lost his direction and his common sense, and now even his instincts were failing him. Worse, he'd begun to second guess himself.

Nadya touched his shoulder. "Are you all right?"

"Stay with Melody. Please. I'm going to search the rest of the ship."

He checked the staterooms, the galley, the engine room, and

finally came up the interior companionway that led into the saloon. Nadya sat on the couch, Melody on her lap, her face buried in Nadya's shirt, weeping exhaustedly. Nadya looked at York and gave a slight shake of her head. York retreated.

Back on the bridge, Chang was smoking.

"That was what gave you away," York said. "I smelled that Balkan tobacco on your clothes."

"Being around Helios has made me careless. The man has virtually no sense of smell or taste. He barely feels pain. He's not even particularly intelligent. He's succeeded through sheer greed and a complete lack of compassion."

"How to succeed in business," York said.

"Marx said much the same thing."

"Helios owns the company that's supposed to move Abu Simbel. If he succeeds in destroying the dam, it won't have to be moved. And I suppose the grateful Brotherhood will sell him the temple to go with his canal."

"Exactly."

"Did you ever consider killing him?"

"Many times. My superiors feel his murder could destabilize the entire Middle East."

"You won't interfere with my killing him?"

"If you do it, we can blame the CIA. I won't stand in your way. But I don't think you have a prayer."

York felt the tidal wave of rage again, so powerful it left him dizzy, the murderous rage that had made Melody scream. "I'll take my chances," he said.

"Just so we understand each other," Chang said. "Saving the dam is first priority for all of us. Then, to whatever extent we can, we help you."

"Agreed. So you're saying you don't trust the Egyptian Army to stop Bisri."

"No," Chang said. "Do you?"

"No."

Chang nodded and flicked the end of his cigarette toward the river. "Filthy habit," he said. "I really should give it up."

THEY WERE THIRTY MINUTES out of Aswan. Nadya was on the bridge, having promised Melody that she would come immediately if she called.

"They have checked the inventory of dynamite," Nadya said, recapping her last radio exchange, "and everything looks correct. They have locked down the shed where they store it and surrounded it with guards. That would be the likely place for Bisri to get his explosives. So maybe we were in time."

"Maybe," York said. "Do they have Bisri yet?"

"Not yet."

York suddenly saw Bisri getting down from the truck at the food souk, his right hand moving involuntarily to his waist.

"What if Bisri had a man on the explosives team?" York said. "They work in the same tunnels. One stick of dynamite here, another there. Over the space of a few months, no one would notice."

"Where would he hide it?" Nadya asked.

The nervous mannerism had stopped, York was sure, after Bisri had disappeared into his apartment.

"It's in his room," York said.

"They checked and didn't find anything. They have a man watching it."

York had smelled dynamite. The nitroglycerin had an acidic odor and the filling smelled like sawdust. He would know it again.

"I want to see for myself," York said.

"Even if he were to get the dynamite," Nadya said, "the channel is deserted now, surrounded by guards on all sides. He would need a truck or car to carry that much explosive. How would he deliver it?"

"I don't know," York said. "But he's thought of something."

YORK SPED ACROSS the Nile, alone in the launch in the darkness. He had left Nadya, Melody, and Chang on the east bank in the care of an Egyptian regiment. Chang had the flare gun from the *Amon Ra*, and had promised to signal if he caught sight of either Bisri or Helios.

Close to shore, York turned upstream and watched for the shack and the makeshift dock where Helios's man had transferred him to the yacht. The weak searchlight on the launch penetrated no more than ten meters beyond the bow.

The shack jumped suddenly out of the darkness. To his relief he saw two Land Rovers parked there and no other sign of life. He passed the shack and gave himself an extra two hundred meters in case anyone was watching the dock. Then he drove the boat onto the beach. He found an old-fashioned boat hook on board with a good, sharp point on it and jammed it into the sand and tied the boat's painter to it. In the tool box under the middle seat of the launch, he found a pair of wire cutters and a big screwdriver, and he stuck both of them in the waistband of his pants.

The Rovers were unlocked, with no keys in their ignitions. The keys were probably in the shack, which was closed with a hasp and padlock. It was easier to hotwire the Rover, and in two minutes he was on his way.

The road was pitted and rocky, but easy enough to follow and free of turnoffs. He recognized the collection of shacks that ringed the workers' estate as soon as it came into view, and he pointed the rover down the alley that led to Bisri's quarters. It had only been a few blocks, he remembered, once the government housing began.

The streets were empty; York guessed some kind of curfew was in effect. He passed the shack made of crates and then the first of the plywood buildings, complete with green cobra stencil.

Three blocks later he saw a government Rover parked in the dirt street across from Bisri's room. He pulled up next to it and saw a young soldier with a mustache and a bright smile. "Do you speak English?" York called to him.

The man shook his head. "La."

"I have an important message from President Nasser. From Al

Rayyes." York set the handbrake and climbed down, leaving the
Rover running. He walked around to the soldier's door, opened it,
and stunned the man with a quick chop to the neck. He pulled him
out and finished him with a knee to the chin, then bundled him
into the back of the government Rover and used the man's own
handcuffs to secure him to the frame.

The doors of the sleeping quarters were strictly for show. York splin-
tered the wood around the lock and was inside in less than a minute.

The room smelled like raw wood and unwashed bodies. Below
that, oddly, he detected the sweetish odor of gasoline, and finally,
at the bottom, the chemical stink of nitro. He searched under the
cheap, steel-frame beds, even though the Army must have been
there before him. Under the fourth and final one he found a wood-
en trunk whose latch surrendered without a fight. Despite an oil-
cloth lining, there was nothing inside. Dirty clothes had been stuffed
on either side of the trunk, and as York threw them aside the smells
of petrol and nitro got stronger.

He shifted all the beds down until he could get at the plywood
panel that the last bed rested on. The screws were loose in their
holes and the panel easily lifted up and out.

The ground under the foundation of two-by-sixes had been hol-
lowed out, and five waxed cardboard boxes were half-buried in the
sand. Three of them held 20 sticks each of brown dynamite with
Cyrillic characters printed on the side. The fourth held caps, wires,
and a radio transmitter that was clearly intended as a detonator.

The fifth box, the largest, held a roll of dark brown rubberized
canvas six feet long and a foot in diameter. York stared at it in puz-
zlement until he noticed the small outboard motor and the greasy
five-gallon can of gasoline tucked underneath. It was an inflatable
boat, wrapped around a rigid transom to support the motor.

It seemed obvious now. Bisri had planned all along to come in by
water rather than by land. He could take the explosives up to the lip
of the retaining wall and blow a hole in it big enough to drown any
hope of finishing the dam by the deadline.

York felt himself start to relax. With no dynamite, Bisri's fangs were pulled. He began to carefully load the dynamite into the trunk, trying to decide if he should simply cart it away himself, or use the radio in the soldier's Rover to find help.

He was nearly done when the lights went out.

The darkness was absolute. He felt his way carefully to the door. The street was dark too, as were the surrounding housing blocks.

York had not stayed alive this long by believing in accidents. He slid under the bed nearest the door and listened to the chug of his Land Rover as it idled in the street. He counted off a minute, then two, then three. Finally dark shapes moved against the lesser darkness of the doorway and a flashlight swept the room. Bisri cursed, the cadences unmistakable in any language, and then, as he found the exposed dynamite, he began to bark orders. Two men ran into the street while Bisri checked the room again with the flashlight.

York heard car doors open and shut, a tailgate fall open. A voice, probably the soldier's, shouted, then broke off under the muffled rhythm of kicks and blows.

Bisri was focused on the dynamite, moving the last of it into the trunk with rustles and clunks. It was just possible, York thought, to slip into the street while Bisri was distracted.

Before he could act, the two men were back, jabbering excitedly. All York saw was their feet, practically dancing with nervous tension. He could imagine what they were saying—the handcuffed soldier, the second Rover—they had to know that York was nearby. Bisri shouted more orders and handed off the flashlight. Immediately one of them shone it under the farthest bed while the other man dashed outside again.

York eased out from under the bed, got his feet under him, and rushed for the door. The man with the flashlight yelled and lunged for him, barely missing. York launched himself through the door and landed painfully on his bare feet in the street. He skidded and then dug in, sprinting for the Rover, and he got 20 feet before he was tackled from behind. He barely had time to raise his arms protectively before the street rose up to smash him in his damaged ribs.

Fighting for breath, he kicked free and got up into a crouch, facing the man who tackled him. The street was nearly as dark as the room. Bisri and the other man were running toward him, Bisri with the flashlight now, vague shadows in the night, heard more than seen. York took out the man in front of him with a high sweeping kick and charged the other henchman with a berserker yell and windmilling arms. The man couldn't decide whether to run or fight, and York took him down before he made up his mind.

In the meantime, Bisri came up from behind and landed a powerful blow with the flashlight to York's right kidney. York gasped, started to turn. Bisri hit him again with the flashlight, this time in the ribs, and the pain was a white light that blinded him. The last blow was to the head, and the white light turned to darkness.

EVEN AFTER HE REGAINED consciousness, as the first waves of an incoming tide of pain rolled across his body, he continued to lie in the street, knees drawn up to his broken chest.

My mission, he thought, was to blow up the dam. That was why I came to Egypt in the first place. All I have to do is lie here, and Bisri will do the job for me. I can take the credit, and go back to Washington, and everything will be the way it used to be.

Except that it wouldn't. The things he'd admitted to himself could not be tucked safely back into the locked boxes in his head.

And it was not York that Bisri was doing the job for. It was Helios, and the thought of Helios was enough to make York open his eyes and slowly pull himself onto his hands and knees.

His stomach lurched and it took yet more willpower not to throw up. He carefully touched his forehead and his fingers came away wet and gritty. Bisri must have left him for dead. And Bisri was not far wrong.

A man, some bystander, stood beside him, apparently asking if he needed help. York ignored him. He crawled to the nearest plywood

housing block and used the wall to pull himself upright, barely reg-
istering the bloody handprints he left behind.

The Rover he'd hotwired was gone. The second Rover was still
there. He glanced in the back and saw that the soldier was dead.
Helping himself along with both hands, he got into the driver's seat.
By the dome light he saw that the keys were gone and the micro-
phone had been torn from the radio.

It was hopeless. Yet he staggered into Bisri's room, searching for
his wire cutters, getting to his knees to look under the nearest bed
before he realized that they were still in the waistband of his pants.

He wandered back into the street and got onto the floor under
the Rover's steering column, where he passed out for a few seconds.
When he came to, he groped at the harness of wires for a long time
before he finally found the two red ones, stripped them, and twisted
them together. He stripped the brown wire and touched it to the
reds, forgetting that the car was still in gear and killing it instantly.

He set the brake, hands shaking now, put the gearshift in neutral,
tried again. The wires sparked and the motor caught.

The car was running, but there was a dead man in back. This was
going to be hard to explain.

He turned the car around in the narrow street. Steering was
harder than he remembered; the machine had a perverse and independent will. In the first block, the Rover ran up against one of the
plywood buildings and cut a long gash into the wood. York wrestled
it back onto the road and nearly hit a man in a long beige galabiya
and turban.

With his left hand, York grabbed himself by the hair and pulled
his own head upright. The pain was like an electric shock. He
pushed the accelerator down, feeling every ridge, every piece of
gravel, every footprint in the road as it reverberated in his ribs and
his kidney and his pounding head.

Twice on the way to the river he lost focus and drove off the
road, barely managing to swerve back without getting mired in the
loose sand. So many things could go wrong. Bisri might have taken

the dynamite in a different direction. He might have found York's launch and stolen or scuttled it. York hoped that he had. Then he could lie down and either sleep or die; he didn't care which.

The loamy, fishy smell of the Nile brought him around. In his trance, he had driven the Rover straight into the water, far enough to kill the engine. He listened to the waves tap against the doors.

There was something important he had to do.

Helios. Bisri. Sixty sticks of dynamite.

He stepped out of the Rover into water up to his calves. In the floodlight that burned on the shack by the dock, his hands were stained dark brown with blood. They stuck to the side of the Rover as he steadied himself against it. "Forgive me," he said to the dead man in back. He thought at first that the dead man had answered, but it was only another hallucination.

He stumbled down the beach. How far away had he left the boat? Too far. He couldn't see it, couldn't see the shore, could only see nauseating flashes of light from the river. Then he tripped over the line tied to the boathook and went sprawling in the sand.

He got onto his knees. He understood that the next few things had to happen in order. First, pull the boathook out and throw it in the boat. He had to rest after that. Then he pushed the boat into the river and collapsed rather than jumped into the bow, one leg dragging in the water. Hate to see the fish that bite that head off, said a voice in his head. He pulled his leg into the launch.

Sometime later he made his way painfully to the stern and, on the fourth try, started the motor, remembering just in time to turn the rudder so that he didn't drive himself up on the bank again.

He saw lights across the river, at the trench where the Army was even now, he was sure, convincing themselves that the threat was over, wondering when they should pack it in and go back to work. It was like seeing his hometown football stadium on a winter's night in high school, driving toward a circle of light brighter than the day, surrounded by nothingness, warm in the car with friends, the cold all around.

He felt the cold seep into his hands and feet as he shot across the water, and he knew he was running out of time.

From one minute to the next he would stare at the distant lights, expecting to see an eruption of smoke and flame any moment, and then he would lose himself in the rhythm of the hull slapping the water, only to start awake, not remembering where he was until the word came into his head again: Helios.

Closer now. He made out pontoon boats tied up along the east bank. Bisri's boat, though, was dark as the Nile, dark as the night, virtually invisible. He drove the launch almost to the shore and then swung downstream, the motor buzzing like a thousand wasps. He switched on the feeble searchlight, wishing the pain would recede enough to let his head clear, if only for five minutes.

He was nearly to the channel. The sand banks had given way to pale granite, looming ten feet higher than the river. There was no sign of Bisri and he knew he should throttle back, but he was afraid of being late, of missing Bisri by seconds and watching his final failure explode in front of him.

Something shot past to starboard and it was a long second before he realized it was Bisri in his raft, that the launch had missed him by ten feet and sent him rocking in its wake. York throttled back and turned around. It was impossible to see Bisri, impossible to know what he was doing. But he would not have come this far without being ready to blow the dynamite as soon as he tied his raft to the rock wall.

York nosed the launch into the cliff until the paint scraped against stone, then gave it more gas, five knots, ten. He was so close to the rock wall that the slightest twitch would smash in the hull. York was sweating now, and when he wiped the sweat away his hands dripped with blood.

The spotlight picked Bisri out of the darkness a moment before the launch shot between the raft and the cliff wall. A single frozen image imprinted itself in York's brain: Bisri crouched in the raft, reaching for the detonators.

York spun the launch around again. If he rammed the raft directly it could set off the blasting caps. He looked frantically around the floor of the launch and saw the boathook a few feet away. He grabbed it, came around the outside of the raft, and as he passed he cut the engine, stood, and threw the boathook at Bisri with every bit of strength he had left, the momentum hurling him against the side of the launch as it bobbed in its own wake.

At that moment a flare exploded overhead and for one despairing instant York thought it was the dynamite going off. Then he remembered something about a flare gun, a signal of some kind.

Helios. It meant Helios was here.

In the light of the flare he saw Bisri dancing on the water. It was a bizarre and impossible sight, and York realized that the boathook had missed Bisri and ripped a hole in the cheap fabric of the raft, that the raft was now spinning out of control and taking on water as it collapsed. A brown wave washed over the side and covered the bundles of dynamite, soaking the blasting caps and detonator, and still Bisri fought for balance, in water up to his ankles, then his knees. As the last of the raft disappeared, Bisri belly flopped into the river, too buoyant to go under. His head came up, his turban still, improbably, in place. As he dog paddled, he fixed York with a stare that managed to be both hostile and resigned.

York started his engine. He could easily run Bisri down with the launch; the propeller would turn him into chum for catfish. The idea had no appeal; Bisri was no longer a threat. The only thing York cared about was Helios. He left Bisri floating there and sped back upstream.

Another flare crawled up the sky and caught fire. York traced the trajectory back to the ground and there, on a patch of beach, he saw Chang.

York ran the boat aground at Chang's feet. He clambered out and stood swaying on the sand. Dozens of soldiers milled around, none showing interest in York or the launch. Between the distant mercury vapor lamps and the last of the flare, he had enough light to read the concern on Chang's face. As he lumbered toward him, the concern turned to fear.

"My God, man," Chang said in English. "What happened to you?"

"Where's Helios?"

"Did you find Bisri?"

York gestured backward with his thumb. "In the water. The dynamite too. The dam's safe. Where's Helios?"

"You need a doctor. You're in no condition to—"

"Do not," York whispered, "argue with me. We had a deal. I did my part. You do yours."

"One minute." Chang grabbed a passing officer and said something to him in rapid-fire Arabic, pointing to the river. The officer glanced at York and quickly looked away again. When Chang finished, the officer started to salute, thought better of it, and dashed away, yelling into a walkie-talkie.

"Helios," York said.

"He landed his helicopter up there, on the foundations of the hydroelectric plant." Chang pointed to the wall of granite above the tunnels where Bisri had worked. "He couldn't resist being here for the show."

"They let him land there?"

"He does it all the time, to watch. He has powerful friends, even here."

"How do we get up there?"

Reluctantly Chang said, "I have a Rover."

"And a gun?"

His hesitation was even briefer as he handed over the pistol that he'd threatened York with on the beach at Abu Simbel, a hundred years ago. It was a Walther P38, tough and reliable.

"I must be completely insane," Chang said.

"I hope so," York said. He wasn't sure what he meant.

Chang led him to yet another official Land Rover, this one with keys in the ignition. "You drive," York said.

"Goddamn right I drive," Chang muttered, and York laughed. The laughter came out with an edge of hysteria and he bit his lip to make himself stop.

Chang took the high road around the pit, inland from the river, climbing into the pale granite bluffs, past the massive girders that supported the floodlights, past the cliffs that had been blasted for rock to build the coffer dam, past the noise and the heat until stars filled the windscreen. York began to shiver again.

"You've lost a lot of blood," Chang said.

"Drive," York said.

The road curved back toward the river. In the distance was a long, gray, level plain, like some grim Greek version of the afterlife. But it was only concrete, and at the end of it winked the green and red running lights of a helicopter.

The road ended at a low gate made of heavy steel pipe, padlocked. York got out of the Rover, the Walther in his hand. He wondered if he had the strength to climb over the gate. Behind him he heard Chang rummaging in the back of the Rover, and ahead of him he saw a massive man standing at the very edge of the concrete slab, staring down into the floodlit pit below. He towered over his bodyguards, one on either side of him. The bodyguards were not in white robes but in full combat gear, including Kalashnikovs and bulletproof vests. Helios himself wore a dark gray business suit and he had already started to turn when York called out to him.

"Helios!"

The gate was four feet high. York crawled over it, stumbled, managed somehow to keep his feet. He was unable to hold the Walther steady. He must have seemed drunk and the thought shamed him.

"Helios, you bastard!"

Helios pointed to each of the bodyguards in turn, pointed to York, and began to walk unhurriedly toward the helicopter.

York was at least a hundred meters away. He broke into a shambling run and fired a shot that ricocheted pathetically off of the concrete.

The bodyguards knelt and took aim.

In a chilling moment of lucidity, York saw that his heroic fantasy had gone fatally wrong. He dropped to the ground and fired again in the direction of Helios.

The rattle of automatic weapon fire cut the night and then there was silence.

YORK FOUND TO HIS SURPRISE that he was still alive. He hurt too much to be dead.

The two bodyguards lay sprawled across the concrete, motionless. Helios stood at the door of the helicopter, looking at something to York's left. He was too far away for York to read his expression.

Using both hands, York emptied the Walther's clip as Helios got into the helicopter and the helicopter lifted gently off the concrete. It rose into the night, turning sideways so York had one last look at the concentric circles of the sun god Ra on the fuselage. Then it turned again and slowly flew away.

He heard footsteps. Chang stood beside him, holding a Soviet Dragunov sniper rifle. York wanted to thank him, only the cold was in his chest now and he could no longer speak. He didn't want to close his eyes for fear that he would never open them again. But the last of his will was gone and his eyes closed anyway.

HE WAS IN A BED, in a room cluttered with broken wooden furniture, chests and tables and wardrobes and cabinets. Dusty sunlight filtered through wooden shutters. He had been there for a while, waking and sleeping, because he recognized the room, though he didn't know where it was.

He touched his throbbing head, which was wrapped in bandages, and then his chest, also wrapped. He was terribly thirsty.

He turned his head and saw a blue enameled pitcher on a cracked nightstand next to the bed. When he reached for it, his aim was poor and it banged and clattered onto the tile floor. The noise set off a chain reaction of barking dogs that started in the next room and spread in all directions.

The floor was laid in an intricate hexagonal pattern, a trompe l'oeil in shades of gray and green that looked like a pyramid of blocks with the light side facing up. Then York blinked and the blocks reversed themselves, the light side now facing down. He was still staring at it when Nadya came in.

"You're awake again," she said. "Do you remember where you are this time?"

"No," York said. Shaking his head seemed like a bad idea.

"You're in Cairo. You've been here five days now. You're staying with a friend of ours who fixes broken things. And sometimes broken people."

"Melody?"

"She's here too. At the moment she's less broken than you are, but you will probably heal faster, God willing."

"Chang?"

"Home in Irkutsk. He is a Hero of the Soviet Union and he tells me he will receive the Order of Lenin."

The next name came harder. "Helios?"

"In Greece at the moment."

"Was he...did they charge him...?"

"Helios was not implicated in any way in the plot against the High Dam. Bisri and his men are in prison and will likely be executed."

"Chang had a sniper's rifle. He killed both of Helios's bodyguards. He should have killed Helios too."

"Al Rayyes was able to cover up the deaths of the bodyguards. He could never have covered up the death of a man like Helios. It would have meant Chang's life, and it was not Chang's fight. He saved your life, and you should be grateful."

"I'll be grateful when Helios is dead."

"York, you must listen to me. If you devote your life to killing Helios, the only thing that will happen is that you will die. Even if you should somehow succeed, which is virtually impossible, one of his sons would simply take over his empire. His sons are exactly like him, if not more spoiled and narcissistic, and nothing would change.

"And you have responsibilities. What happened to Melody is your fault, the result of your carelessness, your selfish desire for gratification. She cannot go back to the life she had, not now, perhaps never. Someone must take care of her, perhaps for quite a while."

York winced. Guilt, fatigue, and pain hammered at him. "If I don't go after Helios, he'll come after me."

"I doubt he even remembers you. Does it matter to you whether you swat a fly or the fly escapes? As long as the fly doesn't bother you again?"

York looked away.

"I know these are hard words. No man likes to be told of his unimportance. Your importance lies elsewhere."

"Where? I can't go back to my old life either."

"No. Al Rayyes has reported you dead to your government, killed while attempting to sabotage the High Dam. He is making quite a stink about it." She smiled for the first time. "Al Rayyes is in fact quite grateful to you. He has arranged accommodations for you and Melody in Khartoum."

"Khartoum?"

"It is quite a beautiful city. Your apartment is in Garden City, which is much like Garden City here in Cairo. I have seen the neighborhood. Stucco houses in wonderful colors, wrought iron balconies like in Paris, very near the river, with many flowers and trees."

"What would I do there?"

"Eventually I imagine you will have to find a job. Maybe you could be an English teacher."

Talking was too much effort. His eyes lost focus.

"I didn't expect you to agree," Nadya said. "Not at first."

On a Wednesday afternoon in December, a black ZIL III pulled up to the central Cairo branch of Barclays Bank. A chilly wind blew out of the eastern desert. A tall, very thin man in a hat and sunglasses got out, carrying a briefcase. The car remained at the curb. Twenty minutes later he emerged from the bank and got back in the car.

A petite, auburn-haired woman shared the back seat with him. She also wore a hat, as well as a veil, like a woman in mourning. She was in her late twenties, with the air of a much older woman.

Another woman sat in the front, next to the uniformed driver. She was tall, with shoulder-length black hair and black-framed glasses. "Did everything go all right?" she asked.

"Fine," the man said. He set the briefcase on the floor, leaned back in the seat, and closed his eyes. "No problems."

"Good," the woman said, and turned to the driver. "To the train station, please."

"Aiwah."

She smiled at the man in the back seat. "Bismillahi rahmani rahim."

The man returned the smile at lower amplitude. "If you say so."

The petite woman covered the man's hand with her own and looked out the window as the car moved away from the curb.

From the mosque at the end of the street came the first notes of the afternoon call to prayer. The call spread from minaret to minaret and echoed across the murky surface of the River Nile.

# AUTHOR'S NOTES

One of the issues I come back to repeatedly in my fiction is violence. Is it inevitable? Under what circumstances does non-violence get to win, and at what cost?

If a discussion about war and violence goes on long enough, somebody's bound to say, "What about Hitler? Would you not have gone to war to stop him?" I was a fan of the old *Mission Impossible* TV show, which not only had the best theme music ever (except maybe for *Route 66*), it made a habit of hoisting the bad guys on their own petards. With that inspiration, I set about trying to answer the Hitler Ultimatum.

As you can imagine, the Internet is full of excruciating detail when it comes to Nazi Germany. If I wanted to know what Hitler's private plane looked like, there were photos. The courtyard of Wewelsburg Castle during the remodeling? No problem. It was a pleasure to have so many photo references to work from—I hardly had to make anything up.

In addition to the web, I relied on a couple of print books for background. I wanted a solid, non-controversial life of Hitler and got just what I was looking for with John Toland's *Adolf Hitler: The Definitive Biography.* For the nuttier stuff I went to *Unholy Alliance: A History of Nazi Involvement with the Occult* by Peter Levenda. His constant mockery of the Nazis startled me at first, but ultimately struck me as a valid way to puncture their pretensions and deprive them of a glamour they don't deserve.

An old friend from Austin, Bill Wallace, lent me his most impressive knowledge of history and the occult, and made helpful suggestions on the story in manuscript. Richard Butner and Orla Swift also provided valuable early readings, and Bill Schafer of Subterranean Press published it in the final issue of his on-line magazine. My thanks also go out to the judges of the Sidewise Awards for Alternate History, who named it a finalist in the short form category for 2014.

## THE NEXT

I talked about this one in the introduction. I didn't read any reference books for it, though I made extensive use of Google Maps. Jim Blaylock confirmed my LA geography and provided corrections on my flora. My favorite lawyer, David Stevens, who is anything but predatory, kept me on the straight and narrow where legal matters were concerned.

## DOGLANDIA

I started this in a Hello Kitty notebook in longhand in 2002 and wrote half of it before I put it aside for reasons now lost to me. Once I started thinking in terms of a novella project, this story came to mind right away—though it proved considerably shorter than the other three.

Thanks again to Richard Butner and Orla Swift for commenting on the first draft.

## DOCTOR HELIOS

This one began with Cairo. It wasn't even an idea, it was just an image, a memory of the city from when I was 12 years old. Clumps of intensely green tropical foliage, ancient buildings side by side with the new, the fierce contrast between the absolute dryness of the desert and the immensity of the Nile. I had no characters, no plot, mafish, as they say in Arabic. But I felt a powerful emotional resonance.

I had been in Egypt and the Sudan from the fall of 1963 to the spring of 1964. My father was excavating early human sites in the area that would become Lake Nasser once the Aswan High Dam was completed. Thus a lot of the detail comes from memory. I rode in a felucca on the Nile, saw an unbelievably huge catfish head floating in the river, and regularly crossed from our home on the East Bank to work sites on the West Bank by means of WWII surplus landing craft. We rode one of those pontoon boats up to Abu Simbel for a day trip before the temple was dismantled and moved to the ridge above, and I used the pictures I took that day with my Brownie camera as reference.

The actual writing of *Heroes and Villains* started here, because I thought it would be the most difficult of the stories. (In fact, that honor went to "The Next," because I underestimated the difference between screenplays and prose.) Once I hit on the idea that it would be a spy story—my favorite genre throughout the 1960s—things fell quickly into place.

I probably would not have been able to write it had I not managed to find a copy of the 1965 book *High Dam at Aswan: The Subjugation of the Nile* by Tom Little, which was filled with great details about the construction of the dam, the layout of the work areas, and the political background of the project.

I used Saïd K. Aburish's superb *Nasser: The Last Arab* as my general reference for the history of the region and time. This is a first-class biographical work, as partisan as it is well-informed, and includes an uncompromising account of the criminal behavior of the CIA in the Middle East.

Also helpful were *Cairo: The City Victorious* by Max Rodenbeck, and a kid's picture book, *The Aswan High Dam,* by Peggy J. Parks.

I used the M.A.S. Abdel Haleem translation of *The Qur'an* (Oxford, 2005) for background, though when it came to translating the opening lines, I went with a more traditional rendition. I used "Koran" rather than "Qur'an" and "Moslem" rather than "Muslim" in keeping with the standard practice of the period.

Wilton Barnhardt, Richard Butner, John Kessel, and Orla Swift all read the manuscript and made insightful comments. Bill Schafer bought the story for his *Subterranean* magazine, and commissioned a gorgeous cover for it from the amazing Ken Laager. I'm proud to have that cover gracing this book.

Lewis Shiner is the author of *Black & White*, the cyberpunk classic *Frontera*, the award-winning *Glimpses*, and other novels. His short fiction has appeared in *Omni, Southwest Review, The Twilight Zone*, and many other magazines, and has been reprinted in a number of best-of-the-year anthologies. He lives in North Carolina.